TAKING TIME

a Tale of Physics, Lust and Greed

Mike Murphey

FROM THE TINY ACORN ...
GROWS THE MIGHTY OAK

This is a work of fiction. References to real people, events, establishments, organizations, or locales are intended only to provide a sense of authenticity and are used fictitiously. All other characters, and all incidents and dialogue are drawn from the author's imagination and are not to be construed as real.

Taking Time

www.acornpublishingllc.com

Edited by Laura Taylor
Cover design by Damonza
Interior design and formatting by Debra Cranfield Kennedy

ISBN-13: 978-1-947392-92-2 (hardcover)

ISBN-13: 978-1-947392-91-5 (paperback)

When H.G. Wells published *The Time Machine* in 1895, I'm sure he didn't know he was creating an entire sub-genre of literature. Nor did Einstein understand how his theory of special relativity would feed the creativity of so many writers grounded in fantasy rather than physics. I believe humans are fascinated by the concept of time travel because it offers the hope of a second chance—an opportunity to go back and do it over, do it better, make the correct choice rather than the wrong one. This is the first in a series of three books. My take on time travel, the story of Marta, Marshall and Sheila, was inspired by my relationship with Nancy—my wife and companion of twenty-five years—and the random set of circumstances that brought us together.

In the third book we meet a man named Sean Brody and a woman named Maggie Stanfield who pass quietly in the night because of a poor choice on Sean's part. This book, like the others, is dedicated to Nancy. Every day for twenty-five years, I've been thankful that, when that critical moment came, I chose correctly.

IN THE BEGINNING . . .

April 2043

GIVEN A CHOICE BETWEEN repeating any part of high school or being gnawed on by badgers, Marshall Grissom would at least consider the alternative. The teen years might be a highlight for some. For tall, awkward kids with little athletic prowess and a fair dose of social ineptitude, though, high school is just an ugly obstacle on the path to real life. And if he'd known that's where this whole secret mission thing was headed, Marshall never would have gotten on the bus.

A HARD ROW TO HOE

October 2044
Global Research Consortium Projection Laboratory

"SO, DO YOU THINK THEY'RE telling us the truth why some of the lemmings didn't survive?" Sheila Schuler whispered from the side of her mouth.

"The . . . what?" Marshall had to replay Sheila's comment one time before he could muster the concentration to make sense of it. As he scanned the computers, lights and lenses while he absorbed stares of scientists, engineers and technicians, though, a single thought consumed him.

We should have practiced naked.

The one time he'd suggested it, several female scientists and computer techs scowled as if Marshall personified the lowest bundle of perverse male hormonal scum on the planet.

The smart guys who represented the conglomeration of competing interests pursuing time travel had considered the question. Would nudity create such a distraction at a critical moment that the mission might be jeopardized?

Marshall recalled a couple of scientists insisting that, just as when the astronauts took man's initial steps into space, *everything* should be rehearsed in precise detail. Every conceivable circumstance should be anticipated and practiced.

Within the Wormhole Project, Marshall now realized,

this philosophy represented a distinctly minority position. Training is fine, conceded the folks putting up the money. As representatives of the various governments and corporations pointed out, however, unlike the swashbucklers over at the Light Speed Project, travelers here at the Wormhole Project didn't fly anything, navigate anywhere, or even push any buttons. They only needed to stand there and live long enough to describe the experience.

As for nudity, any male who suggested some of the rehearsals should take place in the buff suffered an unspoken accusation that he just wanted to ogle a naked woman.

"The lemmings?" Marshall asked, shifting his gaze from computers and cameras to look directly at Sheila. He did his best to concentrate on her eyes, making a futile effort to ignore the spectacular and unambiguously nude body below her chin.

"It doesn't bother you?"

"Um ... but ... but why would they lie?"

Sheila gave a quick shrug, which resulted in a corresponding jiggle.

Marshall understood unequivocally. They should have practiced naked.

Until this moment, with the platform beneath him beginning to hum and a plasma sort of ooze crawling across giant mirrored metal globes to each side of them, Marshall counted on the historical gravity of the occasion to block the male animal's primordial response to the female body. He might have been okay if Marta Hamilton was the only naked lady he had to try and ignore. Attractive in her own way, Marta was relegated to something like optical background noise compared to Sheila. And none of

Marshall's carefully nurtured best intentions would pass this test.

When that awkward moment arrived for the six travelers to remove their robes, the men hesitated. Sheila and Marta exchanged an eye roll, shed their garments and stepped under spotlights illuminating the projection platform. Marshall felt his first warning tingles at the sight of Sheila from behind. When she turned to face the room, though, she eclipsed all the technological wonders surrounding them. Marshall took his place beside her, aware that he was doomed.

That's when Sheila asked about the lemmings.

The first-time travelers were two lemmings wearing sensors and miniature video cameras and recording and tracking devices built into their tiny collars. The scientist's first choice as test subjects had been dogs. Dog lovers among the technical staff had objected, though. Which set a precedent, and the scientists were forced to seek popular approval for the choice of test subject. The only two creatures to which staff people had no objections were lemmings, which are suicidal anyway, and African tree frogs. Because an African tree frog has nothing in common with mammalian anatomy, and because the collars kept slipping off over their little heads, the scientists went with lemmings.

When the scientists waved their wands and pushed their buttons, the lemmings went away—somewhere. The scientists waited a while, pushed the buttons again, and the lemmings returned. The fact of their decapitations, though, dampened any sense of triumph. Both lemming bodies and lemming heads were present, albeit neatly disconnected.

The collars were conspicuously absent.

The second time around, someone suggested the issue, rather than fine-tuning all the calibrations and power settings, might be the collars. They put the instrumentation into lemming vests. This time a head and four legs were all that reappeared. So, the scientists said screw the popular sentiment and went with their original second choice, pigs. The pigs worked out better only because the researchers could barbecue the leftovers.

Finally, they attempted a projection without vests or collars. Both lemmings and pigs returned in good health. The process of time travel, though, acquired a completely unanticipated complication.

"N-naked?" one female traveler candidate stammered when Naomi Hu, the project's chief medical officer, made the announcement.

"That is correct," Naomi said. "Our physicists now believe only living organic matter can be transported through the wormhole. We can't send devices crashing around through time and space to record things remotely. We can't write notes to ourselves to warn of some impending doom. We can only project a living, breathing being, showered and scrubbed free of inorganic matter. And who is completely naked."

"In front of . . . people?" another weak query sounded from somewhere behind Marshall.

Half a dozen female candidates decided they could not abide the nudity and transferred to alternate duties. Marshall considered his options. None of the other male candidates appeared particularly concerned, though, so he felt he could not withdraw without seeming prudish or cowardly. And in truth, Marshall felt he could ultimately deal with the danger. He couldn't, however, abide his fear of making a mistake that might jeopardize someone else.

Not to mention his other problem.

2

FELLOW TRAVELERS

Eighteen Months Earlier

"UM . . . IS THIS SEAT . . . TAKEN?"

Marshall thought he'd lucked out when he saw the empty two-seat row near the back. When he reached it, though, he found a black woman—too short to be seen over the seat backs—staring out the window.

Her size did not imply delicacy. Her sleeveless blouse revealed taut, sinewy arms. Her skin was not nearly as dark as her demeanor. Her eyes bored into him. She craned her neck to consider him as, at six feet and seven inches, he loomed above her.

"Does it look taken?" she asked and turned back to the window.

If he'd had an option, he would have moved on. But this aisle seat was the only one left. He could get off and wait for the next bus, but then everyone would see him marching back up the aisle. He couldn't bear that.

So he sat, scooting as close to the aisle armrest as he could.

Clearly, the woman had no interest in conversation. Fine with Marshall. In almost any social setting, he played the role of interested observer. If circumstances forced his participation, he kept a well-practiced *Oh?* Or *Really?* Or

How interesting close at hand, then withdrew.

So, he contented himself to sit quietly during an interminable journey into the heart of a desert wilderness as apprehensive men and women from the world over practiced the awkward, tentative dance of initial acquaintance. The mix of joviality, posturing, ego, judgment and sarcasm ebbed into an edgy silence as their bus journeyed farther into the sand and cactus and unrelenting sun.

Marshall took comfort in the desert. He'd grown up there. While these people from greener, wetter places began to make nervous comments about *wasteland* and *desolation*, he welcomed the beauty of the Sonoran landscape. His anxiety didn't fully engage until they reached the chain link fences, the razor wire and the guards. That's when he surrendered to his insecurities and began to obsess over what he'd gotten himself into.

After negotiating a double set of sliding gates, with signs displaying little lightning bolts, the bus stopped alongside several others at a paved lot outside an immense two-story building, which exhibited all the architectural charm of an airplane hangar. Giant red plastic letters clamped onto the outside of the structure declared *Global Research Consortium*.

These bus riders had all signed contracts. Marshall signed a week earlier in his cubicle at the public relations firm where he worked in Las Cruces, New Mexico. The contract was sketchy, at best, regarding the job to which he'd be assigned. Forbidden to disclose the contract terms, he committed himself to an obligation of five years, accepted a generous compensation package, and understood he could choose to decline his initial assignment once informed of the details and, at lower pay, select a different job to fulfill his five-year obligation.

The specifics would be forthcoming when he reported for duty.

Marshall and his bus-mates joined a larger group milling about an expansive lobby. Safely indoors, the others seemed to relax, restoring some of the collective bravado. One last bus disgorged its passengers and the crowd, some one hundred strong, shuffled into an auditorium. There, with an absence of fanfare, they learned the stunning truth.

"Welcome, ladies and gentlemen, to the Global Research Consortium," rumbled a man with a black Van Dyke-ish beard and a subtle Slavic accent. "I am Dr. Yunieski Andropov, and I have the privilege of supervising the science staff here. Now that you have signed your contracts, this will be your home for the next five years. Because of the extreme levels of security surrounding our work, we have been able to offer only a vague understanding of our project. If, following this orientation session, you wish to reconsider, we will explain your options."

Andropov pointed to a middle-aged female wearing a little-girl smile and a white lab coat. "I will now defer to our chief physicist, Dr. Gretchen Allen."

A pretty woman who'd thickened a bit with middle age stepped to the microphone. A long dark braid of hair spilled down her back. Her hazel eyes carried the spark of enthusiasm. She cleared her throat. "Look around you, ladies and gentlemen. Because seated here today are the first human beings who will travel through time."

Wait, this can't be right, Marshall told himself. He must have gotten into the wrong line at the motel. There must have been two sets of buses, one taking the confident and competent ones to the time travel secret mission, and another bound for the secret mission involving . . . what? Maybe . . . reading novels and making clam chowder?

When his supervisor at the public relations agency—a woman who did not care for him—told him of this assignment, she'd lent the impression she'd carefully considered Marshall's skill set and discovered something for which he would be entirely suited.

A skeptical Marshall wasn't at all sure he *had* a skill set. But they offered more money. Why would they offer more money if he'd be asked to do something he wouldn't be good at? Marshall couldn't imagine he'd be even remotely suited to travel through time. Unless, maybe, when this woman said travel through time she didn't mean travel through, you know, TIME. Back when they broke up the Soviet Union, maps became full of all these new Such-and-such-istans nobody could keep track of. Maybe he was being recruited to go teach natives how to milk goats in a desperately impoverished country named something like Timeoslovakia.

From the reactions of the people around him, though, he suspected Dr. Gretchen Allen knew nothing about goats. Titters and gasps answered her astonishing declaration. The physicist paused to give the amazement a moment to percolate before she continued. "Over the next few months, you are all going to become intimately acquainted with the musings of Albert Einstein. For now, put simply as possible, Mr. Einstein told us more than a century ago that just as every point in space exists simultaneously, so does every point in time. The future, past and present are concurrent. This is because space and time, when you get down to the pure physics involved, are inextricably bound. Thus, the logic goes, just as we can travel to different points in space, so should we be able to travel to different points in time."

Dr. Allen stole the cordless microphone from its stand and began to wander.

"Ah, but you say, I see these various locations in space. If I am close enough, I can touch them. I can place them on a map and chart a route to reach them. And if I find these places disagreeable I can leave and go somewhere else. Why, then, can I not do the same thing with locations in time? If right now, for example, my existence sucks, why can't I pack up all my troubles in my old kit bag and go to a more pleasant time of life? Why don't I have a map that shows me where five years ago is, or where my future resides?"

Marshall glanced about and saw that Dr. Allen held the rapt attention of her audience.

"The current state of technology limits our powers of observation to the three dimensions that define objects in space. Time exists as a separate dimensional plane which, in our ignorance, has remained hidden. We know it's there. We just don't know how to perceive it. But we are very close to solving that problem."

Dr. Allen paced like an evangelist. "A number of isolated achievements combined to bring us together here. These were building blocks requiring assembly, and the Global Research Consortium provides the context in which that can happen. Our efforts to this point have achieved extraordinary results, and soon we will initiate animal testing."

Holding the microphone with her right hand, she pointed

her left index finger and swept it across the expanse of the auditorium. "Our goal is to project human subjects—that would be some of you—within eighteen months."

The candidates moved from the auditorium to a room arrangement that reminded Marta Hamilton of college class registration. Eight tables—each manned by several GRC staff members—stood along the far wall, letters of the alphabet posted above each table.

Marta lined up at the *G-H-I* sign and felt a towering presence behind her. She glanced to see the goofy man who'd sat next to her on the bus. He acknowledged her glance with an apologetic smile and a timid half wave. She returned her attention to the seated staff member, who explained options to the woman ahead of her.

"You will now be asked to sign one of two contracts. Both will confine you to this campus for the next five years. One contract places you in the candidate pool to become a traveler. The other assigns you to alternate duties at lesser pay. Both contracts include an agreement to disclose nothing of what you have heard or seen here and to authorize ongoing surveillance to ensure your compliance following your tour of duty."

"I'm sorry," the woman said with a quivering voice. "I didn't know—"

"You were told your last chance to withdraw occurred before you boarded the bus."

"But you didn't say *time travel*. You just said—"

"Well, we couldn't tell you about the time travel because that part is secret."

"Do I have to decide this minute?"

"No, you have twenty-four hours to make up your mind."

The woman bit her lip and absently twisted a lock of her hair. "Can I call my mother?"

"Like I said, it's a secret."

"But she wouldn't tell anyone."

"Uh, huh. If you feel you need counseling, go right over there . . ." He pointed to a table in the corner with a growing line.

"Um . . . what if I don't sign either contract?"

The man smiled. "You'll be subjected to five years of intense federal supervision."

The dazed woman took the information packet and wobbled off toward the counselors. The man watched her go, and then turned his attention to his line.

"Name?"

"Marta Hamilton. Spare me the speech. I'm here to join the candidate pool."

The man nodded and handed her a sheet from the pile to his left. With a flourish, she scribbled her name, stepped to the side and challenged Marshall with a glare.

"You will now be asked to sign one of two contracts . . ."

Marshall found himself in line behind the woman he'd sat next to on the bus.

Faced with both her glare and a decision that might be a matter of life and death, Marshall swallowed hard. He willed his eyes away from Marta's, thought of the money, and said to the man, "Does it matter if I'm allergic to anchovies?"

"What? No. Of course, not."

"Oh. Well . . . okay then."

That first day reduced the official travelers' candidate pool from one hundred and four to eighty-two. Marshall wasn't overly concerned. The physicist lady had used the term *some of you.* That implied a competition. That meant some would go, and others would watch. He recalled the sandlot baseball and touch football games of his childhood.

No one ever picked Marshall for anything.

3

ONE GIANT . . . LEAP

October 2044

MARSHALL BECAME ACUTELY aware of a growing wave of murmurs rolling through the projection lab. He had little doubt they were directed at his rising . . . discomfort.

He and the other five travelers stood—in the middle of a vast complex fifty feet below the surface of southeastern Arizona's desert—on a slightly raised elliptical projection platform constructed of twenty-first century polymers infused with an impossibly complex grid of fiber optics, sensors and microchips. An ethereal green glow radiated beneath his feet. From above, surgical-style lighting bathed the platform and its occupants from every angle.

Eight-foot-high seamless globes loomed on each side of the platform, their mirrored metallic skins gleaming. The globes hummed and pulsed with a plasma-like sheen Marshall found creepy. Banks of computers monitoring various mission aspects surrounded this center stage. Rows of video cameras and environmental sensors filled the few spaces computers did not. At the center of the computer array set a control panel made to appear more complex than necessary.

And off to the side, a periscope.

This periscope prompted Marshall's first inkling that

the science of the Wormhole Project competed with other issues.

"What's that?" Marshall asked an engineer the first time his subset of traveler candidates toured the room.

"A periscope."

"What's it for?"

"Nothing."

"I . . . I guess I don't understand," Marshall said.

The engineer laughed. Clearly, he relished telling this story.

"Couple of weeks ago, Michael Huxtable came down— he's the program administrator. We'd just installed the control panel. That's it over there. At first, it was just a flat metal plate with that throttle-looking thing you see, and a switch. When Dr. Andropov showed Huxtable the panel, Huxtable puffed up and said it wouldn't do."

"What, it didn't work?"

"It worked fine. Huxtable said we had to dress it up, though. Lots more lights and switches. And some of those rotating red and blue strobes like on a police car, and an alarm that makes lots of noise. *Think about the first time you're giving an investor's representative this tour,* he said. *Someone spends a billion dollars, they want to see something more complicated than an on/off switch.*

"And he told us to get a periscope. *What would we use a periscope for?* Yuni asks him. *I don't care,* says Huxtable. *Just make sure every time an investor's representative is here, someone's looking through it.*"

As the vibration of the projection platform began to tickle Marshall's bare feet, he glanced to his right and sure enough, a technician had his face glued to the eyepiece as he rotated the periscope through a slow 360-degree turn.

The periscope distraction helped, and Marshall relaxed a little. He sorted through the mental clutter and took stock of the scene around him. Beyond the embellished control panel stood a small stage with three chairs and three banks of monitors. Dr. Naomi Hu joined Dr. Andoprov and Dr. Allen at these seats of prominence. Marshall estimated about forty people present to monitor, manage, fine-tune, and observe the crossing of human history's next era-defining threshold.

History. The mission. The distractions made Marshall momentarily forget he might die during the next few minutes. Now reminded, he retreated to his training. Naomi Hu impressed upon the travelers the importance of positive expectation as they approached this event. *Seek a mental comfort zone. Find your happy place.* To Marshall's dismay, though, right now his happy place mostly involved Sheila's left nipple.

The time machine's thrum graduated to a soft vibration. Sheila's breasts acquired a subtle quiver.

Dreading this moment, Marshall had spent the previous sleepless night considering the ungainly creature everyone would be staring at tomorrow. He towered over everyone. He struggled to weigh enough. His chest barely managed not to be concave. A scrawny butt gave way to spindly legs attached to feet the size of swim fins, the latter conspiring to trip him. Nobody would take notice of *those* appendages, though. Because the stereotype assigned to men with big feet was, in Marshall's case, spectacularly true.

With every reduction of the travelers' candidate pool, Marshall had become more concerned, though he remained convinced he was not destined to be a pioneer. Until the moment fourteen days ago when Yuni announced the six-person primary team. Even after Yuni called his name, Marshall remained in denial. Any time now, someone would admit to the joke and Marshall would put on a self-effacing smile, laughing along with everyone else.

Unlike Marta and Sheila, he lacked a natural aptitude for math or science. Loath to call attention to himself, he rarely spoke during briefings, classroom sessions or training exercises. Rather, he sought out his instructors individually with questions, because his job required that he learn these things, and, despite his insecurities, an impossibly persistent conscience guided Marshall. What if his failure caused the program to be compromised, or worse, resulted in harm to someone else?

So, he worked diligently.

And where had it gotten him? Here. Now. Growing more rigid by the second.

He would find no reprieve.

Poised at the brink of mankind's next frontier, to his mortification, Marshall could not help himself. When Neil Armstrong took that *one small step* onto the surface of the moon, Marshall would bet anything Neil hadn't done it with a hard-on.

4

BEING OF TWO MINDS

"AAAAAAAAAAAAAIIIIIEEEEEEE!"

He issued a piercing shriek, a little-girl scream that if shouted aloud would have called his masculinity into question. Thankfully, Marshall realized, his cry of terror had occurred only in his mind.

He cautiously opened his eyes to find he did not have eyes. Nor arms, nor legs, nor anything else for that matter. His thoughts were the sole remaining aspect of himself.

A blank brightness he could not describe surrounded him. Or, for all Marshall could tell, this brightness might be within him, and everything beyond the boundaries of his missing skin some sort of oblivion. His perceptions shifted like a fickle wind as he tried to define this experience. He felt absolute solitude at one instant, then surrounded by every soul he had ever encountered the next. All-encompassing terror dissolved into a serenity surpassing anything he'd ever felt, then swept back again.

Most disconcerting of all, the experience lasted forever—weeks, years, eons, way beyond the length of his or his unborn children's lifetimes. A cruel unrelenting infinity.

And then, only an instant from the moment Marshall

entered this bright blank space, he returned.

Humanity's first time travelers journeyed one week into the past. The animals—with the exceptions of those wearing collars and vests—had seemed to handle a week okay. And roughly a week prior to the moment of their projection, Marshall and the other travelers, along with a dozen scientists and engineers, attended a pre-mission briefing.

Everyone sat around a broad oak table. Windows along one wall revealed a brightly lit grey concrete corridor more tunnel than hallway. The interior walls were also cast concrete, though someone thought the room would be more tolerable if these walls were painted a light blue, reminiscent of a sky nobody saw.

Dr. Andropov conducted this routine meeting as a final review of the preparation regimen for the first human projection, and to consider how best to spend the last week of training.

"Any specific concerns?" he asked.

Marshall looked expectantly at Raul Hinojosa, Josh Mathis and Felix Werber. The four men had discussed the nudity issue and agreed someone should insist on a full dress rehearsal. Or, *undress* rehearsal, Marshall supposed. Now, though, neither Josh nor Felix would meet Marshall's gaze. Raul, more outgoing than the others and the logical one to raise this question, shrugged at Marshall's imploring glance.

Reluctantly, Marshall cleared his throat. "Um, I know this has been controversial," he said, his voice cracking slightly, "but doesn't anyone else think it will be a mistake if we see each other naked the very first time when we're five minutes away from—"

At that point a week ago, several women glared at him, Dr. Andropov coughed, Marta rolled her eyes, Sheila suppressed a smile, and Marshall retreated, crushed like a bug on a speeding windshield.

This time, Marshall trembled with confusion. He grabbed the table to steady himself as his memory registered a vague but alarmingly realistic image of a naked Sheila Schuler. He felt inexplicable relief at being clothed. He saw Sheila sag backward into her chair with wide, confused eyes that fixated on Marshall in a very uncomfortable way. Marta Hamilton wobbled. Raul gasped. Josh vibrated as if suffering some sort of seizure.

Only Felix seemed unaffected as he stared at his fellow travelers, exhibiting the same puzzled curiosity as the scientists and engineers.

Marshall registered these alarmed expressions of surprise before a mental skirmish overwhelmed him. Two recordings, slightly out of sync with each other, seemed to play in his head. He struggled to focus on one without the intrusion of the other. Marshall's memory of last week's meeting became crisp. His memory of the projection platform and shift into time sharpened as well, though the recollections seemed to trip over each other.

"This meeting is different," he said aloud. "It didn't happen this way." That's when Marshall saw the additional frame of reference snap into place for the others.

"Oh, my Lord," said Sheila. "Why did we come here?"

"So, if we went back to this meeting," Marta asked, "why didn't this happen last week? Why didn't the past change?"

"What are you talking about?" Yuni asked.

"We're here," said Marshall, fighting his way past an alternate confused and frightened consciousness sharing his brain and glancing to the time/date display on the wall.

"The first projection sent us back one week," Sheila said pointing to the date, "so why are we here and not in the projection lab?"

"And why aren't there two of us?" Marta asked.

"Wait, are you saying . . ." Gretchen began. The expressions on the travelers' faces answered her question.

Felix, seated next to Marta, put his hand on her shoulder and one part of Marshall's consciousness cringed. He'd seen Marta react to similar innocent gestures of familiarity with a reflexive lightning snatch and twist that left her innocuous assailant face down on the floor and gripped in a hammerlock.

Marta regarded Felix with wide-eyed paralysis as he asked, "What are you talking about?"

Marta blinked and shook her head, as if to rattle something loose inside. "Why did the projector send us here? And why are we not sharing this conversation with our past selves?"

"Past selves?" Felix said. "You're saying you've traveled here from . . . why don't I remember?"

The scientists' excited babble swayed the bit of Marshall's attention not in conflict with his past.

"You've traveled here from the future, haven't you?" Gretchen asked. "From next week. This is the first projection."

"So, what happens now?" Josh wondered aloud.

"They were supposed to leave us here for ten minutes," Sheila said. "What will happen then? Will we disappear?"

Everyone turned to the clock.

"Quick, get out of the way!" shouted Yuni. "Somebody set up some cameras!"

The scientists scrambled to one side of the room and herded the travelers to the other where they exchanged worried glances. As the seconds ticked toward 2:15, Marshall tasted fear in the back of his throat until Sheila leaned close with a mischievous grin and whispered, "Geez, Marsh, why didn't you tell us you were hung like a horse?"

At 2:18 the confusion stopped.

As if a demon was being exorcised from his body, Marshall felt a tug at his very core. The uncomfortable second presence drifted from his brain and his mind cleared.

The travelers, though, had not disappeared.

They still huddled together with the others staring at them like zoo specimens. A quick glance around showed Marshall the others shared his sense of relief—except Felix who wore a frightened look of urgency.

"We've gone back . . ." Sheila began to say. But the rest of the sentence faded from her lips as Felix grabbed her by the shoulders and repeated, "I still don't know what you people are talking about!"

Yes, Marshall concurred mentally. He remembered clearly the discomforting, sterile sort of eroticism induced by their nakedness. He recalled the projection platform, an unimaginably long and yet instantaneous journey, and then confusion. No sooner had each recollection occurred, though, than it began to crumble to dust settling into remnants of a vague dream.

The travelers had only a moment to exchange worried

glances before questions crashed over them like a wave. Yuni let the cacophony ring for only a moment.

"Quiet! Be quiet or we'll get nowhere."

He turned to Sheila.

"Is Dr. Allen correct? You have completed the first trip from the future, and you ended up here?"

"I . . . I think . . ."

Marshall offered a pleading gaze to the others.

"Something has happened," Marta said. "Unless we've shared some kind of an illusion." She looked suspiciously at the gathering on the other side of the table. "You haven't been conducting hypnosis or dream therapy experiments you're not telling us about, have you?"

"Of course, not." Naomi Hu appeared shocked at the accusation.

"Clearly something perplexing occurred," Yuni emphasized. "You displayed unmistakable signs of disorientation. Are you saying now you don't remember?"

"Yeah, sort of," Marshall managed. "I have a sense of familiarity with what you described. It's more like I dreamed it, though."

"Well," said Josh, "if that's the case, then I had the same dream."

Meanwhile, one week into the future, five of the six travelers flashed back into being on the staging platform of the time projector.

They were naked once more.

Mercifully, Marshall found that his problem had subsided, but quick, half-smiling glances from Sheila and several female technicians threatened to get him going again. He was spared further embarrassment as someone asked, "Where's Captain Werber?"

An onrushing mob of support staff bearing bathrobes halted in mid-stride as all eyes turned to a vacant space on the projection platform. Momentary silence, interrupted only by the clatter of a single computer keyboard, shrouded the lab. Everyone's gaze swept to a lone computer tech, who typed with grim purpose, his frantic expression washed in the glow of a computer monitor.

"Elvin?" Yuni said.

Without tearing his eyes from the monitor, the computer tech said, "I don't have a lifeline, but I'm searching."

"Everyone," Yuni said, his voice thick with emotion, "if you have a job, get back to it. If you are an observer, please leave. The travelers need to begin their debriefing."

As each traveler filed past, Yuni gravely shook their hands. Marshall waited at the end of the line. When he reached Yuni, the Russian leaned forward and whispered, "I'm sorry. I cannot wait. I must know. Where did you go?"

Marshall looked at him with startled disbelief. "You mean, you don't know?"

5

THE SPEED OF LIGHT

SHEILA WANTED TO FEEL distraught over Felix's disappearance. During the previous month, though, the man had proven himself to be an arrogant prick. Like the other pilot, he'd condescended without remorse to the Wormhole Project traveler candidates. And he'd hit on Sheila relentlessly.

None of the Wormhole people knew the two pilots well. During their brief time on this side of the campus, Felix and Josh had kept to themselves, except when they were propositioning women at the Time Warp.

So instead of grieving, Sheila found she had to do her best not to laugh at the pointed lack of eye contact from the three remaining male travelers as they stepped in quick succession from behind the doors of four cubicles where they'd fulfilled the final obligation of their post-projection physicals.

Only an hour earlier these men had practically stretched their eyeballs from their sockets stealing sideways glances at Sheila and Marta. Now, however, Josh, Raul and Marshall seemed fascinated with the simple globe light fixture above them or the carpeting below.

Sitting in a reception area just off Naomi Hu's office,

the other women—Marta, Gretchen and Naomi—did their best to ignore this display of post-ejaculatory awkwardness: that moment when carnal desire is snatched away and things like what their mothers might think momentarily assail the male conscience.

Dr. Allen and Dr. Hu, along with Dr. Andropov, served as the ruling triumvirate overseeing the principal scientific teams for the GRC's Wormhole Project. Yuni Andropov directed mathematics and engineering. Gretchen Allen ran the physics team. Naomi Hu supervised all medical and psychological aspects related to time travel.

Upon their return, Naomi marched the travelers to the infirmary where they were scanned, MRI'd, drained of copious amounts of blood, photographed, recorded, probed anally, orally, vaginally—in the case of those who had vaginas—and ordered to produce semen samples in the case of those who did not.

Naomi described frankly what their post-mission rituals would be. She told the women they could expect something along the lines of a visit to the gynecologist. And as matter-of-factly as possible, she counseled the four males to take their time producing semen samples. Given the stark medical setting, she told them, performance anxiety should be expected. She didn't want anyone to feel rushed.

To her surprise—particularly given the additional trauma of Felix's disappearance—the men exited their cubicles with a minimum of delay. They performed so efficiently the group had to wait at the reception area for golf carts that would whisk them to their next station in the debriefing process.

As they awaited their escort, Sheila whispered to Naomi,

"Looks like that went well. Did you get enough?"

"Enough?" Naomi asked.

"You know . . . stuff."

"Oh. Oh, yes. We got lots."

Sheila winked. "I thought you might."

Gretchen Allen didn't pretend her devastation at the apparent loss of Felix Werber. Like Sheila, she felt no emotional attachment to the German test pilot. Her grief focused on political implications of the tragedy for the program to which she had dedicated most of her professional life.

"We've lost a traveler on our very first mission," Gretchen said to Yuni as they waited for the other five to finish their medical tests. "What would have happened to the space program if Alan Shepard had gotten himself blown up?"

"They would have continued, just as we will continue," Yuni told her.

"Yeah, but NASA didn't have Light Speed Project buzzards sitting on their shoulders, just waiting to swoop up all the funding as they pick through the carrion." She put her elbows on the oak table that dominated the conference room and covered her eyes with her hands. "God, Yuni, I must sound like the most callous asshole in the world. We probably killed a man today, and here I am, worried about funding."

"You told them you had concerns about the projector's power limitations," Yuni pointed out. "But Leonard Rose insisted Felix and Josh be included."

"Yes, and I should have put up more of a fight. What absolutely petrifies me is that it could just as easily have been one of our people instead of one of theirs. I don't know if I could live with myself if—"

"Well, you'd better decide," Yuni said, his tone harsh, "because in all likelihood, we will lose more people before we understand this process. We're stepping off a precipice here without knowing whether there's a safe place to land. And don't be too concerned about funding. Ultimately, travel to the future cannot succeed unless we master travel into the past."

"Not if you listen to Leonard Rose's arguments . . ."

Gretchen stopped in mid-sentence as the five travelers filed solemnly into the conference room and took their seats.

"What did you mean when you told us you went to the conference room?" Yuni asked with the five travelers sitting before him. Although Yuni seemed dour and accusatory, as if someone was lying to him, Sheila took no offense. With his dark Russian features and pointed beard, Yuni Andropov always seemed dour and accusatory.

"Wait a minute," Josh said. "What about Felix?" His tone made the question a demand.

"Yes," Yuni said. "We must talk about Felix. But you've indicated in your medical briefing that your memories of these events you experienced are fading. We are all devastated at the loss of a traveler, but first we must—"

"He wasn't a fucking traveler," Josh said. "He was a test pilot. He survived thousands of hours in the air, and your technology killed him."

"Dr. Allen expressed her concern that the projector's power might be limited," Yuni pointed out. "But Dr. Rose insisted we add two Light Speed pilots to the team. Now, back to my question. What did you mean when you told us you went to the conference room?"

"Just what we said," Marta answered. "We returned to where we were a week ago at two p.m. And you should already know that, because you were all there. You saw us."

"Of course, we saw you," said Gretchen, "but you didn't come or go anywhere. You were there when the meeting started, and you left when the meeting ended. The event was wholly unremarkable."

"Okay, I can understand when we had the meeting last week, none of us was aware that we'd been projected back there," Marta said carefully, "because that was then, and at that point, we hadn't been projected. Now it *has* happened, though, so you should certainly be aware of it."

"And you feel positive the recollection wasn't an illusion?" Naomi Hu asked as she walked into the meeting. "After all, we have no idea what the process of time travel does to the mind."

"A shared illusion?" asked Raul. "All of us appeared to remember things the same way. Back before it all started to fade."

The travelers each offered their own vague accounts. Only Marshall, though, recalled an uncomfortable duality of consciousness, and his recollection stirred memories among the others.

"Yes," Sheila agreed, "I felt so strange. Like two voices competed for influence in a single mind."

"And you all felt something like this?" Naomi asked.

As the others nodded or voiced a timid agreement, Sheila said, "But not Felix."

"Why do you say that?" Naomi asked.

"Because . . . I remember . . . He saw our reactions, our disorientation, and he grabbed Marta and asked what we were all talking about. He had no awareness of today's projection. It's like he was . . . only him. I don't think the Felix from now ever got there."

6

OUT DAMN SPOT

ONLY MARTA KNEW THE SCIENCE and engineering staffs could search all they wanted, but a failure of technology didn't render Felix Werber as dead as Marshall's chances of getting a date.

She knew this because she'd probably killed the guy. A crime of opportunity. A spur-of-the-moment improvisation that might have some blow-back if a body turned up, but nothing could be done about that now. Going into the mission, Marta had been ninety percent certain Werber was a saboteur. She didn't know what form his treachery might take.

Minutes before they stepped onto the projection platform, Marta and Sheila emerged from the women's locker room wearing their sterile white robes. Because the scientists theorized that even minute non-organic particles—like dust—would cause painful burns, the travelers carefully scoured themselves in hot showers. The original protocols called for shower technicians to spray them with high pressure hoses, like in a prison or a carwash, but that's where Sheila drew the line.

"I know you're concerned about dust particles getting

stuck in all the cracks and crevices," she said, "but I'll attend to my own crevices, thank you."

The six travelers strode from their respective locker rooms simultaneously and mingled next to the projection platform. Marta separated herself from the group and kept her attention on Werber, who made a show of solemnity as he shook the hands of each of the other men. Turning to Sheila, he substituted a quick embrace, his left hand sliding under her hair at the back of her neck. Sheila recoiled a little at the gesture, but apparently decided this was the wrong time and place to cause a scene. When Werber turned to Marta, her cold stare stopped him in his tracks.

"Sheila," she said, "can you come back to the locker room and help me with something."

Wearing a puzzled look, Sheila followed.

"I . . . I know this is just my paranoia at work, but, well, I'm . . . nervous, I guess. When I was a kid, my mom always told me to be sure and wash the back of my neck. And I never quite got it clean to her satisfaction, and . . . would you be sure I got the back of my neck?"

"Well . . . okay," Sheila said. Her look of bewilderment morphed into an expression of concern. "You're good. Your neck, I mean. Are you all right, though?"

"Yeah, I'm fine. Now let me look at your neck."

"Marta, my neck is clean. I scrubbed it when I washed my hair."

"Yeah. Well. My mom. You know? And I'd just feel better if . . . I know it's weird. But I'm just a little . . ." Her voice trailed off.

"Sure," Sheila said. "Take a look."

Sheila stood a half-foot taller, so Marta stepped onto the

bench in front of the row of lockers and lifted the blonde shock of hair covering Sheila's neck. A paper-thin dime-sized clear disc adhered to the skin at the base of her skull.

Okay, this is going to be the tricky part.

Marta placed a fingernail at the edge of the disc, then curled the fingers of her other hand around Sheila's hair and pulled.

"Owwww, Marta," Sheila said. "What was—?"

"Oh, I'm so sorry. I slipped, and I just grabbed onto the only thing handy to keep from falling. And you're right. Your neck is spotless."

"Good to know. Now let's get this over with."

They took their places. The spotlights blazed. The cameras rolled. The plasma oozed. The platform glowed green beneath their feet. A flat and unemotional voice offered a countdown. "... three, two ..."

Marta reached to the naked man standing next to her, touched his back and said, "Good luck, Felix."

Werber's head jerked around, his face a mask of panic.

"... one."

During the Wormhole Project's animal testing phase, back in the collar and vest days, the animals' various body parts had not returned on schedule. Rather they showed up randomly over the course of several hours. So, with only half of her attention on the debriefing questions, Marta waited for the other shoe to drop.

A solemn computer tech interrupted. "He's back."

"Is he alive?" Gretchen asked.

"Um . . . Dr. Hu's over there now."

The group hurried to the projection lab where they saw Naomi kneeling next to their fallen comrade. He lay face down, legs and arms akimbo. A dime-sized hole oozed blood in the middle of his back. Her face ashen, her voice quivering, the small Chinese woman said, "I don't understand how this could happen."

"Well, geez," Marta said. "He must have missed a spot."

"So, are you guys gonna quit?" Marshall asked.

Marshall, Sheila, Marta and Raul walked together, counting the correct number of turns left and right that would get them to the travelers' housing section of this underground labyrinth. Although they'd resided here nearly a year and a half, Marshall still took careful note of color-coded arrows and numbers describing where they were and where they should go. Down here, every grey tunnel looked the same except for the science/engineering areas, where offices, laboratories and conference rooms were clearly marked.

Marshall's question broke an uneasy silence.

"Not me," said Marta. "I think this is important. And I don't think the projector killed Felix. I think he was just careless."

"Me, neither," said Sheila.

"Hey," Raul said, "where else am I gonna make this much money? And it's not like they'll let you leave. If you take yourself off travelers' status, who knows, you might be cleaning toilets for half the pay."

Marshall sighed. Felix's death offered a legitimate way out. Anyone could understand, couldn't they? But . . . well. He'd had two previous opportunities to gracefully extricate himself. First, on the day they'd arrived. Second, when the whole naked thing came up. He wasn't anatomically eligible, though, when the third round of traveler corps resignations occurred.

He'd learned of a dozen more female withdrawals when he encountered Marta and Sheila six weeks ago at The Time Warp, a bland nightclub intended to provide the Wormhole Project personnel some semblance of normalcy for single young adults during their five-year confinement underground.

Marshall didn't normally frequent the Time Warp but following a wearying day of classes and training sessions, he entered his apartment to find a warm refrigerator filled with spoiled food.

"What happened to the refrigerator?" he demanded.

"I turned it off," his apartment answered.

"Why would you do that?"

"Because you're morose," the apartment said. "You have no friends. You need to get out more. Have a beer. Get a sandwich. Pick up some chicks."

"You can't say things like that," Marshall said. "It's politically incorrect. Women are not baby chickens. And if a woman ever does come over here, they'll think I taught you to talk that way."

The apartment situation left him no alternative.

As usual, the Time Warp was packed. The club occupied a reasonably large space with a futuristic gleaming oak and aluminum bar along one wall. An ancient disco ball glittered from the ceiling of the portion of the room set aside as a dance floor. Round tables, including some high tops, were crammed under dim lighting throughout the rest of the space. Neon beer signs lined the walls, along with travel posters highlighting beautiful places none of these people could visit for the next five years.

Marshall worked his way into the room. He stood awkwardly until a group of computer techs tossed down tips and abandoned their table. No sooner had Marshall sat, though, than Sheila made her entrance. Just inside the door, she stretched to her tiptoes to survey the room.

All around him, Marshall witnessed a subtle shifting of chairs, the squeezing together of male bodies making room for one more person at *their* table. The three unused chairs at Marshall's post were snatched away. Sheila appeared to ignore the shuffling and fixed her gaze on Marshall. She took a couple of steps, then turned, beckoned to someone with a wave of her arm, and pointed.

Marshall did not see Marta trailing Sheila until they were halfway there. When someone offered Sheila an empty seat along her journey, she said thanks and took the chair with her. Marta didn't wait to be asked. She commandeered the first empty chair she came across.

"Hi, Marshall," Sheila said. "Do you mind if we join you?"

"Um . . . sure?"

As a member of their training group, Marshall shared Marta and Sheila's company each day. Other than small talk during breaks, he found them daunting. Not only attractive, they were clearly among the smartest and hardest-working candidate pool members.

And now they sat at his table.

Marta didn't quite smile, but she did give Marshall a nod of greeting.

"So, did you hear about the latest wave of defections?" Sheila asked after drinks had been delivered. The drinks showed up, unbidden, with explanations that *that guy over there sent this*. Sheila gestured for Marta and Marshall to take their pick of the cocktail assortment. Marta chose something featuring rum. Marshall declined, thinking that drinking some guy's rejected attempt at seduction would be too weird.

"Defections?" Marta asked.

"Yeah, a dozen more women switched over to clerical or technical duties today." Sheila grinned. "The candidate pool is dwindling." She gave Marta a conspiratorial look. "What did you tell Naomi when she asked you about your boobs?"

Marta returned a quizzical stare. "My boobs?"

Marshall did his best to appear interested in his half-empty bottle of beer. He began to calculate an escape strategy.

"Yeah, you know. The implant thing?" Sheila offered Marta a conspiratorial wink.

"Implants?" Marta cupped her small breasts and turned to Marshall, accusation in her voice. "Do I look," she demanded, "like I have implants?"

Marshall's mouth gaped, his eyes opened impossibly wide. "Um . . . no? I mean, I don't know. They . . . they look . . . um . . . Oh, God . . ."

He stared at Marta's chest, feeling like he should surrender to the authorities.

"I'm sorry," Sheila said. "I thought she interviewed

everybody. But, I guess, she just thought—"

"That I'm too flat-chested?" This time Marta addressed Sheila, but her gaze again landed on Marshall. He panicked.

"... I'm ... I'm not a good judge of ... No. You're ... um ... you're ..."

"I'm what?"

"Very pretty ... ?"

Marta snorted.

Sheila told them the story. "Naomi Hu called all ... um ... most of the female traveler candidates into her office individually. When she talked to me, she emphasized that non-organic matter could not be projected through the wormhole. *It has come to our attention,* she tells me, *that the latest generation of breast implants is not detectable by the imaging devices used in your initial medical screenings. We must rely on your honesty.*

"It's those breast implants they've been advertising for the last year or so. The one's they say are completely safe and undetectable by sight, feel or taste—except that Angie Clinton told me when she had hers done, they said flavors are optional. You just have to go back every couple of years to replenish the ..."

Marshall bowed his head and covered his eyes with his hand.

"Anyway, apparently the advertising is correct because the new implants don't show up on the MRIs."

She relayed her conversation with Naomi.

"You put down on your medical questionnaire that your breasts are natural," Naomi said.

"Yep. My dad always told me I should dance with who brung me."

"Everyone put down on their medical questionnaires that their breasts are not enhanced."

"Okay."

"We have a whole department of mathematicians here, and they tell me that, statistically, a certain percentage of women in the demographic group represented by our traveler candidates will have breast implants."

Sheila shrugged and made a palms-up gesture suggesting she couldn't do anything about that.

"If you are lying, you may have been able to escape the scanning devices, but you can't escape the physics. Our best guess is that, during a projection, your breasts will catch on fire."

"So, Naomi gave everyone the option of dropping out of the candidate pool and being assigned to some other GRC job or—no questions asked—they could sign up to have their implants removed."

Marta looked suspiciously at Sheila. "And you're not...?"

"Nope." Sheila pointed to her chest. "All original equipment."

Marshall wished to be swallowed by the floor. Under no circumstance at that moment could he abandon protection of the bar table. Instead, his eyes shifted magnetically to Sheila's cleavage.

As Sheila followed his gaze, he started to stammer an apology, but she intervened.

"Oh, come on, Marshall." Sheila laughed. "They're just boobs."

Marshall nodded and tried to force a weak smile. But he imagined Custer's aide turning to the general and saying,

Oh, come on, George, they're just Indians.

Marshall dismissed the memory of that awkward conversation from his mind, found the questioning gazes of his fellow travelers and sighed once again. "Yeah, I guess I'll hang in there, too."

7

THE SPY

"THIS IS ME," MARSHALL SAID to his companions.

Raul had left them a couple of corridors ago, snapping his fingers and saying he'd forgotten something back at the men's locker room.

As Marshall opened his apartment door, Sheila surprised Marta by saying, "Marta and I might be going to the gym later. You want to join us?"

Marta had never seen Marshall in the gym. She doubted he was the gym type.

"What was that all about?" Marta asked Sheila as they walked on.

"Nothing, really," Sheila said. "I guess I feel sorry for Marshall. I don't know that he has any friends here. And I think under all that shyness, he's a nice guy."

They walked a few more paces in silence until Sheila said to Martha from the side of her mouth, "And speaking of Marshall, what did you think about his performance?"

Marta offered a questioning glance. "Performance?"

"I don't mean during the mission. I mean before the mission." Sheila added a conspiratorial nudge with her elbow. "On the platform?"

Marta seemed puzzled.

"You mean you didn't see? How could you possibly miss—?"

"I was doing my best to remain focused."

"Well," Sheila said with a giggle, "do yourself a favor. Unfocus a little next time and take a peek."

"You going to come by the bar later?" Sheila asked.

"No. I've got things to do."

"Okay, well, toodles."

Marta watched Sheila take a left turn at the next corridor. She wasn't surprised that Sheila, the social extrovert among them, would shower and head to the Time Warp. Marshall would stay home and, well, she wasn't sure what. Maybe he collected stamps or something. She placed her thumb on a glass plate and waited for the clicks and whirrs of the locking mechanism.

Over the course of living together for eighteen months, most of the traveler candidates formed attachments and friendships. A few, like Marta and Marshall, remained apart. Marta's distance was born of professional necessity. She formed relationships when they benefited her work. Even then she avoided attachment. She based her judgments, decisions and actions on purely objective criteria. Emotional involvement clouded objectivity. She'd been doing this for so long now, she found a solitary existence second nature.

Marshall maintained his distance, Marta felt certain, out of a wariness of people in general. No real mystery as to why. Some childhood experience—ridicule or bullying related to his awkward appearance and lack of social grace—made him shun attention. He wouldn't risk embarrassment.

Sheila presented a more complex puzzle. Sheila acted the extrovert. She dated. She sought the company of others. But she possessed a quiet cynicism and was quick to back away. Marta saw clearly that Sheila intimidated nearly everyone she encountered with her beauty, brains and sensuality.

"Good evening, Miss Hamilton. I trust you have had a fruitful and rewarding day, and I take this opportunity to remind you that you still have not chosen my personality setting so I may create the optimum living environment . . ."

Shit, thought Marta. One of the corporate contributors to the Wormhole Project's funding specialized in artificial intelligence and had recently equipped many of the underground apartments with their Happy Home Companion software. The company's representative described the installation as corporate generosity. Marta figured the whole thing was some kind of beta testing.

"If you don't shut up and leave me alone," Marta said in the hardest, coldest tone she could muster, "I will find where they keep your wiring and yank your mechanical intestines through your nostrils."

"I . . . don't have nostrils."

Marta banged her fist on her apartment's built-in bar top and growled, "Wanna bet?"

"Shutting up now," the apartment said.

Marta shed her training jumpsuit and underwear as she padded to her bedroom. She pulled on an oversized t-shirt that hung to her knees. She found a wine glass and a half-full bottle of a red blend called *Rough Justice* that had survived her assault upon the countertop.

She took both bottle and glass to a desk against one wall of the compact living space, pressed her thumb against a small depression that dented the otherwise smooth surface of a metal case the size of a cigarette pack. A virtual screen glowed above the box and a translucent virtual keyboard floated to adjust itself under her fingers. She pushed a set of wireless earbuds into place.

The irony of Felix Werber's death, she thought to herself, *is that in killing him, I might have accomplished his purpose.*

She needed to fix that.

She raised her hands and the ethereal keyboard slid itself into place.

Corporate interests seeking to shift funding from Wormhole to Light Speed Project made their move during initial mission, resulting in death of traveler Felix Werber. Werber's demise was caused by sabotage and WAS NOT, repeat NOT, due to technological failure. Journey one week into past completed successfully. Please inform our representatives to the sub-committee they should resist funding transfer while my investigation continues.

Marta entered a series of commands, reducing the non-sensical encryption of numbers and mathematical symbols. She ordered the computer to time the transmission of her message with the daily technological information dump, where it would be hidden among the weeds of a thousand other dispatches.

Unlike other members of the first travelers' team, Marta came to the GRC campus fully aware of the time travel project, because Sir Rupert Fitzhugh—chief of Marta's branch at MI-6 of the British Secret Service—told her.

By the time the traveler candidates were escorted onto buses and conveyed to the Arizona desert, the time projector and sprawling subterranean infrastructure supporting it had been under construction for almost three years. This secret melding of several governments and some of the world's major corporations—all inclined to compete rather than cooperate—bred suspicion among its contributors. So, many of these entities installed their own spies within the support staff or traveler's candidate group. When Fitzhugh recalled her to London to reveal her new assignment, Marta's competitive nature immediately asserted itself. She was thrilled to be placed at the forefront of this endeavor.

"What should I expect from the other candidates?" she asked her boss.

Imperial, with white hair and heavy, expressive eyebrows, Fitzhugh seemed to carefully cultivate the movie stereotype of a British spymaster. The MI-6 veteran alternated an unlit pipe from hand to mouth and spoke with a theatrical flair. What remained of Marta's island accent made her feel like a Dickens street urchin by comparison.

"Are you familiar with the history of the United States space program?" Fitzhugh asked.

"Um . . ."

"Well, a debate occurred over who should comprise the astronaut corps. Should the program be controlled by the military, or should it be civilian? Should machines or humans do the exploring? If humans, should they be scientists or engineers? Should they be athletes or race-car drivers or test pilots? The disputes were fierce."

"Yes, sir."

"Now, that's one country ruled by one president and one Congress. Multiply that by many countries and ideologies, then complicate it with funding from numerous private interests, and you have all the ingredients for bureaucratic gridlock."

Fitzhugh tucked the stem of the pipe into his mouth. "For the Light Speed Project, they will need pilot astronauts. But for the Wormhole Project, I'm afraid, when they finally got around to deciding who the travelers should be, so many aspects of the program required so many compromises that everyone was tired of arguing. Ultimately, any player with a meaningful stake simply got to pick someone and didn't have to defend their selection very vigorously. We chose you so we could have an unfiltered view of the technology and the politics. You should assume other contributors will do the same."

After interacting with the other candidates for a year and a half, Marta concluded that, in most cases, this flawed selection process produced traveler candidates who were not so much the best and brightest as they were the annoying and inconvenient.

"Just look around the office and think of who you'd like to be rid of for the next five years, and you'll have a good idea of the caliber of people I'm dealing with here," Marta reported to Fitzhugh.

Marta decided she could co-exist with mediocrity to the point that her life depended on someone else's performance. For now, her fate rested with the scientists and engineers. While the travelers themselves might fall short of the right stuff, the technology had clearly been shaped by the best minds on the planet.

But then she recalled the framed quotation hanging among diplomas and certificates on Gretchen Allen's office wall, a quote from some Twentieth Century scientist who observed, "The history of physics is the history of us being completely wrong."

8

VILLAINOUS INTENT

ANDREW GORMLY KNEW IN HIS heart and soul he was not a nice man.

Certainly, he could be nice when niceness benefited him. Just as he could be hard as a puck when the situation warranted. While these chameleon qualities might keep even those closest to him guessing, he made no attempt to fool himself.

He was a duplicitous asshole.

Just shy of six feet tall and built like a radiator putting on weight, he'd been a chunk of granite as a younger man. The accumulation of power and influence, though, made his head-busting past obsolete. He no longer had to be physically formidable to intimidate people who needed intimidating. He could hire muscle. So, he was undergoing the long comfortable process of letting himself go.

Well into his sixties, he retained a thick shock of hair, and not the kind produced by any number of drugs available in 2044. He kept it jet black, however, by artificial means. He refused to have his flattened nose repaired. The crooked beak served as a badge of his violent youth. His eyes were brown dollops buried deep below his forehead.

Comfortable with himself, he had no problem being an asshole, so long as he was a rich one.

Gormly accumulated his wealth by protecting the interests of the Hemisphere Investment Group, a multinational corporation owning a horde of companies representing a broad spectrum of industries and research-and-development firms encompassing almost every high-tech discipline imaginable. As a lobbyist, he held the ear of appropriate governing bodies for twenty-two countries and enjoyed a virtually unlimited budget to assure they paid attention.

If Hemisphere's best interests could not be advanced through either bribery or influence, Gormly employed harder measures. Hemisphere did not officially sanction illegal activities, and Gormly knew why they paid him so generously. He would be the fall guy if anyone got caught unless he could pass that dubious distinction to someone lower on the food chain.

Hemisphere made a huge financial contribution to the GRC and its dual programs, attempting to make time travel a practical—and profitable—reality. Gormly's current assignment—assuring that Hemisphere's interests didn't get lost in all the secrecy at GRC—required the enlistment of disciples. Some he acquired by adeptly manipulating egos and professional jealousies of scientists. The rank and file, though, were usually just greedy.

Nearly two years earlier, Gormly sat at a table with Hemisphere's board chairman, the company's president, and a handful of other key corporate officers and heard the briefing.

"You are crossing a threshold today," the government man told them. "And whether or not Hemisphere chooses to invest in this project, everyone here will be held to the strictest accountability. This is an international undertaking. The stakes are incredibly high. Any violation of security will result in immediate isolation of the guilty party. Don't expect due process. You will be held incommunicado until the program's development phase is complete. So, anyone who wishes to leave this briefing, please do so now."

Gormly knew then the financial stakes would be colossal.

Warren Pitts, Hemisphere's president and CEO, stood. "That's quite a speech. You at least have to give us some idea of the financial stakes here."

The government man didn't flinch. "If you choose not to be involved, my personal belief is that you'll be screwed when time comes to cash in on the most significant technological development in human history."

Okay, thought Gormly, *no question where Hemisphere will land.*

And that's when the government man introduced a physicist.

"Time travel, gentleman," the scientist said. "Someone will do it. We want to make sure it's us. The demise of the fossil fuel era and dawn of the hydrogen age has led to the production of a volatile substance we call enriched hydrogen. And this substance produces such huge quantities of energy per liter that what we couldn't imagine only a few years ago is now possible. The isolation and manipulation of exotic materials such as dark matter, for example. Or constructing a wormhole. Or driving a space vessel capable of approaching the speed of light. All over the world, independent research projects are cropping up, but believe me, gentlemen, no one will invent time travel in their garage. Someone will undertake the ordeal of putting the pieces together. The only way to bear this expense is to create a conglomeration of government and corporate investors. We want to be sure it's made up of the right governments and corporations."

"Okay, but why all the secrecy?" Pitts asked.

The government man stood. The physicist sat. "Besides being incredibly expensive, the cultural, religious and scientific implications of time travel will be hugely controversial. Time in development is critical if we are not to bankrupt ourselves. We simply cannot afford for these issues to become a matter of public debate."

Gormly grinned. *My kind of program.*

The physicist resumed his narrative.

"We will develop two programs, one aimed at the future, another aimed at the past. Travel to the future is no mystery. Einstein's theory of special relativity has been around since the early twentieth century and proves time elapses more slowly in a moving object than it does when we are stationary. This is called time dilation. If we launch a spaceship traveling at near the speed of light, send it on a year-long journey and then return it to the earth, the occupants of that ship will have aged a single year, while the earth will have aged as much as two hundred years. Our astronauts will have skipped two hundred years of history."

The physicist paused to drink from a water bottle.

"Our problem is that we've no way of restoring them to our time to report on what they've found. So, we need a mechanism to return them to the past. Unfortunately, travel to the past is more problematic.

"Einstein also established that space and time are woven into a single entity he called space-time. I'll try to keep the physics as simple as possible. Space-time is like a fabric that is manipulated by gravity. Imagine two locations on a map that are a thousand miles apart. If the geography represented by that map could be folded over on itself the two points would be much closer together. To travel to the past, using something called dark matter, we must fold space-time over on itself and create a shortcut via a wormhole.

"So, the GRC's research will be divided between a Light Speed Project, and a Wormhole Project."

The government man took over. "Should we succeed, the economic benefits are obvious, as are the defense and security implications. Now, because of secrecy attendant to our project, if you decide Hemisphere should be an investor, you obviously will not be able to brief your full board of directors or your stockholders. But I'm sure you have means of directing funds to this program in a fashion that will not arouse suspicion. That will, of course, be a violation of all kinds of Security and Exchange Commission regulations. As an official representative of the highly classified government sub-committee overseeing this program, I am authorized to tell you, don't worry about it.

"And so, gentlemen, do you want in?"

The Hemisphere honchos didn't hesitate.

"How can we lose?" Pitts told Gormly following the briefing. "Whether it works or not, we'll recover some of our investment with government contracts related to the development of the technology. If it does work? Well, if we can see the future, we'll know exactly how to invest. If we can go to the past, the possibilities of manipulating events to our advantage are limitless. So, we're relying on you, Andrew."

For months, Gormly had weighed the decision of where to place Hemisphere's multi-billion-dollar bet. Future? Or past? And with the initial projection into the past only two weeks away, time was running out.

Gormly didn't offer a hint of recognition when Felix Werber stepped into the elevator and shouldered his way towards the back of the car. But he'd pissed Gormly off. If Werber's presence was merely coincidental, then he'd been careless. If not, the risk had damn well better be worth it.

As Hemisphere's designated representative to the project, Gormly enjoyed visiting privileges for consultations with the bureaucrats in the GRC's administrative wing one floor below the desert surface. All the ultra-secret stuff existed a couple of levels below that.

As soon as the elevator began its ascent, Werber said with a panicked voice, "Ach! Please! Please! Stop the elevator. I thought we were descending. I'm assigned to lower levels and am forbidden . . . I could lose my security clearance."

A couple of people in the crowded car groaned at the inconvenience, but a helpful soul slapped the red button arresting their ascent and directed the elevator back down.

"Thank you," Werber said as he left the car.

The elevator resumed its upward journey. Exiting the car, Gormly slipped his hand into his jacket pocket and found the data wafer, a soft plastic object roughly the size and thickness of a postage stamp. He brought his hand to his mouth to stifle a cough and slipped the wafer under his tongue. The guards at the workstation quickly inspected his briefcase, requested that he empty his pockets and directed him through a scanning device.

Gormly walked to the parking lot, unlocked his car and began the long drive to Superior. Well away from the complex, he inserted the wafer into a data slot on his car radio console.

"*Please, Dr. Rose,*" the voice was that of GRC administrator Michael Huxtable, "*we've been through all this before. We fund each project equally. And while your theory is interesting...*"

"*His theory is completely reckless.*" A woman's voice. Probably Gretchen Allen. "*Your assumption risks billions of dollars, not to mention the lives of your space travelers.*"

"*The Wormhole Project is far more dangerous. You're more likely to kill someone than I am.*" Gormly recognized the strident whine of Dr. Leonard Rose. "*And it's entirely unnecessary. We should transfer funding and manpower to the Light Speed Project. We will send our astronauts decades into the future. Can't you people understand how advanced technology will be by then? They will know our history. They will know time travelers are coming. And with their advanced knowledge, they will certainly be able to build a device that can safely return our people to the past. And WE won't have to spend a dime to pay for it.*"

Gormly smiled. *So, the future it is.*

He set about the complex task of issuing Felix Werber his marching orders.

9

CULLING THE HERD

MARSHALL NOTED THE conspicuous absence of Josh and Raul. He wondered why? Had they done something wrong and contributed to Felix's death? Had they failed some aspect of medical testing? Marshall had assumed that if anyone screwed up, it would be him.

Where window blinds in Yuni's office had previously been open to the projection lab, today they were drawn. The group consisted only of Marshall, Marta, Sheila, Yuni, Gretchen and Naomi Hu. Once again, Yuni's expression suggested someone was guilty of something. Gretchen, on the other hand, seemed excited.

During the week following Felix's death, everyone related to the Wormhole Project worked long hours dissecting every iota of data, meticulously inspecting each process and each piece of equipment.

"The sub-committee has approved the resumption of the program," Yuni said. "We're going ahead with the next mission in four days. Tomorrow, you will receive your mission outlines. But we are stepping up security. You are not to discuss any aspect of a mission with anyone but those present here."

"So, what went wrong?" Sheila said. "What killed Felix?"

"Our conclusion is that somehow, he was contaminated with a concentrated bit of non-organic matter resulting in the fatality. Burned a hole about the circumference of a pencil right through him," Yuni said. "We've been through everything. This was not a failure of either the equipment or the process. Human error is to blame."

"You're saying he didn't wash his back?" Sheila's tone betrayed her skepticism.

There followed an awkward silence, which Marshall didn't plan to fill.

"Oh, for heavens' sake, Yuni," Naomi finally said, "you've got to tell them. They're the ones taking the risk."

Sheila's gaze became a grim laser beam aimed at the Russian. He sighed. "We haven't dismissed the possibility that Captain Werber might have been murdered."

Marshall took a long moment to process the statement. He looked first to Marta, whose expression betrayed a distant indifference, then to Sheila, whose mouth had dropped open.

"But why? I mean, Felix was a real dick, but that's no reason to croak the guy," she said.

"What better way to discredit the Wormhole Project and create a shift in funding to light speed than to suffer a fatality on the very first mission?" suggested Marta.

"I thought this was a partnership between the projects," Marshall said. "I thought we each needed the other."

"That's a good organizational theory on paper," Gretchen said. "Until you inject the human element. Leonard Rose is an ambitious man. He wanted to head up Wormhole, because that's the platform where the most fascinating physics research will take place. The Light Speed Project is straightforward—dangerous, and, a lot of us believe, futile. But Rose is stuck with Light Speed, and I think he doesn't want the competition."

She explained Rose's argument that a pathway to the past would be an inevitable result of future technology.

"Well, that's a pretty dangerous assumption, isn't it?" Sheila asked.

"I certainly think so," Gretchen said. "What if we annihilate ourselves and his space travelers arrive in a future where there's no technology left? I can think of any number of possible complications."

Marshall saw Yuni offer Gretchen a warning glance, which again stymied the discussion.

"You said *futile*," Sheila said. "You don't think achieving the speeds necessary to send someone to the future is possible?"

Gretchen resumed her seat, tapped her pencil absently on the table and said, "With oil-based energy resources, or even nuclear energy, building a path to the past was impossible. Enriched hydrogen provided the answer. This energy source allows isolation and manipulation of exotic materials such as dark matter, for example. Or constructing a wormhole. But none of those things violated the basic laws of physics. Some of us believe achieving near light speed in any sort of way that would allow humans to survive the trip will remain beyond us."

"But we've been to the past," Marshall said. "We know that can be done. Why would people still be so fixated on the future?"

"Because," Yuni said, "from both a financial and ethical perspective, glimpsing the future is more attractive than trying to manipulate the past. If you know what will happen, where to place your bets, profits would seem a sure thing—"

"Wait, go back a minute," Sheila said. "Ethical perspective?"

"I'm sorry," Yuni said. "We shouldn't—"

"Yes, we should," Naomi said. "They need to know." Before Yuni could object, Naomi pushed on. "We don't talk about this much, but some of us are concerned about the effect travelers to the past will have on the present. And how will changing the past affect our own future? Travel to the future might set people on different paths, but it wouldn't alter our present."

"Aren't there physical laws that say nothing can approach light speed?" asked Marshall. All the traveler candidates attended lectures regarding the various scientific theories to have emerged over the decades since Einstein began fooling around with relativity regarding the nature of time. Marshall, like most candidates, found these lectures mind-numbing. Sheila and Marta, though, seemed to intuitively grasp the concepts. Marta responded to Marshall's question with a roll of her eyes.

"The faster an object moves," Gretchen said, "the more energy is required to move it. Theoretically, an infinite amount of energy would be required to approach light speed. And not even enriched hydrogen will accomplish that."

"Physics aside," Marshall asked, "do you *really* think Dr. Rose would go so far as to kill someone to limit our funding?"

"And if he did," Sheila added, "why would he choose Felix? Felix was one of his Light Speed guys. In fact, I thought he was kind of the Light Speed Project's golden boy."

Gretchen shook her head. "I don't care much for Dr. Rose, but I've worked with him long enough to believe he's not the sort of man capable of killing someone. And you're right, Sheila, it makes no sense that Felix would be a light-speed advocate's target."

"So maybe the death was accidental, after all?" Marshall said with a hopeful lilt.

"That's right," Yuni quickly agreed. "Now please, we have a mission to prepare for and other issues to discuss.

"Yeah," said Sheila. "Like where are Raul and Josh?"

"We can't rule out," Yuni said, adding a nervous cough, "that Capt. Werber's death was related to overloading the projector. So, to err on the side of safety, we've decided to limit our active travelers' group to you three for the next few missions."

Yeah, right, thought Marta. But she saw no point in arguing. Instead, she said, "So, for those of us who survived the journey, what happened? Did we travel to last week's planning meeting or not? And if we did, why don't you remember your team of time travelers popping in?"

"The results of Naomi's debriefing make it clear," Gretchen said, "what you say occurred must have occurred. Your recollections are similar. So, we must accept that while your experience was real, and our experience was real, somehow, they were not the same reality—"

Naomi interrupted. "I have to say I don't share Gretchen's certainty of the authenticity of your recall. We have long accepted the premise that time travel reality—if time travel is, indeed, possible—may be entirely different from any reality we know. Subjecting you to this device we've created may do nothing more than scramble your bits and produce experiences that are—well, I don't know what. But not what we would recognize as real."

"Or," interjected Gretchen before any of the travelers could raise a question, "another possibility is that you traveled to a place where none of us was present. You didn't go back to *our* conference room at all."

Marta suffered through Gretchen's mini lecture on light speed with as much tolerance as she could muster.

She didn't need Dr. Allen's physics primer, because she'd studied tirelessly to win her place as a time travel pioneer. Her handlers at MI-6 would just as soon she hadn't been selected to the primary travelers' team. They wanted their principal asset on the GRC campus to sit safely on the sidelines as a covert witness to the technology and politics of this multi-billion-dollar undertaking. The British intelligence agency had a huge investment in Marta. She was good at her specialty of industrial espionage and would be difficult to replace.

Marta's innate competitive drive fixed her with an aversion to finishing second to anyone. Since departing the Caribbean to attend university, she'd competed with people who were smarter, stronger, faster—but not tougher, or more determined. In the travelers' program, Sheila embodied the competitive challenge Marta had faced her whole life. Beautiful and athletic, Sheila seemed to grasp these scientific concepts and intellectual challenges being thrown at traveler candidates without breaking a sweat. Marta's advantage, as always, was that she worked harder than anyone else.

Marta understood why she and Sheila made the team. They were simply the best among the candidates. Obviously, Felix and Josh had been installed so the Wormhole Project could harbor no secrets from the Light Speed interests.

Raul, though, brought nothing obvious to the table other than a captivating personality. And Marshall presented an even greater mystery. Quiet. Awkward. Not stupid by any means—probably very bright—but a bit of an intellectual plodder. He usually got there after he back-tracked and covered a lot of extra ground.

Marta typically suffered impatience with people like Marshall, her exasperation manifested by borderline rudeness or outright hostility. Curiously, though, not so much with Marshall. She'd found anger or contempt difficult because the guy was just so… transparent. Completely without guile or pretense. *Or am I utterly off base, and he's the best actor I've ever come across?*

She'd been convinced for some time that someone among the primary travelers' team—besides her, of course—had been planted as a spy. Raul had been her chief suspect, although Felix's unsuccessful attempt to kill Sheila clearly established his guilt.

And Sheila. What about Sheila? Usually, Marta found it helped to work up a quiet animosity for her rivals. God help her, though, she liked this woman.

I hope I'm not losing my edge.

As the three remaining travelers' team members left the meeting, Marta looked carefully up and down the long corridor to be sure the three of them were alone as they walked to the tunnels that joined the research wing with their living quarters.

"So that was suitably vague," she said with a note of sarcasm. "It's like we didn't learn anything at all on that mission."

"Well, I'm pretty happy with what I learned," Marshall said.

"Yeah? And what's that?"

"That when we get where we're going, we're not naked anymore. How awful would that be?"

Gormly could hardly contain his rage. First, his principal asset had somehow managed to get himself killed, and now his emergency backup had acquired amnesia.

"What do you mean, you can't remember?" Gormly growled.

Raul tried to explain. "It's like something we dreamed— all of us. We have a vague sense of memory, and . . . well, I can't offer many details."

"Next time take some fucking notes."

"You . . . you realize that's not possible?"

Gormly answered with his most intimidating stare.

"You understand we're naked? We can't take anything. And we can't bring anything back."

More silence.

Raul had been instructed to hike to a far corner of the underground complex and take a freight elevator opening onto a room at the back of a building still under construction. Bare sheetrock covered the walls, and an untrimmed window looked across the desert to twin sentinels of chain link and razor wire. They sat on folding chairs.

Gormly needed these meetings to be productive. Getting into the inner GRC campus was not easy, and bribes ensuring silence of security people were significant. As Hemisphere's designated representative, Gormly enjoyed access to the main administrative offices, well apart from science or engineering labs. As a participant's representative, however, legal agreements bound him regarding security. Hemisphere would forfeit a substantial bond if anyone caught Gormly drawing outside the lines. But Gormly had never found a security team without at least one member who could use a little—or a lot—of extra spending money.

"And we have another problem," Raul said, reluctance in his tone.

"What kind of problem?"

"They only took three from the traveling team to today's planning sessions. I don't know what they talked about."

"That's not possible." Gormly calculated the small fortune he'd spent to make sure Hinojosa would be along every step of the way. "Listen, we've got a lot invested here. If you did anything to screw this up—"

"All they told us is that the team is being downsized for the next mission. They didn't say why."

"Who are the three?"

"Marshall Grissom, Sheila Schuler, and Marta Hamilton."

Gormly frowned.

Not good news. Gormly had gathered extensive background information on all the initial travelers. Two of these three were not among those whom he considered candidates for blackmail or bribery. Sheila Schuler? Beautiful and smart is not a particularly bribable combination. Gormly instinctively knew he must keep his distance from Marta Hamilton. But Marshall Grissom? *Hmmmm. Not a lot of information available one way or the other. That one will merit a closer look.*

10

GETTING TO KNOW YOU

"SOMETHING ELSE IS GOING on here," Sheila said to Marta as she spotted her at the weight bench. Marta pressed 145 pounds. Impressive for a woman who probably weighed only 105 or so. No way could Sheila lift one and a half times her body weight.

Marta extended her arms and held the weight high over her chest, then let Sheila help her guide it back to its resting place above her. She slid from under the bar.

"Where?" Marta toweled sweat from her face and looked around the makeshift gym. A half-dozen men worked out. Apart from a few long and semi-licentious gazes at Sheila, though, they kept their distance.

"Not *here*," Sheila said. "With the travelers' team. And you are freakishly strong, by the way."

"You mean their explanation about cutting the team by half?"

"Right. Do you believe that stuff about the projector not having enough power to handle more than three people if we're going back longer than a few days?"

"It's not about the projector," Marta said. "It's about keeping secrets."

Sheila glanced quickly to be sure none of the other gym rats had drifted into eavesdropping distance. Marta did the same and continued. "You need to minimize two things if you want to keep something secret, especially here. You have to limit the number of people who know your secret and limit the amount of time you have to keep your secret."

"What secret?"

Marta grinned. She didn't usually get to these places ahead of Sheila.

"Yuni wants to do everything he can to keep Gretchen's theory under wraps."

"Theory? What theory?"

One of the men headed towards the bench press station. Marta's glare warned him away.

"Yuni cut Gretchen off this afternoon. Do you remember what she was saying?"

"Yeah, I thought she was a little cryptic. She said that thing about *your experience was real, and our experience was real, somehow, they were not the same reality.*" The tumblers fell into place and Sheila gasped. "Parallel universe theory."

"And if we truly traveled to a parallel universe," Marta said, "the implications are huge. Because for the purposes of the corporations and governments funding this program, time travel is pointless."

"If we go to a parallel universe," Sheila agreed, "then we can't change anything about our *own* past. We can't manipulate our past in any way that will . . ."

". . . that will produce a profit," Marta finished for her.

"Not to mention blowing the hell out of Dr. Rose's contention that a time machine built in the future will get his astronauts back home."

Marta watched Sheila disappear around the corner, then entered her apartment deep in thought.

"Good evening, Miss Hamilton! And how was your day?" The apartment's voice sounded bright and ebullient.

"Much better than yours is going to be if I hear one more peep."

"Please, Miss Hamilton, my programming requires that I—"

"One. More. Fucking. Peep." She spoke with a snarl.

The apartment said something under its breath.

"I heard that. Don't make me get my gun." Marta waited a good thirty seconds. The apartment remained silent. Marta changed into her t-shirt and opened her bottle of wine.

She again sat before the ethereal 3-D screen and floating keyboard.

In casual conversation, she'd learned Marshall worked for an advertising agency before his assignment to the program. He'd been selected, he said, by some big shot at the conglomerate parent of the company he worked for. He said he really didn't know why he was chosen.

Sheila worked as a television journalist. She told Marta she'd been appointed by an executive of the holding company that owned her station. She didn't really know why. Marta told the others she'd been a British Royal Air Force's science liaison to the Sandia National Laboratory in Albuquerque, New Mexico, before being transferred here. She really didn't know why.

Now that it appeared she would be inextricably bound to Sheila and Marshall as travelers, she wanted more detail, which required a warrant from a British court. Surveillance technology had reached a point of sophistication that privacy now had to be granted. Between information-gathering devices and advanced computer-enhanced psychological profiling, Big Brother had the means to find out just about anything. Fortunately, these advances proved so frightening to reasonable people, who respected basic human rights in the face of exponential technological advancement, courts and economic alliances forbade governments from indiscriminately exercising this power under threat of most severe sanctions. So, Marta needed to go through the process of justifying her request. She quickly made her case for an enhanced level of information retrieval, shipped the request to her supervisors at MI-6, and received permission from a British court within the hour.

She accessed her interactive profile software and entered Marshall's name along with some general parameters for the information she sought. Software matched the photograph Marta provided with the correct Marshall Grissom.

"Marshall Grissom, twenty-eight, is a graduate of New Mexico State University with a communications degree," her computer's electronic voice told her. "He was employed by Sanders and Associates of Las Cruces, New Mexico, one of many branches of Blinker Advertising Corp. Blinker is a subsidiary of Magnum Corp., one of the multinational conglomerates that are significant contributors to the GRC."

"Yeah, yeah, yeah," Marta told the computer impatiently. "I know that. I don't need the background detail. I need to know why Marshall was appointed as a traveler candidate."

The earbuds hummed with electronic noise as the computer took a moment to interpret Marta's request.

"His boss was mad at him," the computer said after a brief delay.

"What do you mean, mad at him?"

"You said you didn't want details. And you should be nicer to the apartment."

God, I hate artificial intelligence. Marta tried to keep the irritation from her voice. "I require detail appropriate to the understanding of my question."

"Marshall Grissom worked as a creator of advertising and promotional campaigns. Executives at Magnum Corp. wish to sell time travel junkets to tourists. They directed the president of Blinker Advertising of Denver, Colorado, to select a traveler candidate who could eventually parlay his or her experience into an attractive tour package. The president of Blinker Advertising of Denver, Colorado, is sharing an unsanctioned sexual relationship with the head of Sanders and Associates of Las Cruces, New Mexico. He allowed this woman, Marshall Grissom's immediate supervisor, to select the candidate."

"Why was she mad at Marshall?"

The computer processed the question for a moment. "Marshall Grissom is psychologically ill-suited for employment by an advertising agency. He is instinctively too honest and is prone to telling the truth. His supervisor believes that some clients are not always best served by the truth."

"So, what happened?"

"Marshall Grissom made a presentation to a major client. He told the truth. His supervisor thought sending Marshall away for five years would make her life simpler."

Marta used a series of keyboard commands and scanned Sheila's photo into the computer.

"Sheila Schuler, twenty-nine, a graduate of Arizona State University. Employed as a journalist at a Phoenix, Arizona, television station—"

"Cut to the chase. Why was Sheila appointed to the traveler program?"

"Say please."

"What?"

"Say please. And don't yell at the apartment anymore."

Marta ground her teeth. "Please!"

"An executive of the corporation that owns the television station which employed Sheila Schuler was mad at her."

"Why?"

"Sheila Schuler refused to participate in an unsanctioned sexual relationship. He decided his comfort level would best be served by sending Sheila Schuler away for five years. Sheila Schuler feared she would be assigned to weather broadcasts in Walla Walla, Washington, if she did not accept the new assignment."

Marta felt a twinge of conscience at having violated her colleagues' privacy. Both, it seems, ended up here as the result of an ethical conflict. That spoke to their strength of character, didn't it? What would they conclude, she wondered, if they were privy to the details of Marta's past? Like nearly everyone else here, Sheila and Marshall thought Marta was a British Royal Air Force officer. They knew she held an engineering degree. And that's all. They would need a warrant for the details.

Marta poured another glass of wine and scanned her own photo into the computer.

"Marta Hamilton, thirty-one, employed by MI-6 Branch of British Secret Service. Specialty industrial espionage.

Raised by single father of modest means on the island of Nevis. Orphaned at the age of seventeen. Driven by unquenchable curiosity, refused to succumb to laid-back lifestyle of the islands. Joined British Royal Air Force as an avenue to a London education. Drew attention of British Secret Service. Jumped at opportunity to enter clandestine world of international intrigue. Aptitude for math and science led her to high-tech espionage. Avoids personal relationships and is known among her colleagues as, and I'm quoting here, a mean mother-fucker."

Marta offered a little smile. The computer made a throat-clearing noise.

"What?" Marta asked.

"Really. The apartment is despondent."

11

FOOLAROUNDUS INTERRUPTUS

ONCE AGAIN NAKED AND DOING his best not to glance either to his right, at the voluptuous Sheila Schuler, or to his left and the lithe body of Marta Hamilton, Marshall stood on the projection platform determined to do better. He would sharpen his focus. He would *not* let his prurient instincts get the best of him.

As she took her position, Sheila's quick glance down and to her left had been furtive. Alas, not furtive enough. And that's what got things started. Then, when Marta's peek to her right produced a double take she could not disguise, Mr. Johnson began to build on that foundation.

Marshall closed his eyes tight and focused on the mission profile.

"Our target date is a month ago Friday, seven p.m.," Gretchen told them in her initial briefing.

"So, will there be two of us this time?" Sheila asked.

"We don't know. If that's the case, try to avoid your past self. Be as unobtrusive as possible. Try not to talk to anyone. Go to the physics lab conference room. We've checked calendars and we know that room is empty at the target arrival time."

Entering the projection lab wearing his white robe, Marshall cringed to see a bigger crowd today. Yuni explained that, given last week's disaster, the Wormhole Project needed to make a statement of confidence, so investors' representatives had been invited. For appearance sake, Yuni filled the room with staff people who sat at superfluous consoles, stared at flashing lights and toggled dummy switches.

The periscope observer had acquired an assistant.

Standing between Marta and Sheila, Marshall felt the stares of strangers. As his own personal tide continued to rise, he retreated to all the gruesome images he could muster as a distraction. He recalled a particularly horrifying mutilation of a pig during the vest era. Its body had been cleaved along its midline, leaving all manner of swine anatomy on display.

For a brief moment, Marshall thought he would make it. Then Sheila sneezed. He cast an involuntary peek. Her sneeze set up a rolling wave. Marshall's surge of response produced a collective gasp from his audience.

Marshall entered the same interminable white oblivion he'd encountered before. Again, his time there seemed to last eternities, but in retrospect registered as only an instant. Now that he knew something of what to expect, the terror he experienced the first time became an uncomfortably overwhelming sense of nonbeing. He perceived himself as utter nothingness surrounded by a vast nonexistence. He could not fathom how all the molecules of himself could ever be reassembled. As the brightness finally began to fade, though, his bits seemed to come crashing together until he found himself whole again.

At the moment of their integration, his past self sat at a small table, still wearing his blue training jumpsuit, trying to convince his apartment he was not suffering from chronic depression.

"You're solemn, indicative of moodiness," the apartment told him. "No one ever visits, and you don't go out. You must be terribly sad."

Although the absurdity of trying to explain his existence to a set of walls occurred to Marshall, he could not bring himself to be rude even to an artificial personality So, he finally agreed.

"Well, buck up," the apartment told him. "You hang in there. It's always darkest before the dawn. Don't do anything foolish. It's a long way to Tipperary."

"That last one doesn't make any sense."

"Sorry. My empathy programming is limited and defaults to my nostalgia mode."

Past-Marshall pondered whether to get a beer from the fridge or just go to bed when a blur of images swamped him. These pictures jumbling through his mind overlaid the image of Albert Einstein with a steamy eroticism Marshall had never before associated with either physics or the frizzy Twentieth Century genius. Future-Marshall, though, recognized the sensations: the disquieting sense of duality of consciousness; the too-full brain; two sets of thoughts;

two sets of memories, all slightly out of sync with each other. With focus, though, Future-Marshall began to separate the duality into two distinct entities. And picking up on the cues, Past-Marshall discovered he could do the same.

"My God," Past-Marshall realized, "I've come from the future. I was going to have a beer, and . . . and I've come from the future."

Simultaneously, another part of his brain offered a knowing, satisfied chuckle. His future self knew things of which his past self had no inkling—what he would do this weekend, how great Sheila looked naked. The delicious prescience began a silent back-and-forth between the two versions of himself he found invigorating rather than frightening and disorienting.

We can do this, he assured himself, then added aloud, "We can do this! And right now, we've got to get to the physics lab."

"Oh, good," said the apartment. "You're going out. Have a good time. Don't do anything another more adventurous and confident sentient being wouldn't."

Sheila found her arrival more complicated.

When future-Sheila burst into the consciousness of her past counterpart, she found herself sitting on her couch, her skirt bunched around her thighs and her blouse on the cushion next to her. Frank Altman stood dramatically before her and unzipped his jeans. Future-Sheila recalled this moment clearly because, given her hectic training and classroom schedule, this scene was prelude to the last time she'd gotten laid.

Anticipating that she might repeat the experience of inhabiting the mind of her past self, future-Sheila flashed off the projection platform with a specific plan for calming her counterpart. Much to her surprise, though, past-Sheila suffered only brief disorientation. Something about the sexual excitement of the moment seemed to block the flood of future information and funnel it into a manageable stream. Past-Sheila even had the presence of mind to be a little irritated at the interruption.

What, they couldn't have picked a more convenient time? she thought to her future self, glancing at the clock above the couch. *Ten p.m.*

This was supposed to happen at seven, future-Sheila apologized. *But they warned us that trying to keep a specific schedule could be a problem until they figure out the time distortion.*

Now Frank stood before her and with one deft movement, tugged down his pants and bikini briefs. "Here it is, baby," he announced. "Here's what I've got for you."

Physically, Frank represented quite the specimen. His dark, sleepy eyes sat in a brooding face that would do James Dean proud. He displayed magnificent musculature, a classic male form crafted by a life of physical labor. Frank was not, however, a towering intellect. Frank's tower stood only about knee-high. Frank represented himself as an aspiring actor. While he certainly had the looks, Sheila thought he'd be in trouble if the script included three-syllable words. His skills as a conversationalist, though, didn't matter a fig to Sheila.

The interest of men like Frank held no mystery for Sheila. She'd commanded such attention her whole life.

Stunning beauty aside, men seemed to intuit her sexual enthusiasm. And certainly, Sheila embraced her libido. She didn't consider herself promiscuous, per se. She just enjoyed sex, knew better than to confuse lust with love, and hadn't found a man who impressed her enough to consider a long-term relationship.

She questioned the practicality of monogamy.

Sheila finally succumbed less to Frank than to sexual boredom. From a physical standpoint, Frank offered the most attractive alternative given their confinement. Because he had other options among the GRC's female staff, and wasn't bright enough to take anything personally, Frank also represented fewer complications than most.

They'd gone out twice for drinks at The Time Warp. Tonight, Sheila had agreed that she and Frank should go back to her place. They'd had sex once before, and while hardly a life-changing experience, she'd conceded to herself afterward that she'd probably do it again.

But tonight, Frank fell victim to some horrendously bad timing.

As willies went, Frank's was fine. In terms of size, he was about average—the five and a half to six-inch standard that, since the dawn of time, has been exaggerated to eight inches by men who take it for granted that most women don't carry tape measures. But as Frank proudly displayed himself for her inspection, future-Sheila began to giggle. And past-Sheila could never apologize or explain to Frank that the last thing her future counterpart saw before being thrust into the white oblivion of the limbo was Marshall. Combined with the pained look of concentration distorting Marshall's face as he tried by sheer force of will to keep from getting harder, the image struck her as hilarious. Past-Sheila shared her future counterpart's vision of Marshall's struggles. As her giggles accelerated to full-blown laughter, Frank withered before her eyes.

"What's so funny?" He pulled at his bikini underwear, trying to cover his shrinking little amigo.

"Oh, Frank, no. No, I'm not laughing at—" she almost said, "your dick," then thought better of it—partly because she *was* laughing at his dick, sort of.

"No, you don't understand."

"You're damn right I don't understand. You didn't seem to have any complaints last time—"

"Frank, please," past-Sheila asserted herself. "It's not you. I just... I just... I thought of something Marshall Grissom showed, um... said to me, and, you reminded me of..."

That's when future-Sheila started giggling again.

"I remind you of a geek like Marshall Grissom? What about me could possibly remind you of him? You see all this and think of some nerd with spaghetti arms and no chest?"

Although past-Sheila wanted to repair Frank's ego, future-Sheila—surprised to discover within herself a growing protective fondness for Marshall—grew angry at Frank's disparaging remark.

"Okay, now wait a minute. Don't bash Marshall. He's a good guy."

"Yeah? If he's such a good guy, how many women do you hear talking about sneaking off to meet *him* in a dark room?"

Future-Sheila conceived a retort but found past-Sheila would not allow it. There followed an uncomfortable silence as past-Sheila beheld the handsome man before her, rekindling her horniness. She tugged at her bra, so Frank could see the dark brown tops of areolas peeking out. He smiled and stroked her breasts. "But hey, what are we arguing about? We've got other things to do tonight."

Past-Sheila, completely prepared to succumb to her sexual hunger, found herself yanked back from the carnal abyss by future-Sheila, who, with a burst of concentrated focus, said to Frank, "Yes, we do have other things to do." She pushed his hands away.

"What, you want me to leave?" Frank asked as Sheila gathered her things.

"I do."

"But why?"

"I have to go meet Marshall Grissom," future-Sheila, now thoroughly in control, said through another giggle. "In a dark room."

Ten minutes later, Sheila opened the conference room door and found Marshall and Marta waiting in the shadows. Marshall looked thoroughly geeky, still wearing his training jumpsuit. Marta wore a t-shirt and a pair of cutoff jeans. They both stared at Sheila's heels, short blue skirt, low-cut blouse, and slightly smeared lipstick.

"What? They missed the arrival time. I had a date."

"Next time," Marta said, "you might want to remember that tags go on the inside of your shirt."

Sheila flushed. She turned and made a quick wardrobe adjustment. Anxious to refocus everyone's attention, she said, "I assume it's like the last time for both of you, too?

We've somehow merged with our past selves?"

"So, do you think this is how it's going to be?" Marshall asked. "Every time?"

Marta frowned. "Yeah. I think so, and this really sucks. I was studying at the library. As soon as I snapped into this time frame, the disorientation hit me hard. I think I—the me from the future—understands what happened. But the me already here can't get her head around it."

She tapped her fist to the side of her head a couple of times.

"Well, I guess I'm lucky, then, because this isn't too bad for me ... us," Marshall said. "Even though I do have a strong sense of division in my brain, the tracks don't twist themselves together as much as the last time. I seem to be able to keep them separate. I can take either track I want, focus on that one and still keep an awareness of the other."

Sheila realized she hadn't yet undertaken an analysis of her own experience. Only now did she understand this event was vastly different from the first.

"I don't have any disorientation," she said. "My past self understood quickly. Each of us recognizes the other, and we have no problem reconciling the two. We've had our moments of disagreement, but—"

"So, what were you doing when integration occurred?" Marta asked. "Maybe there's some environmental factor, or a specific experience that mitigates the disorientation."

Sheila blushed again.

"I ... well," she fumbled, "I was getting ready to ... uh ... I was laughing."

"So, what happened this time?"

A couple of hours earlier, Raul Hinojosa watched as the three travelers returned after their second mission to the past. Then, he'd answered the summons to yet another anonymous grey room smelling of new paint, the furnishings a table and two molded plastic chairs. Again, Andrew Gormly sat as his inquisitor.

"Everybody got back okay this time."

"Did their memories of the event improve at all? Or is this whole exercise just a pointless waste of money?"

"They wouldn't let us into the debriefings," Raul said. "I'll have to wait for the official report to know for sure."

Gormly peered intently at Raul for a moment, as if his glare could discern truth. "Who handles the debriefings?"

"The first time, a lot of people. The technical guys, psychologists. We gave statements for a couple of days. Today, Dr. Andropov, Dr. Allen and the Chinese woman met with them for a while, then they did the medical stuff."

"When are you scheduled to travel again?"

Raul shook his head.

"I don't know, man. Looks like they're sticking with those three for now."

Gormly stood abruptly, sending the plastic chair skidding backward. He leaned across the table on heavy hands and thick arms.

"It's nothing I can control, you know?" Raul said. "It's not my fault."

Gormly turned up the intensity on his glare.

"Anything . . . else?" Raul said.

Gormly responded with a dismissive wave. Raul quickly withdrew. Gormly sat and folded his hands atop the cheap, bare table. He did not acknowledge another opening and closing of the door. Neither did he glance at the janitor who began to wipe the doorknob, table and other surfaces with a damp cloth.

"Why the fuck him and not me? Or you, Josh? You think Marshall Grissom could ever fly a jet?"

Jason Pratt, still wearing his maintenance crew coveralls and appearing every inch the tired, bored drone scientists and engineers and computer wizards perceived him to be, nursed a beer and listened to the conversation taking place just a couple of tables away.

Raul Hinojosa and Josh Mathis, the two surviving disenfranchised time travelers, were deep into their cups and delving into the mystery of why Marshall?

"The guy's a total putz," Raul continued. "He doesn't say anything. He just sits there looking overwhelmed."

Well, he's a weird duck, no question about that," Josh said, "but he's a good enough guy. I mean, he works really hard."

Raul snorted. "Speaking of hard. I'll tell you what it is. It's that monster dick. I've seen pythons that would be intimidated by that thing. I bet Gretchen Allen and Naomi Hu kept him on the team just because they like looking at his dong."

Their conversation dissolved into laughter.

Travelers, scientists and engineers, who all shared a higher security clearance level than the support staff at the GRC, were forbidden to discuss any aspects of their jobs while drinking and communing at The Time Warp. But they did it all the time.

Pratt had picked up all sorts of valuable tidbits for Gormly. He eavesdropped with the help of a powerful directional microphone built into an ink pen he kept in his shirt pocket, and the hearing aid tucked into his left ear.

"The worst thing about it," Raul continued, "is before we were kicked off the team, I think Sheila was starting to warm up to me. I was gonna make my move."

"I don't know," Josh said. "Did you see who she was here with last week? That Frank Altman guy."

"Altman? He's dumb as a stump."

"Yeah, but he looks like he could be on a magazine cover somewhere. If you're looking to get laid by a time traveler, you'd probably be better off focusing on Marta. She's not bad."

"Maybe not," Raul said, "but I'd be worried she might castrate me. She's got a pretty intense attitude."

"The only thing that bothers me about not being included is the money," Josh said. "I agreed to switch over from Light Speed, because every mission is supposed to build our trust accounts. While we sit, not only am I falling behind the other Light Speed guys, I'm not making the money Dr. Rose said I would."

"Yeah," agreed Raul. "The only reason I volunteered to be in this hole for five years is the money. I figured to come out of this thing set for life." He emitted a smirking snort, followed by slurring speech. "Fortunately, I've located a different source of income as well."

Pratt brought the beer bottle to his lips and used the movement to disguise a narrow-eyed glance in Raul's direction. The conversation fell silent for a long moment.

"What do you mean?" Josh finally asked. "They'll throw

your ass in jail and forget you were ever here if—"

"No, no, nothing like that," Raul said a little too quickly. "On the outside. I've got some . . . investments waiting. I'm like you. I don't want to just sit here. If they don't put me back on active status soon, I might just leave."

Josh laughed. "Yeah, right. All you have to do is climb over the fences."

Pratt swallowed the last third of his beer in one long chug, put a few bills on his table, and rose to leave. He smiled at how things were working out.

SECRETS

"I'VE GOT TO FIGURE THIS OUT, Gillis," Marta whispered earnestly as they walked together along one of the endless concrete corridors. "I really don't care for the idea of traveling to the past with someone who might want to kill me."

"Well, the original assassin is dead, thanks to your vigilance. And I think you can trust Miss Schuler, seeing as how she was his target."

Of all her fellow spies slinking about the GRC project, Gillis Kerg, a dapper little traveler candidate representing the Grand Duchy of Luxembourg, was Marta's favorite. He made no effort to hide his desire for Marta, but he suffered her sexual rejections with grace and a sense of humor.

"Yeah. If someone in Light Speed really is trying to screw us, though, I've no reason to think they'll stop."

She agreed with Gillis. She could trust Sheila. That left Marshall, Raul and Josh. Josh had to be high on the suspect list, because, along with Felix Werber, he came over from the Light Speed side. And Raul . . . something about him raised her hackles the moment they met. Marshall she'd dismissed out of hand. No way could Marshall Grissom be a terrorist saboteur, could he?

When she raised her doubts to Gillis, he stopped, checked up and down the corridor and said, "Marta, I have something I think you need to see."

Marta laughed. "No, Gillis. I really don't need to see it. I think I can go pretty much my whole life without seeing it."

"No, no, not *that*. I have something that bears on your current dilemma."

Along with his harmless charm, Marta admired Gillis for his skill set. They knew each other because they'd worked together on a previous assignment involving the interests of both their governments. So, when they ran into each other at the registration session eighteen months ago, they each understood the other's purpose here.

Gillis knew everything about cutting edge security systems, particularly how to defeat them. Few secrets would be safe once he got his covert electronic network operating. The process took a while, though, given the sophistication of security at a state-of-the-art facility like the GRC.

Marta followed Gillis to his apartment where a retinal scan gave them access.

"Welcome home, Gillis Kerg. Ah, and you have a female guest."

The lighting in the apartment dimmed and strains of violins whispered in the background.

"Nobody's getting lucky here!" Marta told the apartment. "Gillis, haven't you figured out how to turn these things off yet?"

"Sorry. I've been working on it, but other issues have taken priority. You'll understand in a moment."

Marta hadn't been in Gillis's living quarters. The

apartment layouts were essentially the same. A living room divided from a kitchenette by an island containing a sink and stove. A bedroom with a bath opened off the main room.

Marta furnished her apartment comfortably—a couch, two chairs, coffee table and 3-D video screen. The main room of Gillis's apartment, though, contained a single cabinet placed along one wall. A large desk precisely centered in the living space and a generic office chair on wheels were the only other furnishings.

"You must introduce me to your decorator," Marta said.

Gillis touched his palm to a scanning device and the main door of the cabinet clicked open. He withdrew an electronic sponge—a standard bit of industrial espionage gear. When activated, the sponge soaked up all electronic signals within a fifteen-foot radius, rendering listening or viewing devices useless and providing protection from eavesdroppers.

"I'll show you the project I've been working on," he said. "I've hacked into the security system and installed my own backup that's fed to a server in the cloud. When any set of security cameras are switched off, my system turns them back on and diverts the feed to my hidden server while the main security monitors remain dark. Security guards switch off cameras scanning certain areas with some frequency. Typically, they're covering for their colleagues who sneak away for unauthorized breaks or clandestine sexual liaisons."

"I'll bet that makes for some interesting late-night viewing," Marta said.

"Yes, but occasionally I turn up something else. Now, understand, I must hack into the system a section at a time, so I'm still adding individual corridors or rooms. And I haven't enabled audio yet. But I found this snippet of video two nights ago. You'll note the time stamp is two a.m."

Gillis touched a sensor on his desk and a 3-D projector lit the room. A virtual keyboard appeared under his fingers. An indistinct image gradually resolved itself into life-like reality.

Marshall Grissom appeared before them. He stood just outside an airlock at the entrance to the laboratory housing the time projector. He bent over something, his legs and arms straining. He stood, and an object protruded back into the corridor. Marta recognized a large plastic trash bin, tilted on two small wheels. An unseen person inside the lab held the bin, balancing it on its wheels. Marshall said something to the unseen person, then bent again to his task. He shoved. The wheels bounced over the metal lip at the airlock's base, and Marshall followed inside. The empty corridor remained on screen another few seconds before a fade to black.

"That's all I captured," Gillis said.

"Shit," Marta said. "I must be slipping. I guess I read Marshall completely wrong."

"When you get this morning's security report, "Gillis said, "you'll find that sometime during the evening or early morning two days ago, Raul Hinojosa disappeared. The security team believes he somehow snuck out of the complex. Which is absurd. I mean, I can get out when I want to, but unless the entire security staff is compromised, Raul would find it impossible."

"Did you guys hear about Raul?" Sheila asked.

"What about him?" Marshall asked through a yawn.

The three travelers sat in a classroom across the hall from Naomi Hu's office, waiting for their memory and focus instruction to begin.

"Were you up late last night?" Sheila asked with a suggestive smile.

"I haven't been able to sleep lately," Marshall said. "I've been wandering the halls."

"What about Raul?" Marta asked as she studied Marshall. *Damn, this guy is good.*

"Since they weren't letting him travel, he bailed," Sheila said

"What do you mean, he bailed?

"He's gone. Snuck out two nights ago."

"Snuck out?" Marshall said. "How do you sneak out? There's no way any of us could get past the security."

"Obviously, there is a way, because he's gone," Sheila said.

"So, what if he wasn't traveling?" Marshall said. "That doesn't make any sense. Does that make sense to you, Marta?"

Marta shrugged. She admired Marshall's ability to remain in character. "I suppose not."

"He *said* he left because he wasn't getting to travel," Sheila said.

"What, you talked to him?" Marta turned to participate more directly in the exchange.

"No. He sent a text to Jolene. You know the blonde with the medical staff? She told me he said since he couldn't travel, he couldn't make the cash incentives to build up his trust fund. So, he left."

"He sent a text?"

"Yeah. I guess he and Jolene had a thing."

"Even if he couldn't make his cash incentives," Marshall said, "he still has all that money waiting for him at the end of five years."

"Except he probably got bored," Sheila said.

"But now he's facing prison. It just doesn't make sense."

"Some people have motivations other than money," Marta said, allowing a suspicious gaze to linger on Marshall an instant too long.

Dr. Leonard Rose pounded the table. "You have to be kidding, Michael. They've suffered a fatality! Now one of their travelers is a deserter, and you still won't shift funding to Light Speed?"

Michael Huxtable, administrator of the Global Research Consortium, sat at the head of a small conference table, refusing to rise to Rose's tantrum. "Yes, Leonard. The sub-committee continues to believe that both projects are necessary. And while light speed is still in the developmental phase, the Wormhole Project is functional."

"You do understand, Leonard," Yuni Andropov said with just a touch of sarcasm, "that we have actually sent our travelers to the past, while your light speed ship only exists in computer simulations?"

"Yes, well, we don't want to kill our astronauts by prematurely subjecting them to human testing," Rose said. "And I've yet to see any data from your projections. So, I don't know whether you've succeeded or not."

"Sorting through a flood of data is an overwhelming

task," Andropov said. "That's one reason we've requested more manpower. We'll make the information available as soon as we've been able to interpret it."

Leonard Rose, though, wasn't the only one upset with the lack of interpretive information regarding the first two projections. Yuni knew all too well members of his own science and engineering groups were grumbling because they weren't getting full access to data.

In an undertaking so complex as time travel, various divisions and departments received their piece of the information, then passed it along where it combined with other data streams to provide a full picture. And right now, the only people privy to the whole truth were Yuni, Gretchen Allen and Naomi Hu. Yuni knew he would spend considerable time trying to calm each group and stave off a mutiny while he continued to stonewall them.

And the first group he had to deal with was his team of travelers. They waited in his office right now, demanding answers. He strode into the projection lab like a horse wearing blinders, adopted his *don't mess with me* scowl, and headed straight to his office. He closed the door, lowered the blinds to cover windows looking out on the lab, and turned to face Marta, Marshall, and Sheila. Gretchen and Naomi sat stoic at the conference table.

Sheila didn't wait for Yuni to sit. "We have questions, Dr. Andropov. It's our asses on the line here, and we want answers."

Yuni stared for a long moment before he sat. "I'm not sure we know the answers yet."

"You haven't heard the questions."

"Yuni," Naomi said with a warning note in her voice.

He sighed and made a waving gesture for Sheila to continue.

"When we arrive in the past, why aren't there two of us? Why do two beings seem to occupy a single body?"

Yuni nodded to Naomi.

"We have a couple of ideas," she said. "One could have to do with matter—essentially precise duplication at a subatomic level. Since you and your past self are comprised of identical matter, Gretchen says it's possible you and your past self must occupy the same space. Since intellect is not matter, the thoughts of your past and future selves compete for dominance in one brain. I tend to think it's simpler than that, though. Just the fact that you share identical DNA—"

"Wait, wait," Sheila interrupted. "You said *compete* for dominance. That doesn't sound good."

"It would account for the discomfort and anxiety you sometimes describe during the integration of your past and future selves. The future being brings the details of events the past being hasn't yet experienced. You understand what's happening. They don't. But the exchange goes both ways. And as the projections take us farther into the past, the past being will be the storehouse of memories the future being has forgotten, or rationalized, or minimized."

"So, there's a psychological conflict?" Marta asked.

"Well, I don't know if *conflict* is exactly the right way to characterize the—"

"Yes, Yuni, it is," Naomi said. "And we have to be careful how we deal with that."

"Okay," said Marta, "if, when we travel to the past, we

occupy the minds of our past counterparts, what happens if there is no past counterpart? What happens, for example, if we try to travel to a point prior to our birth?"

"It may be years," Gretchen said, "before we're comfortable trying to traverse that great a time span—"

Again, Naomi interrupted. "You're right, Marta. I think traveling too far into the past would present a grave danger to a being from the future. And I think that danger exists much sooner than birth. Impacting a toddler's mind, or the mind of a four or five-year old with adult emotions and awareness would be traumatic, even psychologically devastating, to the past being."

"All right," Sheila said, "let's talk about the geographical issue."

Yuni groaned. Clearly, these two women were more intuitive than he'd given them credit for. He saw Gretchen turn to him with questioning eyes. Again, he frowned and nodded his assent.

"You're right," Gretchen said. "If, as has been the case in our first two projections, the traveler goes to the physical location of his or her past counterpart at any given time, we may have a problem. We thought we were dealing with travel through time. If we are traveling through both time and space, though, we have to consider the projector's power limitations."

"During the earliest phases of testing, though," Yuni said, "that shouldn't be an issue. We won't send you to a time frame beyond the past eighteen months, when you've all been on the GRC campus."

"And when the missions go beyond eighteen months?" Marta asked.

"Frankly," Naomi said, "that's one reason the three of

you are here. We've done our best to piece together histories of the animals used in testing. We believe that we successfully retrieved the subjects when their past counterparts were within five hundred miles distance of this facility. The three of you have lived within five hundred miles for much of the past decade."

"So, what if you pick a time in the past when we were on vacation?" Marshall asked.

"We'll be careful not to do that."

"I've got to tell you, Dr. Andropov," Sheila said following the next morning's mission planning session, "everybody's suspicious of the secrecy surrounding the initial debriefings. Everybody knows we're withholding something. And it doesn't help that you dismiss everyone else at the end of these planning sessions. You've got some of the smartest people in the world out there. How long do you think you can fool them?"

"Fool them?" Yuni asked, trying to disguise his irritation.

Coffee cups and empty soft drink cans littered the oak table. Marta was glad Sheila had taken the initiative. Together, they'd decided this confrontation had to continue. The full science team had shared the mission planning session, until, as Sheila said, Yuni called the meeting to an end, asking Naomi, Gretchen and the three travelers to stay behind.

"After each meeting you coach us on what to say," Sheila said. "Why don't you just tell them?"

"Tell them what?" Gretchen asked. She exchanged a troubled glance with Yuni.

"Parallel universe theory," Marta said. "You three think we're traveling to a parallel universe."

"You are jumping to a dangerous conclusion, Miss Hamilton—" Yuni said.

"Oh, come on, Yuni," Gretchen interrupted. "I've argued all along that the travelers need to know. We'll understand much more quickly if we have informed observations."

Yuni scowled, crossed his arms over his chest, and turned away.

"Wait a minute, please," said Marshall. "Parallel universe? I've missed something again."

"Do you remember my lecture on causality?" Gretchen asked him.

"Oh, yeah," Marshall said with relief. "That killing your grandfather stuff."

Sheila playfully punched his arm. "Yeaaaa, Marshall!"

Marta nearly smiled.

Gretchen applauded. "Go ahead and tell us about it, Marshall."

"Well, they used to think travel into the past was impossible because of causality." Marshall pointed at Marta. "That's where one thing causes another. And that creates the grandfather paradox. If you go to the past and kill your grandfather before he has children, you and all your descendants cease to exist. But if your existence is eliminated, then you wouldn't be around to go back and kill your grandfather in the first place."

"There is a way out of the paradox, though," Sheila said.

"And that," added Marta, "would be a parallel universe."

Gretchen beamed. "Actually, *universes*. Theoretically, an infinite number of them. Quantum theory suggests that, rather than the past of her own world, a time traveler would find herself in the past of an identical—parallel—existence. And if you killed your grandfather there, you and your descendants in our universe would be unaffected. The kicker is that the arrival of the time traveler would theoretically disrupt parallel histories of the two universes and send that other universe off in a different historical direction."

"So, if that's what's happening," Marshall said, "why are we keeping it secret?"

"Because we don't know anything, yet," Yuni said. "We haven't proven anything. Until we know for sure, we can't let rumors get back to the investors—"

"But you've got a whole group of people here ready to embark on a Light Speed Project that will cost billions, because they think we've got a time machine that can return travelers to their native time—and universe," Sheila said.

"Yes, but here's the other side of that coin," Yuni countered. "If the investors get even the hint of a rumor we're dealing with parallel universes, and they can't manipulate either the past or the future of *our* universe for profit, most of them will withdraw their funding. The whole project could collapse."

"The Light Speed program," said Gretchen, "is a morass just waiting to suck up funding and leave nothing to show for it. Light Speed advocates think just because we have this enriched hydrogen energy source, we can bludgeon the laws of physics into submission."

"You don't think it will work?" Sheila asked.

Gretchen shrugged.

"What I know is that we have a functioning mechanism

providing access to the past. This device offers opportunities never before possible to explore the nature of the universe. To turn our backs on this prospect for whatever reason would be a crime against science. If we must keep some secrets among ourselves to protect that opportunity, I'm all for it."

"And you're convinced we're going to the past of a parallel universe?" Marta asked.

"I am . . ." Gretchen said, but her voice trailed off.

"Except?" Marta probed.

"Except, some theories also suggest that an exchange of matter between two universes would create problems."

"What kind of problems?" Sheila asked.

"One or both universes would be boiled away in a cataclysmic explosion."

"What?" said Sheila. "You mean we're fooling with stuff here that could destroy universes?"

"Theoretically."

"But you said there's no exchange of matter—just intellect," Marta said.

"Theoretically."

"We really do need to know more," Yuni offered.

"Well, I guess," Sheila said.

Despite their best intentions, Marta knew Yuni, Gretchen and Naomi suffered a naiveté that threatened them all. "Okay," she said, "now let me tell you what else is happening out there. Nobody can keep secrets in a place like this. It's nice to think everybody does what they're told, and everybody's goal is purity of the science. From the day these doors opened, though, political factions have been lining up. Right now, rumors are rampant, and the political intrigue has been dialed up to a whole new level.

"Leonard Rose is really pissed because he and the other physicists no longer share the debriefings. If he hasn't already filed a formal complaint—" Marta knew that he had. "—he will any day. All that's keeping us afloat right now is the bureaucratic morass he has to wade through before anyone gets around to processing his grievance. And I'll guarantee you, he's planning some kind of end run around the bureaucracy. Sooner or later you'll have to tell them about parallel universes. And you must tell them before they find out independently."

Yuni shook his head. "At worst, such a disclosure will mean the suspension of our budget. At best, our funding will be reduced. Very few of our benefactors want to bankroll pure research."

"So that's the tightrope we have to walk," Marta said. "We must withhold the parallel universe thing while you try to find proof, and yet know when they are close to figuring it out on their own. If they find out before you announce your conclusions, I hate to think what's going to happen to the six of us. We almost certainly will be prosecuted for a variety of crimes. And you won't be doing much research from a prison cell."

"Wow, Marta," Marshall said. "How do you know this stuff?"

"The place I worked before was just like this."

13

WHO IS THAT MASKED MAN?

"EVERY INSTINCT TELLS ME Marshall is just who he seems to be," Marta told Gillis. "And that worries me. My perceptions are usually dead on."

The Wormhole Project conducted eight more projections over the following month, each consisting of ritualistic baby steps. The goal of each mission, to penetrate a little farther into the past and cautiously extend the travelers' time there.

Marta and Gillis used each journey to try and build their case against Marshall, hoping he would make a misstep, hoping fervently they'd catch him before he, or someone, could carry out another attempt at sabotage.

Gillis checked both directions down the long concrete hallway to determine he and Marta were beyond hearing distance of any casual eavesdroppers passing by.

"What better disguise for an assassin than a bumbling, good-natured dolt who makes every effort not to call attention to himself?" he asked.

"Yeah, but that's the other thing. Physically, he's the absolute center of attention. He can't just recede into the shadows now, can he?"

"Remember, though," Gillis said, "none of us came to

this project expecting nudity to be a job requirement."

"Before taking any action, I'd be much more comfortable if you could provide a little more video."

Taking action? What did I mean by that? I didn't act knowing Felix's death would be the result. I acted on impulse. I only wanted to do to him what he was trying to do to Sheila. I didn't know the result would be fatal. Or did I? And do I feel remorse at taking a life? No, because ultimately, facts justified my action. But, Marshall? How far do you have to stretch things to rationalize self-defense?

"Well, so would I," Gillis said. "And to that end, more and more of my system is online every day. But let's review what we do know. You and I both agree Raul is not capable of getting out of this facility on his own. We have Marshall Grissom outside the projection lab at two a.m., when the security cameras have been taken off-line. He is clearly working with a confederate, pushing a wheeled trash receptacle *into* the lab. The effort required makes plain the receptacle is full of something heavy—like a body. I think the evidence is clear."

"I just don't know, Gillis. I am the most mistrusting, cynical person I know. But I just don't . . . Sometimes I think I actually like the guy."

"Then there's your entry point," Gillis said. "Be friendlier, more inclusive. Get closer to him. Meanwhile, I keep looking for a corroborating video."

"I'm sorry. It's just hard for me to imagine that Marshall Grissom has an ultimate plan . . . about anything."

Gillis grasped Marta by the shoulders and looked squarely into her eyes. "If I'm right, you and Sheila are joined at the hip with a killer. You'll be susceptible at every

MIKE MURPHEY

turn. Just think how easy it would be on a mission for him to engineer an accident with absolutely no witnesses in this time and place."

Marta almost asked *but to what purpose?* She knew the answer, though. With billions of dollars at stake, both nations and corporations might be completely willing to sacrifice any number of lives to slant the future of the technology to their benefit.

105

14

FIGHTING INFLATION

WITH EACH MISSION, GRETCHEN and Yuni quietly gleaned any and all evidence regarding their parallel universe hypothesis. Naomi instituted a series of mental exercises designed to help the travelers' recall of mission details. And with each projection, the travelers became more comfortable, although integration with their past selves remained a sticking point.

Marshall's other problem, unfortunately, failed to abate with experience.

At first, many of the lab personnel—particularly the women—did their best to appear not to notice, though Marshall knew too well that they did.

My good lord, how could they not?

Every furtive glance fed the fire. And as Marshall's struggles continued, the staff's polite comportment began to deteriorate. Marshall would close his eyes and try to block Sheila's incredible presence, but titters and gasps seeped through this mental barrier. Marshall would peek out to stares of . . . *ridicule. It had to be ridicule.*

The better he knew Sheila, the more he loathed himself for his inability to control his response. His erections, he decided, conveyed the message that he reduced this woman—whom he liked and admired—to a sexual object. He feared his misguided boners gave Sheila an entirely incorrect idea of who he was. Not to mention Marta. Marshall stood in awe of Marta's focused self-discipline and intellect. *God, what if Marta thought . . . ?*

Finally, he mustered the courage to talk to Naomi.

"Dr. Hu?" He rapped on the frame of her open door.

Naomi cringed and said from behind her office desk, "Please don't call me that, Marshall. I prefer to be addressed as Naomi. How can I help you?"

The tiny woman with characteristic Chinese eyes, porcelain skin and ebony hair motioned for him to sit in one of two overstuffed chairs facing her desk. She stepped around to occupy the other one.

"I . . . I'm not sure that I'm suited for this. For time travel, I mean."

"Nonsense, Marshall. Why would you think that?"

"Well, for one thing, I'm allergic to anchovies."

"You're . . . Um . . . so far nothing has come up to lead me to believe that's an issue."

"I break out. Big hives all over."

"Okay . . . I'll make a note of that in your file. But honestly, my psychological assessment indicates that, if anything, you are *more* suited to time travel than the others. You handle transition into your past self more smoothly than anyone else. You cope well with the limbo. I'm intrigued by your ability to retain memories longer and more specifically than the others . . . and we've yet to encounter a single anchovy."

"Yes, I know. But I seem to be more and more of a . . . a distraction?"

"Oh. That."

Marshall fidgeted and studied the ceiling.

"Marshall, it's a perfectly normal reaction. Both Sheila and Marta are attractive women."

"That's the point. It's *not* a perfectly normal reaction. When other guys get up there with Sheila and Marta, *then* it will be a perfectly normal reaction. With me, it's not, because I'm . . . not perfectly normal!"

He folded his lanky frame with elbows on knees and stared past Naomi to the professional certificates displayed on her wall.

"No, I suppose I would have to concede you're not. Many men would take a certain . . . pride, I suppose, in being . . . large."

"Ha! I never thought I would be the guy up there everyone watches. When I found out what the program was about, I figured I'd just hang around and help out for five years while more qualified people did the traveling. Now, this . . . this . . . it's just so embarrassing!"

"I'm sorry, Marshall. We must do it this way. Travelers must be naked. If we could find any other . . . you remember when we tried the curtains and they caught on fire? We can't have fires in the projection lab."

"Well, can't something . . . medical . . . be done about . . . you know?"

Naomi shook her head. "Unfortunately, Marshall, medical science has devoted countless resources over the past sixty years to enabling erections. Nobody's thought much about curing them."

"Aren't there drugs?"

"Yes, but they're bad for you, and, besides, we go to a lot

of effort to be sure travelers are devoid of any foreign substances. We have no idea what complications even the mildest of drugs might present during a projection."

Marshall sighed and smoothed the nap of the upholstery along his chair's armrest.

"At first, you know, everyone tried to be polite about it. Then half-disguised whispers and laughs started. If it's just the women, that's one thing. But now it's everyone. And nobody's really trying to hide it."

"Oh, Marshall, I'm sure you're exaggerating—"

"No, I'm not. Yesterday, when I got ... well ... one of the guys at the monitors jumped up and did a little fist pump. And three of the women near the cameras slapped high fives!"

"I can certainly talk to Yuni about proper decorum—"

"No. He'd write a memo and that would just make everything worse."

"You have to understand, this isn't directed at you because there's anything wrong with you, Marshall. You can't help that you've got a ... that you're ... um ... you. This is human nature at work. We have a group of bright people confined to this facility, and, frankly, they're bored. They're apt to grasp at any distraction as a form of entertainment."

So, Marshal remained on his own. He recalled the Japanese adage warning that the protruding nail will be hammered down—and his nail protruded more than anyone's.

At the completion of each mission, Marshall only wanted to hide. Thankfully, this day's debriefing process had been short. He walked from the locker room, intending to go straight home and assure his apartment of his mental well-being. A stocky man wearing an expensive suit stood near the elevators. Marshall nodded politely as he made his way past.

"I must say," the man said with a grin, "I found your performance today impressive, Mr. Grissom."

Almost genetically incapable of being rude, Marshall stopped and gave a self-deprecating shrug. If ever a situation existed where Marshall wished he could dismiss someone and walk away, this was it. He didn't know this man. And he wasn't sure whether the guy was complimenting him on his time traveling skills or making a sarcastic comment about his dick. As he looked closer, though, the man seemed vaguely familiar. Marshall worried that he *should* know his name. Not recalling the name of someone he'd already met *would* be rude.

The man resolved Marshall's dilemma by extending a hand. "My name is Andrew Gormly. I'm the corporate representative of the Hemisphere Investment Group. I observed today's event. I admire your courage, young man."

The name meant nothing, but the context making the face familiar snapped into place. Marshall had seen this man talking with Raul Hinojosa way back at a reception soon after the traveler candidates arrived at the GRC campus. And he remembered Raul referring to the Hemisphere Investment Group a couple of times.

"Oh, yes," Marshall said. "You're a friend of Raul's."

The man seemed startled, and Marshall winced. Given Raul's recent desertion, Raul might not be someone this Mr. Gormly wanted to acknowledge.

"I'm sorry. Raul?"

"Raul Hinojosa? One of the other travelers?"

"Of course. Mr. Hinojosa. I met him along with several other candidates when you all arrived. I'm sorry to say I don't know him well, though."

"Oh, I just assumed—"

"I wanted to take a moment and tell you that you're performing a great service to humanity." He continued as Marshall shook his head. "Do not be modest, Mr. Grissom. I wish you continued good fortune and look forward to talking with you again."

The elevator arrived. The man stepped inside, bound for the desert above.

"Friend of yours?" Sheila asked as Marshall turned from the closing elevator door.

"Just some guy from one of the corporate contributors," Marshall said. "Um . . . I've been meaning to ask you. Right after the missions, have you noticed, like, a smell?"

"What, do I need to use more deodorant?"

"No, no. Nothing like that. More like a good smell."

"Well, we're very clean. Because of the showers."

"Not that kind of smell. It's something familiar. I just can't put my finger on it."

"I'll make it a point to smell you next time," Sheila offered. "For now, though, I'm glad I caught you." She linked her arm in his. "We need a break. Us three, the Time Warp. Nine o'clock."

Imagining all the stares and titters that would come his way, Marshall tried to decline.

Sheila would not have it. "Hey, I finally talked Marta into coming out of her room. She said she'd be there if you would."

Marshall scanned the crowd and found the women at a table way back against one wall. He forged a trail through the throng as unobtrusively as someone so tall could. The three of them shared small talk while Marshall nursed a beer. A veritable parade of men steered themselves toward Sheila, duplicate drinks in hand, only to alter their route as they encountered the razor sharpness of Marta's glare.

Finally, though, one brave soldier waded into hostile territory. The short, round man wore blue jeans and a long-sleeve shirt, half untucked, with a black t-shirt showing at the open collar. His unkempt hair was in retreat. He wore glasses and sported a three-day stubble.

"This is a private party," Marta said, scanning him up and down.

"I need to speak to Marshall," the man said.

Sheila seemed surprised.

"I need to speak to Marshall," the man repeated. "Over there." He pointed to an empty table. "Please."

Marshall looked to both Marta and Sheila. Marta scowled. Sheila shrugged.

"Um . . . okay," Marshall said. "I'll be right back."

"I'm Elvin Detwyler," the man said as Marshall joined him. "I monitor the lifeline displays during the projections."

"Yes, I've seen you."

"Yeah, well, I need to talk to you because me and some of the guys need your help. And there would be money in it for you. We'd split the pot. You'd get half."

"Half? The pot? I'm sorry, I'm not following—"

"The betting pool. We've got a special side bet with the female lab techs." Elvin pointed across the room to a table near the bar where a half dozen clearly inebriated women laughed and leaned against each other. When they saw Elvin point, they smiled and raised their drinks in a sarcastic toast. Then they succumbed to another wave of laughter. One of them fell out of her chair.

"What betting pool?" Marshall's voice acquired a low, menacing tone surprising even him.

"Oh, my God!" Elvin's laugh conveyed disbelief. "You mean you don't know?"

Marshall attempted an intimidating glare and failed.

"The erection pool?"

Marshall's face fell. "You're betting on . . . what?"

"Your erections. You know, how hard? How fast?"

Marshall slumped and felt a wave of despair. "Why would anyone—?"

"Hey, man, I'm sorry. I honestly thought you knew. But listen. There's a big side bet and if we win, we'll split it with you. We just need you to, you know, tone it down the next three times out."

"Tone it down?" Marshall said with exasperation. "Tone it down? You think I do this on purpose?" He stood abruptly, gave a dismissive wave with his hands and started back to Sheila and Marta.

"Look, just come and talk to us tomorrow," Elvin called after him. "We think we may be able to help. What have you got to lose?"

When he returned to the table, Marta stared at him for a moment. "That looked like an upsetting conversation."

Marshall frowned. "You wouldn't believe me if I told you."

Marshall awoke determined to have nothing to do with Elvin Detwyler and his gang of perverted computer thugs. So, he could not account for finding himself next to Elvin's bank of monitors a couple of hours later. Although no projection was scheduled today, several techs worked to interpret data from the last event.

"I want you to know," Marshall said as Elvin glanced from his computer, "this is very much against my better judgment."

Elvin smiled, did a quick survey of the lab. "Follow me." He tapped the backs of two other computer techs, who accompanied them. The small procession ducked into an office off the corridor just outside the lab.

"Marshall Grissom," said Elvin as he closed the office door, "I'd like you to meet—"

Marshall paid no attention to the others. He looked only at Elvin. "You said you could help."

"We have some ideas. And, as I indicated, we'll share the—"

"I don't care about your money. Just tell me."

Elvin described the betting pools. He accepted bets right up to the moment Sheila took off her robe. The winner had to come closest to a combination of degree of hardness and elapsed time to total erection at the instant Marshall *left the building*. Elvin had worked out an algorithm that provided a score of the combined criteria.

Marshall could only offer an incredulous stare.

"You don't get all the way ... up ... all the time, you know? That's what keeps it interesting."

"How can you ... How do you measure ...?"

"Oh, sure, we have disputes. Sometimes we replay the video. We pick judges."

Marshall's chin fell to his chest, a gesture of abject defeat. "I do not believe this."

"So, here's the deal. We were drinking with the ladies the other night, and the subject of woodies came up. They wouldn't shut up about how the male animal has no control. And we couldn't just sit there and take it. I mean, we had to defend the gender, right? We disagreed, and it worked out to this side bet. They say you're helpless. We say you're not."

"I *am* helpless!"

"Not true. The bet is about total erection—time lapsed from flaccid to proud. And there've been lots of times you've been projected before you're ... complete."

"It's a pretty dumb bet," Marshall said.

"We were pretty drunk," one of the computer techs offered.

"It's not as one-sided as it sounds," Elvin said. "We agreed to take the average of the next three projections. You've got three shots at this, starting tomorrow."

Marshall exhaled heavily, leaned down to put his hands on the empty desk next to Elvin, and shut his eyes.

"So, you have ideas you think might help." He said the words as if making an accusation.

"Jerk off," said another of the computer techs.

"I beg your pardon?"

"You should jerk off."

"Surely you must, I mean, from time to time," Elvin said.

Marshall stared with consternation. He couldn't believe he was having this conversation.

"In the locker room, when you take your shower," the other computer tech advised.

Marshall turned and left without comment.

The next day, though, as he stepped into the shower, Marshall peered cautiously at the empty lockers and bathroom stalls and thought, "Well, it couldn't hurt..."

Shielded by his robe, he strode into the projection lab more acutely aware than ever of expectant expressions. Some of the women were wide-eyed with anticipation, which threatened to get him going again.

He breathed deeply. Nothing. Marta dropped her robe and stepped forward. He still dangled. Sheila gave him a big smile as she dropped her robe and followed. *Uh oh*. Marshall felt that pleasant surge begin. *Do it, do it now. Push the damn button.*

And he was gone.

Twenty minutes later—as the projection lab clocks measured the interval—Marshall returned safely to his native time, relieved by the hope he'd found a solution. Until ordered to produce the post-projection semen sample when he found he didn't recharge that quickly.

"What's wrong?" a male doctor called gruffly through the door as he waited for Marshall to finish.

"I...I don't think it's going to happen."

When the door swung open and the doctor's face appeared. "Why not?"

"Geez, Doc," Marshall protested as he tried to cover himself.

"For Christ's sake, I'm a physician. What's wrong? Are you sick? I'll line up some tests and see—"

"No. No, nothing like that. It's just that I, um, I masturbated just before the mission, and I don't think I can—"

"You did what?"

"I... you know what my problem is out there. It's embarrassing to have everyone see me. I was just trying to—"

"Well, don't! We need this information. This will leave a gap in our database. I'm going to talk to Naomi."

The male betting pool participants were thrilled, though.

Until the next projection when Sheila's robe slipped to the floor as she was handing it to a technician assisting her. Having become accustomed to her nudity she bent over without thinking and picked it up. Marshall watched from behind and lost any semblance of control.

"What happened," Elvin asked upon Marshall's return. "Didn't you—?"

"No."

"Why not?"

"They won't let me."

So, the wager came down to the third projection.

"We doubled the bet," Elvin told Marshall.

"Why? I told you it's a really dumb bet."

"Meet us tomorrow morning. The media room, two hours before the projection," Elvin said. "We've got a lot riding here."

"Don't you people have a shred of human decency?" Marshall asked, and stomped away.

The next morning, though, two hours before projection, Marshall walked into the media room.

117

He glared at Elvin. "This is against—"

"Yeah, yeah, I know. Your better judgment. I think we've got it this time. Sit down right here."

Marshall sat in the mini-auditorium, lights dimmed, and a 3-D projector lowered from the ceiling behind him. There followed a half hour of the most perverse and grotesque sexual scenes Marshall had ever witnessed. Ancient pornographic films depicting swarthy men with ape-like body hair, wearing black socks, having sex with swarthy women who had mustaches. Sex between swarthy men and swarthy midgets. Select scenes from a 1944 Army film entitled "Radical Field Treatment of Venereal Disease." An instructional video featuring a swarthy, obese, leather-clad disciplinarian named Arturo and a woman bearing an uncanny resemblance to Ma Kettle. And finally, selected scenes from a surgical procedure to remove a skateboard accident victim's crushed testicle.

Marshall sat stunned as the lights came on.

Elvin slid into the seat behind him and clapped a hand to Marshall's shoulder. "Hey, man. We just want to help."

When Marshall strode to the projection platform a half-hour later, a queasy uneasiness lingered. Taking his place between Sheila and Marta, though, he remained flaccid. He closed his eyes, inhaled deeply, blew out a cleansing breath. *Still limp.* He heard the projection mechanism start to whirr. He was going to make it.

Until he heard a chorus of eight women call out, *"Marshall!"* He opened his eyes and saw eight female technicians lift their shirts to expose an amazing assortment of bare breasts. The variety, combined with the sheer enthusiasm of the gesture, could not be ignored.

"Shit!" Elvin said just before Marshall jumped into the limbo.

15

THE PLOT THICKENS

DR. LEONARD ROSE COULD FEEL his future slipping away. He'd wanted the Wormhole Project. When he didn't get it, he shifted his campaign to the Light Speed Project and loudly disparaged the opposition. *The past is just a pipe dream, a fairy tale. Wormholes? Dark matter? Quantum dimensions? Theories and mythology. Physics' equivalent of the abominable snowman.*

They could follow a straightforward path to the future. Go fast enough, you'll get there. And he was dead serious when he called the Wormhole Project superfluous. Technological advances over two hundred years would be exponential. A solution to retrieve his astronauts from a distant future would exist without anyone lifting a finger in this current time and place.

But then Gretchen Allen and Yuni Andropov had gone and done it. They were traveling to the past. Or so they claimed. They weren't sharing data, so how could anyone be sure? Where was the proof? He knew they wouldn't dare create a fiction from whole cloth. But they could certainly exaggerate.

He'd anticipated that possibility and drawn on his

political advocates to install Captain Werber and Captain Mathis on the primary travelers' team to learn just how much of the Wormhole Project was smoke and mirrors. But Werber's death and Mathis's exclusion again left him in the dark.

Werber's demise, regrettable as it was, should have killed the Wormhole Project deader than Lazarus. But like Lazarus, somewhere Gretchen and Yuni had found a savior. And with each mission in which they claimed success, Light Speed faded a little bit more.

His resentment grew with each projection as the Wormhole triumvirate drew their cloak of secrecy ever tighter around the three remaining travelers. At the end of each projection, the three scientists and three travelers cloistered themselves. Then the travelers emerged to be debriefed by everyone else. To Rose's ear, their responses seemed too similar, too . . . sterile.

Rose considered himself clearly superior to Gretchen Allen as a physicist. And though he made early key contributions to every aspect of these programs, he feared destiny would relegate him to footnote status—one of hundreds of supporting characters.

The utter unfairness of that prospect brought him to this clandestine meeting with Andrew Gormly. They shared a booth at a café bar on the outskirts of Superior, Arizona. As a senior scientist, Rose could request time off the GRC campus, provided a security agent accompanied him. His official reason for going to Superior was to visit his ailing mother, who resided at an assisted living facility. But his security agent moonlighted on Gormly's payroll.

"Yuni persists in a concern that the projector is only

powerful enough to handle three or four travelers over geographical distances up to five hundred miles or so," Rose explained. "And that creates another problem. Now that they've got projections scheduled going back more than two years, geography becomes an issue."

"Geography?"

The pendulum light hanging from a low ceiling over their booth was apparently burnt out, and Rose struggled to decipher Gormly's facial expressions through shadows.

"When projected to the past, travelers appear to share the physical bodies of their past counterparts," Rose explained. "So Yuni insists those counterparts need to be within a five-hundred-mile radius of the projector. And two years ago, most of our traveler candidates were scattered all over the world. Of the six chosen and trained for early missions, Grissom, Schuler and Hamilton are the only three who meet that criterion."

"What about candidates who weren't chosen for the initial missions? What if we could find someone among them who would fit this geographical requirement? Could you make an argument to include that person among active travelers?"

Rose thought for a moment. "Yes. Yes, I think I could."

"Good. Get me names and profiles of anyone among the other candidates who would qualify. I'll apply some pressure. Then we'll know if, as you suggest, these Wormhole scientists are holding something back."

On the same afternoon Leonard Rose and Andrew Gormly cemented their conspiracy, Marshall Grissom's complicated existence became a little more so.

"Thanks for stopping by, Marshall," Naomi said. "I'm sorry to interrupt your afternoon break." She directed him to one of the leather chairs and closed the door behind him.

He'd never had a summons from Naomi. "That's okay. Um . . . did I do something wrong?"

"No, Marshall. Not at all." Followed by an awkward pause.

Marshall brightened a little. "Did you think of something to help with . . . you know?"

"No, Marshall. I wanted to see you because I'm afraid you might have a much bigger problem than . . . I'm sorry. I mean a much more serious problem than . . . *that*."

"Well, *that* doesn't sound good."

Naomi took a seat in the other leather chair. "I really don't know how to say this. This is so foreign to almost everything I believe about openness and . . . well, I need to take you into my confidence. I'm worried that perhaps I'm jumping to a wrong conclusion. But . . . I think you might be in danger."

"I think I already know that," Marshall said. "It's a frickin' wormhole, for god's sake."

"I mean, besides that."

She studied her hands. "Following Capt. Werber's death, we've spent a great deal of time dissecting video of the fatal projection. There's so much to review that we split the tapes among several of the science groups. By happenstance, among the tapes I was assigned is something disturbing. So much so, I've withheld it. No one has seen it but me, and now, you."

Naomi lifted a remote device from her chair's armrest and pointed it toward her desk. A 3-D image of the projection lab filled the space between them.

"This is the camera from directly behind the platform," Naomi said.

The scene, absent audio, showed six travelers and several technicians milling about in front of the platform. The travelers, clearly nervous, wore their white robes and appeared to exchange small talk.

"Now, watch right here."

Marshall cringed a little, anticipating the sight of his own nudity and feeling a pang of guilt for the charge he felt seeing Sheila and Marta's full-frontal exposure before they turned.

"Marta does an odd thing," Naomi said. "In our pre-projection simulations, she chose a position immediately to your left, with Raul to her right. Here, she positions herself next to Felix, instead. And now..." As the countdown clock above the observation platform facing them hit two seconds, Marta reached out, said something to Felix, and touched his back. Felix jerked his head around. His responsive expression was not one of just surprise. To Marshall, for that final split second, Felix appeared to be terrified.

Naomi pushed a button on the remote, and the images dissolved.

"I...I don't understand," said Marshall.

"This gesture of physical contact with Capt. Werber is so far outside Marta's psychological makeup as to be alarming. Marta, as you've undoubtedly noticed, is not a touchy-feely kind of person. She protects her physical space and has made no emotional displays—other than a very controlled anger—since I've known her."

"Oh, I don't know," Marshall said. "She's always been nice to me. Sort of. Well, you know. She hasn't thrown me to the ground or anything. I like Marta."

"I like Marta, too," Naomi said. "She's got a lot going on, a lot of inner turmoil, I think. But she's a much deeper, more feeling person than she lets on. Most disturbing of all, though, is the spot where Marta taps Felix on his back is the point of his fatal injury."

Marshall's mouth gaped. "You can't believe," he said carefully, "that Marta somehow killed Felix. She would never—"

"This scene can be interpreted several ways," Naomi said. "I could be reading meaning into things that are perfectly innocent. Or, Marta could have, with malice aforethought, killed Capt. Werber. Studying the video, though, I can construct a third scenario in which Marta acted in Sheila's defense."

Naomi chose another point in the video.

Wearing her robe, Sheila stood in profile at the far right of the group.

Felix stepped into her space, placed his right hand behind her neck, and attempted an awkward hug. Sheila appeared startled. She stiffened, then stepped back. Her expression suggested the seed of an angry response, but she took a deep breath, mouthed something that looked like *thank you* and turned away.

"I'll run it again," Naomi said. "This time watch Marta."

Naomi's laser pointed to Marta's position at the middle of the scene. Marta's attention seemed riveted on Felix as he approached Sheila and offered the hug. Her eyes remained on him as he turned to face her. His expression changed to one of apprehension as he met her eyes. Then he quickly retreated and spoke to Josh Mathis.

"Now," Naomi said, "we see Marta approach Sheila. They have a brief conversation, and they leave to return a few moments later. Sheila and Marta shed their robes first, and step to the platform . . ."

"Okay." Marshall nodded.

"What if Felix placed something dangerous on Sheila's body when he touched her? Marta saw this and took Sheila to the locker room to remove whatever it was—"

"And then at the last minute did to Felix whatever he was trying to do to Sheila?" Marshal thought for a moment and added, "But why? If she saw something dangerous, why wouldn't she have just pointed it out, called a halt to the projection and accused Felix instead of killing him?"

"That's what I'm unsure of," Naomi said. "To blame Marta now might destroy her career and send her to prison. I can't bring myself to do that when she may have saved Sheila's life. And that's another question. Was Sheila's involvement innocent? Or is her relationship with Marta— and Capt. Werber for that matter—more complicated?"

"So, what will you do?" Marshall asked.

"Nothing right now. I'll watch both Marta and Sheila more closely. For the moment this is our secret. I wanted to at least make you aware you could be in danger."

"What should I do?"

"Be vigilant," Naomi said. She paused in thought for a moment. "I know you like to keep mostly to yourself, Marshall. But you might try being more sociable with Marta and Sheila. See if you can get a read on where they stand in all this."

16

DEALING FRANKLY

Two Weeks Later

MARSHALL DIDN'T SEE HOW the others did it.

The meetings seemed interminable. They would be in one room with one set of scientists while hours dragged past, and then tromp to another room where a different cast of characters waited, because that meeting should have started ten minutes ago.

And Marshall had to pee.

So, he was last to arrive at the small conference room off Yuni's office where he saw Gretchen practically glowing with excitement.

"What's going on?" he asked Sheila from the side of his mouth as he chose the empty chair between her and Naomi.

"Yuni's decided to let Gretchen have her mission," Sheila said. "The staggered projection."

"That's correct." Yuni overheard their conversation. "Now, if we can get started."

"Isn't that the one everybody thinks is too dangerous?" Marshall whispered.

"Yes," Naomi whispered back. "But it's also the one that could provide some definitive answers about . . . you know . . . that thing."

"I thought we were building up to that one a couple of months from now," Sheila said to Yuni.

"So did I," Naomi agreed with a rather severe glance at the Russian.

"We must do it sooner or later," Yuni said. "The physics group says we're ready to project travelers in different time frames."

He deferred to Gretchen.

"This will be by far the most complicated projection we've attempted. Travelers will be projected five minutes apart. Rebooting the projector takes that long."

"Are you sure we're ready for something this complex?" came one voice from the far end of the oak table.

"We've heard rumors that some parties both inside and outside the science group feel we're going too slow, being too timid," Yuni said. "We need to stretch the capabilities of the technology. Eventually we must be able to project a traveler while other travelers are already engaged."

The mission sounded simple enough, Marshall conceded. Sheila would be projected first to an evening two weeks previous. Marta would go last. Marta recalled she had been studying in the facility's library. Sheila said she wasn't entirely sure, but she thought she grabbed a sandwich in the lunchroom. Marshall didn't have to guess. "I was home." They were to meet at Marshall's apartment.

The full science team, Marshall knew, believed this mission would test projection technology. For Yuni, Gretchen, Naomi and the three travelers, though, the real question was whether he, Marta and Sheila would show up in the same universe.

They worked at memory training exercises the day before the staggered projection mission. Yuni swept into the room, practically pulling Gretchen along with him. Marta found these memory exercises tedious, so she welcomed a break when Yuni gestured to Naomi and her minions that they should follow him.

As Yuni peered carefully about before shutting the door, Marta thought his pointy beard showed more grey than just a couple of days ago.

"You know that *end run* you were talking about, Ms. Hamilton?" he said. "I was just summoned to the administrator's office, and we have a problem."

Marta's clandestine responsibilities included familiarity with the political, as well as technical, lay of the land at the GRC. She knew that as the highest-ranking scientific officer, Yuni's activities were subject to approval of a very short list of people. At the top of that list stood Michael Huxtable, administrator of the facility. Yuni might be the bureaucrat supervising the science, but Huxtable served as bureaucrat supervising everything. As such, he controlled the money. With a budget running to billions, a large contingent of lesser bureaucrats presided over that Herculean task. And countless opportunities existed within the nuances of that humongous budget to fudge a little here, shift a little there, and monumentally screw anyone who didn't get along with the wielders of the purse.

"Yuni?" Naomi asked with concern.

Yuni closed his eyes and drew one more deep breath. "Courtesy of Dr. Rose, we have acquired a new traveler for our team."

So, our days are indeed numbered, Marta thought.

"Rose is behind this?" Sheila said. "So, he's just planting someone here to find out what we're doing?"

"Exactly," Yuni said. "I managed to buy us some time, though. I convinced Michael not to instate our new team member until after we've completed the current mission. I told him this mission is complex and slowing things just to bring a new man up to speed would waste both time and money."

"How did Rose convince the administrator we need someone else?" Gretchen asked.

"Michael has heard complaints we're withholding information. He's concerned."

Marta shook her head and smiled. She found it ironic that the man directing the entire GRC program had a lower security clearance than the science team and the active travelers. She'd said so to Gillis, and Gillis explained that top-level bureaucrats liked it that way. The arrangement offered protection from blame when things went wrong.

"Then you've got the opening left by Raul Hinojosa's defection," Yuni continued. "They plan to prosecute him under the Consortium Security Act when they find him, by the way. And Rose argued that a fourth active traveler would add depth should someone fall ill or suffer injury or be . . . lost."

"So, we get Josh?" Sheila asked. "He'd tell Rose in a heartbeat—"

"No," Yuni said. "Josh doesn't fit the geographical profile. Very few candidates besides you three were living within five hundred miles of here prior to eighteen months ago."

"Who are we getting?" Sheila asked, her tone betraying her trepidation.

"Frank Altman."

"Frank Altman?" protested Naomi. "Frank Altman is . . . is . . . He's done nothing to distinguish himself."

"Very diplomatic, Naomi," Marta said. "What you mean to say is that he's not particularly bright."

"Regardless," Yuni sighed, "Frank has lived in Phoenix his whole life."

"You didn't get him included?" Gormly demanded of Rose. "You said you could get him qualified."

"And I did. Just not for the next mission. After that, Altman is a full member of the team."

Again, they shared a booth at the bar near Superior. Gormly's cold anger chilled Rose.

"Those three scientists, whatever their names are, they have enough pull to get Huxtable to do whatever they want?"

"The names are Dr. Andropov, Dr. Allen, and Naomi."

"Naomi who?" Gormly asked. "I thought they had to be doctors."

"Naomi holds several doctorates—"

"Fine, what's her last name?"

"Hu."

"You don't give me a straight answer, I'm going to have someone cut your nuts off!" Gormly used a napkin to swipe at a water ring on the tabletop.

"Look," Rose said. He took the napkin from Gormly and wrote on it *Dr. Naomi Hu.*

"She's a psychologist and a medical doctor and bioengineer," Rose said. "She insists on just being called Naomi. People laugh when anyone calls her Dr. Hu."

"Stupid name." Gormly crumpled the napkin. "So, you're sure after this next projection, Altman will be inside."

"I'm sure."

"And he understands what he's supposed to do." It wasn't a question.

"As I've already told you, Mr. Altman is not among our brighter traveler candidates. I would have chosen someone a bit more . . . evolved. But yes, he knows he is to report to me."

"We considered approaching Marshall Grissom—"

"Oh, no," Rose said. "That would be a grave mistake. My impression is he's just about the straightest arrow you'll find around here."

"So, we can't choose, can we? We have Altman. And," Gormly added ominously, "we have to make that work."

"I'm sure," Rose said, anxious to end this conversation, "Frank will do fine."

The two men left money for drinks and departed. When their waitress came to clean up, she found a napkin. As she bent to retrieve it, she saw something was written there. She smoothed the napkin flat and found a flowing script that read *Dr. Naomi Hu.*

The waitress knew Naomi Hu. Naomi used to come into the restaurant while waiting for the government to finish building that facility no one would talk about.

So why, the waitress wondered, were those two men talking about Naomi?

She carefully folded the napkin and slipped it into her pocket.

(17)

VISITING THE MARSHALS

THE PROJECTION LAB ATMOSPHERE had grown festive.

As they became more confident in the technology, scientists and engineers and technicians no longer displayed the grim demeanor of executioners. They adopted a party attitude. Being something of a party girl herself, Sheila couldn't help but appreciate this vibe.

Sheila viewed herself, for the most part, as a considerate person. She felt bad for Marshall's embarrassment over his erectile problem. She had grown fond of Marshall in a sisterly sort of way, albeit a sister amazed at the sheer size of her brother's dick.

Eeew, she thought. That's gross.

She quickly revised her analogy. *A sort of female best friend.* It was okay for a female best friend to be amazed at her buddy's winkie.

Today, though, her mischievous nature got the best of her. After all, she had drawn fifteen seconds in Elvin's erection pool. So just before stepping onto the platform, she leaned over and whispered, "Gee, Marshall, this time you get to just watch."

And as she took off her robe, she added a lascivious

smile.

Marshall shed his robe five minutes later, beyond help.

Just before he blinked off into the past, he watched Jolene the medical tech dance a happy little jig.

Even Marta felt a bit festive. Normally she stood next to Marshall during projection and, not wanting to be *too* obvious, had to experience the wonder that was Marshall through the mask of peripheral vision.

This time she witnessed a full-frontal extravaganza.

Oh, my God, she thought, *I have got to get out more.*

"Oh, good. You finally have company. Do you have a breath mint?"

A firm knock at the door followed his apartment's observation. And when he answered, Marshall found himself completely unprepared to find Sheila there.

He'd just changed out of his blue training jumpsuit. He wore only a baggy t-shirt and a pair of loose sweatpants cinched around his skinny middle by a cord running through the waist band.

"Sheila. What can I . . . ?"

She pushed past him, walked straight to his couch and sat.

"Welcome!" the apartment said with enthusiasm. "Please stay. And don't be put off by Marshall's melancholy. He doesn't mean to be morose."

"Why are you morose?" Sheila asked.

"I'm not," Marshall said, "but the apartment doesn't

believe me."

Back when they were new to the program, Marshall did his best to avoid Sheila, a beautiful, smart and remarkably self-assured individual. While he found women fascinating, the entire gender tended to put Marshall on the defensive— beautiful, bright, self-confident women most of all. To voluntarily place himself in their company was only an invitation to embarrassment.

Avoiding Sheila became impossible when they were both selected to the first travelers' team. Then the whole naked stuff complicated things further, followed by the possibility some of his fellow travelers might be out to kill him. Recently, though, as he tried to follow Naomi's advice and engage both Sheila and Marta more, his insecurities began to soften. Marshall began to cautiously hope he and Sheila were, maybe, becoming friends.

At work. But not in his apartment.

Sheila regarded him with an intensity that violated his personal space, even though she sat on the other side of his living room.

"So, are you, you know, just you?" she asked.

Marshall glanced over his shoulder, then back again. "Yes?"

She plucked an autographed baseball from its stand on Marshall's end table. Rolled it on her fingers. Put it back.

"Could I get you something to drink?" Marshall asked.

"No, thank you."

She continued to look at him. He continued to be looked at. The silence grew awkward. He felt frozen, afraid anything he did or said would be the wrong thing. *Why did she of all people have to drop by?* And yet, now that she was here, he found he wanted her to stay.

Finally, unable to tolerate this tension any longer, he shifted his weight to his other foot and asked, "Is there something I'm missing here?"

"I didn't want to worry you," Sheila said. "Probably there's nothing wrong. You know how they haven't been able to account for time distortion."

"What? Wait, you mean this is a mission? And I'm supposed to be . . . but I'm not? Oh, God . . ." Marshall felt a wave of fear sweep over him like a cold wind.

Reading the anxiety on his face, Sheila stepped close and put a hand on his shoulder. "No, no. This is the staggered projection. So, we left at different times."

"The staggered . . . you mean the one everyone says is too dangerous?" Marshall swallowed through a dry throat.

"I don't mean to frighten you. The mission profile called for us to meet here. I'm sure everything will be okay."

The intimacy of her gesture became all tangled in Marshall's head with an overwhelming recollection of her naked magnificence. Marshall realized that in seconds he would appear to be wearing a circus tent.

He retreated to his couch and pulled a throw pillow into his lap.

Sheila sat at the opposite end and tried not to notice. She failed.

Marshall found the awkward silence deafening.

Finally, Marshall shook his head and, carefully avoiding any eye contact, said, "Despite what you might think, I don't regard you as a sexual object. I see you as a very intelligent and compassionate human being."

"Marshall," Sheila said, allowing herself just the hint of

a smile, "don't you find me just a little bit attractive?"

"Do I find you attractive?" He offered a humorless laugh. "If I didn't find you so damned attractive, I wouldn't be the laughingstock of this entire program!"

Sheila slid closer. The movement demanded he meet her eyes. Something had changed. Where her expression had seemed to convey a teasing sort of amusement, now he saw concern.

"Do you ever look at them while they're laughing? I mean really look at them?" she asked.

"Are you kidding?"

"No, I'm serious. Next time pick out a few of the women and look closely. You'll see lust. And the men . . . well . . . you'll see pure envy."

She peered even more intently into his eyes. "You're still not here, are you?"

He shook his head no.

She stepped back.

"Marshall. I'm the one who should be sorry. I guess I've never appreciated how difficult this is for you." Her voice trailed off. "By the way," she added, "she's gone now."

"So, either I went someplace else," Marshall said, "or something really bad has happened."

Sheila glanced at the circus tent. "Would you mind," she asked, "if we just hung out for a little while?"

Marta could study at her computer, comfortable in her apartment with a nice Malbec. One pleasant surprise she'd found at the GRC, though, was a regular library with actual physical books. Marta loved the weight and smell of books.

Being surrounded by silence, tucked away among the stacks, gave her the same comfort she imagined a believer must find sitting alone in a chapel.

She re-read a particularly daunting paragraph regarding string theory for the third time when she heard a shuffle of footsteps and saw Marshall walking toward her. She'd never seen him here. Rather than feeling annoyed at the interruption, she found herself pleasantly surprised.

She'd forced herself to take seriously Gillis's theory that Marshall was some sort of super-spy-assassin. She'd followed his suggestion that she warm to Marshall a little. Try and get into his head. She'd expected to encounter more of what Marshall presented on the surface—a retiring milk toast sort of character, unwilling to risk anything.

Rather than cowardice, though, as she chatted with Marshall during breaks and walked with him through hallways, she'd intuited something very different. Marshall had an innate politeness about him, a hypersensitivity to boundaries. He didn't want to be a bother. Unless someone was willing to go out of their way to invite him, he simply would not intrude.

And if all that was an act? Well, it was a damn good one.

As he approached her secluded library table, she decided her smile of response was genuine.

"Hi, Marshall."

He stopped a comfortable distance away, his body language expressing apology. "I hope I'm not interrupting something important."

"Quantum mechanics," she said, pointing to the heavy book on the desk before her. "String dimensions. Trying to figure out the limbo. Believe me, I could use a little interruption."

Marshall edged closer. "And so, you're . . . alone?"

Marta looked over her shoulder when understanding dawned. "Oh. I get it. You're here from the future, aren't you? Where am I? Oh, wait. Let me guess. This is the mission Gretchen's been talking about. Projecting us at different times. Yuni finally decided to give his approval?"

"Yes, and I don't mean to frighten you, but it's been a while. You and Sheila were supposed to meet at my apartment, and then go back. But neither of you showed up."

They waited. Fifteen minutes. Thirty minutes.

Marta hoped she disguised her concern.

"You know they still haven't worked out the time distortions," Marshall said, but his comforting words dissolved into a little gasp.

"What?" Marta said.

"He's gone. What do you think it means?"

"It means that something bad happened," Marta said, "or we've proved Gretchen's theory."

Marta Hamilton re-read a particularly complex paragraph regarding string theory and quantum dimensions for the third time when her future self snapped into her consciousness. Following several minutes of queasy disorientation, Future-Marta and past-Marta came to an understanding.

"*Okay, which mission?*" past-Marta asked.

"*The staggered projection. We're supposed to meet Sheila at Marshall's apartment.*"

When she knocked, Marshall answered his door wearing a loose-fitting pair of sweatpants and a t-shirt.

"Marta?" he said with surprise.

"Hi, Marshall. Can I come in?"

"Um . . . sure . . ."

Marshall's apartment offered some sort of inane apology concerning Marshall's mental state.

"You should turn that thing off," Marta said.

"I didn't know I could."

"Well, yeah. I guess I've just got mine too intimidated to say anything anymore."

At this moment, future-Marta was—as usual—all business. Past-Marta, though, just being along for the ride, so to speak, had the opportunity to let her professional focus waver and with a quick, unintended glance at Marshall's crotch, recall the sight teasing her peripheral vision at each projection. And that quick glance momentarily distracted future-Marta as well, for it had been only a few minutes ago that she'd confronted the hard reality.

She blushed through her dark skin.

Marshall reddened, too. He directed Marta to his single chair, and he took refuge on his couch, which included a couple of pillows.

"Um . . ." he said. "Can I get you anything? A glass of wine?"

"No, no," Marta answered, "I encourage my past self not to drink while I'm traveling."

She found her eyes inadvertently shifting quickly down again.

As an attractive female, albeit a forbidding one, Marta was accustomed to men's quick appraising glances at her various body parts. She typically dismissed ogling as a weakness genetically encoded into the male psyche. So, she felt surprised at herself, and a little embarrassed that Marshall had noticed her glance.

"You mean right now? You're the other you?"

Uh oh, Marta thought. *He's not here.* "No, I'm still me, or sort of both. You know how it is."

"So, where am I?"

"I'm not sure. We're using three different projection times, and we're supposed to meet up. I embarked last. But you're not here. And I don't think Sheila is, either."

"And that's not good, is it?"

"Well, we don't—"

"Because if Sheila and I aren't here, there was an accident of some kind and we . . . we . . . didn't make it."

Mindful of Gillis's suggestion that she cultivate Marshall's friendship, Marta moved to the couch and put a hand on his shoulder, the intimacy of the gesture foreign and awkward. "Or else the two of you are fine somewhere else, which means we've confirmed parallel universe theory."

"And the investors are going to pull the funding?"

"Oh, I can't believe," Marta said, "they'd be so short-sighted."

She realized her hand still rested on his shoulder. Some strange involuntary force pulled her eyes back down to Marshall's lap.

Oh, shit. I did it again.

A drop of sweat trickled down Marshall's forehead.

"Maybe they won't figure it out," he said. "Maybe we can keep it covered up long enough to think of something."

"Yeah. No telling what might happen if the wrong things are uncovered. Too soon, I mean."

"No telling." Marshall squirmed.

Marshall regarded his ceiling tiles. Marta became intently interested in her shoes.

"Oh, and by the way," Marta said eventually, "she's gone. I'm sure you and Sheila are okay."

"Sure. Um . . . I don't suppose you'd want that glass of wine now?"

Marta thought about saying yes.

"I think," she said after too long a pause, "I should find Naomi and tell her everything before the memory starts to fade."

"Oh, right."

Marshall didn't get up to see her to the door.

Robed and waiting, Marshall stared with growing apprehension at the empty projection platform. Theoretically, they should have simultaneously returned to their own time and place. Sheila arrived first, joined by Marshall a couple of minutes later. Now, ten minutes had passed. Naomi *had* to be wrong about Marta. She might be a little testy at times, but she wasn't a ruthless killer. And he worried she might be in trouble.

"Remember," Naomi said quietly, "time distortions we don't understand are involved here. We don't know what happens to disrupt the flow of time during projection."

"I'm sure she's all right," Yuni added, a lack of conviction betraying his own concern.

They waited for another minute before Elvin Detwyler called out, "We've got her!"

Always having been a part of the main show, Marshall

had never witnessed a return. Now he saw the silvery globes crackle with their blue and green amoeba-like pulsations. And Marta appeared. No flash of light. No thunderbolts. No portals opening or closing. No glimmer of materialization. One instant she was not there. And the next she was. Marshall had another revelation as well.

Like Marta and Sheila, when it came to noticing the nudity of his fellow travelers he used the subtle technique of peripheral vision. And since Sheila was clearly the feature attraction, most of his attention had gone to that periphery.

He realized his difficulties had just multiplied.

18

A SQUIGGLE OF HOPE

YUNI HERDED THE TRAVELERS to their private debriefing.

"We have confirmed parallel universe theory!" Gretchen proclaimed, shaking both her fists over her head. "We may not understand what it all means, but we have confirmed the existence of at least three universes completely separate and identical to ours."

By his nature, Yuni was less celebratory. "But what variable caused our travelers to land in different destinations? We must find what—"

Marta hated to be the one to damper Gretchen's exhilaration.

"It means," she interrupted, "we've run out of options. If we lead everyone to believe we all ended up in the same place, when the truth finally comes out—and we know it will—the six of us will probably be prosecuted by some secret court."

"If we say what really happened," Yuni countered, "the business and government people will understand the implications in only a matter of days."

Marta waited for someone else to pick up the baton.

"I'm open to suggestions," Yuni appealed.

"I don't see that we have any choice," Sheila said.

"Please," said Gretchen, "we've just made one of the great discoveries in the history of science. We have to find a way to continue this research. There *must* be a way to keep everybody committed. Let's at least risk one more day to think about it."

Elvin Detwyler enjoyed the confrontation with a detached sense of amusement.

Dr. Andropov lied. Dr. Rose seethed.

"So, what's the story?" Rose demanded. "I understand the travelers did not arrive simultaneously."

"We're delaying the full debriefing," Yuni told Rose. And as an entourage of scientists and technicians crowded around him, he said more loudly, "We'll do the full debriefing tomorrow."

"Why not now?" Rose demanded.

"We have issues to sort out. We don't want any premature conclusions . . ."

Elvin couldn't hear what Rose whispered to Yuni, but Andropov's response was to stare Rose down before stalking away. Elvin suffered disappointment they hadn't come to blows. He could probably get three-to-one odds on the Russian.

Gradually, the throng dispersed as Sheila, Marshall and Marta walked to the medical suite for their post-mission exams. Lingering behind, Elvin took a position a few feet from Gretchen. When the physicist finished a mumbled conversation, he sidled next to her.

"You know you won't get away with this much longer, Dr. Allen."

Elvin thought he saw a fleeting moment of panic before the physicist gathered herself.

"I'm sorry..."

"It's Elvin. Elvin Detwyler. I'm one of the techs on the lifeline monitors."

"Elvin. Of course. As Dr. Andropov said, we'll have a full debriefing tomorrow. I simply can't—"

Elvin interrupted. "Let's wait and give everyone time to clear out. I want to show you something. And if you won't hang around long enough to hear what I've got to say, I'll talk to Dr. Rose. Then he'll know what the six of you have been hiding."

Elvin insisted they return to the now-deserted projection lab.

"Okay," Gretchen said when they were finally alone, "I'm listening."

"You may or may not know my job is to monitor the energy thread," Elvin said, referring to the energy stream that kept the travelers connected between past and present.

He directed her to the array of computer monitors, which displayed data from the previous projection. Stepping closer, he pointed a stubby finger at the bright red thread of light that ran vertically down the middle of the central monitor.

Elvin did not easily suffer amazement. From the day he'd assumed his duties at the GRC, he'd marveled at the technology allowing travelers to be retrieved through the wormhole. Every person radiates energy in the form of a magnetic field, an electrical charge and an aura of light resonating in a range of scientific instruments could not detect until the energy breakthroughs during the third decade of the twenty-first century.

Scientists used the same technology that made fossil fuels irrelevant to boost these three fields. When combined, the three create a unique identifier of each individual human being. This data is used to track each traveler with a tiny thread of powerful energy linking present and past via the time projector.

"I am fully conversant with the lifeline and its functions," Gretchen said, her impatience showing.

Elvin responded with indignation of his own. "What you don't pay any attention to, and know very little about," he mustered his most severe tone of condescension, "is all the other stuff our monitors tell us while travelers are out there."

He pointed to his monitor again where a series of other lines of various widths and colors danced on either side of the lifeline. Unlike the bold, rock-steady red demarcation, these lesser lines wiggled and wavered. The further to the right or left, the less distinct these other lines became until those at the monitors' extreme edges appeared as fat bands of indistinct, shaky resolution seeming to fade randomly from dim to bright.

"We know they represent various aspects of the wormhole," Gretchen said. "And we've been able to define a couple of them. That's what the Wormhole Spectrum Identification Task Force is for."

"Right, they're working their way out from the middle. They've paid no attention to these vague bands at the farthest extremes."

Elvin pulled up recordings of monitor activity for today's projections. He asked Gretchen if she noticed anything.

At first, these two bands at opposite sides of the monitor seemed identical. They pulsed with the same rhythm. They wobbled from skinny, purplish lines to fat, blue, almost completely transparent lines as if mirror images. Presently, the two patterns became slightly unsynchronized. Not far off. Not enough difference that the deviation became obvious, but different, nonetheless.

"I noticed this phenomenon a couple of months ago, and it piqued my curiosity. I started running some analyses, and I've come to conclusions today's projections seem to confirm."

"And those are?"

"Ah, not so fast," Elvin said. "I have some requirements."

"Mr. Detwyler, I appreciate your effort here. I can get you an audience with the committee, and you can tell them what you've found."

"Ha! The Wormhole Spectrum Identification Task Force will still be puzzling over that pathway when you and I are getting our retirement checks. They don't have a clue as to what's really happening there. Anything I told them would be buried on their agenda for years."

Gretchen smiled a patronizing smile and turned to go. "Well, I'm busy. The anomaly you've identified is interesting. But odds are strong that, for purposes of our primary research, they are meaningless."

"I've named those outlying bands. I call them the universe identification squiggles."

Gretchen stopped.

"If you want to know more, as I said, I have requirements."
She sat again.
"Universe identification . . ."
"Squiggles. Parallel universe theory?"
"Wait. Who said anything about parallel universes?"
She attempted a laugh.
"Certainly not the six of you," Elvin said. "These
patterns at the edges of my monitor say everything about
parallel universes, though. And if we're going any further
with this, I want in."
"In? In where?"
"Look, we can sit here and bullshit each other all
afternoon, but we both know what the six of you have
figured out. And we both know that for some reason you're
keeping quiet about it. Now I can talk to you, or I can go to
administrators, or individual corporations, or even some of
the physicists who are pissed off about being left outside
your secret circle. I'll bet they'll be happy to cut a deal with
me."
Some twenty minutes later, Elvin watched with smug
satisfaction as Dr. Gretchen Allen, one of the world's half-
dozen premier theoretical physicists, sat gaping with
amazement at the monitors before her.
"How did you . . . we have the most brilliant physicists . . .
how could you possibly have seen this when no one else
did?"
"Physics and quantum mechanics are kind of a hobby of
mine." Elvin shrugged.
"A hobby?"
"Yeah. I read. I watch the Science Channel. I fool
around with quantum theory when I've got a few minutes.

It helps me relax. That and blackjack. They kick me out of most casinos, though."

"You do know," she told him, "if this is a scam, if somebody has put you up to this for God-knows-whatever reason, we'll see through it. Once we do a thorough analysis, you won't be able to fool the caliber of minds you're dealing with here."

"You guys can't be all that smart if you didn't notice it."

"And you hold what graduate degrees?" she asked.

"Two years of community college and a bachelor's of computer science I took online."

Gretchen stared again at the monitors. "Community college?"

"So, I'm not the most industrious guy, okay? I needed at least an associate degree. I picked something easy. That doesn't mean I'm stupid."

"So, what does it mean, *you want in?*"

"I want to know what you six know. And I want to work up front. Not from the back row."

"Elvin, you're not qualified. We have dozens of scientists here who would be way ahead of you for that kind of position."

"Based on what? A doctorate? Publications? How many of your published doctors of physics figured this out? Everyone out there is speculating about what the six of you are doing. Who else has come up with anything solid at all? I can keep up with anyone you have. Hell, I can keep up with you."

"I suppose we could figure something out," she said, searching his face. "That is, if you can convince me this is something more than just pure speculation."

So, he did.

Elvin took a tiny sim card from his shirt pocket and used one of the big computers next to the monitors to bring up a sequence of images representing all time projections to date. He'd made three recordings for each projection, tracking Sheila, Marshall, and Marta separately. He picked several at random.

"Notice please that each recording shows the two exterior lines to be identical until ninety-seven seconds into the projection. And they *are* identical. I know this because I've broken them down into several fascinating subcomponents.

"At ninety-seven seconds the variations take place. While these variations are miniscule, detailed analysis shows they are distinct and quite measurable. Now, compare these three recordings, and you'll see that the variations are not random. Rather, the variations themselves are identical for the tracks of all three travelers."

He used the eraser end of a pencil to point at the screen.

"Always, ninety-seven seconds. Regardless of whether the time distance we traverse is a day, or a month, or . . . I'm betting, a hundred years."

Gretchen's eyes told Elvin she was hooked. He could see wheels turning, and he knew her excitement and amazement grew as she began to consider the implications.

"You realize, of course, we'll have to go back over everything you've done and be sure—"

"I've documented my observations carefully, done the math. My calculations are right here in case you want to check and be sure I remembered to carry the one."

He dangled the sim card by two fingers—just beyond her reach.

"You can bet I'll be checking your math."

"As I said," Elvin said, "I want to sit up front with the three of you and share the credit. And no, you can't take my sim card back to your little group first. You decide now, or I go to someone else. And understand there are things I haven't told you yet."

Gretchen stared hungrily at the tiny card. She slowly nodded.

"One other thing," Elvin said. "I want money, too."

Gretchen chuckled. "Oh, I don't think money will be a problem."

They moved to Gretchen's private laboratory where Elvin repeated his performance for Yuni and Naomi. Again, Elvin enjoyed observing these eminent scientists traverse a path from disdain to skepticism to awe.

Elvin grinned. He would get whatever he wanted.

"We must assign a team to research this phenomenon immediately," Yuni said eagerly.

"Why?" Elvin asked. "It's there. We know it works. People will probably be bogged down for decades arguing about how and why all this takes place. Undoubtedly, some theoretical physicists will build entire careers sorting through the details. I, for one, don't care why it works the way it works. I just care that it does."

"That," Yuni replied with an edge of frost to his voice, "might be the difference between a true scientist and someone who views science as a hobby."

"Exactly. And that's also why, while you're screwing around with theories and papers and research committees, I'll be learning how to map parallel universes."

"Map?" Naomi asked. "What do you mean?"

"I mean I'll prove that when a traveler goes to a parallel universe, we can differentiate that specific universe from the others. Even define it for future reference. Just like mapping DNA back in the day. And, if we can do that, we should be able to send a traveler to the past of that specific universe whenever we want to."

Yuni and Gretchen shared a glance of disbelief.

"And how do you go about identifying a specific universe?" Gretchen asked.

"If we accept that the transit time through the limbo as measured in our universe is precisely ninety-seven seconds, we must go to the data and see what happens at precisely ninety-seven seconds."

He loaded his sim card into Gretchen's computer and brought up Marshall's journey earlier that day.

"Watch the outermost bands at each side of the monitor. Although it's difficult to discern with the naked eye, at the start of a projection these two squiggling bands are identical. Then at exactly ninety-seven seconds—at the instant our traveler is arriving in the past of a different universe—one of these bands changes."

Elvin froze the display and pointed to the monitor.

"This squiggle over here is us. And this squiggle to the left is the other universe."

"You are leaping to some conclusions here." Yuni frowned. "And *squiggle* is hardly an acceptable scientific term."

"Well, I like squiggle, and I discovered it. So, it's either going to be a squiggle or an Elvin. That's a deal breaker."

Yuni rolled his eyes. Gretchen shrugged.

"So that's us," Elvin repeated, again pointing to the right. "That's the unique Elvin of our universe."

"Let's go with squiggle," Gretchen said.

"Anyway, when these bands show their subtle shifts, they are displaying the unique squiggle of whatever universe the traveler has reached."

Yuni scoffed. "That is the rankest of speculation."

"Until today," Elvin said, "I would have agreed."

"And today?" Naomi asked.

Elvin pulled up Sheila's and Marta's data to stand alongside Marshall's. He isolated the outer bands and displayed them.

"Here is our pre-projection squiggle," Elvin said. "Now, at ninety-seven seconds we see the shift."

Each screen showed a subtle change of squiggles at the outside of the band.

"Now," Elvin said, "I've come to a conclusion. You haven't discussed the details of what happened today with anyone beyond yourselves, right?"

Yuni glanced at the others. "That's correct."

"So, there's no logical way—other than my analysis of these outer bands—I could know our three travelers found their way to different destinations. The three squiggles are different."

Gretchen gasped. "Oh, my God."

Yuni gestured to the shimmering bands at the edges of Elvin's monitor.

"How can we even begin to interpret this?"

"I've already worked out a mathematical interpretation. There's still a lot we must do to refine it. I've gotten this far with my own computers. Give me some real computing power . . ." He waved at the array of towers around him. ". . . and we'll see what's possible."

Gretchen, still staring at the shimmering bands, asked, "And what makes you think we can match one of these . . . squiggles and somehow target the universe it represents as a destination for time travelers?"

"Why not? Right now, the projector is a shotgun. We fire it. If we accept parallel universe theory, it flings the travelers off to some completely random destination. You're smart guys. You've got a lot of smart guys working for you. It doesn't take a lot of imagination to think we could come up with a way to refine the projection process to the point we could hit a specific target."

"Do you realize," Yuni asked Gretchen and Naomi, "what the others will say when I tell them I've given Elvin Detwyler a title and boosted him a half dozen pay grades?"

Naomi held a thin file folder. She sat beside Gretchen on an old brown couch Yuni used for napping when things were too hectic to return to his apartment.

"What others think may be the least of our worries," Naomi said. "I'm afraid Elvin is something of a volatile character."

"What choice did we have?" Gretchen asked. "This is the answer. This solves everything. If other universes do, as we can now hypothesize, have historical paths parallel to ours, then when we send our travelers to alter some event in that universe's past, we can assume they will be sending travelers to our universe to effect the same changes. Meaning we *can*, after a fashion, manipulate our own past."

"We can make that theoretical argument, anyway," Naomi agreed, "and that should keep the investors interested at least for a while."

Following their meeting with Elvin, Yuni and Gretchen agreed to give Noami a couple of hours to gather information from the GRC's personnel records.

"So, Naomi," Yuni said, "who is this guy to whom we've handed the keys to a time machine?"

"I've studied the interviews, and it's clear Mr. Detwyler didn't take them seriously. And that in itself provides information. While I don't have everything I'd like, I think I can offer a generally accurate psychological profile."

Naomi referenced the screen of a small electronic notebook.

"Elvin Detwyler, thirty-two years old, the son of a pair of college professors. Lots of disruptive behavior while he was young, though he did manage to stay out of jail. We know from observation of his behavior here that he is a . . . hustler, I think would be the correct term."

Yuni raised his eyebrows.

"He runs the Marshall Grissom erection betting pools."

"That's Elvin who does that?" Gretchen asked. "You know, I nearly won last week. Missed it by about seven seconds and . . ."

She withered under Naomi's disapproving glare.

"Sorry," Gretchen said. "I didn't mean to interrupt."

"As far as school is concerned, Elvin failed both socially and academically. I believe he is a classic example of the child so bright he's simply bored. And, when he reveals his true intellect, he scares the hell out of people with formal educations. I believe Elvin holds a deep resentment for people like us. If *we* display behavior out of step with societal norms, *we* are regarded as eccentric. When Elvin does it, he is regarded as weird, and he will be bitter about that double standard."

Naomi swiped to the next page of her electronic file.

"He appears to be an unrepentant gambler. He has little sense of decorum. He is utterly convinced of his intellectual superiority, yet he is hampered by insecurity. My guess is that he is sexually frustrated. Women who combine intellect and beauty, like Sheila Schuler, will intimidate him completely. The interaction between the two of them will be interesting.

"Since he is overweight, disheveled and, some might say, generally unattractive, his appearance and his social inepti-tude have rendered him obnoxious by many standards. I am afraid we can expect him to fulfill those expectations by raising obnoxiousness to a whole new level."

Yuni put his elbows on the table and covered his eyes with his hands. "Oh, God," he lamented. "What have we done?"

19

LAYING A TRAP

LEONARD ROSE SAVORED YUNI Andropov's expression as the chief scientist walked into Michael Huxtable's office and saw Frank Altman standing against the wall off to the side. Rose did not give Yuni the opportunity to question Frank's presence. Even before the three scientists could be seated, Rose attacked.

"Clearly," Rose said as he stood and pointed at Yuni, "you are withholding data from the scientific team. You hold your secretive debriefings and offer the rest of us some laundered version of what happened."

"Leonard, please," said Huxtable. "Let's try and have some decorum."

"Michael," Yuni interrupted, "what is Mr. Altman doing here? He doesn't have the security clearance to—"

Huxtable leaned forward in his high-backed leather throne and barked, "All right, both of you, settle down. We will hold a discussion, come to some agreement and quit squabbling so we can get back to work."

A scowling Rose retreated, crossing his arms over his chest. Yuni settled three chairs away, adopting the same posture.

Huxtable looked back and forth between them.

"Leonard, we'll address your concerns momentarily. Yuni, you are correct. Mr. Altman's presence does violate security protocols. Mr. Altman is here to remind you he is now a full member of your travelers' team and should be treated accordingly."

Frank augmented an embarrassed smile, topping it off with a *what can I do?* shrug.

Rose directed a satisfied smirk at Yuni.

"That's fine," Yuni answered. "We fully intend to integrate Frank into the active travelers' program."

"All right," Huxtable said, "Mr. Altman, you may go."

As Frank closed the door behind him, Huxtable turned back to Yuni. "I, too, have been uncomfortable with the information flow from your group. Now, what about Dr. Rose's accusation? Have you been filtering information from debriefings?"

Yuni took a deep breath. "Yes."

"There, you see!"

Huxtable raised a warning hand to Rose.

"This is not a decision we made easily," Yuni said. "As events began to unfold, the three of us agreed initial results could be misleading if we drew conclusions too quickly. Any of the individual funding entities can withdraw their support at any given time if they hear unfounded rumors or incorrect interpretations of our progress. And," he added with a sharp look at Rose, "the implications represented significant complications to the Light Speed Project."

"You have hijacked the science." Rose pounded the padding on the arm of his chair. "You are squandering brain power here with your secrecy."

Again, Huxtable signaled for Rose to back off. "Yuni, you and I have worked together for a long while. I respect your judgment. Giving you the benefit of the doubt, I will assume you have good reasons for restricting information to the rest of the scientific team. Whatever those reasons are, I'm no longer comfortable with the situation."

Rose stood again, leaned forward with one hand on the table and pointed an accusing finger with the other. "Dr. Andropov, members of this consortium have invested billions. Every participant knows this is a highly classified project. Nobody would benefit from a breach of that security. But investors are getting restless. They need to believe that those guiding the science and technology are being held to some level of accountability. We must know whether progress is being made."

"We?" said Gretchen. "Sounds to me as if you might be getting pretty cozy with some of the corporations, Leonard. That's not supposed to happen, either."

"I don't sequester myself," Rose said. "I try to see the whole project, not just my scientific niche."

"All right, people," Huxtable said. "When the consortium was established, those of us drawing up the participation agreements tried to insulate science from the money. That was wise. The science should be pure. Its interpretation shouldn't be contaminated by the interests of the individual governments and corporations. At the same time, we *do* have to provide some level of accountability, and I am that level. I do need a clear sense of where we are."

Yuni glanced quickly at Gretchen and Naomi. "We have, in fact, reached a critical point," he said. "Our progress has been significant, and the implications of our findings could be instrumental to the project's future. We wanted to be sure of the facts behind those implications before discussing them with the rest of the scientific team. I'll be glad to offer a broad outline of those details with you. I would prefer that Dr. Rose wait until we are ready to make an explanation to the entire team. We need one more day."

Rose bristled. "My security clearance should be every bit as high as yours."

"One more day."

"What about Elvin Detwyler?" Rose said.

Again, the looks crossing their faces pleased him.

"Don't act so surprised. Plenty of people have noticed Detwyler's disappearance into your inner sanctum over the past couple of days. I'll ask you point-blank. Have you told him things you haven't told the rest of us?"

"I'm not prepared to discuss Elvin at this point."

Again, Huxtable intervened.

"Yuni, I don't have to tell you what a serious breach of security that would be."

"I'll tell you how serious it would be," Rose said. "It could rise to the level of a felony. You won't give me information, but you'll take some computer tech—"

"We haven't told Mr. Detwyler anything he didn't determine on his own," Yuni said quietly.

Huxtable propped his elbows on the table, made a small tent of his fingers and covered his nose as his eyes shifted back and forth from Andropov to Rose.

"I must ask you to leave, Leonard. Under the condition that you and the others will be fully briefed within twenty-four hours. And you, Yuni, are going to remain here and convince me why I shouldn't have security confine the three of you."

From the hallway, Marta watched Yuni, Gretchen, and Naomi march grim-faced toward the projection lab. They suspended their conversation as the three scientists strode toward them. Marta read their expressions. Before she could say anything, a doorway flew open across the hall. Marta and Gillis watched Leonard Rose charge out.

"I'm warning you, Yuni, I won't put up with this any longer! You don't get to run this place like some sort of emperor who . . ."

Yuni whirled and took a menacing step toward Rose.

"The briefing will take place tomorrow," he said as he advanced.

Rose took two quick steps of retreat. "It had better!" He slammed the door.

Yuni, Gretchen and Naomi resumed their march without acknowledging Marta and Gillis.

"Leonard Rose is a total dick," Marta said from the side of her mouth.

Gillis took her elbow. "Speaking of Leonard Rose, follow me."

"Welcome home, Gillis Kerg. Ah, and the young lady is back—"

"If you can't turn that thing off," Marta snapped, "just give me your gun, Gillis, and I'll shoot it."

"Gun?" said the apartment. "Firearms are forbidden!

May I speak with you in private, Gillis Kerg?"

"Sure," Gillis said. "Go ahead."

"But . . . she's still here."

"She promises not to listen."

"She promises?" The apartment sounded skeptical Marta growled.

Gillis laughed.

The apartment said, "Never mind."

Gillis touched his palm to the scanning device on his desk. A drawer clicked open. He withdrew an electronic sponge to ensure the security of their conversation. Next, Gillis disappeared into the apartment's bedroom, then returned holding a crumpled napkin, which he handed to Marta. Carefully taking it with two fingers, she cast a questioning glance.

"Open it."

She flattened the napkin, turned it over, and saw handwriting spelling out Dr. Naomi Hu.

"I must begin with a confession," Gillis said. "Occasionally I slip away to Superior for recreational purposes."

Marta wasn't surprised Gillis could defeat the GRC's entry-exit security.

"You risk imprisonment just to chase some tail?"

"Not that much of a risk. What else can I do, though? You are so protective of your own lovely tail, I'm reduced to criminality."

"Right. So where is this going?"

"The young woman I meet there is a waitress at a local bar. She cleaned a table last week and found this napkin."

"And she gave it to you?"

"The people of Superior have questions about this

facility. They gossip and make assumptions about what we do here. My friend also happens to know Naomi Hu works at this facility."

"How would she know that?"

"Back when people were first arriving—a couple of years before we traveler candidates showed up—the completion of some housing areas was delayed. The scientists had to stay in town a few weeks while their quarters were finished. My friend got to know Naomi when she came to the restaurant. Now, being aware of the secrecy, she wondered why someone would be writing Naomi's name. She gave the napkin to me."

"That is interesting."

"It gets better. She said two men were sitting at the table where the napkin was left. And one of them, I believe, was Leonard Rose."

"Why do you think that?"

"My friend also works from time to time at an assisted living facility where Dr. Rose's mother resides."

"So that's how Rose gets permission to leave the campus."

"Exactly. He visits his sick mother."

"Doesn't a security officer have to . . . ?"

"That's the protocol."

"So, who was the other guy?" Marta asked.

"That's the important question, isn't it?" Gillis said. "My friend thinks she's seen him before. I asked her to get a picture with her phone if he comes in again."

"This is fascinating," Marta said. "I think catching Leonard Rose in the act of violating security regulations might create all kinds of opportunities in the days to come."

20

SECRETS REVEALED

ELVIN DETWYLER TOOK HIS PLACE alongside the top three scientists behind microphones on the auditorium stage. Sitting among the audience, Marshall thought the scruffy computer tech seemed to be savoring the reactions of the people filing into the room.

Since yesterday's announcement of a "briefing of significant findings," rumors had run rampant. At the Time Warp the previous night, Marshall and Sheila overheard speculation regarding what this impending statement could be. And today, Elvin's place on the auditorium stage seemed to compound the muttering and whispering.

"Ladies and gentlemen, please, let's get started." Yuni gestured to his right. "You have, of course, noticed the presence of one of our former computer technicians, Elvin Detwyler. I have named Mr. Detwyler special assistant to Dr. Allen. Mr. Detwyler will hold a senior research position with the physics group."

All around, murmurs again bubbled, more than a few harboring a note of anger as Elvin rose and greeted them with a sarcastic bow.

Yuni cast a warning glance at Elvin. "The reasons for

this promotion will become evident."

Yuni took a deep breath, and almost smiled. "I have asked myself time and again how rare is an opportunity to stand before one's colleagues and announce a discovery that will change our entire perception of the universe?"

The room fell into dead silence.

"I know many of you have grown impatient, and perhaps even suspicious, of our activities the past few weeks. I know some of you believe the mission briefings you've received were censored. Well, that's exactly what's been happening. I'm sure you'll agree, though, that our caution has been justified . . ."

Yuni paused for effect.

". . . because with Mr. Detwyler's help, we have clear evidence confirming parallel universe theory."

A moment of boggled silence erupted in a roar as a hundred voices spoke at once.

Yuni raised both hands. "Quiet! Please be quiet and listen for a moment. Since the first projection using human travelers, Dr. Allen has suspected—as, perhaps, have some of you—the travelers were being projected to the pasts of parallel universes. Because the implications of that possibility are so profound, we decided to limit access to that information while undertaking subsequent research."

The whining voice of Leonard Rose cut through another round of excited murmurs. "How dare you presume to keep such an important breakthrough from us? We represent the world's greatest scientific minds. We contributed to anything you—"

"Unfortunately," Yuni said, "brilliance doesn't make any of us immune to gossip. How many of you sat at the

Time Warp last night, holding speculative discussions about what would happen today?"

The curtain of silence descended again.

"And how many others beyond this group might have overheard elements of that discussion?"

Marshall recognized several scientists from the night before as they exchanged sheepish glances.

"Gossip and speculation are facts of human nature. And though this is supposed to be a secure facility, we all know practically every government and corporate entity involved is making a concerted effort to learn each new development and finding."

"That has nothing to do with—" Rose started.

Yuni cut him off again. "Tell me, Leonard, do you understand the full implications of parallel universe theory vis-à-vis the funding of our continued research? For everybody's benefit, I'll ask Dr. Allen to spell it out."

Gretchen replaced Yuni at the microphone.

"If, indeed, time travel sends us to a parallel universe, the bottom-line implication is—where most of our financial backers are concerned—time travel is of little value. Any changes imposed on the past mean nothing to us, because they apply to a different universe. We can't alter our past. And implications for the Light Speed Project are clear if any time machine you encounter in the future can only return your astronauts to a different universe."

Naomi stood and asked Gretchen for the microphone. "Furthermore," Naomi said, "we create a very real ethical issue. Each time we travel to the past, we may be altering the reality of another world. Would we want some other society, some other civilization, to indiscriminately alter our future?

Or manipulate our universe for *their* profit? Because we risk that possibility as well."

"So, are you saying you think this project—all our work, the remarkable things we've achieved here—will be abandoned?" a physicist called from the back of the room.

"No." Yuni smiled. "Had we openly discussed our initial suspicions, I think that could have been the result. Premature rumors could have resulted in our financial supporters making a rash decision. By maintaining secrecy," Yuni shot a vitriolic glare toward Leonard Rose, "we bought ourselves time. And now, thanks to Mr. Detwyler, we think we've discovered something that will keep our backers interested. I'll let Mr. Detwyler explain. Elvin? If you will?"

"What remotely qualifies this man to speak?" Rose said.

"I'm smarter than you," Elvin said, abandoning any pretense of tact as he claimed the microphone. "I know that pisses you off, Leonard. You make it painfully obvious that you regard technicians as mental midgets. The fact is, though, even without benefit of your graduate degrees, I can think circles around you, so sit down and listen. That's the way we learn."

Marshall didn't mind seeing Rose's blood pressure rise to a boiling point, but he sensed Elvin had gone too far. The other scientists were not necessarily fans of Leonard Rose. Although Marshall's ego didn't have much of an appetite, he also understood that few people achieve remarkable things without a self-confidence bordering on arrogance and fostering a driving need for recognition. Rose wasn't the only one here who regarded technical staff with condescension. And the travelers as well, for that matter.

Marshall paid rapt attention while Elvin dialed down

his rhetoric. Using charts, graphs, and formulas projected in three dimensions, he laid it all out. Yuni, Naomi, and Gretchen filled the gaps regarding the travelers' experiences along the way.

"Ladies and gentlemen," Yuni said when Elvin finished, "we have a great deal of work to do. Elvin believes we may be able to pinpoint the specific... um... squiggles of individual universes and *aim* our projections at a precise target. If we can do that, a traveler from our universe might be able to effect a desired change to the past of another universe while reciprocal travelers from that other world might be able to effect the same change here. Getting to that point will take a huge effort. And for that, we need all the funding we can get."

"Parallel universes, huh?" Gormly muttered. "And they think it might still be possible for us to manipulate our own past?"

"It won't be easy," Rose said. "But at least the theoretical base for a solution is being established."

"And Huxtable will let them get away with having kept this information from the rest of you?" Gormly raised his empty glass to the waitress.

Rose nodded and appeared defeated. "If an announcement had been made initially, I have to concede the implications might have driven away a number of you folks providing the money. Secrecy gave them time to further research the issue and come up with a possible solution. And they've put our Light Speed research on hold to transfer most of our physics and math staff to the Wormhole Project."

"What about you?"

"That's the worst thing of all. Michael Huxtable named me Gretchen Allen's assistant. I should have been named co-director with Andropov."

"This is not what Hemisphere signed up for," Gormly said. "This whole thing is veering way off course."

"Wait, now," Rose said with a note of alarm. "There's no justification for stopping the project just because these complications might not fit our preconceptions. As with the Manhattan Project, as with the space program, we have no idea what practical applications this research will ultimately yield."

"Yeah, as long as you get to spend someone else's money."

Gormly didn't care a whit about how much money these scientists and engineers spent. His employers weren't shortsighted. They wanted to own more of the project, not back away from it.

A few *parallel universe* rumors circulating among funding governments and corporations were fine with him. Some, he knew, hoped for an excuse to back away from their financial commitments. If they left, so much the better. So long as a sound theoretical basis supported a possibility that the past could be manipulated, the Hemisphere Investment Group stood more than ready to grab a bigger piece of the pie.

Sheila corralled Naomi as the others filed out of the auditorium.

"Explain about altering the reality of another world each time we go to the past," Sheila demanded.

"If we accept quantum theory," Naomi said, "then we must accept that these other universes have been proceeding along identical historical paths to our own. But the intervention of a time traveler in another world would, theoretically, set that world on a different historical path."

"How different?" asked Sheila.

"I don't know. I would conjecture that a single, brief visit would change little—except for the lives of the people directly affected by the visitor. But frequent and longer visits might change things significantly."

"So, each time we travel to the past, we are manipulating lives?" Sheila asked.

"Well, yes. I think that's possible."

Sheila shook her head. "That's not right."

21

SEX AND BASEBALL

"MARSHALL, STOP SNIFFING ME!"

"What? I wasn't . . ."

"Yes, you were," said Marta. "Do I have BO or something?"

Sheila giggled. "He hasn't told you about the smell yet?" she asked. "He says there's a smell when we come back from a mission."

Marta regarded Marshall curiously. "Like, really . . . fresh and new?"

"Ha!" Marshall said to Sheila. "She smells it, too. I told you!"

"Please, people," Naomi said with an uncharacteristic hint of frustration, "Let's stay on task. What about September of 2041?"

Marshall sighed and sifted through the pages of calendars, diaries, credit card receipts, time sheets, and other data before him.

Once the full scientific team came on board, parallel universe fever ran rampant and mission profiles quickly became more ambitious. Maybe a bit too ambitious, Naomi cautioned at every opportunity.

Initially these research missions represented deliberate progressive steps into the past—a day, weeks, a few months. And because the traveler candidates arrived two years ago, only animal test subjects had stretched the geographical limits of time travel beyond the boundaries of the GRC campus. The next mission, though, would take the travelers to both a time and place before any of them knew they would become time travelers, and before they knew each other.

The physicists insisted the technology was up to the task. Elvin pushed hard to gather a bigger block of data for study as they sought to map parallel universes. The science team dissected every nuance of the forces blurring and squiggling across their computer screens behind that bright red line that meant life and death to the travelers.

Only Naomi balked and that worried Marshall.

"I'm not sure the travelers' past counterparts are psychologically equipped to deal with the blast of information our people will inflict on them," Naomi told them.

Still, here they were, searching their calendars for a date before they'd come to the GRC campus when all four members of the traveling team were within reasonable proximity to each other, and within a 500-mile radius of the time machine.

"I was working in Phoenix," Sheila said, scanning the image of a tattered appointment calendar. "Except for Labor Day weekend. I was in Sedona that weekend."

"Sedona? Really? I went to Flagstaff over Labor Day weekend," Frank said.

Marta smiled. "Labor Day 2041," she said without consulting any of her personal reference material. "Aztec, New Mexico."

"Not bad," said Naomi. "Still within a few hours' drive of northern Arizona."

They peered anxiously at Marshall. They'd been at this for hours and this was the closest they'd come to a date during the past three years that put them all within a reasonable geographic grouping at the same time.

"Las Cruces," Marshall said. "I didn't travel much . . . oh, wait, 2041? Labor Day three years ago. I think . . . I need an old Diamondbacks schedule." He tapped out a quick search command on his pocket computer. "Phoenix! The Cardinals played the Diamondbacks. I drove over for a couple of ball games."

"Excellent," Naomi said. "We could designate Flagstaff as the meeting point, and you'd each be within a reasonable drive time following your projections. Now, let's see if we can sort out what you were doing."

Marshall and the others appreciated the necessity of brutal honesty in mission planning. Naomi didn't want to project travelers into past beings who might be involved in a situation—like driving or skydiving or defusing bombs—where the distraction of integration with a future self might be fatal.

"So, do you remember details?" Naomi asked, her pencil poised.

Marta's smile remained fixed. "Sex."

Marshall turned to Marta with surprise. Although Marta had thawed a bit, she still maintained her distance. She seemed to be spending more of her free time with Gillis Kerg, but she hadn't previously volunteered any hints about whatever personal life she might have.

Sheila laughed and playfully punched Marta's arm. "Way to go, Marta!"

"What, you think you're the only one who gets some every once in a while?"

"No, no, I didn't mean—"

"It's all right. Granted," Marta said, "it doesn't happen much. A guy I know from London came to visit. We have a thing that goes back a while. We don't really like each other that much, but the sex is great."

"Okay, what else besides sex?" Naomi asked. "Sightseeing, shopping, any excursions . . ."

"Nope. Just sex."

"Okay," Naomi said. "I'll put down *personal fulfillment* for Marta. Sheila?"

"Sex," Sheila said with a laugh.

Marshall didn't care for the trend here.

"I was dating a guy from the Maricopa County prosecutor's office. We did some hiking, but we'd been going out just a few weeks so we were jumping each other like every other minute."

"OK. Hiking and *personal fulfillment* for Sheila. Frank?"

"Sex. Mostly late at night after the bars closed. The rest of the time I slept late and hung around the university campus."

"Picking up coeds?" Sheila asked. "Were they at least of age?"

"Hey, it's a great place to meet girls. I don't ask for ID."

"Okay, I'll put down *debauchery* for Frank," Naomi said. "That's not fair . . ."

"Marshall?"

Marshall mumbled.

"What?" Naomi asked. "I didn't quite get that."

"Baseball. I watched some baseball games."

Their expressions suggested they expected more.

"Geez. I'm a baseball fan. I like to go to a weekend series in Phoenix or Denver."

"No sex?" Sheila asked.

"I mostly just hung out during the day. One afternoon I went to the zoo."

"The zoo?" Frank snickered.

"I'll put down *baseball* for Marshall."

Three days later, four travelers waited their turns to step between two gleaming silver globes bracketing the projection platform. Technicians stared at computer screens or adjusted dials.

Elvin split his attention between fuzzy squiggles behind the bright red lines bisecting four monitors, and medical technician Jolene Drew, who circulated through the room collecting the last-minute bets for today's erection pool. Once Elvin achieved his new station, he decided handling the money just prior to a projection would be inappropriate. Not that he had a lot to do. His work didn't really begin until the mission was under way and he could start analyzing data.

He coped with his pre-mission jitters by studying the travelers' routines. Marshall paced a short course, back and forth, eyes squinted, brow furrowed. Elvin figured any fear Marshall felt was swallowed by his single-minded focus on willing himself flaccid. Frank showed no sign of concern. For a moment, Elvin felt impressed with Frank's cold calm. Then he realized Frank probably wasn't smart enough to understand the extent of the peril he faced.

Sheila had turned on her *party girl* act as she buried her distress behind a façade of flirtatious laughter, winks and thumbs-up gestures—a nervous actress preparing for her big nude scene.

And finally, Marta. A quiet study in focus. She sat apart, gathering everything with her eyes and ears. Almost unblinking in her concentration. Marshall seemed to be of particular interest to her.

Elvin turned to the monitors and listened through his headset to cracks and pops and static noises associated with activity simmering behind the crisp red lifelines.

Although he'd witnessed every projection thus far, including the animal tests, this one was different. He knew many skeptical eyes watched him and more than one of the physicists probably hoped he'd screw something up.

"One more time," he heard Naomi say to her four wards. "We are projecting you to a point before any of you knew anything about time travel or this program. Your past selves will have no foundation, no inkling of what's happening."

Naomi had determined Marta's past self—given her military training, her intuitive grasp of much of the science involved and her off-the-charts self-discipline—best suited to cope with the trauma of a future version of herself leaping into her consciousness. And she would be safe and relatively isolated when she jumped into her past self—behind a locked door at a small bed and breakfast in Aztec, New Mexico.

So, Marta would go first and arrive—the scientists hoped—a day ahead of the others. She would drive to Phoenix and be present when Marshall joined his past self at the baseball stadium. The two of them would drive to Sedona and help Sheila with her transition. Finally, they would all go to Flagstaff to assist Frank through his maiden voyage.

Each traveler recalled cell phone numbers from three Labor Days previous. If problems arose, they would communicate among their past selves by phone to manage any last-minute adjustments.

Naomi feared the length of time the travelers would spend in the past. They would each exceed any previous experience, and Marta could be there as long as forty-eight hours.

"Remember the explanations you'll have to make to your past selves," Elvin heard Naomi say. "When you return, you leave these past selves with knowledge as to their own futures."

The ethical issue raised by Naomi added a new aspect of mission planning. By simply being projected into an alternate universe version of yourself, Sheila wondered, were you bestowing that past being with your total consciousness? And if so, were you arming that being with information concerning his or her own future that could affect the path of that future?

"So what?" Leonard Rose had countered.

"Leonard," Sheila said, "think back over your lifetime. Think of a choice you made that seemed to be a mistake, but in the full context of your life, ultimately led to something rewarding. I know some of the worst things that have happened to me regarding relationships or career choices have led me to some of my happiest and most satisfying experiences. I hate to think what would have happened if, forewarned about the immediate result, I made a choice denying me these long-term benefits."

Leonard harrumphed away her concern.

Although he wouldn't admit it, Elvin agreed with Leonard's sentiment. Elvin felt impatient with any issue that compromised his ability to gather more data.

Marshall, as usual, spent his pre-projection moments conjuring the most anti-sexual images he could muster.

Sumo wrestlers oiling each other. Nuns. Old withered nuns with rulers, threatening my eternal damnation. Small, brown, squirming, tail-wagging puppies being cast into a wood chipper . . .

He relaxed a bit. How could anyone get an erection when puppies were being massacred?

Then Marta stepped onto the platform and turned to face them under the lights.

Another puppy fell into the grinder.

Without question, Marta had become a significant contributor to Marshall's misery.

Beyond that pleasant pre-boner glow, though, puppy mutilation seemed to be doing the trick.

For her part, Sheila watched Marshall with subtle glances, as she always did. His predicament served a purpose. The distraction granted her an outward calm that was a lie.

As she came to know Marshall better and appreciate him as a friend, she promised herself she would not stir the pot for pure entertainment value anymore. Until a moment later when Frank slid behind her and whispered, "I'm looking forward to seeing you up there, babe. We haven't spent any time together for a while, and," he nodded toward Marshall, "you've had to hang around with dweebs like that."

Frank allowed his robe to fall open just enough that, when Sheila turned to him, she saw his pubic hair had been trimmed. His skin glistened with body oil that would set up a glow under the bright lights of the projection platform.

A few moments before, Sheila was content to let Frank be Frank. *So long as he leaves me alone.* With Frank's disparaging reference to Marshall, though, Sheila fumed. Her best intentions fled.

She turned slightly so Frank could hear her whisper.

"You've never seen Marshall being projected, have you, Frank? You might want to pay careful attention. He's a pro at this stuff. And, oh yeah, there's no need for you to feel intimidated."

Frank smirked as Marshall stepped out of his robe, his back to them. Sheila heard Frank laugh aloud at their shared view of Marshall's nearly nonexistent butt propped on stork legs.

"Like I'm going to be intimidated by that guy," Frank whispered.

"Yeah? Well watch this."

As Marshall completed his turn to face the cameras, Sheila winked and mouthed, "Good luck," parted the front of her robe, and did a quick Marilyn Monroe curtsey: hands on thighs, knees tucked into each other and slightly bent, then, just the slightest twist of her torso that sent ripples through her breasts.

She smiled the most dazzling smile she could manage, then glanced back to Frank.

Frank's smirk evaporated as his eyes were drawn to the enormity of Marshall rising. Sheila enjoyed Frank's expression of pure dismay.

"Oh, and Frank," Sheila added, "that body oil? Are you sure it's completely organic? If it isn't, at the very least you'll get some pretty bad burns. At worst, it might just fry that little weenie of yours right off."

22

AN ENTHUSIASTIC RECEPTION

FUTURE-MARTA'S FLASHING ENTRANCE into past-Marta couldn't have been timed better. Past-Marta sat impaled atop Nigel Smythe in the throes of full orgasm. Future-Marta had carefully rehearsed the presentation her half of the brain would make to ease her past counterpart's shock. When she arrived, though, all future-Marta could do was catch the escalating wave and enjoy the ride.

For her part, past-Marta thought this strange duality was some new level of sexual experience. She screamed her approval. "Oh, God! Oh . . . oh . . . Aaaaahhhhhhh!"

Nigel moaned as Marta's enthusiasm brought him to his most intense peak of the day.

Covered by a fine sheen of perspiration, Marta collapsed onto his chest where she lay purring while Nigel tried to catch his breath. Marta basked in the silent afterglow until her eyes popped wide.

"Oh, my God."

"What, you already started again?" Nigel asked.

"Something's happening . . ."

"Not yet, please? Just give me a few minutes."

Future-Marta, who hadn't shared the company of a man

for some time, felt a little upset about the interruption of the afterglow. But she came to her senses and quickly shushed her past self.

"I know you don't understand, but you've got to be calm. You've got to process this. You can't say anything to Nigel."

Past-Marta put both hands to her head.

"Are you all right?" Nigel asked.

"No. I'm . . . I'm feeling very strange. I've got to—"

She leaped off him and sprinted to the bathroom.

"What's happening to me? past-Marta wondered with a touch of panic. *Nigel's always said that someday he would actually fuck someone's brains out . . ."*

"The first thing we have to do is be calm," the voice occupying a part of her mind cautioned. *"You'll understand soon."*

Past-Marta leaned on the sink and stared into the mirror. She forced herself to breathe deep, slow breaths. She felt her heart rate settle. She closed her eyes and focused her attention inside her head.

Where she found the explanation. The travelers' program, the GRC, parallel universes. Marshall, Sheila, Yuni, Naomi, Gretchen. Snippets of the next three years revealed through a torrent of images all underscored by a single, remarkable realization.

"I will travel through time," she said aloud to the mirror.

"That's right, and right now, we have a mission to accomplish. We have to make an explanation to Nigel."

". . . and get to Phoenix as soon as possible," past-Marta completed the thought.

"Although," future-Marta suggested, *"given the time distortion issue, the schedule is probably flexible enough to spare another fifteen minutes."*

Past-Marta, at first concerned that her future self seemed willing to let her rigid sense of duty slip even momentarily, opened the bathroom door, saw a grinning Nigel Smythe propped on one elbow still tangled among bed sheets, and understood the wisdom of her past counterpart's suggestion.

Elvin leaned over the computer tech's shoulder and studied data emerging from Marta's monitor. He clamped his hands over the earpieces of his headset to try and further muffle the competing outside noise.

"There—did you hear that?" he asked the tech.

"Hear what?"

"You have to listen closely."

Elvin pushed a button to reset one of a half dozen devices recording projection data.

"Listen, during the ninety-seven-second interval right after projection . . . Wait—there!"

"I did hear something. Very faint."

"Okay, let me run it back again. Now, here it comes." He listened, smiled. "Now is that the theme song to *I Love Lucy* or not?"

The tech laughed. "Damn, I think you're right. Wait. Let it run . . . it changes. I think it's still music, but it's different . . ."

Elvin reversed the recording again and played with an alternate combination of filters. No question. The theme song from *I Love Lucy*. And then . . .

They looked at each other. "*Bonanza!*"

Elvin ran the whole projection sequence. At exactly

ninety-seven seconds into the projection, *I Love Lucy* became the theme song from *Bonanza*.

Gretchen planned to have Marta arrive at her destination at 2:00 p.m. Friday of the Labor Day weekend. The actual arrival time was 3:32. Not bad, Marta thought. Considering the distance in time and space they were navigating, the projection team had done a remarkable job.

Once she untangled herself from Nigel Smythe, she stepped into the shower and performed some quick mental calculations. Extrapolating the same time difference to Marshall's projection, give or take an hour, would place his arrival at tomorrow's Phoenix Diamondback's game at just about 6:00 p.m.

Marta had plenty of time to drive to Phoenix and meet Marshall. The projection profile called for her to contact him by cell phone prior to the game, somehow convince him he should let her accompany him and explain what was about to happen. Marta would have no trouble getting a seat close to Marshall's. These were, after all, the Diamondbacks.

She stepped from the shower and reached for her phone.

"Hi, this is Marshall. I can't take your call right now. Leave a message and I'll get back to you."

"Bugger." She waited for the beep.

"Mr. Grissom, my name is Marta Hamilton. I must talk with you concerning a matter of utmost urgency."

She left her number.

Reluctantly, the Martas bade Nigel farewell.

23

GLBRXXXPFFT

MARSHALL'S PAST COUNTERPART made his way through the crowd exiting Imodium Multi-Symptom Relief Ballpark in downtown Phoenix when future-Marshall came crashing into his consciousness.

Past-Marshall wavered for a moment, clamped his hands to his head and sagged to his knees. Marshall's companion, Bob Stoops, who occupied the cubicle next to Marshall's at their Las Cruces ad agency, bent to assist him.

A woman behind Marshall put her hand to his shoulder and stared at his eyes.

She said, "Glbrxxxpfft, ssssss, nsmqulrdax psss, ffffffffffffffsssssssss?"

Which Future-Marshall clearly understood as, "Are you all right, sir? I'm a nurse. You seem very pale."

Bob stared with alarm and said, "SSSSS, prblxgronkle."

Future-Marshall, taken aback by the strange noises emanating from Bob's mouth, thought he understood his friend to say, "Hey, man, you only had one beer."

Obviously dazed, Marshall peered from one to the other. Something wasn't right here. For one thing, both Bob and the nurse looked a lot like lizards. Granted, he found the nurse attractive, but lizardish nonetheless. Bob wore a white baseball jersey with the familiar classic slanted bat logo of the St. Louis Cardinals. Instead of the familiar red birds, though, pterodactyls perched on either end of the bat.

At the same time, a rush of images and impressions assaulted Past-Marshall as his mind seemed to be running off somewhere of its own accord.

"Ga . . . ga . . . gavlbrossssssssssppppfffft . . ." was the only response he could manage.

Meanwhile, back at the projection platform, Elvin took the computer tech's place at Marshall's monitor and gleefully twisted dials, seeking the combination of settings that made the *I Love Lucy* theme and its eventual transition to the song from *Bonanza* most clear.

There! Only seconds into Marshall's projection, unmistakably, *I Love Lucy*.

And—bam—at ninety-seven seconds Elvin held his breath, listening intently for the orchestral sounds that cued the Cartwrights' ride across a golf course where the opening scene to *Bonanza* had been filmed.

"Three, two, one . . ." he mumbled as he fiddled with the dials again and heard . . . some weird music that, had he not been a devoted fan of the Broadcast History Channel, Elvin never would have recognized as the theme song from *My Mother the Car*.

With a puzzled frown Elvin focused on the outer bands dancing at the screen's periphery. The foreign universe squiggle seemed bizarre in comparison with previous projections.

"Something's off here. I think Marshall may be in the wrong place."

Losing a traveler during his first mission as one of the honchos would not look good on Elvin's resume.

"I think we should bring him back." Cutting a projection short had never been done before. An automated computer program performed the process of retrieving travelers. Their journey to the past simply played itself out over a predetermined duration.

"What did you do?" Leonard Rose said.

Elvin's face flushed beneath his two-day whisker stubble. He felt his heartbeat race. "I didn't *do* anything. I'm seeing some puzzling data here. I see no reason to take any chances . . ."

"Are you sure, Elvin?" Gretchen asked. "Because we don't have an emergency protocol programmed."

"You're kidding?"

"Retrieving travelers is a deliberate procedure," Yuni said as he peered over Elvin's shoulder at the monitor. "The process involves a number of steps that must be done at precise intervals and sequences. The computer's execution of that process is flawless. And the computer only initiates the return process at the point we've planned for a mission to end."

"That's not real smart." Elvin began to sweat as the rogue band of light continued to contort itself.

"No one thought to do anything else, because until you came forward with your findings, we had no way of knowing whether a traveler had missed a target," explained Gretchen. "We didn't know there was a target to miss."

Elvin pointed to the strange flutter on Marshall's monitor,

which had adopted a previously unseen color combination. "We'd better do something. At the very least, I know Marshall didn't end up where Marta did, and I've never seen anything approximating this pattern."

Sheila, who had just shed her robe and was stepping onto the platform to begin her journey, leaped down and ran to Elvin's side. "What's happening?"

Elvin turned to her and suffered a momentary lack of brain function at her naked proximity.

"Sheila," Gretchen said, "get your robe."

Sheila covered herself. "Is Marshall okay?"

Yuni turned to Gretchen, who shrugged. "The lifeline's still good."

"Yes, but for how long?" Elvin pointed to the edge of the monitor. "These universe identifiers are different—I mean a whole lot different—than anything we've encountered before."

"So, what does that mean?" Sheila demanded.

"I think we should do whatever we have to and get him out of there," Elvin said.

Rose pointed to the lifeline. "There is no sign of physical distress."

Naomi joined them.

"Mental trauma is the real danger here," she said. "I agree with Elvin."

"We've never done a manual return," Rose protested, his dark eyes casting their allegations. "We've never even practiced it . . ."

"*Get him back!*" Sheila shouted.

Marshall felt the two halves of himself begin to settle into awkward cohabitation.

As the pretty lizard nurse hovered over him, future-Marshall saw the tiny shimmering scales of her bare skin. She wore a tight halter top and a short skirt. Her features were clearly reptilian and past-Marshall was unquestionably attracted to her.

Future-Marshall beheld a throng of strange beings around him. They all had some sort of *human* quality to them. They walked upright. They wore hats, shoes, trousers, skirts, shorts . . . but they seemed to loosely represent a wide variety of cold-blooded species.

His own hands and arms were covered with light scales of a decidedly greenish tint.

We're lizards, he thought.

"What! We don't use that word," an angry internal reaction snapped. *"Are you all bigots in the future?"*

"No, I'm sorry. What are we then?"

"We are Reptilian Americans."

To his left, Marshall saw a toady creature approach.

"Fzzz, sppetlec, graclecet sppppffffts?" Marshall's ears heard the creature ask. His brain decoded heavily accented English: "I'm a doctor. Can I be of assistance here?"

"No, no," Marshall said. "I'll be fine."

"So, what is he?"

"He is an Amphibian American."

"Like . . . a salamander?"

"Why would you say such a thing?" an appalled past-Marshall replied. *"Enlightened beings don't employ ethnic slurs . . ."*

While the doctor shined a tiny flashlight into Marshall's

eyes, a hulking dinosaurish creature slinked behind the woman accompanying the doctor. Suddenly the dinosaur grabbed at her purse and loped into the crowd. The doctor's wife, apparently wary of post-ballgame thieves in downtown Phoenix, had wrapped her purse strap around her shoulder. Entangled by the strap, her arm was yanked completely from her body.

"SSSpppthhn! SSSpppthhn! Grbblefriz mxstfnsssss?" – Mable! Mable! Are you all right?

Future-Marshall was shocked beyond response until past-Marshall pointed out, "*No big deal. She's an Amphibian American, too. Her arm will grow back in a couple of weeks.*"

As the doctor and several others took off after the dinosaur creature, past-Marshall finally had a moment to examine the part of his brain revealing future-Marshall's world.

"*Oh, my good Lord! You're hideous. Is that . . . is that hair? Gag me with a spoon! Ooooh, I do like this Sheila person, though.*"

At the same time, future-Marshall understood his past counterpart's attraction to the nurse attending him. She projected a sultry air that Marshall found most discomforting. Their eyes met. Marshall felt a warm wave wash over him as future-Marshall sped back into the limbo, his uncomfortable lust for this exotic Reptilian-American nurse hanging over him like a steamy cloud.

"So, did we get him?" Sheila asked.

"Just wait," Yuni said.

Sheila felt helpless as the projection team carefully

checked through the recall protocol, attempting to time each task precisely. Elvin glued his attention to the unwavering red line bisecting Marshall's monitor. Finally, the projection platform crackled to life, and Marshall appeared, lying on his back.

Sheila ran to him.

"Marshall?"

"Grbbleflexxx," he said.

"Oh my God! He has brain damage!"

Naomi pushed Sheila aside and directed the beam from a small penlight into Marshall's wide eyes.

"Marshall, try and talk to me."

"I said I'm fine."

"Well, I hope you're fine. But that's not what you said."

"Of course, I did."

Then his eyes became frantic. He jumped to his feet and called out, "Is the recording equipment running?"

Elvin waved from his console and nodded.

"Grbbleflexx. SSSSSfttpfgarblex fffffsptffff sssssssspt!" Marshall said loudly.

Sheila grabbed his arm and held her breath to keep from sobbing as she hoped the medical staff could save him.

"The pronunciation isn't exactly correct, because Reptilian Americans have a completely different set of vocal organs," Marshall said, "That means, 'I'm fine. Somebody, get me a robe and stop staring.'"

"Reptilian Americans? You mean they were lizards?"

"Please, Naomi. We don't use that word. It's offensive."

The staff robed Marshall and rushed him to Naomi's medical lab as a grim Sheila turned to Gretchen and said, "Okay, let's get me back there."

"You mean we're still gonna do this?" Frank asked, his voice shaky. "What if we get sent to lizard land, too?" Frank had returned from a quick dash to the showers to wash off his body oil just in time to witness Marshall's bizarre behavior.

"It's what you signed up for," Sheila said with disgust as she stripped off her robe.

"Perhaps," Yuni said, "we should delay the next two projections until we at least have time to set up a computerized emergency protocol for returning the travelers."

"Yeah, I like that idea," Frank said.

"Marta's already out there somewhere," Sheila countered. "She'll be finding our past selves and expecting us to show up. She'll tell them things about their futures that may change their lives. I'll take my chances."

"She's right," said Gretchen. "We need to get to Marta early and keep her from contacting Marshall at the baseball game."

Yuni frowned. "All right, Sheila, go ahead. If we see any signs of trouble, we'll go through the process manually again and get you back."

Sheila nodded, dropped her robe, and whispered to Frank, "As for you, you pussy, you'd better have the balls to step up here and meet us at that bar in Flagstaff."

24

THE THREESOME

FOR THE FIRST TIME DURING A projection, Elvin didn't leer at Sheila as she winked away. His attention tracked between his headphones and Sheila's monitor. He'd quickly become adept at finding the faint *I Love Lucy* music accompanying each projection, and . . . yes!

He'd positioned Marta's monitor next to Sheila's to compare the outer band configurations. He nervously counted through the ninety-seven-second interval until opening chords of the *Bonanza* theme coursed faintly through his headphones. Squiggles on the two monitors seemed identical.

"All right, I'm ninety-nine percent sure Marta and Sheila are in the same universe."

Yuni nodded. "Do you have the emergency return protocol sequence entered into the computer yet?"

"A couple more minutes," a computer technician called.

"Okay. Frank, get ready. As soon as the protocol is uploaded, you're going."

"Don't you think we should maybe just get the girls back and try again tomorrow?"

"You're a member of the team now," Yuni said. "Our

job—your job—is to research time travel phenomenon. If we don't go now, we'll be squandering an opportunity."

"Finished!" the computer tech said.

"We should do this now," Elvin said as the Bonanza theme still rang through his headphones.

"So, are you going to be a member of this team or not?" Yuni said pointedly to a pale Frank Altman.

Frank dropped his robe, covered himself with both hands and, eyes cast downward, slunk onto the platform.

Sheila needed time to think.

Her friend from the Maricopa County prosecutor's office opted for a morning run, so Sheila hiked alone on a trail in the cool early hours of Arizona's northern mountains.

She had to decide what to do about the executive from the company that owned her television station. His veiled innuendos had become more direct. On the surface, her decision was easy. She didn't do married men.

Certainly no prude, Sheila didn't want to be married to anyone, and she genuinely enjoyed sex. Traffic-stopping beauty made getting laid easy. Although, surprisingly, she often had to settle for men who didn't fascinate her. The problem with being stone-cold gorgeous is that the most interesting men—quieter, more intellectual and introspective guys—were often too intimidated to ask her out. That left brash, pretty-boy, ex-big-man-on-campus types who found rejection easy to shake off because a willing substitute usually sat just a few bar stools away.

Sheila had no doubt that if she bedded Roland Timmons,

she would occupy an anchor chair within a year. He was certainly applying the pressure. Yes, this was sexual harassment. Yes, she could file a lawsuit. And yes, after threats to sue she might get some kind of settlement. If she did, though, covering snowplow races and frozen pipe jamborees in Minot, North Dakota, would be her professional destiny.

If she didn't sleep with Timmons and if she didn't file a harassment suit, she'd simply maintain her place among a rank and file of attractive, ambitious female reporters. Because certainly someone else would succumb to his offer.

She didn't do married men.

"We've got a lot to go over and not a lot of time to do it!"

Past-Sheila wobbled and sat heavily on a fallen tree next to the trail. She looked around to see who had spoken . . . no, not spoken. Thought. Someone was thinking in her head.

"Oh, my God, I've got brain cancer!" past-Sheila exclaimed, her heart rate leaping, her hands flying to her temples.

"What? Why would you think you've got brain cancer?"

"Oh, no. Oh, no. This can't be happening. I have to find a doctor."

Future-Sheila recalled her interview with a young man who, out of the blue, started hearing voices. Afraid he was going crazy, he'd consulted a physician. Doctors discovered a brain tumor in time for surgery and chemotherapy to save his life.

"That's the trouble with medical stories," future-Sheila admonished her past self. *"You do a story about coronary artery disease, and suddenly every bump and flutter becomes the onset of a heart attack. I'm not cancer. Just sit here for a moment and pay attention to your thoughts."*

"Hmm, this is certainly a very calm and rational brain tumor. At least the voices aren't telling me to run naked through a crowded room. Oh . . . wait . . ."

"That's one of the new things you might want to set aside for right now. Focus on the part about what we have to do here."

"Wow! Who is this Marshall guy?"

A half hour later, Marta's cell phone rang through to her Mercedes. She pushed a button and said, "Marta Hamilton."

"Marta? This is Sheila? Do you know who I . . . ?"

"Sheila? Why are you already here?"

"It's wonderful to know we're both where we're supposed to be." Marta could hear her relief.

"Why? What happened?"

"Things have changed. Marshall ended up in some Jurassic Park universe. The Marshall you're supposed to meet at the baseball game isn't involved anymore."

"Jurassic Park?"

"I'll explain later. Right now, get to Sedona as quickly as you can. Same hotel. I'll be ready. Then we go to Flagstaff and collect Frank. His arrival has been moved ahead, too."

"Is Marshall okay?"

"Yeah. Except that he speaks reptile."

"Ooookayyy . . . I passed the Sedona exit off I-17 about twenty minutes ago. Give me an hour."

"Here's another one: 'SSSSpffftblglk, fffffssssspttt, mffffs-glrbked.' That means 'It's hot, you need to go inside.' Or I guess it could be, '*You're* hot, *we* need to go inside.' I think the difference has to do with the tongue flicks."

The members of Naomi's psychological team huddled around Marshall, furiously taking notes.

"We're getting this recorded, right?" one of the scientists kept asking.

As soon as Naomi found Marshall to be of mostly sound mind and body, psychologists and biologists swarmed him. The realization that he was now bi-lingual thrilled Marshall. As a Southwest native, Marshall felt he was not a genuinely literate person because he hadn't learned to speak Spanish. And now he could converse with lizards . . . "Bgsssverflux," he swore, as the remaining reptilian aspect of his brain recoiled at the slur.

The medical team devoted the debriefing's first half hour to language and jargon of Reptilian Americans. Then the whole thing began to fade. Of the three travelers, Marshall had proven most adept at recalling events that occurred during projection. Marta and Sheila could offer specifics for only a few minutes before the experience receded into a nebulous haze, although their recall improved with each journey. Marshall, though, clung to details longer. These were general memories, though. Times, places, descriptions, sequences of events, conversations. Retaining the subtleties of a second language, or details of math or technology, slipped away more quickly.

After forty-five minutes, Marshall once again had to content himself with English.

The biologists took over.

"They were reptiles?"

"Well, yes, sort of. Like reptiles with humanoid

features. Sort of a cross between the two. They walked on two legs. They had hands and arms. They wore clothes, shoes . . ."

"Preposterous!" Dr. Peter Billis said with an air of condescension. "You're saying somehow mammals and reptiles mixed their gene pools? That's impossible. Even different mammalian species can't interbreed. Cross-breeding between mammals and reptiles is absurd."

"We must stop thinking so narrowly where parallel universe theory is concerned," Naomi interjected. "Dr. Allen has been surprised that thus far the physical laws of our universe seem to apply to the others we've visited as well. They expect at some point to confront bizarre laws of physics elsewhere. Why shouldn't we anticipate the same thing biologically?"

"I thought parallel universes implied identical worlds," Billis said.

"Clearly, we have to re-think that. Perhaps we are only talking about parallel histories. The biological evolution of a world is the result of many tiny random events over the eons. One small change millions of years ago could have set the evolution of the inhabitants of a parallel Earth along a different path."

Sheila and Marta walked into the blare of a crowded bar two blocks from the Northern Arizona University campus. Sheila peered anxiously through the gloom.

She did not see Frank Altman. She did see dozens of college-age men and women in various stages of substance-induced celebration. The place featured a long bar down one side of a narrow room, with a variety of alcoves and nooks breaking up the opposite wall. The sparse illumination came from track lighting along the exterior walls with the fixtures pointed upward to mute the reflected light off a black ceiling.

The sound system emphasized bass speakers that loosened the floorboards. Conversation required shouting at a decibel level that could make ears bleed.

This noise did nothing to affect crowd response as Sheila entered. She felt eyes rivet onto her. She'd swapped her boots for a pair of boat shoes. She still wore her hiking clothes—cargo shorts and a tank top.

Still.

"Christ, Sheila," Marta shouted, "it's a good thing I've got healthy self-esteem or one of these days you could give me a complex."

"How do you know they're not looking at you?"

"Oh, yeah, right. Everyone ignores the cover girl to stare at the short, frizzy, flat-chested one."

As the buzz regained its momentum, eyes still followed as Sheila and Marta walked deeper into the shadows.

"There he is," Marta said. "Back there. Next to the last table with those two . . . My God, they're children!"

Sheila tracked Marta's gaze and found Frank. He sat with two young women who couldn't have been a year removed from high school.

"So how do we do this?" Marta yelled.

"I'll take care of it."

Sheila walked to the table and waited for the inevitable full-body scan from her target.

". . . and I'll show them to you," Frank was shouting, "All

my notes are back at my hotel room, just around . . . oh my goodness."

"Hi, Frank. We need to talk."

"Um . . . okay."

A puzzled look entered his eyes as if he were trying to understand how this woman knew him. Sheila smiled. Frank's confusion became moot.

"Aw, you mean we don't get to see your etchings?" one of the girls screamed.

"Some other time. This appears to be . . . an emergency."

"Etchings?" Marta shouted.

"Yeah," said the other girl. "They're, like, pictures. You know? Like, art?"

"And he thinks you two could be models," Marta hollered.

"Yeah. Like, uncanny. How'd you know?"

"I'm psychic."

"You are?" Frank asked.

Marta rolled her eyes and tugged at Frank's arm, guiding him toward the door.

Sheila paused at the table

"You two have got to be smarter than this," she said to the girls. "You're in college, for God's sake. He's a landscaper and a gigolo."

"A what?"

"Look it up," she yelled, and followed her two companions.

Sheila joined Marta and Frank in the welcome relief of quiet outside the bar. "You have a room?" she asked.

Frank gaped, but only for a second.

Sheila imagined the sweaty images churning through that vacuous brain. Another man might be skeptical of what appeared to be a blatant proposition falling into his lap. She concluded that Frank Altman's ego would quickly overwhelm any analytical impulses his limited intellect might bring to bear. Why wouldn't a gorgeous woman and her friend be so swept away at the very sight of him they couldn't wait to hustle him off to bed?

"Just down the block, ladies. I've got some wine you will—"

"Don't talk," Marta said. "Just take us to your room."

Frank grinned. "Oooohh, the quiet one is the domineering type."

Marta rolled her eyes.

Frank fumbled a moment with his key card and opened the door to reveal a budget motel space featuring a king-size bed and a black velvet painting of the Pope.

"Lie down, Frank," Marta ordered. "I'm going to tie you up."

"Whoa. Not that I've got a problem with a little bondage. Shouldn't we ease into it, though? Have a drink? Maybe loosen some clothing? And . . . how do you know my name?"

"Loosen all you want."

"Don't mind Marta," Sheila said. "She's just impatient. Wine would be nice."

Frank opened the box and splashed the drinks into plastic motel water cups. Sheila smiled again, dipped a finger into the amber liquid and suggestively put the finger to her lips. She found the wine austere, with subtle notes of kerosene.

Frank drooled a little.

"So why don't you lie down and let us take it from here?" Sheila added a sly wink.

From her jacket pocket, Marta took four lengths of stout cord. She looped one end around Frank's right wrist and secured the other to the headboard.

As Sheila reached for his other arm, he said, "Wait. Are you going to tie my legs, too?"

Sheila smiled her most seductive smile. "Why, of course. That's a real turn-on for us."

"Okay, well, shouldn't I take my pants off before you do my legs? I mean, it would be pretty hard to—"

"Fine," Marta snapped. "Take off your pants."

"I've only got one hand free." Frank waved his arm. "I'll need some help."

Marta rolled her eyes again, grabbed at the snap and zipper of his jeans, and reached to his pant cuffs. With one violent yank, she relieved him of his trousers. He didn't wear underwear, his enthusiasm evident.

"Mmm," said Sheila as she bound his other wrist.

Marta took the remaining lengths of cord and secured Frank's legs to the metal rail at the foot of the bed. "Okay, now can we cover that thing up?"

Sheila took one of the pillows and placed it strategically.

Frank adopted a puzzled frown. "Now, what?"

"Now," Sheila said, "we wait. Marta, why don't you see what's on TV?"

"Hey! What is this? I thought we came here to have a threesome."

"We know what you thought, Frank."

"And how do you know my name?"

"There's no point going into some drawn-out explanation," Marta said. "If things happen the way they're supposed to, you'll understand soon enough."

Like the slightest hint of a rising sun over a dark and vacant landscape, the idea began to dawn upon Frank Altman that laying naked and bound to a bed in the company of two strangers might be cause for concern.

After a couple more minutes of his protests, Marta said to Sheila, "So if *our* guy doesn't show up, how are we going to explain ourselves to *this* guy? We could be in a little bit of trouble here, you know."

"What? What trouble? What guy? What are you talking about?"

Sheila wrinkled her nose. "Well, if worse comes to worst, I'll figure something out."

"All right. If you two aren't going to get naked right now, I've had enough of this—"

Frank's brain exploded into a chaotic muddle of impulses and images. Voices assaulted him in senseless fragments. These mental scenes included the two women who were here with him, and they *were* naked. The vision was so real he was surprised to open his eyes and find them clothed. That elusive string of clarity snapped, though, as a man wielding an impossibly large penis, erect and threatening, leaped at him from a dark corner of his thoughts. Frank screamed. A tangle of senseless images banged relentlessly inside his skull as he thrashed and struggled against ropes binding him in place.

"Help me!" Frank gasped. "There's ... someone ... What did you do to me?" Only the ropes kept him from making a break for the door. He began to whimper. "Please . . . please let me go. I can't—"

"Yes, Frank, you can."

When his whine trailed into long mewling cries Sheila grabbed his shoulders and shook. "Just be quiet for a moment and pay attention. Be still and listen to the other voice."

The whimpers subsided. A wild-eyed Frank searched the room, settled on Sheila, shifted to Marta, and then back to Sheila. "Tell me honestly, did you give me something? Some weird date rape drug or something? Just let me out of here. I promise I won't—"

"Listen to me, Frank," Sheila said. "The stuff in your head is real. Quit fighting it and pay attention."

The two tracks drifted apart and one became familiar. That was him, here, now. But the other track was him, too. Only everything there was a revelation.

"The . . . the future?" His eyes begged for understanding.

"Now you're starting to get it," Marta said.

"I'm a time traveler? That's impossible. I . . . I have a pickup truck . . ."

Frank closed his eyes tight and screwed up his face as if this level of concentration presented an excruciating ordeal. Marta replaced the pillow that had bounced to one side of the bed during Frank's struggles.

"Okay," Sheila said, "now do you understand what this means?"

Frank dared to open one eye.

"It means . . . it means . . . we aren't going to have a threesome?"

Distracted by Frank's whimpering, Sheila didn't notice Marta bend over and put her hands on her knees until Marta groaned.

"Marta, what's happening?"

Marta shook her head. "I don't know. I've been back here for more than twenty-four hours now. I really haven't gotten any sleep. But—"

"You're tired. Anyone would be."

"No. Something else is happening. I'm having lapses."

Marta took deep slow breaths.

"Lapses?"

"Just now, everything went blank . . . about the future . . . I . . . I . . ."

"I don't understand."

Marta seemed to relax. She stood and shook her head.

"For a minute there I—my future self—went away. I was alone here. And I preferred it that way. If you hadn't been talking to Frank about the mission, I'm not sure I would have come back. Not sure *she* would have let me come back. Even now, it's a struggle to remember there's a part of me that belongs somewhere . . . sometime, else."

For several hours, Elvin had been able to relax. The Marshall crisis was behind them. Not Elvin's fault. He was regaining his confidence when he swallowed hard and felt his heart rate leap again as Marta's lifeline began to quiver and curl into a series of s-turns.

"We have another issue!" he said.

Yuni, Naomi, and Gretchen followed his pointing finger to Marta's computer display. They stared without breathing until the pattern reversed itself, shimmered, and settled back to normal.

"What happened?" Yuni demanded.

"I don't know," Elvin said. "We've never seen that before. The connective threads have never wavered."

"The emergency protocol is programmed," Yuni said in a grim voice. "Let's bring them back."

Sheila diverted her attention from Marta long enough to cut Frank free.

"What is it with you two?" he said. "If a flaming nerd like Marshall can do this, I can, too!"

"Shut up, Frank." Sheila switched her focus to Marta. "They'll return us soon."

"This is difficult to describe," Marta said. "All I want to do is let my mind relax. Be who I am. But something tells me if I don't hang onto what I know of the future, that I . . . I don't know."

Elvin scanned frantically from one to the other bright red thread while the technical team stood anxiously just beyond the platform as computers clicked methodically through each step of the return protocol. Threads linking Sheila and Frank to this time and place did not waver. Marta's lifeline continued to shift slightly from the sharply defined thread to a slightly fuzzy track.

Hang in there, Elvin silently appealed to Marta. *You're the tough one. You, of all people, can't be who screws this up for me.*

Frank underwent the transition first.

"Oh, thank God," Sheila heard him say. "I was afraid I'd be that way forever."

Sheila didn't allow herself to divide her attention from Marta for more than an instant. She continued to talk quietly, describing their mission and their future lives until mercifully, she saw tension melt from Marta's face.

"Who are . . ." Marta began. "Oh, wait. You're that woman from the—but that's crazy."

"Don't you know me? We've been talking about our mission. We came here from—"

And now Sheila was alone within herself.

"We came here from Sedona where I drove to pick you up," Marta said. "I was . . . for some reason, I was driving to Phoenix to meet some man. And then I had to get you, and we came here to talk to him."

She nodded at Frank.

. "That's right. You can remember—"

"I remember what we've done. I'm just a little fuzzy about why."

Sheila started to explain, and realized she had trouble making sense of it as well.

She was pleased to have met Marta. She found within herself an unaccountable animosity toward this man named Frank. She remembered they had taken his clothes and tied him to the bed. Which at this moment seemed a serious lapse of judgment.

Marshall scanned the faces around him, recalling World War II movies in which ground crews scattered about the English countryside anxiously counted B-17 bombers returning from missions over Germany.

After showering and dressing, Marshall returned to the lab and walked into pandemonium.

"Naomi, I want a medical team . . ." Yuni shouted.

"Already here."

Marshall ran to peer over the shoulders of computer technicians.

"You're sure you've never seen a lifeline pattern like that?" Marshall heard Naomi ask Elvin.

"No, I . . . I don't know. Maybe. During the early animal experiments. Some of the ones we didn't get back."

Marshall felt an adrenaline rush as Elvin's uncertainty heightened his own concern. It didn't help when Elvin added, "Honestly, I wasn't paying that much attention to the variations. Not with the animals."

"You have to go back and review those recordings," Naomi said.

Elvin and Naomi shifted their attention to the computer screens, the displays ticking through the return protocol. When the final task light switched from red to green Marshall felt the air pressure dip as thirty-five sets of lungs took deep gulps and did not exhale.

Plasma crawled across the metal globes and Frank appeared. Techs handed him a robe and practically threw him off the platform. Even Sheila's return, for once, failed to take center stage. She stepped to Marshall's side.

"Why are they arriving separately?" one of the techs asked.

Elvin silenced him with a glare.

The plasma surged again, and Marshall took a quick inventory. *Is she whole? Yes. Is she standing?*

Marshall reacted a split second before anyone else, vaulting past the technicians with waiting robes to crush Marta in a hug. "Are you all right?"

"Fine, Marshall," she mumbled, her face buried in his chest. "Um . . . kind of naked here."

"Oh, geez." Marshall quickly stepped back, allowing Marta to cover herself. He turned crimson, realizing he'd just embraced a nude woman in front of the entire projection lab.

"I'm sorry. I was . . . we were worried . . . I would never . . ."

"It's okay, Marshall. I need to get to debriefing while I still recall some things they have to know."

That evening, Andrew Gormly waited at the bar. When Dr. Rose failed to appear, Gormly was only a little perturbed. Emergencies arose. Last-minute meetings were called. Getting off the campus and all the way to Superior wasn't a simple task. He checked the clock one more time, paid for his drink and left. He took no notice of a waitress across the room holding her phone.

"Marta," Sheila whispered, "after the mission yesterday, did you notice anything unusual about . . . your toes?"

"My toes?"

"Yeah, did you look at your toes?"

"I guess I don't pay much attention to my toes."

"Well, look," Sheila said.

"What, right now?"

They sat alongside Marshall and Frank at a table before a panel of the various group leaders representing all program specialties. Elvin joined Yuni, Naomi, and Gretchen at a table apart from the veteran travelers. They waited for Yuni to convene the meeting.

"Just look," Sheila said.

Marta rolled her eyes, reached surreptitiously to the floor and slipped off her workout shoe. Sheila leaned to peer down.

"Just toes," said Marta with a wiggle.

Sheila frowned. As she toweled off alone in the women's locker room after yesterday's mission, she found that her toenails were perfectly pedicured and painted a lovely shade of pink. When had that happened?

She dismissed her toe issue as Yuni called the meeting to order. The travelers—aided by transcripts of their immediate debriefings—did their best to answer questions.

"The problem is," Marta explained, "we don't remember many specifics of the event. By now, everyone should understand that once a traveler has returned, any recollection of what happened quickly regresses."

"And what about your hosts from the past universe?"

"We have reason to believe the host's memory also becomes transient," Naomi said. "Sheila, would you please tell them."

"I was the last of the three to depart," Sheila said. "The past-Marta clearly was confused about what had just happened."

"If my recollections are correct," Marta agreed, "I believe

my wavering lifeline coincided with my loss of awareness that I had come from the future. Only Sheila's prompting and reminding kept me there. I'd been there longer than the others. My sense is that from the time a traveler enters the past, the essence of a future being starts to be . . . for lack of a better term . . . absorbed by the past being."

"We have considered Marta's report carefully and are concerned about the effect of prolonged exposure to a past environment," Naomi said. "Following each of our previous missions, the travelers have talked about uncomfortable sensations of duality both past and future entities experience. And they've all talked about how that sense of discomfort eases with the passage of time. We think it possible that the stronger of the two entities—the being comfortable in its own body and universe—could eventually displace the consciousness of the visiting entity."

"To the extent that the being from the future would lose awareness of his separate existence?"

"Yes," Marta said. "And I think as that awareness is exhausted the lifeline tying that traveler to this universe wavers."

"And that would mean . . . ?"

"That *could* mean," Elvin said, "we wouldn't be able to bring our guys home."

25

I LOVE LUCY

SOFT BUT PERSISTENT KNOCKING roused Marta from a sound sleep. Understanding what woke her took a couple of minutes. She got out of bed, found the t-shirt that draped down to her knees and shuffled to her apartment door.

"Gillis, for God sake, you can't possibly think that waking me at this unholy hour will get you an invitation to my bed."

Gillis smiled and raised his hands as if to ward off a blow.

"Dear, dear Marta, that particular itch was scratched just a couple of hours ago. I come bearing gifts."

"At two in the morning?" Marta yawned, rubbed her eyes with the back of her hand and stood aside so Gillis could enter.

As he crossed the threshold, Gillis adopted a puzzled look.

"Your apartment personality system," he said. "I've been trying for weeks to figure out how to shut the damn thing off. How did you do it?"

"I didn't," Marta said. "I intimidated it."

"What, it's scared of you?"

"I threatened to kill it."

"I'm not sure that would work for me," Gillis said.

"Well, you do need a certain presence."

Although their stature and wiry builds were similar, Marta regarded Gillis as almost dainty. She knew from experience he didn't lack courage, nor did he succumb to the bluster of larger, louder people. He had a fastidiousness about him, though—an understated sort of elegance—which compromised his masculinity. Only when he smiled did he seem dangerous.

"I've discovered information related to our discussion about Leonard Rose's off-campus activities," Gillis said. "I thought you might be anxious to see it."

Marta questioned neither his professional capabilities nor his judgment. As an electronic surveillance expert, Gillis was Luxembourg's senior operative. He knew everything about the cutting edge of espionage technology—both how to operate it and how to defeat it.

"So, you snuck under the wire tonight to meet your friend?"

"Several wires actually. And yes, we had a lovely evening. At the end of which she told me she'd used her cell phone a couple of days ago to surreptitiously take a picture of the man Leonard Rose meets in Superior."

Wide awake now, she directed Gillis to a small sofa and sat next to him. "Show me."

"Ah, if you only meant that," Gillis said with a sigh.

He withdrew his pocket computer and the bent-nosed face of a heavyset man floated before them. The image looked vaguely familiar.

"She doesn't know his name?"

"No. She tried checking credit card receipts, but he pays with cash."

"I've seen this guy," Marta said. "I can't remember when or where, but my gut reaction is that the context wasn't pleasant."

"Well, I have one more context to offer," Gillis said. He produced a sim card and plugged it into one of the computer ports. "I ran the photo though my face recognition software, searching the pirated security video in my system. I've only gone back a few weeks, but this is what came up."

Marta saw a hallway scene, the elevators closest to the projection lab. Marshall Grissom stopped to talk with a stocky man dressed in a suit. The security camera showed the man's back. Marshall shook hands with him. As the man turned to board the elevator, they saw a clear view of his face. Without question, this was the same man photographed by Gillis's waitress, the same man conspiring off-site with Leonard Rose.

"Oh, Marshall," Marta sighed. "Who are you?"

"So how is this Elvin Detwyler experiment working out?" Michael Huxtable asked Yuni, Gretchen and Naomi during the weekly science and technology briefing to the director. Although Yuni usually handled this task alone, Huxtable wanted to hear from everyone. Naomi felt uncomfortable with this arrangement. She feared it implied Rose was gaining traction in his campaign to undermine Yuni.

"Despite what you may have heard from Dr. Rose or a few others," Yuni said, "Elvin is making a valuable contribution. We've made real progress towards a navigation system whereby the destination for a journey into the past is targeted to specific universes."

"And you've no doubt we are not traveling to our own past?" Huxtable swiveled his high-backed chair in Gretchen's direction.

"None," Gretchen said.

"We are also making progress on the geographical questions," Yuni continued. "We've initiated a series of missions pushing the physical boundaries farther and farther. This, of course, allows us to shift more candidates to travel status."

Huxtable nodded. "I'm also concerned about a political situation you folks seem to be hatching down there."

"Political . . . Oh, you mean the ethics discussion."

"Isn't *discussion* putting it a bit mildly?"

"Some people have become passionate on both sides of the issue," Yuni said.

"They tell me Sheila Schuler is one?"

"Sheila is not shy about speaking her mind, as is the case with a few of the scientific team. They question our right to manipulate the pasts of other universes. And a few, like Leonard Rose, are militant in their assertion that we are the primary universe, and others exist at our pleasure. He comes right out and says *screw the ethics* to anyone who will listen."

"What about the rest?"

"I think most members of the scientific and medical staffs have a good-faith concern over the rights of individuals to determine their fates without interference. At the same time, they revere the scientific process. A new frontier demands exploration. All human progress arises from such curiosity, and a certain number of people have always been casualties of exploration. Most of us accept that it comes down to human nature. We have never been content with what we know and who we are. We always want to know and be more."

"What about Grissom and Hamilton? Where do they stand?"

Yuni lowered his vision as he formulated his answer. "I guess I don't really know. Marshall is not one to fling himself at controversy. Marta also appears to keep her political views to herself. Although Naomi might have better insight than I."

"What about it, Naomi? You've been quiet. Do you have anything to add?"

"No, I think Dr. Andropov has accurately characterized the situation."

Naomi didn't care for the tone of these questions, or the entire conversation for that matter. Yuni was being undermined.

"You can convey to Ms. Schuler my belief that her campaign is doomed to failure," Huxtable said. "The debate between ethics and profits has historically produced a pretty one-sided result. Yuni, don't let this thing get out of hand."

Meanwhile, some one hundred feet below Huxtable's plush office, Leonard Rose underwent a briefing of his own.

"What do you mean, the key is *I Love Lucy*?" Rose demanded with a growl.

Wearing his white lab smock and polished wingtips, Rose glared at the disheveled, unshaven lump of a man before him. *Jeans. Ancient high-topped Converse tennis shoes he must have dredged up from the garbage bins at some museum. And those damned rock band t-shirts. How long would it take for everyone to see through this pretentious fraud?*

Since their public confrontation the day Yuni, Gretchen and Naomi revealed the reality of parallel universes, Rose had refused to speak directly to Elvin. He planned a campaign of ridicule and backbiting. To his dismay, though, other physicists seemed gradually to be succumbing to Elvin's nonsense. Rose's derision found a smaller and smaller audience. Finally, Gretchen told Rose he could no longer ignore Elvin by *pouting in the corner.* She ordered Rose to meet with Elvin and review his team's progress.

"We think we can use the old television show theme songs as a shortcut to locate and identify the other universes," Elvin said.

"You know, Mr. Detwyler, I think you've just summarized your whole approach to the scientific process. Shortcut. You're always looking for some gimmick . . ."

"Exactly. *You* want to be the big shot who publishes the paper. I just want results. As I told Gretchen and Yuni, I don't care why it works. I just care that it does."

Rose wished he could walk from this room with a recording of Elvin's heresy.

"Here's how we'll define and locate parallel universes," Rose said. "We will systematically understand the mathematics of each dimension. Using what we know of our own universe, we will painstakingly determine the unique electronic, magnetic, gravitational, and quantum identifiers that *must* uniquely characterize them."

"Yeah. I can see how that would work. Eventually. Or we could just listen to the music—the old UHF waves created by television broadcasts before the advent of cable and satellite TV."

Rose rolled his eyes and extended his arms in a plaintive *why me* gesture.

"As I'm sure you know, Dr. Rose, radio and television signals don't just stop. Theoretically, everything that's ever been broadcast over the airwaves is still bouncing around in space."

"The strength of any such signal—particularly a signal that's seventy or eighty years old—would be so weak as to be undetectable," Rose said.

"Yet over and over again," Elvin said, "the monitors have picked up the *I Love Lucy* theme song during projections. Just consider how our projection lifelines work. We are essentially clamping onto the unique energy field generated by one human being. Only a couple of years ago, we all would have said that field is too slight to be detectable. But with the energy resources now at our disposal, we use that signal to hang onto individual travelers through god-knows-what obstacles and distances of time and space."

The crux of Elvin's theory was that somehow these old UHF waves got tangled in the borders of the physical limbo separating parallel universes. "We've learned just where to look for it, and how to amplify it. The Lucy music lasts only the ninety-seven seconds it takes the time projector to make its connection to the past."

Returning from her meeting with Huxtable, Gretchen walked into the conversation. "But you've heard other music as well," she said.

"Yes. Twice we've heard the *Lucy* theme transition into

Bonanza. And there was that *My Mother the Car* thing when Marshall showed up in lizard land. And we've found the *Dick Van Dyke Show* theme, too. Reviewing recordings of those projections, we find that transition into the second theme song occurs precisely ninety-seven seconds after the Lucy theme appears."

"Why would you hear this transition only sporadically?" Gretchen asked.

"Because given this weird dimensional spectrum we're dealing with, you have to know just where to search. Only now are we understanding how to do that."

"You've attached way too much significance to random ancient television signals," Rose said with a dismissive wave.

"No, I'm not, Leonard. Going over recordings we've found Bonanza five times and Dick Van Dyke three times. We've compared the destination universe squiggles with the music. All five Bonanza squiggles are identical to each other, as are the three Dick Van Dykes."

"And this musical connection to a specific universe happens why?" Gretchen asked.

"Could be lots of things. I think it has to do with the number of transmissions of any given UHF signal. *I Love Lucy* still runs every day. I think there's an *I Love Lucy Channel* in your basic cable package. Of course, that's cable, no UHF signal involved. So, while we get *I Love Lucy*, and maybe the oldest and nearest or most similar parallel universes get *Dick Van Dyke* and *Bonanza*. And the weirdest and most dimensionally remote universes get the leftovers, like *My Mother the Car* or *Branded*."

"This is excellent work, Elvin," said Gretchen. "We're getting into a series of missions now to incrementally test the projector's geographic capabilities. I want your team to prioritize finding these associated theme songs on every projection. Tell me if you need additional people. This could be the key to aiming the projector."

"Or," Leonard Rose said over his shoulder as he walked away, "it could be a colossal waste of money and time."

Meeting with Gormly the next day, Rose never got around to telling him about Detwyler's latest idiotic scheme. Rose wanted only to escape the man's wrath as quickly as possible. Had there not been a handful of other patrons scattered through the dreary bar, Rose thought Gormly might even be moved to violence.

"What do you mean Altman won't be included? Your job was to get him there so we would have someone—"

"None of the primary team will travel for the next series of missions. These are routine missions to gather data regarding mapping of universes. They want to involve more travelers."

"So, it's not because you or he fucked up?"

"No. When missions become more complex, I'm sure they'll use the primary team. And I'll see that Frank is included. Frank's involvement isn't critical anymore, though, because Yuni Andropov is no longer able to hide things."

"I'm sorry. I don't share your faith. Listen very carefully. You *will* find a way to get Frank Altman included in these projections."

"So why aren't we going this time?" Marshall asked. "Did we do something wrong?" Despite embarrassment concerning his erectile issues, he found himself anxious at the thought of being replaced.

"No," Naomi said with a laugh. "All these missions are routine. You'd be bored."

In truth, Naomi's urging had convinced Yuni and Gretchen to have the primary team stand down as new candidates became active travelers. She didn't trust Marta. She feared a scenario in which Marta would target one of the new travelers for another *accident,* and her active participation would only make that easier.

Naomi glanced left and right, then leaned into the small gathering that also included Sheila and Marta. "We're telling everyone it's an opportunity to initiate more travelers, and it is. The bottom line, though, is your expertise makes the three of you too valuable to risk on these no-brainer missions."

"Frank gets to go," Marshall protested.

"Yeah, well, Leonard Rose made a big deal about that. He said since Frank joined the primary team late, he needs the experience. And we don't have a problem with that."

"Relax, Marsh," Sheila said, poking a friendly elbow into Marshall's ribs. "Now we get to watch a whole bunch of other people be naked. I'll bring popcorn. It'll be fun."

"What's wrong, Marshall?" Sheila asked as Marta sat with them in the observation gallery overlooking the projection platform. "You seem, I don't know, glum."

"Glum? Who uses words like glum? You sound like my apartment. I'm not glum."

"Well, you're something," Sheila said, surprised at his pissy attitude.

For nearly two weeks now, the three of them watched novice travelers wink off into the recent past. Naomi was right. From the travelers' standpoint, this was an exercise in tedium.

"You're not still upset because we aren't the ones up there freezing our bare fannies off, are you?" Sheila said.

"No."

"What's wrong, then?" Marta asked. "I agree with Sheila. I think you're glum."

Sheila stared at Marshall. Marshall squirmed a little.

"Oh, I know!" Sheila said triumphantly. "Marshall, that's just silly."

"What?" Marta said.

"Don't you know why he's glum?"

Marta shrugged.

"We've been watching travelers all week, and no one else has gotten a boner."

"Sheila!" Marshall said.

"Well, it's true, isn't it?"

Marshall slumped.

For this series of projections, Elvin and Gretchen targeted the newly dubbed Dick Van Dyke and Bonanza universes. Unlike the journeys taken by the veteran trio when they stepped onto the platform and were spirited away, this round of projections was more monotonous and considerably colder for those involved. The traveler teams had to stand naked under spotlights while Elvin and his group searched patiently through the netherworld of old television transmissions for the theme to *The Dick Van*

Dyke Show or *Bonanza*. Because Elvin wasn't exactly sure yet how to do this, travelers could stand there for a long time. As with any environment housing many computers, the projection lab was cold.

So, the whole thing had been a litany of limp dicks and erect nipples.

"I just thought," Marshall said finally, still directing his gaze at the ceiling tiles, "once the other guys got involved, I would at least have some company. That it would seem more normal for someone to . . ."

Marta patted Marshall's arm.

"You're forgetting one very important thing. Sheila's not up there with those other guys."

Sheila smiled at Marshall and batted her eyelashes. "What can I say?"

From his station at the computer bank, Elvin squinted into his monitor and called out, "Okay, almost got it, almost got it . . . here we go! No . . . damn. We slipped off into *The Gong Show*."

Frank was always mindful of the video. As if standing there naked while Elvin fiddled with his television theme song search wasn't bad enough, Frank knew a dozen cameras recorded from every angle to capture each nuance of the process.

"Christ, Elvin, we're freezing here," he called across the room. "Can't you hurry it up?"

Frank couldn't believe how things had changed. Here he stood next to a lovely nude woman, his magnificently sculpted body displayed for every female to drool over, and his sexual confidence was completely shot. He snuck a peek at Carla O'Neill, embarking on her second mission. A satin-skinned redhead, Carla displayed full, freckled breasts. She wasn't Sheila, but she wasn't bad.

Frank, though, hung goose-bumped and shriveled. At first, like the other men, he'd made fun of Marshall's inability to control his body as he stood between Sheila and Marta. And like the others, he'd secretly worried he, too, would be unable to stifle the reaction when his turn came. Now, though, Frank found himself concerned that he wasn't hard. Not even a little. During the half dozen missions he'd completed during the past two weeks, he'd accompanied four women—any of whom he'd have bedded at a moment's notice—without a twitch.

His worry mounted. Peeking at Carla, he forced lustful fantasies, hoping for a response from his once-faithful companion. Here stood these women. While he couldn't begin to compete with Marshall for size, he wanted with some urgency for them to see all the possibilities he had to offer.

But under the glare of lights and the nip of air conditioning, not to mention anxiety associated with being flung off into God-knows-when, his willy was worthless. Forget about the launching pad. He couldn't even get his rocket out of the Vertical Assembly Building.

While Elvin's projection team had become more proficient at hitting their targets, Frank suffered more than his share of nightmare forays into distant nooks and crannies of the cosmic ether.

Naomi's speculation that not all universes would share identical biologies proved correct. The *Tonight Show* universe was no sweat. Easy target. Everything familiar. Citizens of *The Gong Show* universe, though, looked as if they'd been painted by Pablo Picasso—and the impressionist art movement produced works resembling digital photographs. At *The Gong Show* Sheila had three breasts, each of them lovely. Beings from the *Welcome Back, Kotter* universe appeared normal enough, but they squawked like parrots. And humanistic insects populated *The Many Loves of Dobie Gillis*. That one gave Frank nightmares for days, although he had to admit, even as a praying mantis, Sheila was hot.

"They've been up there a long time," Yuni said while Elvin fiddled with his dials and switches. "If you don't hit it pretty soon, we'll have to give them a break."

"I know." The correct theme song stubbornly eluded him, and his frustration grew. "All right, stand down. Let's take ten minutes. This one could be important."

Frank and Carla stepped off the platform and grabbed robes.

"I don't want to miss this one," Elvin said to Yuni as he stood and bent backward to address a gnawing kink in his spine.

"We don't want to miss any of them."

"Yeah, but we do, don't we? We still haven't gotten this down. We're only hitting our destination universe about half the time. And I think this one could be a big deal."

"Which one?" Yuni asked.

Elvin grinned. "*Gunsmoke.*"

Yuni seemed puzzled.

"Oh, right. You're from the Ukraine. Gunsmoke, Matt Dillon, Doc, Chester Goode, Festus Hagan? Longest-running TV western in the history of television. Bigger than Bonanza."

Yuni shrugged.

"Anyway, I first picked a faint signal three days ago. And I've found it a couple of times since. Each time, the signal seems stronger."

"And you believe this is significant?"

"Next to *I Love Lucy*, *Gunsmoke* might be the most broadcast show in history. Now think of all these parallel universes arrayed alongside each other. A sort of bandwidth—like FM radio. That might place the *Gunsmoke* universe very close to us—as opposed to, say, the *Pete and Gladys* universe, or the lizards."

Yuni glanced quickly over his shoulder. "Don't let Marshall hear you use that word."

"Right. Which would be out at the edge of the spectrum somewhere."

Elvin sat and resumed his tinkering.

Static and vague musical tones drifted over the projection lab sound system.

"There. There it is, very faint, right around here . . ."

The *Gunsmoke* theme blared forth. Other technicians wearing headphones jerked them painfully from their ears. All eyes snapped first to Elvin's workstation and then to Carla O'Neill.

"Oh, my God!" yelled Carla. "Oh, my God!"

She sank to her knees.

Naomi rushed to her side and helped her to a sitting position.

"Speak to me," Naomi said. "Tell me what's wrong."

"I've . . . I've been joined." Carla's eyes were wide with alarm. "I'm here. From the future. And . . . and there's been a catastrophe."

26

JOEY, WE HARDLY KNEW YE

"WHAT DO YOU MEAN, 'FROM the future'? We're the future! Every place *else* is the past." Leonard Rose's piercing whine reminded Elvin of fingernails on a chalkboard.

"And they used to think the earth was the center of the universe, too," he said.

"Why, Leonard?" Gretchen joined the argument. "Given maybe an infinity of universes, isn't it a little arrogant to think everything started with us?"

"You mean you think we're the spinoff of some other universe's tampering?" Rose said.

When Yuni had called for a break, Marshall and Marta took advantage of the opportunity to leave through the airlock that remained closed during projections. So, they knew nothing of the unfolding drama. Only Sheila remained as advisor to the novice travelers.

"That's an interesting way to put it, Dr. Rose," she said. "How does it feel to think your chubby existence at this moment, and the direction of your future, might be the result of a plan cooked up by a bunch of yahoos from some other dimension?"

Rose's response was cut off by Carla.

"You have to listen to me! We've got to act quickly."

Naomi raised her hands, calling for quiet. "We're listening, Carla. Tell us."

"A disaster! The people from *Gunsmoke* think we might be able to reverse it."

"What's happened?" Yuni demanded.

"There's no time for that! Elvin will be here at any moment, and he'll know what to do."

"What?" demanded Elvin, who took for granted someone else would handle whatever this crisis was. "What do you mean, *Elvin will be here*? Elvin is already here!"

"I mean they're sending the *Gunsmoke* Elvin. He knows what's happened, and he'll know what you guys have to do."

"Whoa," Elvin said. "I'm not a traveler. I can't... I wouldn't... It's just not safe. I'm the intellectual property, remember? I'm one of the ones we can't afford to risk..." He turned quickly to Yuni. "I am on the list now, right? You did update the list since you realized I'm a genius?"

"Elvin, there's no list. And I'm assuming if our *Gunsmoke* counterparts are projecting you into this plane of existence, they must consider the circumstance extraordinary."

"Shit!" Elvin said. "They can't do this!"

"Well, they are," Carla said.

"Shit. There's a good chance they won't even get me here."

"They know all about the *I Love Lucy* universe," Carla said. "They say it's an easy target. Remember, they're ahead of us..."

"Fuck!" Elvin began to bob and weave around the projection lab.

"Elvin," Sheila said, "settle down. It's not like you can duck."
Overcome with panic, he bolted for the door.

Run, just run, just . . . wait a minute . . . I can't get away from them that way . . . what else can I . . . ? Elvin felt every eye as he stopped, turned and stared at a digital clock counting off seconds above his workstation.

Five minutes! It had been five minutes since future-Carla had arrived.

Ha! I'll bet they missed! They missed! Fuck this. Let some other Elvin from some other universe get raped by the future. The folks in Dick Van Dyke *or* F Troop *or wherever the hell that other Elvin ends up can deal with whatever problem these* Gunsmoke *yokels are having . . ."*

Elvin cautiously took a step toward his computer, then another. His confidence grew with each second that flared onto the clock and then expired. Finally, he pulled himself to his full height, attempted to tuck half his shirt tail into his pants, and risked a deep breath. At that instance Elvin's eyes rolled back and a bloodcurdling scream—one that seemed to come from some part of him he did not know—shattered the silence.

"You cocksuckers!" he shouted, "I'll get you for this! If it's the last . . ."

The diatribe halted mid-curse. Sitting heavily at his workstation, Elvin blinked and surveyed the lab.

"Holy shit, I'm here, aren't I?"

"Shitfuck!" Elvin answered himself as his future counterpart's thoughts and experiences tumbled through his brain. *"Why did you let them . . . ?"*

"Back off, dipshit. I'd hardly characterize it as letting them. They ganged up."

Once more, Elvin tried to run. He leaped from the chair

and his stubby legs pounded toward the door. He managed a half-dozen strides before Sheila tackled him.

"Let me go! I refuse to . . ."

Sheila rolled Elvin to his back and straddled him, her hands around his throat.

"So help me, Elvin, if you don't tell us what's going on here, I'll . . ."

Elvin's eyes bulged and all the fight went out of him.

"Let me go," he said. "I understand. We've got to send Frank back, right now."

During these histrionics, Frank had withdrawn to the fringe of the group surrounding Carla. From his perspective as a spectator, he found this unfolding drama faintly interesting until thirty-five sets of eyes whipped from Elvin and Sheila to him.

"Send Frank?" he asked.

Carla stood and pulled her robe tighter around herself.

"There's been a horrible tragedy. Naomi and Dr. Andropov—uh, not this Naomi and Dr. Andropov, the ones from . . ."

"Yeah, yeah, I understand who you're talking about," Frank said, waving his hands with a rolling motion to urge Carla to the point.

"They know you're here ready to go, and they want you to try and stop it."

"Stop what?"

"Okay," Elvin said, realizing he had to step back and let future-Elvin explain. "Remember our concerns during the early projections that if matter from one universe contacted matter from another universe one of the universes might be destroyed?"

Color drained from Gretchen's face. "There is no exchange of matter . . ."

Elvin raised a cautionary hand.

"They aren't just sending a traveler to this other universe," he said. "They're exchanging travelers. And apparently the timing was such that these travelers met themselves in the transition zone. The limbo. Something catastrophic happened, and this other universe—*The Joey Bishop Show*—seems to have been, well, canceled."

Sheila glared at Rose. "Screw the ethics, huh? Screw the ethics? How many billions do you think we just killed?"

Rose squirmed under a host of accusing eyes.

"*We* didn't kill anyone. Those people from that other universe—"

"We *are* those people," Sheila yelled. "You don't grasp it because you haven't traveled. We are them! They are us!"

Yuni called for quiet.

Elvin again had the floor.

"Right now, they want us to project Frank two hours into *Gunsmoke*'s past. He has to disrupt the timing of the projection. As they are initiating the projection, Frank is outside. He's supposed to be inside observing, but he snuck out to the hallway to smoke a cigarette."

Naomi drilled Frank with a glare. As a condition of participation, nicotine-using traveler candidates signed agreements to abstain during their five-year tour. The issue wasn't so much one of concern over health—cancer having mostly been rendered treatable—but the way nicotine tended to skew key biological data Naomi's team monitored.

"Hey, sometimes I bum a smoke when I'm nervous."

"We'll discuss it later," Naomi said.

"Well," Elvin said, "it's a good thing he's there. They don't want to target someone inside the projection lab again. They projected into Carla before they realized the danger if she met herself on the way. They chose me because of my technical knowledge, and I'm not a traveler. And they know Frank's outside smoking."

"That won't work," Yuni said. "Mission rules prohibit anyone entering or leaving the lab during a projection because of the airlock."

"Yeah, well, we—they—thought of that, too. Apparently, Frank has a sporadic thing with the receptionist—Betty? And he's supposed to be able to talk his way past her."

From across the room came, "What about Betty?"

Elvin recognized the voice of Alex Whitfield, a large bio lab tech who shared an apartment with the aforementioned Betty.

"No, wait," said Frank.

"That still won't work, or it shouldn't. Only me, Dr. Allen, and Naomi have the codes to open the airlock under those circumstances," Yuni said. "It's for security."

"Frank is to have Betty contact Naomi. They think Naomi is most likely to listen and bend the rules. They just want to try and delay the projection a moment. If we don't stop this thing, the *Joey Bishop Show* universe will melt down again and two travelers will perish as well."

"Who are the travelers?" demanded Sheila.

"They don't want to get into that right now. We don't know for sure."

"That's the real point, isn't it?" Sheila said. "We don't know what we're doing!"

"We're trying to fix it," future-Elvin told her.

"Can you find the right theme song?" Yuni asked.

"*I* probably couldn't manage it quickly enough," present-Elvin said, "but my future counterpart can nail that sucker with no sweat."

"All right," Yuni said. "Let's go."

Everyone scrambled except Frank.

"Wait a minute!"

Everyone stopped.

"We just found out that two travelers got fried," Frank said. "Should we maybe think this thing through before we send someone?"

Behind him, Frank felt a looming presence.

Alex Whitfield growled, "Get up there, asswipe."

Frank stood alone bathed with light. Despite the air conditioning, he felt perspiration beading on his arms and forehead.

"So, you know what you have to do?" Elvin asked him. "Get Naomi to delay the projection."

"Yes, I've got it. Let's just get this thing going."

At his station, present-Elvin sat fascinated as he allowed future-Elvin to deftly manipulate the squiggles shimmering on Frank's lifeline monitor.

"We've got it," Elvin said aloud. "Here we go."

The projector hummed. Frank winked away. Strains of the *I Love Lucy* theme song replaced the hum as every head turned to the countdown timer above Elvin's workstation. At precisely ninety-seven seconds, the music changed.

"*Gunsmoke*?" Yuni asked anxiously.

"*Gunsmoke*," Elvin confirmed.

He took a moment to silently congratulate his future counterpart and realized the other Elvin had gone.

"Damn," he murmured to himself. "I had a whole lot of stuff I wanted to ask you."

Frank typically coped with the limbo's eternity by letting his mind go slack, a condition he achieved easily. He thought of himself as simply conscious energy that would, eons from now, coalesce back into—he hoped—a familiar body inhabiting some other universe.

This time, though, he couldn't keep his mind slack. The limbo fostered a cruel honesty, and Frank understood his colleagues thought of him as a not-very-bright man with little purpose or conscience. And, to a large extent, he conceded that truth. But he was not indifferent to the plight of billions of innocents in other universes. Most of them. He didn't care what happened to the lizards or the bugs. Humans like him, though, were a different matter. Somewhere, a Frank would explode into oblivion. And that Frank had a mom and dad and brothers and sisters, who wouldn't survive unless he could fix this.

So, as he burst into the consciousness of the *Gunsmoke* version of himself, he felt consumed with urgency. And while the Frank from *Gunsmoke* wanted to whine, panic and bemoan his fate during the adjustment process, *I Love Lucy* Frank would have none of it. He gave himself a mental slap and ordered, "*Man up. We've got a job to do.*"

He found himself standing under a bank of exhaust fans that served as air exchangers for the underground complex. He allowed past-Frank one last drag on his cigarette, marched into the reception area and confronted—not Betty. In her place sat a thin, blonde woman with glasses and a carefully cultivated air of officiousness.

"Where's Betty?"

"She had a doctor's appointment," the blonde said.

"Is she okay?"

"I don't know. I'm a temp from the administrative secretarial pool. May I help you?"

"Yeah. I'm Frank Altman. I'm a traveler, and I need to get into the lab."

"Well, if you're a traveler, you know the rules, don't you?"

"Of course, I—"

"And the rules are that once the mission checklist has started, no one enters or exits. That's what they told me."

"Yes, but this is an emergency."

"They didn't say anything about emergencies. They said no one."

"This is a life-and-death emergency."

"Nothing I read made any distinction about life and death."

"Life and death on a scale you can't even begin to imagine." Frank glared with bared teeth. "They are about to make a horrible mistake, and I've been sent to warn them!"

She peered at him over her glasses. "You're the guy who was out there smoking?" She gestured to a video screen next to her showing a long slow camera pan from one end of the hallway to the other.

"Yes, I am."

"So, on your way to rescue us from imminent calamity, you had time to stop and befoul the air we all breathe."

"Listen, I don't have time for this. I don't have time to explain—wait. Wait, just go to the intercom and ask for Naomi. Tell Naomi Frank Altman is outside and has a vital message from the *I Love Lucy* universe."

The blonde studied Frank for a few seconds more.

"Please!"

"I'm to ask for Naomi?"

"Yes."

"Naomi who?"

"Yes."

"What?"

"Go get Naomi!"

"Naomi who?"

"Yes. Naomi Hu!"

"That's what I asked you. If I am to find this Naomi person, I must know her last name."

"Hu!"

She regarded him another moment. "You're a nut. Go away, or I'll call security."

And with that a whole universe—home to planets and entire civilizations and dolphins and kittens and spiders—once again melted into oblivion.

"Send me," Sheila demanded of Yuni when Frank returned with news of his failure.

"No," Elvin said. "They are adamant. It has to be Frank."

Sheila walked to Elvin's side and whispered, "Ask your buddy from the future if he knows what an idiot Frank is."

"He's gone. And I don't know what he thought of Frank. He had other things on his mind."

Sheila watched helplessly as Frank tried three more times. He returned to tell them he found Betty at her desk, too angry to speak to him; that Betty took a bathroom break and one of the security guards manned the desk; or that the intercom wouldn't work. And every time, The *Joey Bishop Show* bit the dust.

"Yuni, please," Sheila begged. "You're the one who makes the call. Not Elvin. Is Frank the guy you'd pick to save the universe?"

Yuni looked at Elvin. Elvin shrugged.

"Okay, Sheila. Get ready."

"There's no point. It won't work."

Sheila whirled, ready to angrily defend her plan, when she saw a tear trickle down Gretchen Allen's cheek.

"We can't change it." Gretchen's voice quivered. "Elvin and I have discussed historical intransigence for a while now, and this only bolsters our suppositions. I think we could go through this exercise a hundred times and the outcome will be the same."

"Clearly the past is *not* intractable," Naomi protested. "Look at the variations we've encountered during these attempts. Each projection had subtle differences."

"Yes. *Subtle* differences. But the major overwhelming historical fact—the death of a universe—remains unchanged."

Elvin stepped away from his bank of computers and took up the explanation.

"I've been running computer models which support what Dr. Allen is saying. While we don't have enough data to know for sure, we have a theory."

"And?" Yuni asked.

"Think of time, of history, as a vast river with a strong current. Hardly an original analogy, I know. But anything caught in the mainstream of that current will be swept along with inevitable results. At the edges of the river, though, close to the shore, you'll find backwaters and eddies—contradictions that allow peripheral objects or events to find alternative paths."

"So, the major events don't change?" Yuni asked Elvin.

"Right. If you're John Kennedy, you are right damn smack in the middle of the strongest current. And no matter what happens, Lee Harvey Oswald will shoot you dead. If you're a janitor at the Texas School Book Depository, though, one version of history might have you cleaning toilets when Kennedy is assassinated. Another universe might have you mopping a floor in a completely different part of the building. You don't matter to history. So, the subtleties of your life are more flexible."

"Did your future counterpart agree with your theory?" Leonard Rose asked.

"We didn't discuss it," Elvin said. "We were busy."

"So, we're just going to let it go?" Sheila demanded.

"We have no choice," Gretchen said. "We can't change it. We can only make things worse."

"Which is basically what I've been arguing all along," Sheila said. "We've got to stop. We've no right—"

"We have every right!" Rose said. "We've got more than a right. We have a duty. We have a scientific imperative. This is no different than any other frontier mankind has confronted."

"And on what other frontier did we destroy entire universes?" Sheila shouted. "We don't know what we're doing. We've got to slow down!"

Gretchen took Sheila's arm. "Sheila, every day, with everything I see, I'm becoming more sympathetic to your point of view, that we have to be more careful, that we must be mindful of consequences. But remember, this is history, too. This is the next chapter of human endeavor. We can't just walk away. I'll bet you anything that if we tried, history wouldn't let us."

"Yeah? Well, I can walk away. Just watch me."

"If you do," a red-faced, glowering Rose said, "you'll forfeit everything. And I'm not about to let you just march out the door. With your attitude you'd be the biggest security risk we could—"

"Shut up, Leonard," Yuni said. "You're not in charge here."

He turned to Sheila.

"Your experience is critical to this program. And you may be correct. We have a whole process to pursue before we can responsibly come to that conclusion. We can't just arbitrarily declare the realm of time travel off-limits."

"You can do what you want. I'm through."

"Please, Sheila," Gretchen said, "you have become our nagging conscience. Yours was a quiet voice that has suddenly become loud. If anything, your responsibility to this program—and your obligation to honor your contract—has become greater than just a few hours ago."

Sheila stifled angry tears. She would not cry here!

"Sheila," Naomi said softly, "you can't leave. The best place to give voice to your cause is from within. Once you step outside, you have no voice at all."

"And you think anyone will listen?"

"We will," said Naomi with a gesture that included Gretchen and Yuni. "Believe me, we'll listen."

The projection lab fell silent except for the persistent, furious tapping of one computer keyboard. Sheila turned to see Elvin hammering away. He briefly glanced up and said, "Yeah, Sheila, I'll be more careful, too. Right now, though, I have to get a whole lot of things written down before they drain from my head. How long do you think I've got?"

"I'm assuming it's all of a highly technical nature? You've probably got about ten minutes before it melts."

Elvin milked the fading information from his brain for nearly half an hour. Sheila waited. When his fingers finally slowed to a stop, she pulled his chair from the desk, turned it on its rollers and placed her face inches from his.

"Who were the travelers?"

Color drained from Elvin's face, casting it a peculiar shade of gray. "The . . . travelers?"

"Who died?"

"I'm sorry, Sheila. I don't . . . know."

"Yes, you do. There's no way a person would be able to keep the emotional response to that kind of tragedy out of his head. No way it didn't get transferred to your brain."

Elvin started to open his mouth with another protest.

"And don't say you can't remember. I've been through this a dozen times. I know what things stay with you the longest. Emotional memory lasts far longer than intellectual concepts. Who . . . Was . . . It?"

The last three words boiled from her mouth as if Elvin confronted the Reptilian American version of Sheila from Marshall's lizard universe.

Elvin lowered his eyes to the projection platform.

"Carla."

"And who else?"

"Marshall and Marta were also members of the team."

"You said two travelers were killed," Naomi said.

Only Marta survived," Elvin said. "Marshall didn't make it back, either."

Sheila realized she had to stay.

27

DYING TO KNOW

MARSHALL TOOK NEWS OF HIS death badly.

"Dead?" He took a quick glance at his hands to see whether he'd missed something. "Does that mean I'll die in other places, too?"

"No... Maybe. We don't know," Gretchen said, reaching to squeeze his shoulder. "All we're sure of is the *Gunsmoke* version of you, and the *Joey Bishop Show* Marshall, have apparently perished. Which means you can't travel to the *Gunsmoke* universe from this point forward, because you have no equivalent being to share."

"Which raises another issue," Sheila said. "We have no assurances that our counterparts from any universes to which we are traveling are still alive. Some of us might have been killed in accidents we know nothing about yet."

"Or," Leonard Rose said, "it could mean just the opposite. The continued survival of Mr. Grissom and Ms. O'Neill here could be proof that Elvin is wrong, and the mainstream of history—to use his analogy—can indeed be altered. By any standard, this program is among the most significant historical developments of all time. And as a principal traveler, Mr. Grissom has to be a figure of great significance."

This is the first time, Marshall thought, *that I can remember hoping Leonard Rose is right about anything.*

Marshall felt thankful not to be left alone during the hours following his demise.

Naomi arranged for Carla's friends to meet her at The Time Warp. She also reserved a couple of tables for those closest to Marshall. Sheila, Marta, Gretchen, Naomi and even Elvin attended. Marshall settled back into the edges of the glow cast from various neon display signs around the bar and listened to reassurances from his colleagues.

"Here's the big flaw in your logic," Marta said to Elvin. "If history is as unforgiving as you say, why isn't everybody dead? If the *Joey Bishop Show* Universe is destroyed, wouldn't that mean destruction of all other universes must follow?"

"Well, obviously not. Maybe there's some sort of historical imperative of survival on a grand scale. If a catastrophe is big enough, history lets it go so history and time can continue."

"Or maybe," Sheila said, "history is not very prompt. And eventually, each universe will perish."

"The death of our universe is inevitable," Gretchen pointed out. "But on a billion-year or so time frame."

"Suppose this is the first domino creating that inevitability," Sheila said.

Marshall sighed. "Who's to say Elvin's calculations won't be off during some future projection, and I'll end up in *Gunsmoke* with no place to land?"

"Look, Marshall," Elvin said. "I spent the afternoon

going through information my future counterpart left with me. What I learned is a targeting breakthrough. We won't be shooting in the dark anymore. With just a little more practice and research, I'll have a ninety-percent chance of hitting what I'm aiming at."

"The only way to be sure we don't make *any* more mistakes," Sheila countered, "is to stop projecting anyone at all."

Gretchen stared into the amber contents of her glass. "Sheila, we agree we have some mind-boggling issues to consider here. We agree we don't know what we're doing. And we know we must be more careful. But we can't stop."

Even Naomi, who Marshall judged a stronger advocate for the travelers' well-being than any of the others, didn't want the program shut down.

She stared hard at Marta as she spoke.

"We must do our best to understand this new territory. That's the essence of science. We explore. We test. We can't just walk away. Mankind has always paid dearly to satisfy its curiosity. Right or wrong, it's a fact. Psychologically, it's who we are."

Marshall listened to the discussion and began to examine his own feelings about the delicate balance between safety and exploration.

"You know what we're most afraid of right now?" Gretchen asked Sheila. "We're most afraid they'll *make* us stop. That companies and governments will withdraw their funding. Because once they conclude a big payoff might not materialize, that's exactly what will happen. So, for as long as the funding lasts, we've got to learn everything we can."

"Of course, Marshall," Naomi said, "you could step

away. You could finish your five-year tour as an advisor to active travelers. Everyone would understand."

"Well," Marshall said with an apologetic glance to Sheila, "the truth is I don't want to stop, either."

As the group dispersed, Naomi plucked at Marshall's sleeve. She stood and leaned to his ear.

"Don't you think it's interesting," she said, "that *Gunsmoke* Marta was the only survivor?"

"That's crazy," Marshall whispered. "How could Marta engineer the destruction of a universe?"

"I'm not suggesting she did," Naomi said. "But what if she took advantage of an opportunity? Who will question two more deaths when billions die?"

Despite the tragedy, Elvin walked out of the Time Warp with a bounce in his step. He knew how to do this. He had his notes, and if he worked all night, he could probably write a step-by-step universe targeting primer by morning.

"Stop strutting around as if you've accomplished something!" Leonard Rose's angry voice arrested Elvin in his tracks. "All this is a gift given to you by someone from the future."

Elvin turned.

"Leonard, what is your problem? Do you dispute my data?"

"By your own admission, the data is a result of revelations planted in your brain by a future counterpart."

"Right! *My* brain, because it was—or will be—me who figures it out!"

"You can't prove that."

"The science is elementary," Elvin said, "so even you should be able to understand. We've proved time travel. Einstein said more than a hundred years ago that time and space are woven of the same fabric. Future, past, present each exist simultaneously. It doesn't matter in what order things occur. It doesn't matter whether I reached my conclusions today or ten years from now. I still will have done it."

"Okay. Now that we know there is a future version of this same project, how do we know this is your work at all?" Rose said. "How do we know Gretchen or me or the team as a whole didn't achieve these breakthroughs? And how do we know your future counterpart didn't hijack our work? How do we know this Elvin from the future hasn't journeyed here more than once and given you our work so you could claim it?"

Elvin offered a long angry glare before turning away. The bounce was gone, though. He'd come to a realization. Leonard Rose would work hard at planting and cultivating his seeds of doubt. The scientific community would long debate whether Elvin Detwyler was one of history's great minds, or whether he was just an intellectual thief.

28

STEPPING UP THE PACE

"AND HOW IS YOUR MOTHER?" Andrew Gormly asked Rose.

The inquiry took Rose by surprise. To his experience, Gormly didn't express concern for anyone.

"She's the same. People suffering dementia usually don't get better."

"Physically, though, she's doing okay?"

"Yes."

"Good. If anything happened to her, I don't know how we'd get you off the campus for these discussions." They shared a booth in the familiar Superior bar. The glow of an antique jukebox chased their shadows. "So, is the Schuler woman still causing trouble?"

Rose scowled and plucked at his necktie, loosening it enough to unbutton his collar. "It's gone well beyond her. The incident has given her ethics argument a lot of traction."

"They want to stop?"

"They want to be more careful. I think you'll see some significant changes—a lot more deliberation and a slower pace."

"Jesus Christ. How much slower can they go?"

"I don't know. We've got several committees now."

"Wait a minute!" Gormly said. "Wait just a minute. That could be the answer. Here we are, pouring money into all these missions, each one just a tiny step forward. We're not getting anywhere . . ."

His voice trailed off. Rose waited while Gormly drifted into his own thoughts. A Pacifico beer sign flashed on and off over his head like an idea balloon in the Sunday comics.

"The ethical issue as they see it," Gormly finally said, "is that each time we undertake a projection, we disrupt the history of some other universe, right?"

"Yes. But we believe by taking the right precautions we can minimize—"

"So, if we really want to minimize the interference, fewer missions would be better."

"I suppose . . ."

"So, fuck baby steps. Everyone providing funding is frustrated with the pace of the research. Fewer missions would be cheaper, and we'll get our questions answered a lot faster. Dr. Rose, you will become the chief advocate for minimizing our impact on the historical paths of other universes."

Before Rose could ask questions, Gormly shifted gears.

"Give me more detail concerning this death thing with Marshall Grissom."

"Well, of course he's not really dead. This is just another of Elvin Detwyler's harebrained theories. The version of Marshall from another universe apparently died. Detwyler believes if something happens to a historical figure in one universe, that person's fate is sealed everywhere else as soon as history has a chance to catch up. Which is absurd, because our Mr. Grissom is just fine."

"So Detwyler concedes he was wrong?"

"Oh, no. The great Elvin Detwyler could *never* be wrong. He adjusts his theories after the fact to suit his convenience. The last time we talked, he suggested that because Grissom's death occurred in our future, and because we are now forewarned not to reconstruct the same circumstances, history will jump out and zap him some other way."

"Like some random accident or something?"

"Who knows," Rose said. "It's all hokum."

"Some of your colleagues take Detwyler's theories seriously, though?"

"Yes, although for the life of me, I can't understand why."

Gormly remained after Rose left the bar. He withdrew his phone and tapped out a text message to be encrypted for Jason Pratt.

"Mr. Grissom might still be a threat. The circumstances are such that people would not be surprised should he suffer a fatal accident. Loose ends are always a concern."

"It won't be safe," Sheila protested from her seat at the conference table two days later. "We haven't even begun to approach a projection of that distance."

Marshall sat quietly. He preferred to remain at the periphery of these heated discussions of the newly constituted ethics committee. He, Marta and Sheila sat on the committee along with several others, including Leonard Rose.

"You say we must minimize interference in other histories," Rose said, "so here's the perfect solution."

"You're not the one being flung back further than we've ever attempted. There are a thousand things we don't know yet . . ."

"So, your ethics have their limits?"

"We agreed to be more careful," Marta said.

Rose remained undeterred.

"A single mission—a jump back ten years—would substitute for what we originally envisioned as a ten-mission process. That's one-tenth of the opportunity to impact other universes. Yes, while the risk to our travelers is greater, the risk to other universes is minimized. And our investors could have an answer as to whether the past can be changed to benefit the future."

Much as he distrusted Rose, Marshall conceded to the logic in his argument. But ten years . . .

"You mean whether the past can be manipulated for power and profit," Sheila said. "Why don't you at least be honest about what this program is really designed for."

"What ivory tower do you live in?" Rose shouted. "Investors need a profit and you pretend there's something wrong with that! Every exploration ever undertaken has a profitable return as a motivating factor. You choose to believe there is some evil intent at work here. Our backers genuinely want to create a better future."

"At the expense of some other world . . ."

"How do you know that to be true? Have we been somewhat heavy-handed so far? Maybe. That doesn't mean we can't find ways to make the scientific discoveries we seek and still have a minimal impact."

"Which is why we're here," Marta said. "Please remember, though, while we're being more careful of our impact on other worlds, we travelers would also like to survive the process."

"It's what you signed up for," Rose said.

"Dr. Rose," Yuni said, "while I understand your logic, I must agree with the team. Such a big leap could be—"

"No, he's right," Sheila said, much to Marshall's surprise. "It is the best way. The least intrusive way. But there's no need to endanger the others. I'll go alone."

"No, that won't work," Rose said. "You're biased. You want the mission to fail. Frank Altman should be the one who . . ."

"May I remind everyone," Naomi interrupted, "we have a set of mission rules, and those rules require a *team* of travelers for very good reasons. How many times have we avoided failure or tragedy because one traveler could assist another? We certainly won't suspend those rules on the most dangerous mission we've confronted. Whatever we do will involve the full primary team."

Andrew Gormly cursed as the phone continued to ring.

"Goddammit, Pratt," he said to himself, "pick up the fucking phone!"

The call kicked over to the GRC's messaging system. Gormly hung up. He couldn't take the risk of leaving this message. He dialed again.

An answer followed the third ring, "Yeah?"

"Call it off," Gormly said. A moment of silence followed as Pratt digested the surprise of such a direct contact.

"We'll have him in another five minutes," Pratt said.

"He's on his way now, and I've got everything set . . ."

"We can't risk it. Rose just gave me the mission outline. Everything centers on Grissom. They might shelve it if something happens to him. I need to think about it."

Jason Pratt stared at the phone. He'd have to reach his contact in security. All calls entering the GRC system from the outside world were recorded. The digital record wouldn't be reviewed until tomorrow, though. Erasing the call would be a simple matter. Calls made within the complex were not reviewed. The only record of the message he'd left for Marshall Grissom would be on Marshall's phone.

"Um . . . I got a call saying you'd found my notebook?"

Pratt turned to see Marshall standing at the doorway to the storage room. Pratt glanced automatically to the pocket computer he'd taken from Marshall's locker. The device rested on a chair next to a tall shelf loaded with heavy canisters marked by radiation hazard labels.

"Yeah. I found it on the floor in the men's locker by the projection lab. I hope you don't mind, but I turned it on to see if I could tell who it belonged to."

"No, that's okay." Marshall stared at the canisters. "Um . . . shouldn't those things be somewhere . . . safer?"

Pratt laughed.

"No, they're empty. They use them to store the waste from the reactors . . . and they've got lead linings.

"Oh. We'll, thanks again, I'll just . . ."

Pratt blocked Marshall's way.

"Let me get the notebook. The floor's slippery over there. I just mopped."

Marshall reviewed the mission outline and worried at its complexity.

A ten-year leap into the past. Four travelers arriving at four different geographic locations, each with a specific task aimed at changing some aspect of the past. And—if the theories were correct, their counterparts from that universe would try to effect the same changes here.

"How can we take another universe's actions for granted?" Marshall asked during the morning planning session.

"We have chosen the *Star Trek* universe as our target," Elvin explained. "Like *I Love Lucy*, *Star Trek* was huge in syndication, so we think we can assume they are a biologically identical universe to ours. And I'm confident we can get everyone there without any trouble. At the same time, it's a place we haven't visited yet, so its history should be running parallel with ours. While we plan this mission, Star Trek *must* be doing the same."

"With us—our universe, I mean—as their target? In an infinity of universes?" Marshall asked. "Seems like a long shot to me."

"What if it's not a long shot at all?" Sheila countered. "What if our histories are running along parallel paths right down to the smallest detail? Once again, we'll risk the possibility that a traveler will meet himself in the limbo."

Mission planning debates remained centered on Sheila's disconcerting hypothesis a week later.

Marshall glanced at Frank, who dozed next to him. For once, Marshall sympathized as the scientists argued endlessly about the nuances of timing, and the reality or unreality of coincidence.

"Just to create a tiny divergence, I still think the smart thing is to send a traveler to *Star Trek* before the main mission," Naomi argued. "Just a brief visit—maybe even suggest which one of us should go first. Certainly, that couldn't upset . . ."

"To that point, wouldn't the historical paths still be identical? So, they'd be doing the same thing, so that traveler would meet him or herself . . ." Gretchen argued.

"A possibility," Elvin said. "But we can also safely assume they aren't any more anxious than we are to blow someone else up. And that they, too, are being just as careful as we are. They know if we're going to do this, one of us has to act first, and the other universe will follow."

"So, who goes first?" Sheila asked.

"We go first, of course," Rose said. "We shouldn't give up the initiative to—"

Frank fell out of his chair. "Holy shit," he groaned.

Marshall knelt over Frank and watched his eyes flutter as he helped him to a sitting position.

"Frank? Frank? What's happening?" Naomi asked.

"They say they want us to go first," he grunted.

When *Star Trek* Frank popped out of *I Love Lucy* Frank, the science team quickly extracted enough of the *Star Trek* plan to recognize its remarkable similarity to their own.

Leonard Rose expressed suspicion. "We're just going along with this?"

"Why, Leonard, what's wrong with the plan?" Gretchen asked.

"I don't think your trust is warranted. I won't concede they are ahead of—"

"Clearly, in this instance they *are* ahead. Besides, I believe Sheila is right. It's not *them* and *us*. It's just us."

"It doesn't feel right," Rose said. "How do we know Frank got it straight?"

"Hey," Naomi answered. "He's your guy. I'm sure the *Star Trek* version of you lobbied to have him carry the message, just to eliminate your fear of bias."

As a matter of fact, Rose conceded silently, he had been formulating that precise argument when his *Star Trek* counterpart beat him to the punch.

"So, we're agreed?" Yuni said. "We go in one week. If we are successful, they'll project their team here."

"How could you people accept this hideous idea?" Sheila demanded. She'd marched to Naomi's office following the revelation of the mission profile. "There must be a hundred other events we could choose from."

"We've gone over the past decade of all your lives and this jumped out at everyone," Naomi said. "I don't like using Marshall's past this way, either. But the timing is right. And it's the right scenario."

The travelers could each recall or reconstruct with reasonable certainty where they were during May of 2035, and the geography worked for all four travelers.

Sheila was a nineteen-year-old student at Arizona State University, finishing her sophomore year. Frank, age twenty-two, also lived in Phoenix, working construction near Cave Creek. Marta, twenty-three, had recently taken her position at Albuquerque's Sandia National Laboratory. She remembered a camping trip with friends near Silver City early that May. Marshall, counting down the final weeks of his senior year of high school, lived at home in the little eastern Arizona town of Whittier.

"So, the group of you decided to exploit a tragedy from Marshall's life?" Sheila accused.

"The whole point is to see if any aspect of the past can be changed. Ethically, we feel bound to select something that wouldn't upset the balance of history in some unseen way. And the results need to be unambiguous. The death of Samantha Kennedy meets all the criteria."

If she'd known beforehand what the scientists would ask of them, Sheila wouldn't have been so quick to support a single ten-year leap into the past. When she spoke up, she thought she would be volunteering herself. What resulted, though, would put everyone at risk and worse, it would subject Marshall to terrible emotional jeopardy. She felt desperately guilty about that. She needed to find a way to mitigate the danger.

"We need some kind of panic button to get us out of there if everything goes to hell."

"Like what?" Marta asked.

"I don't know. Ten years is just too much . . ."

"So, talk to Elvin and Gretchen."

"They'd more likely listen to you than me," Sheila said.

"Why?"

"I'm the biggest controversy going right now. Anything I suggest is going to be suspect. And we need this."

Given Gillis's suspicion concerning Marshall's potential treachery, Marta liked Sheila's idea. A traveler needed a quick way out if things started to fall apart around them.

"The problem is," she said to Gretchen, Elvin and Rose, "when I had my Flagstaff lapses, I was just stuck there until you guys figured it out."

"We saw the flicker of the lifeline," Elvin said. "Now we know exactly what that means."

"I had issues before the monitors picked it up, though. An experienced traveler can recognize signs of trouble before you can. And a few minutes could be the difference between getting someone home safely, and a breakdown that could compromise the whole mission."

"Or lose someone altogether," Sheila added.

"What we need," Marta said, "is a way for a traveler to initiate the retrieval."

"You can't take anything inorganic with you," Elvin said. "There's no kind of device we can send . . ."

As his comment trailed off, Elvin wandered away within himself. By now, the others were familiar with these lapses as Elvin listened to all the little synapses making their connective sparks through his brain.

"Unless we use a device that's already there!" Elvin snapped back to the moment. "It's simple. I should have thought of this weeks ago."

"Maybe you already did in the *Gunsmoke* universe," Rose said.

"Eat shit and die, Leonard." Elvin turned back to Marta and proclaimed, "Tasers."

"Tasers?"

"Right. Among other things, the lifeline tracks a traveler's individual magnetic field. Anything sufficiently disturbing the magnetic field should show on our monitors."

"And," Marta said, "a nonlethal electrical shock will scramble the magnetic field."

"I'm sure it'll work," Elvin said. "You just have to add that to the list of things you do as soon as you arrive. Go find a taser."

"Shouldn't we test it?" Marta asked.

"Right."

While gearing up for the Whittier mission, the team still undertook quick and minimally intrusive data-gathering projections. Elvin, Sheila, Gretchen and Marta peered across the lab where Frank sat waiting to guide two new travelers through just such a journey.

"Hey, Frank," Elvin said, "I've got one more thing to add to the mission profile."

"You want me to what?"

"Come on, Frank, it's no big deal," Marta said.

"You want me to tase myself?"

"Don't be such a pussy," Marta said. "I had to get tased as part of my military training."

"Yeah, with plenty of medical guys around if you went into cardiac arrest."

"Sure, the first time. Then a bunch of us did it for fun after that."

"No way I'm going to tase myself. Where will I find a taser?"

"Just proposition the first woman you see on the street," Sheila said. "I'm sure she'll be glad to help you out."

They watched Frank's lifeline with care. Marta didn't recognize the little shudder of variation, but Elvin did. "It works!" he said. "I can train the others on what to look for."

"May I remind you," Gillis said, "you'll be in the past for as long as a week. Marshall will have any number of opportunities to eliminate someone else. And if I were him, you would certainly be my top priority target."

"Yes, well, at least I now have the means to get myself out of there if I see something going sideways," Marta said.

"Not quickly enough, though," Gillis countered. "Suppose he's drawing down on you with a pistol? How long will it take Elvin to recognize your distress signal, and then, how long for the computers to get you out of there?"

"Look, as soon as I arrive, I'll be sure my past self is armed. I must admit I've come to like Marshall as I've spent more time with him. But if I have to shoot him to save myself and the others, I won't hesitate."

"Marshall," Sheila said, "you don't have to do this. You can give me the information—everything you remember—and I can deal with Samantha. Marta and Frank and I can do this."

Marshall's response carried a hint of anger that surprised her.

"How can you possibly think, given a chance to save my friend . . . that I could refuse?"

"You know the odds are very low—"

"The odds don't matter. I still have to try, don't I?"

"All right, people," Yuni said to the small gathering of scientists and travelers, "I want to emphasize that all of you need to stand ready to support Marshall's task. That's the priority. Frank and Marta, you each know your secondary assignments."

Marta nodded.

Frank looked bored.

"You remember the name of the company?" Yuni pointedly asked Frank.

"Yes. Vantage Solar. I find a stock guy and buy a few shares. How complicated could that be?"

"A broker. Not 'a stock guy.' A broker."

"And Marta, yours is simple. Use the internet to place the longest odds bet you can find—one in which you can recall the outcome—then place anything you win in a bank account. Sheila, your primary job is to support Marshall and be ready to assist the others through any difficulties.

"Sheila has provided us with her cell phone number of ten years ago. Call as soon as possible to establish a network of communication. You are to check with each other at regular intervals. Sheila, please be sure and take the time to get oriented. Don't try and make the drive from Phoenix to Whittier until you feel comfortable with your integration."

Easy for you to say, thought Sheila. The moment of integration represented the biggest risk, and she would face that moment alone. Sheila would find a way. No matter what happened, she would be there for Marshall on the night of May 9, 2035.

29

WHITTIER

A RITUAL SEND-OFF THE NIGHT before a mission had become a tradition among the travelers. All active travelers and candidates attended. The primary team abstained from alcohol for a twenty-four-hour period prior to projection. The others attended for well-wishing and companionship, and they seemed determined to drink enough to compensate for their comrades' sobriety.

Sheila, Marta and Marshall shared a table along with Wanda Mays, a novice traveler who'd made benign training bumps into the near past. This evening, Wanda had gradually attached herself like a leech to Marshall's arm.

Marshall didn't mind for the most part, because Wanda kept grinding her right breast into his elbow and staring up at him with lustful, increasingly glazed-over eyes. He enjoyed the attention. As Marshall began to realize he'd become something of a rock star in the eyes of many female traveler candidates, who made it a point to join the betting pools at each of his projections, he felt a little unsettled concerning the unwanted attention, but decided to see what would happen.

Tonight, though, Wanda was in the way, as were the

others. His conversation with Sheila and Marta had to weave itself through best wishes and lame jokes from their drunken colleagues.

They sat tightly together at their crowded table. The jukebox played songs from the 1960s, a musical era that happily continued to insinuate itself into hearts and minds of generation after generation. Thankfully, Frank had removed himself to the periphery with a group of admiring women.

"This isn't right, you know," Sheila said, peering into Marshall's eyes. "This is too much for them to ask."

Marshall jumped a little as Wanda's right hand clamped onto his thigh.

"How can I not do this?" he asked, directing a startled glance to Wanda. "I have a chance to save the life of someone I . . . knew."

"Someone you cared about," Marta said, scooting closer.

Marshall leaned forward as well. The foreheads of the three nearly touched. He experienced a stark realization: he truly valued his relationship with these two remarkable women. He started to say so, but Wanda chose the moment to snuggle closer and bite his left earlobe.

"Ow!" He pulled away before Wanda could draw blood. She offered a glassy, seductive wink and ran her tongue suggestively over her lips.

Embarrassed, Marshall forced his attention back to Sheila, who echoed Marta.

"Someone you cared about, maybe even loved?"

"She was . . . a friend."

Emotions ten years buried had been resurrected since Marshall learned the mission profile.

Marshall knew Samantha Kennedy was far out of his league. This beautiful girl lit his life as a distant beacon. And while the high school social strata of a small town relegated Marshall several rungs below her, Samantha usually acknowledged him with kindness. They'd been buddies when she moved to town in the third grade. For a few years, the Kennedys lived across the alley from Marshall's family. One summer, Marshall and Samantha built a fort along his back fence. Their relationship began to fade by sixth grade as Samantha and Marshall gravitated toward their respective social echelons. It was pretty much gone by junior high school when Samantha's parents divorced, and she moved with her mom to the other side of town.

Gradually, they resumed a limited interaction during their senior year of high school.

They'd even gone out once. A date. Sort of.

Samantha was usually booked. She held elite social status and bent herself to pressures of popularity. One Wednesday, though, between Thanksgiving and Christmas breaks during their senior year—Marshall still couldn't remember how he'd managed the courage to ask her—she'd agreed to a Coke date, which consisted of going to Bud's Drive-In, getting a couple of cherry cokes delivered to Marshall's Toyota, and cruising the one-way thoroughfare that bisected their small town.

At one point, a car full of jocks pulled alongside and Steve Bransom called from a rear window, "Hey, Samantha, do you need rescuing? We've got beer!"

Samantha scowled across at Steve and rolled up her window.

She and Marshall had been talking about aspirations and books and music, and Marshall could have sworn she'd enjoyed it. She confirmed his hopes when she turned away from the hooting crowd next to them. "Let's go someplace where we don't have to listen to jerks like that."

Through a dry throat, Marshall suggested, "We could go out to the dunes. I don't think anyone else would be there tonight."

He almost flinched as he waited for her rebuke. To his utter amazement, she said, "That would be nice."

Just a few miles east of Whittier, several acres of rolling red sand dunes interrupted the lush Sonoran Desert. They waxed and waned according to winds that swept the landscape during late-summer's monsoon season. The haboobs—roiling walls of sand and dirt that occasionally swarmed into Phoenix—gathered their fuel here. During most of the year, though, the dunes were a quiet playground for families during the day, and for teenagers seeking carnal solitude after sundown.

As he pulled off the narrow pavement and onto a patch of hardpan tucked behind a sand hill, Marshall fought a crippling fear he would say or do something to spoil the perfection of this unexpected moment. Above the sandy summit, an impossibly huge desert moon was buoyant, dimming a thousand stars that glowed around it.

And they talked. That's all. An unmistakable connection was forged, though. Marshall could feel it. Finally, summoning all the courage he'd ever had to muster, he asked with trepidation, "Samantha, could I... would you mind, I mean ... could I kiss you?"

She offered him a crooked smile and took his hand.

"Could we just hold hands? For now? You don't know how many guys have tried to . . . well, you know . . . out here. It usually comes with beer, or a joint. And this has been . . . so different . . . could we just hold hands?"

Marshall remembered the odd mixture of disappointment and relief. But she'd said *for now,* two words he clung to. A crucible of hope. The day would come when Samantha Kennedy would see the truth about pretty guys with cruel intentions and look to the purity of purpose in the heart of a tall, skinny geek.

When he finally walked her to her porch that mystical evening, she opened the front door, turned to him and said, "Marshall, if you want to kiss a girl, don't ask her. Just do it."

Marshall's jaw dropped, and he stared for an awkward moment too long.

"Well, okay." She smiled and went inside.

They didn't go out again. He didn't call her. But the smiles and brief comments they shared in halls and classrooms told Marshall he'd reached something within her, even if she didn't understand it yet.

A few months later, though, only weeks before graduation, fate shattered Marshall's fantasy of their shared destiny.

What Marshall knew of the events that night came from news accounts.

The party was at Donnie Court's house on a Wednesday night, May 9, 2035. Donnie's parents were gone. Drugs and alcohol were involved. And at some point, talk turned to fast cars. Not toned-down hydrogens and electrics everyone drove, but gasoline behemoths with monstrous horsepower from the previous century. Donnie's dad collected antique automobiles.

A race took place between two of those cars, out by the dunes.

Samantha and Donnie both died in the crash.

This was Marshall's assignment: an attempt to save a young woman's life. The mission planners grasped nothing of Marshall's emotional entanglement with Samantha Kennedy beyond the fact that he knew her. While largely a matter of curiosity to scientists and governments and corporations awaiting an outcome, the fate of Samantha Kennedy again thrust itself onto center stage of Marshall's past and future.

And, yes. What they were asking was unfair. Unconscionable. He did feel anger. And helplessness. He could not turn away. One day, she smiled at him between classes. He awoke the next morning to digital footage of a crumpled, burned relic of the Twentieth Century, and an impossible realization that Samantha was gone forever.

Only a couple of his best friends knew of the evening he and Samantha had shared. Kids who were closer to Samantha seemed to lay exclusive claim to anguish over her death. Had Marshall attempted to voice his own grief, he knew they would view him as some kind of emotional stowaway, seeking to insert himself into a tragedy they regarded as exclusively their own.

Though years had passed, and Marshall had matured both emotionally and intellectually, seeing Samantha alive again was almost too painful to contemplate. He had to do it, though, because this grotesque experiment might give her another chance.

Marshall said good night to the crowd at the Time Warp, abandoning Wanda, who, thankfully, was too drunk to notice.

As Marshall trudged away, Sheila anguished over the conflict within her. She knew how much Marshall wanted to save his friend. His success, though, would mean at least some aspects of history could, indeed, be changed. And if that happened, big-money backers of the project would sink their claws even more deeply. Any future concerns regarding the ethics of manipulating the lives of billions of people populating universe after universe would be reduced to the buzzing of an irritating insect.

"Okay, everyone," Yuni called from his seat overlooking the projection lab.

Sitting at the center of an array of computer monitors, Elvin looked warily at Sheila as she prepared to step out of her robe.

He saw Sheila go to Marshall. With an uncharacteristic expression of sadness, she whispered something to him. He saw Marshall shrug, then read Marshall's lips as he answered, "I have to."

Sheila shook her head, stood on tiptoe and kissed Marshall's cheek. Her chest heaved, and she whispered something else. She slipped out of her robe and nodded she was ready.

Marshall suffered no erection pool today.

For one thing, Sheila had threatened to emasculate

Elvin if he organized one. "This one time, you little snot-weasel, you leave him alone."

Elvin had carefully cultivated his bad-ass-irreverent-nerd image and could cope with Sheila's wrath, but he had no heart for it today. Irritating as the realization might be, he found he held a nagging respect for these three travelers, and he wouldn't mess with any of them.

The last thing Marshall wanted was to be seventeen again.

But here he was, engulfed by the stark white wasteland of the limbo as he endured an eternity fearfully anticipating the version of Whittier High School awaiting him in a different universe.

Now that he knew what to expect, the limbo's interminable blankness had become something of a refuge, a quiet millennium where Marshall could fine-tune his philosophy of life, or sort through the great mysteries of being, or lament the weakness of character that reduced him to lustful fantasies about Sheila and Marta.

This time, though, he was on a mental treadmill of adolescent insecurity and dread. His adult mind—which should have offered the refuge of perspective—seemed to have abandoned him. While occupying himself with the happy anticipation of seeing friends and family and bringing his mature perceptions to the party would be perfectly reasonable, he instead couldn't escape premonitions of disaster and humiliation. Although his awkwardness had eased by the time he was a senior, the hard-learned survival path for a skinny dork from his earliest days of junior high was: when outside your immediate peer group of fellow dorks, keep your head down and do nothing to call attention to yourself.

While the young Marshall ached to show the world the person hiding behind his silence, any attention he drew merely provided opportunity for upper echelons of the high school caste system to point out his limitations in a very public way.

And sure enough, as Marshall came crashing into the consciousness of his seventeen-year-old counterpart rushing from one class to another burdened by a backpack full of laptop computers, electronic notebooks and even a real book or two, *Star Trek* Marshall sprawled to the floor of a crowded hallway, throwing a body block at Donnie Court. Donnie toppled with the impact.

"Goddammit," Donnie sputtered as he pushed himself off the floor. "Watch where the fuck you're going . . ."

"It was an accident, Donnie," came a sharp voice from somewhere above Marshall. He rolled over to see Samantha bending to help gather the spilled items.

"You never tripped?" she admonished Donnie.

"Shit . . ." Donnie muttered, glaring daggers to stifle ripples of laughter that escaped onlookers.

Under any other circumstance, the *Star Trek* Marshall would be mortified. By this time young Marshall had nurtured a quiet dignity he carefully protected from those who found amusement in other people's embarrassment.

And the young Marshall would have found this incident—completely of his own making—a total humiliation.

Suffering the terrifying presence of future-Marshall, though, past-Marshall barely noticed. Instead, his perception of the world around him submerged beneath a decade's worth of sensation and experience engorging his brain.

Marshall looked at Samantha with blank confusion. She responded by dropping to her knees beside him.

"Marshall! Did you hit your head?"

At the same time, a voice within him commanded, "*We'll sort through this. For now, though, just get up and let's get out of here.*"

"No, no . . . I'm all right . . . I'm just . . . dizzy, I guess. I don't know . . ."

He had trouble focusing, when he sensed a familiar, supportive presence and felt a hand take his.

"It's all right," Sheila said to Samantha. "I'm his cousin from Phoenix. I'll take care of him."

The hall cleared as the tardy bell blared.

Marshall wasn't sure why, but he trusted this vaguely familiar woman.

"Really . . . Sammy . . . I'm fine."

Samantha's expression of alarm dissolved into just a hint of amusement when he used her third-grade nickname. Reluctantly, it seemed, she rose and said to Sheila, "It's nice to meet you."

When Samantha had gone, Sheila said, "Don't try to talk. This won't be easy. For now, let's get you out of here."

With her help, Marshall stood.

His brain seemed a minefield exploding with too many images to process. Visions of a future life ripped past in a frenzied collage. Each time he sought to single out one scene, a dozen more crashed by to push it away.

Ten years is too much, the *Lucy* half of Marshall's psyche realized. He almost surrendered to a moment of terror as he understood that young Marshall would suffer some kind of mental overload if future-Marshall couldn't extract the seed of dread taking root.

"Focus on why we're here," Sheila whispered as she guided him along a hallway toward the front door.

Past-Marshall knew he needed to slam his younger counterpart with an image so powerful, it could survive the onslaught of everything else. As they walked out wide glass doors toward the parking lot, information overload had put the young Marshall at the verge of incoherence when one grotesque picture blared into his brain quashing everything else.

An image of a mangled automobile, with the words "Samantha Kennedy, eighteen" and "double fatality" forming a surreal black statement below it.

"Sammy's gonna die?" he asked in a ragged whisper.

"Maybe we can save her," responded the intrusive yet familiar entity sharing his mind. *"For now, though, get hold of yourself and deal with this other stuff."*

"Sammy's going to . . ."

He found he couldn't say it again.

Sheila helped Marshall into the passenger seat of the car she'd driven from Phoenix. She sat behind the wheel. To his relief, he found while he'd been suffering the traumatic revelation of Samantha's fate, he slowly came to grips with the gush of information regarding his future.

The *Lucy* half of Marshall realized how dangerous this information overload had been and how easy it would be for young Marshall to be drowned by the torrent. Indeed, future-Marshall believed only his experience with previous projections—along with Sheila's comforting presence—allowed him to withstand it.

"Do you think Marta and Frank can handle this?"

"Frank's fine," Sheila said. "Turns out he faced a mental collage of ten years' worth of sexual conquests. The *Star Trek* Frank wasn't overwhelmed at all. He just kind of laid back and enjoyed it, I guess. Marta, I don't know. My phone shows I missed a call from her, and she hasn't called again. I'm a little concerned."

"And how about you?"

"Rough. I was asleep in my dorm when we integrated. I'm not sure I want to go through anything like that again."

"So, what happens if you don't hear from Marta pretty soon?"

"I'll call Frank and tell him to go to Silver City."

"We're closer," Marshall said. "We could get there faster."

"Yes, well, you're seventeen, and you can't just disappear from school without drawing attention to yourself . . . and besides, the key assignment of this mission is here. It requires you to be here and me to provide support."

"Frank's not—"

"I know, I know," Sheila said. "But it's no big deal for him to leave work. He's got his own vehicle. He can drive there."

Marshall's disorientation surged and waned like waves against a shore.

Again, trying to achieve some kind of focus, he peered across the car seat at Sheila. The nineteen-year-old version was no less stunning than the adult, though she'd done her best to tone things down. Her makeup sparse, she'd pulled her hair into a ponytail and wore loose-fitting jeans and a baggy shirt.

She was still incredible.

Marshall's younger self contemplated Sheila with something between total intimidation and an awed disbelief. The wave pulled back, out toward the depths of his disorientation. The older Marshall didn't want his younger self to be submerged again. *Time for more shock therapy.*

"Did I ever tell you," future-Marshall asked Sheila, "how absolutely beautiful I think you are?"

Sheila couldn't have been more surprised. She'd watched with both amusement and satisfaction as Marshall finally began to understand the possibilities afforded by his celebrity status. Apart from the whole erection thing, though, he'd never shown a hint of coming on to her, or anyone else she knew of.

"No, Marshall," she smiled brightly. "You never have." She almost laughed at the strange juxtaposition before her.

The Marshall she knew had come to terms with his tall, awkward body. He was carefully groomed, and his face—which no one would describe as handsome—had acquired a bright and calm demeanor that pleased her.

The adult Marshall had a bewildered sort of dignity and did his best to keep his emotions hidden in a shallow reservoir. He presented to the world an analytical silence. Sheila had been chipping away at this facade and found herself really liking the guy underneath.

This boy, though . . . His height mocked him because he utterly failed to meet the stereotype. He was the tall kid who couldn't dribble. Sheila could envision him slouching when he walked, or slumping when he sat, trying to escape notice.

His dark hair refused to be constrained. A few wispy strands wandered back and forth, slaves to the constant static electricity in this dry, windy climate. A zit blossomed off to the side of one cheek.

To find the man he would become, though, Sheila had only to look into those eyes. And that's what she was doing when this awkward boy leaned across the car seat and kissed her—the act so unexpected she didn't react initially. At the point she might normally have pulled away with disapproval, she found herself enjoying the experience.

Marshall held this rather chaste kiss for several seconds, then sat back.

"Holy shit!" said the boy, his eyes wide.

"Holy shit, indeed," said Sheila with amusement.

"I can't believe I . . . he . . . I did that."

"Me, neither."

"It was . . . um . . . an emergency measure sort of a thing . . . you know?" future-Marshall tried to explain.

"I'm glad to assist," Sheila laughed, and kissing Marshall lightly on the cheek added, "For now, though, I'd better leave you alone and undistracted. I found it helpful to close my eyes and sit quietly. Let the jumble of memories find their own way. And besides, I have to find a place to stay."

"About the only decent motel is just off the Lordsburg Highway," Marshall said, and before he could suppress it, his younger self added, "You could always stay at my house."

Sheila laughed again.

"No, I couldn't. Your mom knows for certain I'm not your cousin. And I'm fairly sure you don't have girls sleep over very often. How would we explain ourselves to her?"

Marshall reddened. "Oh . . . yeah."

Marshall retreated to his own car and sat for nearly an hour while two halves of his consciousness came to terms.

"*Okay*, future-Marshall thought, *today is Monday. We have two more days before the crash. We've got to convince Sammy not to show up . . . or at least not to get into the car.*"

"*How do we do that? I haven't even called her since that night at the dunes.*"

"*We have to make her understand. Look, our last class has already started. Let's hang out here and meet her at her car.*"

"*No. She won't be alone. She could even have that creep Donnie with her.*"

"*Hey, we're supposed to try and save Donnie, too.*
Yeah, right."

As he waited for the day's final class period to end, Marshall's dual personas marveled at the revelations within them. Young Marshall became fascinated and overwhelmed by details of the decade that lay before him. He could not fathom older Marshall's promise that in just a few short days, he would recall none of it.

Future-Marshall was no less absorbed as distant memories popped into fresh reality. Routine details of this day—and yesterday and the days and weeks before which had been only the vaguest of shadows—became crisp and concrete. Apart from the tragedy looming before him, he found he suddenly relished this opportunity to retrace his steps.

He closed his eyes, settled back, and let these two tracks run.

A sharp rap at the drivers' side window startled him. He turned to see Doug Martinez motioning for him to roll down his window. Everywhere students flowed through the parking lot.

"Hey, dickweed, where were you? Ferris's quiz? I hope your nap was worth it, because now you'll be spending the weekend writing your make-up paper."

"Shit," Marshall said.

Mr. Ferris, their physics teacher, was highly suspicious when students missed his class on quiz or test days. Rather than allowing a make-up test later—with the benefit of further study—the offender could only avoid an F by writing a detailed report requiring serious research.

"Shit is right," said Doug, who was among the small group of Marshall's close friends. "I need you to help me with my computer simulation this weekend. You've gotta be there."

Marshall couldn't tell Doug—a total computer nerd—that it didn't matter, because no one would show up for his computer simulation. The entire high school community would come to a standstill because of the accident.

As that thought drifted across one track of his consciousness to the other, younger Marshall offered a startled protest.

"But we're going to keep Sammy from getting killed, aren't we?" past-Marshall thought.

That's when his younger self began to realize the implications of his impressment into this multi-universal physics experiment.

"Wait a minute. You're going away, back to your future. I'm who'll be stuck here with the consequences of whatever happens."

"Um . . . well . . ."

"So, we cut a class, no big deal. You don't have to write the make-up report, I do. You make me seem like a total klutz by knocking Donnie down. All of a sudden, I'm back to being an uncoordinated doofus, and you hop off to the future where nobody remembers stupid stuff you did in high school."

"Isn't it worth it if we can save Sammy?"

The internal debate ended abruptly. But future-Marshall added an appeasement.

"We'll do the report before I go. It'll take a half hour, tops. I know this guy named Elvin, and he sits around expounding about theoretical physics over a couple of beers. Just off the top of my head, we can write a report that will blow the socks off a high-school physics teacher."

Doug reached through the open window and punched Marshall's arm.

"Hey man, where'd you space out to? Why'd you miss class?"

Two rows over, Marshall saw Samantha and three of her fellow hotties heading toward Samantha's car.

"I can't talk right now. I have to catch Sammy before . . ."

Doug followed Marshall's gaze toward the four girls.

"Now it's *Sammy*? Dude, don't even try. You'll just get trampled."

"No, I've gotta go."

And before the younger Marshall could be taken over by dread of yet another public humiliation, future-Marshall pushed forward with a somber sense of purpose.

"Samantha! Wait up a minute."

She turned, as did the other members of her troop. Seeing Marshall, they exchanged glances as if sharing a private joke.

"I was worried," Samantha said. "When you didn't make it to class, I thought—"

"No, no, I'm fine. I sat out here until my head cleared. I mostly just feel stupid."

The other three girls shared that look again.

Samantha scowled at them. "Sorry about Donnie."

"Hey, no. It's okay. Listen, before you leave, can we talk for a minute?"

Marshall sensed Samantha's discomfort.

"Um, sure . . . see you guys later."

When the other girls had gone, she said, "Your cousin is very pretty."

"My cousin? Oh, right. She's from Phoenix. Visiting. She was at school because . . . because . . ."

"The two of you must be very close."

"Well, we're good . . . um . . . we've always been friends . . ."

"Marilyn said you kissed her."

"What?"

"Mr. Boston let Marilyn go to her car and get her English book. She saw you and your cousin kissing."

Marshall found himself without a response.

"She's not your cousin, is she?"

"It's a long story."

Quickly, Marshall took Samantha's hand and drew her closer. The younger Marshall was appalled at the forwardness of the gesture. Future-Marshall remained determined.

"I need to see you Wednesday night."

Samantha pulled her hand away.

"What would your cousin have to say about that? Don't you think you should take it a little slower, at least while you're new to this? Maybe just one girl at a time?"

"No, Samantha. It's not that way. I need to see you."

"Marshall, I didn't mean to give you the wrong impression when we went to the dunes. I like you—as a friend. And clearly, your cousin is who you should be asking out."

Marshall was puzzled by the slight tone of anger tinging Samantha's voice. Almost as if she was jealous.

"Please, I'm not asking you out or anything. I just need to talk with you. I haven't called you since that night, because I understand it was nothing more than just a very nice time between friends. I know you don't feel anything more for me. But I need to talk with you."

"And your cousin?"

"Never mind her. She's just a friend. It's complicated, and—"

"I can't see you Wednesday. I've got a big test."

"Sammy, I know you're going to Donnie's house Wednesday night."

"How do you know that?"

"I ... um ... you guys are kind of going together. I just figured—"

"I am seeing Donnie Wednesday. And I'm not going to bail just because—"

"Tomorrow then."

"I can't tomorrow night either. And how did you find out I'm going to Donnie's house? Is he telling people?"

"No. How I know is part of what I have to explain."

"Just tell me now."

"Believe me," Marshall said, "telling this story will take more time than we've got here. Please, Sammy, give me a half hour, and then if you don't want me to, I'll never bother you again. We were close once. Can't you please trust that friendship one more time?"

She rolled her eyes. "You know what I've liked so much about you? You're one person who doesn't pressure me to do anything or be anything. And now, here you are. Same as every other guy. Everybody wants something."

"All I want is for you to listen to me."

"I can't tomorrow. I've got drama club. Mr. Campbell is casting the senior skit for the graduation assembly. I can't miss it, and I don't know how late it will go."

"Then tonight," he pleaded.

She stared at him intently for a moment and gave a sigh of resignation.

"My mom's going out tonight, and I have to babysit my sister. Mom will be back by nine-thirty or so. I can sneak out after they go to bed. I'll meet you down at the park some-time between ten and ten-thirty. That's the best I can do."

"Thank you," Marshall said with relief. "I'll be there. Please, please don't forget."

30

ALIENS

NEITHER THE YOUNGER NOR THE older version of Frank was happy when Sheila ordered him to Silver City. Young Frank had a date that evening with a woman in whom he'd invested two dinners. As well as his older counterpart could recall, tonight would provide a memorable return.

"Tomorrow," Frank said.

"Today. Right now."

"So, who's gonna pay for this?"

"Oh, for Chrissake."

"Hey, I'm a working man. And I went to the stock guy's office this afternoon and gave him a check for that solar battery stock . . ."

"Which will probably end up making you rich when you get back to 2045. Just use the money you were going to spend getting into that poor girl's pants tonight. You're Leonard Rose's guy. You think he'll be happy that you passed up a chance to go make sure Marta's doing what she's supposed to?"

"How do I even know where to look?"

"I'll make some calls and find out where Marta and her friends are staying. I'll call you while you're driving over. I'm concerned about her, and you should be, too. Now go!"

Sheila calculated the timing.

Driving to Silver City would take Frank at least five hours. She had more than enough time to call motels, or hospital emergency rooms. Sheila eventually found her—in jail.

"Jail?" Frank asked over the phone. He was still an hour away from Silver City when Sheila finally tracked Marta down.

Working from a threadbare motel room on the outskirts of Whittier, Sheila had gone through the Silver City motel and hotel listings. Marta hadn't been admitted or treated at the local hospital. Finally, Sheila called the police to ask about automobile accidents.

"What was the name again?" the police receptionist asked.

"Marta Hamilton."

"I think I heard something come over radio traffic this afternoon," the receptionist said. "Call Deputy John Fiske at the Grant County Sheriff's Department. They might be able to help you."

Fisk was not particularly helpful.

"Yeah, she's in jail."

"What happened?"

"Are you a relative?"

"No. I'm a friend."

"She's got a couple of other friends here. You can talk to them. Her bail hearing is set for tomorrow morning."

"Can't you at least tell me what she's charged with?"

"She assaulted a police officer. And she had a weapon in her possession."

"Um ... a taser?"

"No. A handgun."

And he hung up.

"Wow," Frank said when Sheila called to relay the conversation, "that cop must have really pissed Marta off. Where would she get a gun?"

"They won't let you see her tonight," Sheila said. "Find someplace to stay. I'll be there by morning."

"If she'd been injured she'd be hospitalized, even if she was under arrest. If they've got her at the jail, she's probably okay."

"Physically," Sheila pointed out. "We have no idea what kind of mental damage might have occurred when she arrived."

Marshall marveled at how little his hometown had changed. He'd last been here to see his mom a few weeks before entering the travelers' program. He found the decade-earlier version of this place nearly identical.

Whittier originally existed as a small agricultural community, producing mostly cotton and cattle. With the success of the mining industry one county over, it gradually had become a town of commuters who worked for the mining company.

The Sonoran Desert provided a beautifully rambling landscape of browns and greens wandering along dry riverbeds and over dramatic rocky crags. Given a wet winter, the desert bloomed with an extraordinary spectrum of color. Ancient saguaro cacti stood watch over varmints that scrabbled out their existences below.

When he walked into the kitchen to find his mother standing at the sink, the Marshall from *Lucy* had a hard time believing she'd ever been so young. She said hello to him without interrupting the peeling of cucumbers. He just stared, and as his gaze lingered, she turned to face him.

"What's wrong?" she asked with a note of suspicion.

He shrugged off his backpack letting it fall to the floor. He wrapped her with a hug. She seemed to enjoy the embrace for a moment, then leaned back. "All right, what did you wreck this time?"

"Nothing, Mom. What, I can't just be glad to see you?"

"Hmm."

They stood quietly regarding each other before she asked, "Are you planning to mow the lawn this afternoon?"

Future-Marshall was surprised at his young counterpart's reaction to this rather innocuous question. The pleasure of seeing his mother seemed to boil away. Why? The last time he'd been home, he hadn't minded mowing the lawn. But then, he'd been twenty-five years old.

He wanted to say, "Sure. I'll go do it now." Instead, he complained, "Oh, Mom, I've got stuff to do. And it doesn't need mowing yet."

"Please, Marshall, I don't ask much of you. It does need mowing. And this time run the trimmer around the edges."

Marshall felt a black mood settle over him like a shroud as he looked out the window at the hot afternoon and the broad-leafed grass his mom stubbornly nursed through the cauldron of each eastern Arizona summer.

"We shouldn't even have grass. Everybody else has a desert landscape. It saves water."

"Mow the lawn."

"Last time I couldn't get the mower to start."

"This time put fuel in it."

"Jesus Christ . . ."

"Prayer won't help. We're agnostics."

While pushing the mower back and forth across the broad stand of grass, Marshall puzzled over his response to his mom's simple request.

Mowing and trimming the lawn takes maybe an hour. That's not hard. I don't have anything else I need to do.

A glowing point of realization began to burn amid his conflicting emotions.

"Oh, my God," he said aloud, understanding for the first time, "I'm a teenager. I'm an obnoxious, self-absorbed, whiny, pathetic teenager."

Even more startling came a realization that, in the conflict between the maturity his future self brought to this relationship and the bedlam of adolescence, the adolescent was beginning to prevail.

Marshall had, of course, heard Marta's unsettling description of her attempt to hang onto her future consciousness during the Flagstaff mission. He apparently had an affinity for time travel that some of the others did not. Before today's arrival, he'd never even come close to losing himself.

Now, though, he began to understand the danger.

The further the distance between future and past, he decided, the stronger the influence a past being has over this fragile relationship. Initially, the intimidation of mental turmoil made the past counterpart a willing, if fearful, participant in this shared adventure. Once confusion wore off, though, the past being was stronger and, Marshall realized, could assert itself. Maybe withdraw from the whole scheme. Perhaps even extinguish the future counterpart altogether.

Marshall remembered returning from college late in his junior year at New Mexico State, walking into his mother's house and being able to appreciate rather than resent this oasis that was his refuge during his lonely journey through adolescence.

He'd found his mother reading.

"Mom, I don't know if I've ever told you how much I appreciate all you've done for me. I can't imagine how hard it must have been for you after Dad died. And . . . I guess I've been, well . . . I'm sorry. I should have helped more, or . . ."

She put down her book, laughed, and wiped at a tear.

"Marshall, you were such a sweet little boy. You were so willing to please, and then you turned fourteen. I just kept telling myself that you'd been replaced by an alien, and I knew that one day they'd give you back."

"An alien?"

"It's okay. Part of a teenager's job is to give his parents grief. Somehow, experimenting with being a perfectly rotten human being is part of the growing-up process."

"An alien?"

She had smiled again. "Welcome home, son."

Marshall sighed at the future memory and pushed the lawnmower with a renewed vigor. He vowed to be better this time around.

"Stay there, Mom," Marshall said, following supper that evening. "Let me get the dishes tonight."

"I ... what?"

Suspicion gripped Marshall's mother. Aliens were not considerate. Aliens ate quickly and silently, then slithered off to their rooms where, behind closed doors, they used the Internet to conspire with other aliens and plot innovations in annoyance and procrastination. Either that or look at pornography.

All the time Marshall washed dishes and wiped down counters, she dreaded what surely must come next. What disastrous announcement was he preparing her for? What girl had he gotten pregnant? What impossible favor would he ask?

When he bent to kiss her cheek, she flinched, and with one eye squinted shut, watched him walk to his bedroom.

"Goodnight, Mom."

She wondered what he meant by that.

Marshall waited until the television's glow winked away. He allowed another fifteen minutes for his mom to settle into her bed, then slipped out the back door. He wouldn't risk starting his car. Instead, he wheeled his old bicycle into the alley off the garage and pedaled a mile to his rendezvous with Samantha.

Mission planners had given much thought to the approach he should take with Samantha and Donnie. Ultimately, they determined, he must do anything he could, including telling them of the time travel project and his journey from the future. Only as a last resort, though, because his contemporaries obviously wouldn't believe him. Another problem would be the effect that story would have on young Marshall, who would not be skipping off into the future when the experiment ended.

While the younger Marshall would quickly become oblivious to his encounter with the future, everyone around him would know what he'd said and how he'd behaved. If Samantha and Donnie survived, Marshall would not be just the tall, geeky kid who didn't quite fit. He'd be the tall, geeky lunatic who made up bizarre stories about the future. And if Samantha and Donnie could not escape their history, Marshall's prediction of the event might make people wonder if he'd somehow caused their accident.

The first to arrive, Marshall took a moment to see this place he'd known his whole life. Whittier's City Park covered four square blocks a half-mile beyond the center of town where ancient elms and cottonwoods produced a green canopy that stood as a contradiction to the desert climate. He turned to his left and saw a cinder block structure at one corner of the park, the Community Building, a place for wedding receptions and reunions and civic meetings. Beyond the municipal swimming pool sat a rough but lighted softball diamond. At this hour the lights were off, games over. This forested space was warm, black and silent save for the pool's security lights.

He settled into darkness and with each passing minute, became more fearful that Samantha would not appear.

Finally, the *click, click, click* of a bicycle coasting to a stop caused him to turn.

"You rode your bike, too," he said as he smiled.

"And if you tell anyone, I'll strangle you."

"Bad for the image, huh?" The older part of Marshall couldn't help the little jab.

Then he thought to himself that nothing could make Samantha look bad. She wore cutoff jeans and a dark t-shirt. Her hair was disheveled from the ride and a slight sheen of perspiration lent a glow to her face as it reflected distant pool lights.

She appeared the epitome of vibrant youth.

"I'm here. What's so important?"

Marshall issued a heavy sigh and glanced at his shoes.

"I've thought about it for days now, and I haven't any idea how to say this."

She offered a snort of exasperation and started to wheel her bike away. "If my stepdad catches me, I'll be grounded until graduation."

"That would be the best thing that could happen."

She stopped.

"What are you talking about?"

"Please, you can't go to Donnie's Wednesday night. If you do, something terrible will happen."

"Oh, you're psychic now?"

"Don't ask me how I know. I just know. There will be a race, out at the dunes. Phil Barret and Donnie with two of his dad's muscle cars. And . . . and . . ." he shifted his gaze into her eyes, "they'll kill you, Sammy."

Her bicycle clattered to the ground. She took a long stride toward him, put two hands to his chest and shoved hard. "Is this some nerd computer game challenge or something? Scare the shit out of someone?"

Marshall saw a gleam of tears reflected in the glow of security lights.

"You asshole," she hissed. "You fucking asshole!"

She swiped at her eyes and glared. The young Marshall wanted to leave, go hide somewhere for the remaining school year, but future-Marshall wouldn't allow it.

"Have Donny and Phil been talking about the cars?" he asked.

"Apparently you already know the answer to that question. What are you, some kind of creepy voyeur, too? Have you been following me around?"

Marshall knew from news accounts Phil and Donnie had debated for several days who was the better driver. A distraught and guilt-ridden Phil told police these arguments resumed the night of the party when everyone gathered at Donnie's house was drunk or high.

"I know because—what the hell? You already think I'm a fucking asshole—I know because ten years from now we figure out how to travel through time. I've come from the future to try and keep you and Donnie from being killed."

Samantha closed her eyes and shook her head. "Oh, Marshall." She picked up her bike.

"Sammy, please. I haven't bothered you since the night we went out. I haven't called you or followed you around. I've hardly told another soul about it. If I was just trying to impress you or get your attention, don't you think I'd come up with something more believable?"

She stopped.

"I'm afraid, Sammy. It's no secret that I care for you. I've been through this once already, and I don't know if I can stand losing you again. You don't have to like me or talk to me or . . . or anything. Please just—"

The bike fell to the ground again as Samantha bowed

her face into her hands. Her shoulders began to shudder. These were not angry tears.

Young Marshall stood awkwardly for a moment until his older counterpart reached to Samantha in a careful, almost paternal hug. She responded by clinging to him with all her strength, burying her face against his chest as she sobbed.

Standing in darkness under cottonwoods and elms, young Marshall hoped the world beyond would never intrude again. Samantha finally put both hands on his chest, tapped him twice with open palms, and pushed away.

She wiped at her eyes. "Thank you, Marshall."

"So . . . you believe me?"

"No. I don't."

"But you're not completely sure, right? You're thinking maybe . . ."

She put a finger to his lips and peered into his eyes.

"I believe you genuinely care about me . . . All the rest of it . . . I guess I believe that for some reason, *you* believe this. At first, I was just mad because . . . it seems I'm always angry nowadays. Everybody's pushing me one way or another to make some decision. What college? The whole sex thing. Don't talk to that guy. Let's try this drug or that drug . . ."

She took both his hands in hers.

"Being with you at the dunes was so easy. And now you're willing to make yourself look like a loon, because you're worried about me."

"A loon?"

She nodded.

"So, you won't go to the party?"

Now her face clouded again.

"Marshall, just don't go there. Don't push your luck."

He sighed. She shook her head and resumed their embrace.

After a couple moments of silence, he screwed up his courage and asked, "Sammy, why do you hang out with that guy? Why the partying? Why the drugs?"

This time when she looked at him, he saw suspicion creeping back into her face. Marshall retreated a couple of steps.

"When they do the ... the autopsy ... they find traces of alcohol, grass and cocaine ..."

"I've never touched cocaine."

Marshall did not back down. "Apparently you will Wednesday night."

Samantha turned away again. Marshall waited.

Finally, still facing away, she said, "Don't you ever drink or smoke pot, or take pills?"

"I've had a few beers. And I smoked with Doug a couple of times. Frankly, I don't see the attraction."

Samantha seemed to be trying to make up her mind about something.

"Marshall," she said after another interval of silence, "did you ever wonder why we moved out of the house on Sixteenth Lane, back when we were kids?"

Now her voice became a whisper. He had to step closer to hear. He had the eerie impression he was talking with the third grader who'd been his friend. Despite the warmth of blackness around them, he felt goosebumps rise on his arms.

"Well sure, I guess I must have. Probably because your folks wanted a better house?"

"We moved because my mom kicked my dad out, and

she wouldn't stay in that place where we'd lived together."

Marshall knew Samantha's parents had divorced and her mom remarried a few years later.

"She kicked him out because of me. He was ... touching me. And she caught us. And nothing's been the same since."

The younger version of Marshall felt his knees buckle. He closed the gap between them and embraced her from behind. "Oh, Sammy, I'm so sorry."

Meanwhile, things were clicking into place for future-Marshall, thanks to college psychology classes: a victim of sexual abuse; insecurity that breeds a need for approval from male figures in the victim's life, often involving promiscuity; delayed stress syndrome, the effects of which are frequently anesthetized through alcohol or drug abuse; a conviction within the victim that she is somehow to blame. His eyes glistened with tears of his own as she turned within his embrace to face him again.

"Have you ever seen anyone, Sammy? I mean a doctor, a psychiatrist ..."

"No. My mom couldn't stand it if anyone knew. And she's been through too much already."

"You have to see someone! This wasn't your fault. A doctor won't tell anyone what happened. He can't. It's confidential. We can find someone, Sammy. You don't have to feel this way your whole life ..."

"Well, according to you that won't be an issue. Maybe a car wreck's the best thing that could happen."

"Don't say that, Sammy. I'm here because we can change it."

Samantha shook her head again.

"One minute, Marshall, I think you're the most

understanding guy in the world. And the next, I think you're from some other planet."

"Like I said before, Sammy, why would I invent something that makes me seem so . . . so . . . geeky?"

She laughed and brushed aside more tears.

"You've got me there, kid. Maybe you really believe what you're saying. And that makes me worry about *you*. Have *you* been to see a psychiatrist? Maybe we can go together."

Marshall smiled.

"If you're from the future, tell me something that happens tomorrow."

He shrugged. "I can't. My future self is seeing all this through ten years of memory. I can't remember what happened on a given day a decade ago."

"Oh, well . . ." Samantha sighed, but her smile made it okay.

Present-Marshall wanted desperately just to leave it that way. Future-Marshall would not let him.

"Please, Samantha. Don't go to Donnie's Wednesday."

And sure enough, Marshall felt the wall go back up. The little girl left, and a wary cynic returned.

"Look, Marshall, don't try to control my life. Several of us are going there to study for finals. We already made plans. If I see something dangerous, I'll leave. Give me credit for having some common sense."

Samantha kissed his cheek, turned away and picked up her bike. "Good night, Marshall. Thanks for caring."

As she faded into darkness, Sheila stepped from the shadows.

"How long have you been here?" he asked.

"Long enough."

"I didn't know what else to do," Marshall said, his voice quivering.

She took his hand and squeezed.

"And it wasn't just the half of me that gets to fly away who made that decision," Marshall added with sudden realization. "It's the kid who has to stay here who decided. And I'm not sure he understands what he's gotten himself into."

Sheila sighed. "You are as good a person as a teenager as you are when you grow up, Marshall." She hugged him. "The kid's in love. There's nothing easy about that."

31

SPINNING THE TRUTH

EIGHT HOURS LATER SHEILA DROVE into Silver City, a small university town in the southwest corner of New Mexico, tucked into rolling, forested hills that spread north and east to become the magnificent Gila Wilderness.

As they had arranged, she met Frank at the parking lot of the Grant County Courthouse, a 1930s-era, two-story stone building, which overlooked downtown from atop an urban hillside. The parking lot remained mostly empty at this early hour, and Frank was out of his car standing next to Sheila's window when she stopped.

"The jail's not here," Frank said, "and I don't think we can see her before the arraignment hearing at 10:00 a.m., which *is* here."

"Then I'll go to the jail," Sheila said.

"Yeah, good luck with that. I already tried, and the guy said visiting hours don't start until afternoon."

"Hmm. We'll see about that."

Suspecting she might need the benefit of all assets at her command, Sheila was not the toned-down version of herself she'd presented at Whittier High School. She wore her tight jeans and a clingy shirt with a scooped neckline emphasizing cleavage.

Clearly, Frank was impressed.

"Geez," he said, staring down at her. "I'm surprised they let you walk around loose when you were nineteen."

"Where's the jail, Frank?"

"Follow me."

They drove to a depressing cinder block fortress presenting a drab gray face with glass doors. They stepped into a small foyer that separated them from a larger room painted institutional green featuring a reception counter. The place smelled of industrial strength floor cleaner. Sheila fluffed her blonde hair and tugged at her shirt so the scooped bodice rode even lower. Only when she'd entered the main room did she realize the person attending the counter was a broad-shouldered woman in her late twenties wearing a grumpy frown.

Sheila stopped so abruptly that Frank bumped into her from behind. He grabbed Sheila to steady her.

From the side of her mouth, Sheila said, "You didn't tell me it was a woman."

"A fat guy with hairy arms was sitting there just an hour ago," he whispered back.

"Can I help you?" the woman asked. Her tone reflected bored skepticism.

"Yes," Sheila said. "We were hoping we could see Marta Hamilton for just a moment before her arraignment hearing."

The woman pointed to a sign above one of the doors behind her that read *Visiting Hours: 1 p.m. to 4 p.m.* "No."

"Please, it's . . ." Sheila started, but Frank stepped around her, nudging her with an elbow as he did so.

"Ma'am, please pardon my sister. She doesn't understand about regulations. She's a freshman at Arizona

State, and, well, you know. She doesn't have a clue as to what life is like for those of us who have to work for a living and—" He gave Sheila a castigating sideways glance, "—follow the rules."

The woman at the desk shifted her gaze from Sheila and took stock of Frank. Sheila also glanced at Frank, wondering when he'd had time to undo the top two buttons of his khaki work shirt.

Frank offered the woman a most compelling smile and added just a hint of a wink.

The woman smiled back before she caught herself. She did her best to recapture the bored frown while adjusting her posture to emphasize her breasts through her deputy's uniform.

"Say, you didn't grow up around North Phoenix, did you?" Frank asked. "The Sunnyslope area? You seem so familiar."

"Nope." Now the deputy did smile. "I grew up right here. I have some cousins over there, though."

"Oh, wow." Frank increased the voltage on his smile. "My high-school girlfriend had a sister a couple of years younger than us. Man, was she ever hot. And there's such a resemblance."

Now the deputy laughed.

"Right. I'll bet that works on a lot of women, doesn't it?"

Sheila expected some sort of curt dismissal.

"Sometimes," Frank said. "You do remind me of her, though."

"Okay." The deputy sighed. "What can I help you with?"

"Oh, nothing. We'll wait until visiting hours. We're

just worried. Marta's our friend, and she's never been in any kind of trouble before. We're not even sure what she did."

The deputy turned to her computer, cranking up her posture another notch as she did so. She pecked a few keys.

"A couple of friends were trying to get her to an emergency room, and they were driving too fast . . ."

"Emergency room?" Sheila said. "What happened?"

The deputy appraised Sheila with a scowl and returned to her narrative, directed exclusively at Frank.

"She was confused and disoriented. When our man stopped the car, she jumped out from the passenger side and demanded that he use his taser on her."

"Did she appear injured?" Frank converted his expression to one of grave concern. He leaned closer to the deputy, leading with his eyes.

"Oh, no." Her tone reassuring. "The report says she was hysterical. Her friends said they were frightened she might hurt herself."

Frank leaned back and patted his chest with relief. "Thank God. What happened then?"

"The officer tried to calm her, and she kept demanding he use the taser. So, he decided to cuff her. When he got close, she kicked him."

"Oh, Lord, I hope he's okay."

She clicked further down the report. "Yes, he's fine. Just a bruise. Once she assaulted him, though, he didn't have any choice."

"The taser?"

"Yep, he put her down. After the arrest officers found a handgun in their car."

"You've been very helpful," Frank said. "I don't suppose . . ."

The deputy offered an expectant smile.

"Um . . . would you consider letting me show my appreciation by buying you a drink once your shift is over?"

"You're just full of surprises," the deputy grinned. "I thought you'd take one more shot at getting me to let you see your friend."

Frank raised both hands. "We'd hoped to see her, but I understand completely. And you've done so much already."

"Yes. I'll meet you for a drink when I get off." She leaned closer to Frank. "As long as your sister has someplace else to go."

"Of course. She has to drive back to Whittier right after the arraignment."

He smiled again and backed slowly away, maintaining eye contact.

"All right," the deputy conceded. "Wait right there. I'll see if we've got time to bring her up before they put everyone on the bus."

"Thank you. And why don't we make that dinner as well as a drink?"

"You got it."

Frank and Sheila were ushered into a sterile, closet-sized enclosure with a telephone on each side of a thick, stained plexiglass partition. As they waited for Marta to appear, Sheila said, "I hope you're not going to stand her up."

"The deputy?"

"Who else?"

"I'm looking forward to it. Trust me, she's ready to roll."

Sheila had never seen Marta Hamilton display fear. But the woman who sat on the other side of the plexiglass was clearly scared. Her eyes were red and the flesh around them puffy. Her dark skin seemed a shade paler displayed against her orange jail jumpsuit.

"Do you know who we are?" Sheila asked.

Marta regarded them blankly at first, followed by a spark of recognition.

"You're ... Sheila? And he's ... I should know, shouldn't I?"

"Are you okay?" Sheila asked.

"Well, I don't think I'm going crazy anymore ... You, and him, too, you were in my dream. And I was ... I had to get away, because ... no, she had to get away because she was afraid I'd be injured if she stayed ..."

"So, you had to get the policeman to use his taser," Sheila said. "I know it seems like a dream, but it wasn't. The experience fades. That's one of the effects of time travel."

"Time travel, yes. She ... that other me, she came here from the future. Ten years. And his name is Frank ... what happens now?"

Sheila shook her head and saw pain on Marta's face through the distortions of the plexiglass panel.

"Unfortunately, this is a part of this whole time-travel thing no one gives much thought to. We don't know what happens now. Within a few days you won't have any memory or awareness of your future self ..."

"But everyone around me will be completely aware I acted like a lunatic and got myself arrested for a reason I won't be able to explain!"

Marta's grip tightened on the telephone receiver.

"Yes," Sheila said. "Our past selves are left to live with consequences of the things we do during the time projection process."

"And you guys think that's acceptable?"

"No. As they always tell us, though, it's what we signed up for."

"I didn't sign up for anything yet. I have a career that's important to me. I can't get arrested and maintain a security clearance where I work now. This trip will change my whole life. A decade from now, I probably won't be in any position to even be considered for your time travel project."

Sheila held the phone away from her ear so Frank could hear Marta's end of the conversation. He took the phone.

"You're one of the four lead travelers," Frank said. "You're making history with every trip. Elvin says nothing can change that."

"Although I hate to say he's right about anything, I do think Frank is right about this," Sheila said, reclaiming the handset. "You are a traveler. Whatever happened here will be inconsequential to your future. Things will work out."

Cynthia Osborne served as arraigning judge for Grant County District Court that week. Cynthia enjoyed a strict routine. Up at 5:00 a.m. and off to the gym, where she did either the spinning class or yoga. Then a shower, coffee with a handful of friends, and on to the courthouse.

This morning, though, the buzzing alarm clock startled her from a particularly erotic dream involving Joaquin, her yoga instructor. She briefly considered rousing her husband, Al, to the task, but he was inert. Morning sex was not his forte. She arose and entered their walk-in closet, complete with washer and dryer. A pile of dirty clothes blocked her path. She shoved them into the washer and proceeded to scrub her face, apply the minimum of makeup to be seen at the gym, pee, pack her gym bag and pull on her shorts and exercise bra.

The washer went into its spin cycle.

Cynthia smiled at the memory of youthful experimentation with an unbalanced load. Though she turned to walk away, the flickering images of her fantasy encounter with Joaquin gave her a second thought. She turned back and put her hand to the washer. She felt the vibrating buzz of the spin cycle flow through her fingers.

She peeked around the corner of the closet to see Al in a deep, sleepy state of total uselessness.

She bit her lower lip. The spin cycle was a long one. She leaned into the machine and felt the buzz penetrate her shorts, setting off a lovely pelvic glow. She backed away, peeked around the corner again, and boosted herself on top of the washer, where she sat with one corner of the jittering machine ground tightly into her crotch.

Gratification came with immediate intensity. She stifled a small scream and hung on until the rinse cycle.

So, the judge was late to the gym. Which made her late to the courthouse.

Before arraignments began, she had a pretrial motion meeting with a couple of lawyers. Only the week before, Cynthia had berated one of them for being tardy to a similar session. So, rather than driving around back to her usual parking spot, she stopped in a no-parking zone, ran up the steps, took the elevator to her office, handed her keys to her court clerk and asked him to move the car.

The clerk returned holding a parking ticket.

"My car was only there for five minutes..." Cynthia protested.

"The officer already put the ticket under the windshield wiper," her clerk apologized.

"Did you tell him it was my car?"

"He said he'd already hit the send button and the computer had it. He said a judge should know better. He said he couldn't unwrite a ticket."

She studied the offending police officer's signature. *Owen Kirkpatrick.*

Judge Osborne's pleasant memory of her early-morning gratification had nearly offset the unsettling disturbance of her routine. The parking ticket, though, was more than enough to tip the balance.

Her mood remained surly as arraignments began. She hammered the first two defendants who came before her, setting steep bail with no hint of sympathy. Marta and the public defender appointed to represent her stood when Marta's case was called. Judge Osborne peered sternly over a pair of reading glasses.

"Assault of a police officer?"

Marta hung her head.

That's when Cynthia scanned further down the police report and saw the arresting officer's name.

"Is Officer Kirkpatrick present?" she asked her bailiff as she scanned a nearly empty courtroom. "I want to hear from him."

The bailiff seemed surprised. Normally arresting officers

were not expected to be present at arraignment hearings. "I saw him a little while ago having coffee in the cafeteria, Your Honor."

"Go get him. We'll wait."

The judge ruthlessly dispatched two more arraignees before Officer Kirkpatrick arrived.

Again, Marta stood.

"Now," the judge said, "tell me what happened."

"Your Honor . . ." the attorney began. But Marta tugged at his sleeve and said, "I'm not sure, Your Honor. I suffered some sort of anxiety attack, I guess. I became frightened and hysterical, and I . . . I was afraid I'd do something awful, so I asked the police officer to stun me with his taser."

Again, the judge consulted the report, before glaring back at Owen Kirkpatrick.

"You tased this young woman?"

"Well, yes," Owen said as he stood in the gallery. "But not because she asked me to."

"Why, then?"

"Because she kicked me!"

"Kicked you where?"

"My shin."

"Hmm." The judge added an almost inaudible, "Too bad."

"You outweigh her by at least a hundred pounds. You couldn't subdue her any other way?"

"No. After she kicked me, she grabbed the taser off my belt and pointed it at herself. I had no choice. She could have injured herself. So, I took it away from her, and I tased her."

"So, she wouldn't injure herself?"

"Um ... well ..."

Marta waited, the only sound the click of the court stenographer's machine.

"Miss Hamilton, I see there's no record of you having any previous legal difficulties. Were you drunk?"

"No, Your Honor."

The judge swiveled her gaze to Owen. "Did she agree to a breathalyzer and a blood test?"

"Yes, Your Honor."

"And?"

"No alcohol, no drugs."

"Miss Hamilton, do you promise never to kick an officer again?"

Marta nodded vigorously. "Oh, yes, Your Honor."

"Do you promise not to sue anyone over getting tased?"

"Absolutely," Marta inscribed an X over her heart with her index finger.

"Then have a nice day."

Outside the courthouse, Sheila, Frank, and Marta were joined by Marta's companions, Melanie and Olga.

Sheila pulled Marta aside.

"Forgive me," she said, "The Marta I know doesn't really have 'friends.' Who are these people?"

Marta regarded Sheila with suspicion that dissolved to an expression of helplessness.

"You don't know how much I hate feeling this way," Marta said. "How much I hate not knowing what's happening here ... *you're* supposed to be my friend. In the future. Right?"

"Yes, well, you kind of change—"

"And by the time we meet up again you will have forgotten this? And so will I?"

"I'm surprised you remember this long."

"As you said, it's fading pretty fast. But this one thing, she . . . I . . . was pretty emphatic about . . . Sheila, I work for British Intelligence. Industrial espionage. I don't blow things up or anything. I just process information. I don't know Melanie and Olga. Not really. I work with them at the lab. And single women my age are supposed to have friends . . ."

"A spy? Marta, that's so cool."

"When you get back to where you came from, there's something you need to remind her . . . me . . . about. She found something while sharing my memory that seemed to get her attention."

"Okay."

"Tell her we know the man in the picture. We see him sometimes at the Sandia Lab."

"What man?"

"The man . . . I don't know. This is so frustrating. I know it's important. I just can't remember why. Tell her. Help her remember."

"Okay, guys," Marta turned to Melanie and Olga—who had been chatting happily with Frank— "I think it's time to go."

"And you're sure you're well?" Olga asked Marta, putting a hand to Marta's forehead. "No more hallucinations?"

"I'm fine."

Frank joined Sheila, standing apart from Marta's reunion with her companions.

"So, what about the bet?" he whispered.

"Marta—our Marta—is gone," Sheila whispered back. "Obviously that part of the mission is dead."

"Dr. Rose warned me you guys might pull something like this—just go through the motions."

"Nobody's going through the motions. Marta bailed—as she should have—for her own survival. This Marta can't act on any foreknowledge because she has none."

"What bet?" Marta asked. Her friends had gone to get their car, and Marta had hung back for a final goodbye.

"Forget it, Marta," Sheila said. "You just get back to Albuquerque. Take care of yourself and keep out of trouble. We'll see you in a decade or so."

Sheila guided Frank to their cars.

"You think you'll be okay getting back to Phoenix? Are you having any confusion yet? Any trouble remembering there's a future half of yourself still here?"

"I'm fine," Frank said. "But I'm not going to Phoenix. You've reminded me that I'm Dr. Rose's representative here. I'll call and get a couple more days off. I'll keep my date with the deputy, then I'll meet you in Whittier."

"Look, Frank, nobody deliberately tried to screw up this part of the mission. We tried to manipulate the past, and for whatever reason, we failed. You and Dr. Rose just have to accept that."

32

THE PRICE OF THE PAST

SAMANTHA AND MARSHALL DIDN'T speak to each other the next day at school.

The only morning class they had together was English. Marshall kept his distance. The one brief glance she cast his way offered no encouragement. His imagination interpreted her gaze as regret she'd told him her secrets, fear he might tell someone about her father; and skepticism over his time travel story which, he knew, could only seem ludicrous in the light of day.

And as the younger aspect of his being continued to gain dominance, Marshall was more than happy to leave it alone. Until Sheila and Frank forced his hand at lunch.

When Marshall and Dave headed to the parking lot for their usual quick drive to Bud's for a burger, they found Sheila and Frank waiting.

"Um ... Dave, I don't think you've met my cousin, Sheila," Marshall said.

"No." Dave offered his hand. "Wow, you're hot."

"Thank you, I guess." Sheila completed the handshake.

"And this is Frank," Marshall continued. "He's ... um ... he's Frank."

"Listen, Dave," Sheila said, "Marshall and I really need to talk. Do you mind . . . ?"

She smiled an impossibly captivating smile.

"Oh, sure. Catch you at fifth period, man."

"So, how are things going?" Sheila asked as they climbed into her car, Frank relegated to the back seat.

"They're not. Sammy's avoiding me, and frankly, I don't blame her. What would you do if somebody fed you such a goofball story?"

"What about the guy?" Frank asked. "What was his response?"

"Donnie?" Marshall was taken aback. "I . . . I haven't talked to Donnie."

"Why not?"

"I can't talk to *him*. He's a jerk. I don't like him, and he doesn't like me. Never has. There's no point."

"Your mission is to save *them*—not just her," Frank said. "You're not trying . . ."

The seventeen-year-old facet of Marshall's being felt only intimidation from this underwear-model-looking guy. The older Marshall, though, became angry. During this whole conversation, future-Marshall found himself unable to interrupt the younger Marshall's responses. His irritation, though, finally allowed him to break through.

"Fuck you, Frank. Samantha is my friend. She's someone I care deeply about. I will do anything I can to save her . . ."

Marshall's ire bled into embarrassment at the uncharacteristic outburst, but he saw Sheila grinning with surprise. "Way to go, Marshall."

"Are you sure?" Frank shot back. "Because Sheila's your

friend, too, and if you save Samantha, you know what will happen. Sheila's ethics crusade goes tits up."

Marshall's heart thudded to his stomach. "Oh, my God. He's right, isn't he? This whole thing puts you in an impossible position, doesn't it?"

"Marshall," Sheila said, "I don't care what Frank thinks. I will do anything I can to save that girl. So will you. And that includes talking to Donnie. You save him, then you save her, too."

Marshall stared across the gravel parking lot, into the waves of spring Arizona heat shimmering up from the hoods of a hundred cars.

"Yeah. I know. I'll catch him after fifth period, before he goes to weights."

The jocks took their PE classes during sixth period—the day's last class—so they could get a jump on whatever team practice the season called for. Donnie and some of the football players used the hour to lift weights and screw around.

Marshall waited for Donnie along the pathway to the athletic field house, cutting his second class in two days— something Marshall simply didn't do.

The field house stood at the end of a narrow walkway passing between the back of the band building and a set of *temporary* modules that had been used as classrooms for as long as Marshall could remember. He sat on the steps of a module, shaded from the intense Arizona sun. Between buildings, thick, green jasmine vines peppered with tiny white blossoms climbed trellises. Waves of their thick, sweet aroma rode the breezes that coursed through the narrow passage.

Closing his eyes, Marshall's future self sent a strong message to the present that quiet desert moments like these were not to be taken for granted. Memory simply didn't do them justice.

Movement along the sidewalk commanded Marshall back to his task. The first group of athletes paid him no notice. A couple of guys among the next knot of jocks offered a wave, and one added, "Hey, Marshall, how's it going? You taking a break this afternoon?"

Marshall smiled back self-consciously.

"Yeah. Long year . . ."

And they were past him.

More boys passed, concerned about beating the tardy bell. Still, Donnie wasn't among them.

Marshall issued a sigh of relief, rose and headed back along the sidewalk. He reached the point where the concrete ended at a door to the main building when Donnie shoved the door open on a dead run. For the second time in two days, Marshall and Donnie collided. They ended up entangled by jasmine vines and a broken trellis.

Marshall was first to regain his feet and extended a hand to help Donnie extricate himself from the plant. Donnie slapped his hand away.

"What the fuck are you doing in the middle of the sidewalk?"

Marshall suspected the question was rhetorical but answered anyway. "Walking."

Donnie pulled his right arm from a tangle of vines and wood lath. He bled from a scratch along his forehead.

"Um, you've got a cut up there..." Marshall said, pointing.

"Shit." A trickle of blood dripped off his eyelid. "Get me something to ..."

Marshall withdrew a handkerchief from his back pocket. Donnie eyed it suspiciously.

"It's clean," Marshall said.

"I'll get it back to you," Donnie pressed the white cloth to his wound and turned to go.

"Donnie, wait," Marshall felt his heart race and his palms go damp. "I need to talk to you about Samantha."

"Right." Donnie's voice dripped with sarcasm "I understand you guys are buddies now."

"Do you care what happens to her?"

"What I care about and don't care about hasn't got anything to do with you."

"Well, I do care. And if you pressure her to take drugs, you're going to hurt her."

"What, you're her mother now?"

Every instinct within him urged Marshall to turn and go. Reaching Donnie was impossible. Retreat was the only rational option. The nagging presence of future-Marshall, though, forced him to stand his ground. He took a deep breath.

"You've got a little more than twenty-four hours before you wreck your dad's Corvette and kill yourself. If you're determined to do that, fine. But you'll kill Samantha, too, and I'll do anything to keep that from happening."

Donnie stared coldly at Marshall for a long moment, then hammered Marshall's stomach with a quick thrust of his fist.

Marshall collapsed to a knee, scrabbling for breath.

Donnie bent over him and said softly, "Leave me the fuck alone, asshole."

And Donnie was gone.

From his knees Marshall slowly rolled to a fetal position, until, finally, he could pull in a breath. He sat up and said, "Well, we tried."

"You didn't try hard enough," Frank complained later that afternoon.

"Hey, you're welcome to talk to him if you want. He's not about to listen to anything I say. I'll go over there tomorrow night and pull Samantha out of the car if I have to, but I'm done talking to Donnie."

Sheila thought for a moment. "That's not a bad idea, Marshall. Frank and I will talk to Donnie. And maybe we can make life a little easier for you after we've gone."

An hour later, Sheila and Frank parked just off the road near one of Whittier's few traffic lights along Donnie's likely route home from school.

Unlike her more modest approach the day before, Sheila was dressed to leave the most indelible impression she could. Light makeup. Tight jeans. A tank top. She wore a sheer bra that did little to disguise the thrust of nipples through the fabric of her shirt. Her hair spilled over her shoulders.

She sat in the passenger seat and endured Frank's undisguised ogling.

Finally, she said, "Frank, please. You've seen me naked, what, a dozen times now? How about some professional courtesy and decorum here?"

Future-Frank might have tried to comply. Of the present-Frank, though, whose glimpses of her nude body were limited to future-Frank's memory, Sheila knew she had probably asked the impossible.

"Gawd, I can't believe we really do sleep together," he groaned.

"Yeah, well, I guess that will be another test of whether the future can change the past."

Frank looked away for a moment. But only a moment.

"Hey, here he comes," Sheila said.

As Donnie's pickup truck swung down the street from a block away, Frank drove to the light and ignored the green. Donnie came to a stop behind him and blasted his horn. Donnie's expression of irritation quickly resolved to one of unmitigated lust as Sheila exited her car and walked to his passenger-side window. She wiggled her index finger, instructing the boy to roll the window down.

"Hi, Donnie. I'm Sheila. We need to talk."

She took his gaping, staring lack of response as an invitation, pulled open the door and slid into the passenger seat.

"Let's go somewhere we can chat. The park maybe?"

Donnie could not seem to pry his eyes away from her breasts.

She snapped her fingers.

"Here. Up here. Read my lips. We need to drive away now. The light is green."

Donnie glanced at the intersection ahead. The car blocking him was gone.

"To the park?"

"Yes. We'll talk there."

He pulled into the empty parking lot behind the Community Building, turned off his engine, and squirmed as he again fondled every inch of Sheila with his eyes.

"Do you know who I am?"

"You're . . . you're that girl who was at school . . . oh. Oh, you're Marshall's cousin."

"Well, yes and no. I am that girl who was at school. I'm not Marshall's cousin."

The reference to Marshall seemed to break the hungry trance gripping Donnie and his irritation surfaced. "What is it with you guys? Why the sudden interest in me and Samantha? I haven't said two words to Marshall all year, and now the dork's all over me."

"It's because we asked Marshall to talk to you and Samantha," Sheila said.

"Who's 'we'?" Donnie demanded.

At that moment, Frank tapped at the driver's side window. Donnie jerked his head around.

Frank pulled open the door and pushed the button that rolled down the window. He shut the door and, elbows on the window frame, leaned into the conversation.

"This is Frank. We asked Marshall to talk to you. We're the ones who told Marshall what will happen to you and Samantha if you throw your party tomorrow night."

Donnie eyed Frank with apprehension painted on his face.

"Where do you get off having someone tell me I'll get killed?" he said, turning back to Sheila.

"You have less than twenty-four hours," Sheila said with no compassion in her voice. "You've caught a break, though, because you've become the subject of a physics experiment.

An experiment to see if people from the future can change the past."

"From the future?" Donnie's tone was derisive.

"Here's the deal. A decade from now, a secret program enables us to project people through time. That process is complicated. Right now, we're trying to determine whether the past can be changed. And you are a lucky subject of our experiment."

"What, did I win some sort of lottery or something?"

"No. You have the good fortune to know Marshall Grissom—or rather, Samantha has the good fortune to know Marshall Grissom. You're just along for the ride."

Donnie snorted a half laugh, half sneer. "Why Marshall?"

"Because we chose him. He thought we were nuts, too. But he cares enough about Samantha that he's willing to risk having people think he's crazy if it means saving her life."

"Forget Marshall," Frank interjected. "You'd better think about yourself. Here's what you've got planned for tomorrow. Your parents are out of town. You and your buddy Phil have asked Samantha and Phil's girlfriend to come over, right? Along with a few others? You've told them you have booze and grass.

"What you haven't told them is that you've scored some coke."

Donnie paled, clearly shaken by Frank's reference to the cocaine he'd purchased last weekend.

"You plan to get the girls wasted and have a party. I can relate to that. But you and Phil have also been arguing about which of you is the better driver, and you've been thinking about racing a couple of your father's cars. Tomorrow night, you get that argument mixed up with booze and drugs, and you and Samantha are toast."

Donnie's attempt at a reply was cut short when Frank held up his hand and warned him with a cold glare. "I don't care what you have to say. You know what I said is true. Live or die, Skippy, it's up to you. Let's go, Sheila."

This day—the day Samantha Kennedy and Donnie Court were, perhaps, fated to die—had tortured Marshall. Both Samantha and Donnie ignored him at school, and nothing could ease his fear of the evening ahead.

Now he, Frank and Sheila sat parked a block away from Donnie's house. A late-spring sun glowed low to their right, turning the western sky into a broad splash of crimson and yellow, interspersed with the most piercing shade of blue Marshall could remember. The low-light angle made adobe walls and fences throughout this old neighborhood glow like neon.

"So, do you think you got through to him?" Marshall asked for the tenth time since Sheila and Frank had relayed their conversation with Donnie.

Frank grunted.

Sheila reached from the driver's seat and patted Marshall's arm. "We've done everything we can. All we can do now is wait."

"And if they get into those cars . . ."

"We call the cops and send them to the dunes," Sheila said.

"What if cops don't get there in time? What if they're all somewhere else? This is a small town. The police here aren't—"

"It's what we're here to find out," Frank said. "There was never any guarantee you could change anything."

"That's what's shitty about this." Marshall shifted his gaze out the car windshield. "For all these years, I've felt awful about Samantha's death—because I lost someone I cared about. Now, though, if she dies it will be my fault. And I'll have to live with *that*."

"Think about it, Marshall," Frank said. "A couple of weeks from now the reality will fade."

"I don't think so, Frank. For me, recollections of each mission have grown clearer and stronger. I'm learning how to remember. And I'll remember this."

They were quiet for another half dozen minutes.

"I bet she doesn't even show up," Frank said.

He was wrong.

Only minutes later, driving her mother's car, Samantha passed them and pulled into Donnie's driveway. Phil and some of the others had already arrived.

As darkness settled in, Sheila moved their car directly across the street from Donnie's driveway. They waited another hour before doors to a four-car garage slid opened spilling light as a red mid-sixties Pontiac GTO rumbled forward followed by a white 1979 Corvette convertible.

Phil drove the GTO, his girlfriend beside him. Donnie, however, sat alone at the Vette's wheel. He pulled himself above the level of the windshield and turned to yell something into the garage.

Marshall stared with pounding heart as Samantha reluctantly emerged, her arms folded across her chest.

"Goddamn it, get in!" Donnie yelled at her.

When she took a step back, Donnie attempted a cop-show leap over the car's closed door. He landed awkwardly and fell, scraping his head along the driveway. A stream of blood flowed down his face. When he got to his feet, he was laughing.

"Donnie, you can't drive," Samantha yelled.

"Bullshit I can't drive. You just watch me drive. This fucker will hit one-forty. I've done it before."

"You go to the dunes like this and you'll get arrested."

"You believe future boy's shit, don't you? And those other two nutjobs. What's wrong with you? You used to want to have fun."

Samantha took a long look into the night sky, then trotted to the driver's side of the Corvette. She opened the door and got behind the wheel.

"I'm driving. I won't let you drive when you're like this. You'll run into something or hurt someone . . ."

The moment she got into the Corvette, Marshall was out of Sheila's car at a dead run. Donnie stood laughing beside the driver's-side door and tried to shove Samantha across the seat to the passenger side when Marshall knocked him to the ground.

"What the fuck!"

"Samantha," Marshall pleaded, climbing to his feet. "You can't. Please don't."

"Marshall, go away."

"It's happening, just like I said . . . right? You can't deny it."

"No! It's not! I didn't take drugs. I'm fine. But I can't keep him from going out there. I'll drive to make sure he docsn't get hurt—"

Donnie hit Marshall from the side with a full tackle that

scraped both of them painfully across the driveway's brickwork design. Donnie got to his knees astride Marshall and launched a fist at Marshall's face. When Marshall jerked his head aside, Donnie's hand pounded into the bricks.

Donnie's drugged state, though, must have masked the pain. He was poised to strike again when Frank wrapped him from behind and pulled him away.

"Nobody's going anywhere," Sheila said, stepping between Marshall and Donnie. "We've called the police. If either one of you takes these cars out of this driveway, they'll be all over you. You want to take a sobriety test tonight, Donnie? How about you, Phil?"

Phil shut down the GTO's rumbling engine. He tugged his girlfriend out the door. "Fuck this. We're out of here."

Marshall saw resistance fade from Donnie's body under the increasing pressure of Frank's grasp. Frank released him, and Donnie sagged to the grass.

"Get the keys to both cars," Sheila told Frank. "Donnie, go inside and stay there. Samantha, you should go home."

Samantha spun on Sheila with fury.

"Fuck you! Fuck all of you. Leave us alone. Just go away and leave us alone."

Marshall stepped toward her.

"Please, Sammy, I only want—"

"Marshall," she said with cold rage, "I will never speak to you again."

Marshall, Sheila, and Frank sat outside Donnie's house all night. Samantha's car remained when the sun came up. On

Thursday, May 10, 2035, though, Samantha and Donnie were alive.

"So, what now?" Frank asked.

"Now we can go," Sheila said.

"Some of us can," Marshall sighed.

"Marshall, I'm so sorry you're left to cope with this," Sheila said. "You did save her, though."

"Yeah." Marshall's adolescent heart choked with feeling for a girl who would forever despise him. "At least we did that."

The mission profile called for the travelers to return Thursday morning. Elvin was shooting for 7:00 a.m. Marshall, Sheila, and Frank drove to Whittier City Park and waited under the twisted elms. Their departure occurred at 7:18, leaving the counterparts of three travelers alone with themselves.

They regarded each other blankly for a moment. Sheila felt the accelerating decline of her future cognition. Soon they would be three strangers with a decade's worth of personal evolution ahead before they'd become the people each of them would eventually know.

"So that's it?" Marshall asked. His voice betrayed that he was drained, both physically and emotionally. "Now it just sort of fades away and we meet each other ten years from now?"

"I guess so," Sheila said. "Where do you want me to drop you?"

"At school."

"Don't you want to take a day off?"

"No . . . what would be the point? I can't miss any more classes. I still have to graduate, you know."

"How will you handle Donnie and Samantha?"

"I leave for Las Cruces in a month," said Marshall, who was enrolled in the summer session at New Mexico State University. "Dealing with Samantha apparently won't be an issue. And Donnie? Who knows? I guess he'll do whatever he'll do. I won't hide from him."

Sheila gave Marshall a hug. "Good for you."

She turned to Frank. "I'll drop you at your truck."

Frank flashed his best babe-magnet smile. "You want to get some breakfast first?"

"No. No, I don't. I just want to get back to Phoenix. And Frank, please don't call me."

She would be more than happy to remove Frank Altman from her life for another decade.

This time, Elvin hit the markers with precision and all three travelers simultaneously congealed into being. As always, technicians rushed forward with robes while medical techs stood by ready to deal with dizziness, disorientation, and the process of medical debriefing. Their task was simpler with this corps of veteran travelers.

Marshall felt the comfortable aloneness that always represented such a welcome contrast to the shared consciousness of projection. He also felt a sweeping relief knowing they'd done it! Samantha—at least the *Star Trek* Samantha—had been spared her fate at the dunes.

He quickly sorted through his memory and, indeed, clearly recalled seeing her—his heart aching all the while—walk across the stage at Whittier High School's graduation ceremony.

So, he smiled a weary smile when he saw Marta and Naomi rush to him.

"I'm here for you, Marshall," Naomi said.

Marta hugged him hard. "Me, too," she whispered.

"Hey, what about me?" Frank said, appearing alongside Marshall and spreading his arms wide. "I'm back, too."

They didn't even acknowledge Frank's presence. That's when Marshall saw the tears streaking Naomi's cheeks.

"Oh, no," Sheila said almost to herself. "It didn't work."

"I don't understand," Marshall said.

Then, he did understand.

The image of Samantha, so beautiful, wearing her smile and her cap and gown, crumbled into a memory of... *a funeral. Rushing back from Las Cruces. Wearing that damned suit in the heat of midsummer.*

Marshall's time traveling heroics had bought Samantha Kennedy an additional two months. The coroner called her drug overdose an accident.

"Send me back," he said with a quaking voice. "I can stop her. I can fix this."

"No, Marshall," Naomi said softly. "You can't change it. We may not be able to change anything."

Marshall studied Naomi's kind eyes for a moment longer and turned away. His memory led him next to Donnie. Their efforts had granted Donnie another four months. Donnie could have used Samantha's death as a pivotal axis to a constructive life. He could have been shocked into maturity and responsibility. With stark clarity, though, Marshall recalled their conversation, standing alone at Samantha's grave.

"You did this to her," Donnie had told him. "All that crazy shit you scared her with."

Only a few weeks earlier, the young Marshall would have allowed himself to be bullied into accepting the guilt.

"Fuck you, Donnie," he answered. "I loved her. I did everything I could to save her. And what did you do? Kept up the pressure, right? The drugs. The sex. Tearing her down instead of building her up. For once in your life, take some fucking responsibility."

Donnie shoved him hard.

Marshall had staggered back but he did not go down. Instead, he balled his fists and stood his ground defiantly next to Samantha Kennedy's tombstone, waiting for Donnie to pulverize him.

Breathing hard, Donnie took one step toward Marshall, then turned and walked away.

That evening, Marshall learned through friends, and for many of the evenings to follow, Donnie got very drunk. He died at the wheel of a white 1979 Corvette, out by the dunes, racing with his friend, Phil, who was driving a Pontiac GTO.

Marshall's suit stayed in the closet of his dorm room at New Mexico State on the day they buried Donnie Court.

The three travelers entered the Time Warp and drank quietly. Though Marshall hadn't wanted to come, Sheila and Marta insisted. They needed to be sure their friend was okay. They talked about things other than physics and history and time travel. They talked about details of their lives, which they thought good friends should know.

Barriers slipped away, and they simply became three people who cared for each other.

Marta couldn't remember experiencing anything like it. She felt only a little apprehension at the thought she might be heading to a place she hadn't planned to go with these people.

Very late that evening, Sheila and Marta escorted Marshall to his apartment and saw him safely inside. As they turned to go their separate ways, Sheila snapped her fingers. "Oh, yeah, I nearly forgot."

Marta walked back to her.

"You're a spy." Sheila grinned.

"I'm a . . . what?"

"Oh, don't worry. She told me. And she asked me to be sure to remind you of a memory you recognized through her mind."

Marta's eyes grew wide. "Yes. Yes, there was something. Something important . . ."

"She said it was about the man in the picture. She said you knew him from the Sandia Lab."

"The picture," Marta said to herself. "That's it."

Then she told Sheila, "Thank you for remembering. I have to go. See you tomorrow. Don't tell anyone I'm a spy."

Marta raced down the hall before Sheila could ask Marta once more about her toes. Sheila was concerned. This time her toenails were painted purple, with little green hearts in the middle of each one, even the tiny baby toes.

33

BREAKING THE FAST

MARTA POUNDED AT THE DOOR of Gillis Kerg's apartment. She waited a moment and pounded again. The knob turned. A crack emerged between door and door frame where a single bleary eye squinted out.

"Gillis, let me in."

"At last." He smiled. "You've come to your senses."

A man who didn't care for the confinement of pajamas, Gillis had wrapped himself with a towel before coming to the door. When he stepped back and placed his hand on the towel, ready to pull it free with a dramatic flair, Marta raised a restraining hand.

"Down, boy. This is business."

Gillis yawned. "Then I'll put on some pants."

He returned momentarily, wearing gym shorts and a t-shirt.

"Show me that picture again. Of the guy with Rose at the bar."

Gillis touched a small pad atop his desk. Marta heard a soft click. Gillis opened a bottom drawer, withdrew a file folder and handed her a grainy eight-by-ten photo.

"I know this guy," Marta said again. "He was at the

Sandia National Laboratory when I was there. I just have to think . . ."

"What jogged your memory?"

"The mission we just completed. I wasn't able to stay. I couldn't cope with the trauma of transition into my past self. She was completely overwhelmed. The memory transfer goes both ways, though. I was confronted by a whole set of fresh memories. Things I had forgotten. One was the image of that man and, for a moment, everything else stopped. I saw him clearly. He wasn't around much. But I saw him at the Sandia facility more than once."

"Okay, so you remember this guy who was somehow on the fringes at the National Laboratory, and is now an acquaintance of Leonard Rose . . ."

"Not just an acquaintance. This guy is meeting with Rose at a bar in Superior. That's forbidden."

"The security man who accompanies Rose off campus would have to be involved." Gillis absently straightened a pile of folders on his desk. "So, either Rose or this other guy has enough money or influence to compromise security protocols."

"How would he be connected and have access to both the National Laboratory and the GRC?"

"He could work for the government," Gillis said. "I'm sure some people transferred from there . . ."

"No, not the government. Private corporations. Both facilities conduct classified projects. Both facilities are government-initiated and government-regulated, but corporate entities are involved as well."

"Either way the guy would have an office. Even if he was in administration, you or I would know of him."

"Not necessarily. At the National Laboratory, the biggest corporations had liaisons assigned to whatever project they supported. Those guys just dropped by from time to time. The same arrangement exists here."

"So, if that's the case, he'd work for a corporation common to both facilities. That should narrow the search."

"Some," Marta agreed. "A lot of the same corporate players are at both facilities."

"So where should we go with this?"

"Leonard Rose is a slimy guy. My instincts tell me this mystery man is a sleazeball, too. If we can get some dirt to hold over Rose's head, we have a valuable tool at our disposal as the political battle unfolds here."

"I couldn't agree more. I think the place to start is with corporate reports and personnel rosters. See if we can find out who this other guy works for."

"I'll be tied up with debriefings and discussions regarding the Whittier mission. I'll owe you big time if you can handle that part of it for now."

"Oh, I like the sound of that." Gillis smiled.

Sheila had no illusions about the impending post-mission debate. She walked into the gathering of scientists and travelers the following morning with no intent to compromise.

"What more do you want?" she demanded as she stood and scanned an array of troubled or angry faces. "It didn't work. We can't change the past. There's nothing to accomplish here. It's time to stop!"

"That is not your call," Leonard Rose snapped from the

other side of the table. "When we make our formal report to the investors, we need to include a recommendation that emphasis be shifted to light speed research—"

A chorus of groans rolled around the table.

"Leonard," Gretchen said, "we have at our disposal a working time machine. Simple physics tells us that achieving the kind of speeds to make travel into the future possible—even with the energy sources now at our command—is unlikely . . .'"

"Travel to the past was *unlikely* five years ago," Rose parried.

". . . and even if the effort was successful, you still have the issue of getting anyone, or any information they might have gathered, back to the present. A time projector can't get them back to their originating universe."

"All we can do," Naomi suggested, "is report honestly the results of our work thus far. Our attempts to manipulate the past have resulted in the alteration of a few details. To this point, though, we've made no substantive changes. With continued research—"

"You think if we go to the board with this conclusion there will be any more research?" said Rose. "Nobody will keep throwing money at this if you tell them there's no return."

"There's plenty of opportunity for return," Gretchen said. "It's just not the instant gold mine everyone envisioned. Consider the pure research opportunity. And history. Learning from history has always been crucial to mankind's future. If used carefully and judiciously, we have a tool that can be—"

"So, you're willing to put time travel into the hands of

something like the National Geographic Society?" Rose gave a sardonic laugh. "If you treat it like the public library, it will be funded like the public library."

Sheila could stand it no longer. She slapped the table with her open palm. "Listen to yourselves! Past, future, none of this is right! The only recommendation we should make is to stop before we do any more damage."

Rose made a dismissive gesture, a comment on the irrelevance of her argument, and that infuriated her.

"You know, I could walk out of here right now and let the world know what's happened," she said. "Put this whole debate onto a much larger stage—"

"And spend the rest of your life in prison," Rose said.

"Maybe, maybe not. I'm thinking most people won't be very happy to know you're fooling with forces that could wipe their whole universe out of existence!"

Rose scowled, turned away from Sheila and appealed to Yuni.

"We need to plan another mission. We need to explain to the investors this was not a fair test. Too many aspects of the Whittier mission were compromised by the bias of—"

"Bias?" Sheila said. "Bullshit! It. Didn't. Work!"

"No attempt was made to place the wager!" Rose jumped to his feet as well. "And we did keep the two young people from dying. We did change the path of history!"

"Only temporarily," Naomi pointed out again. "And—whatever the reason was—you can't get around the outcome where the bet was concerned. Marta didn't realize an economic benefit from a manipulation of the past."

"Because she failed to carry out her assignment," Rose said.

"Because she followed mission protocol that precluded her carrying out her assignment," Elvin said, pointing his pencil at Rose. "And you agreed to that protocol, right along with the rest of us."

Sheila was surprised. Elvin had made his opinion clear enough. He did not want to see exploration of the past stymied. He thought Sheila's position went entirely too far.

"The other protocol everyone agreed to," Elvin continued, "is keeping the influence of investors separated from the science. You've lost sight of that altogether, Leonard. I care about physics research. I don't want some corporate asshole telling me how to do it."

"Even if you disregard my inability to carry out my assignment," Marta said to Rose, "let's not overlook Frank. His stock investment didn't produce any results either."

"It would have if . . ." Rose began.

"But it didn't."

"Only because Frank's an idiot," Rose retorted.

"Hey, wait a minute," Frank said, roused from his boredom at the far end of the oak table.

Rose scowled at him.

If, indeed, Frank's stock investment had been allowed to stand, he would be a wealthy man. Six months after he bought his shares for $200, though, the stock price made a small surge and past-Frank, seeing the opportunity for a trip to Vegas, cashed out for $1,000.

Yuni stepped into the fray and redirected the discussion.

"Elvin, will you please give us your summary regarding the results of our team's actions in the *Star Trek* universe?"

Much to his discomfort, soon after the return of the

travelers Elvin suffered a visitation from his *Star Trek* counterpart. With minor discrepancies, the Elvins concluded, the outcomes in each universe were the same. Elvin offered his summation to the group and sat down to an uncomfortable silence.

"We have to do it again," Rose said finally. "A new mission, new goals. We can't make a recommendation to the board without more evidence."

"Then you'll do it without me," Sheila said. She knew she wasn't speaking for Marta or Marshall. She didn't care. She was done. Whatever the consequences, she would take this battle to other fronts.

As the others continued to argue, she glanced sadly at Marshall, who sat at the edge of the pandemonium, staring at the wall opposite his chair while the debate ricocheted around him.

Everyone stopped talking when he finally said, "I want to try again. I think we learned some things. I think I could go back and keep her from—"

Naomi did not look at him when she said, "We can't, Marshall."

"Why not?"

"Because," Rose said, "this team of travelers became too emotionally entangled here. You've lost sight altogether of our purpose. The point of the experiment isn't to save one girl from the result of her poor choices. The point is to determine whether we can change the past of our own world. We will have to undertake a different mission with a different set of travelers."

The meeting broke up with the debate unresolved. Rose hurried directly to his office, where he opened his top desk drawer and took a new, preprogrammed phone out of its plastic packaging. He pushed a single button. "I'm clear."

He left the physics wing and descended another layer further beneath the desert. One more elevator up, one more door, and he faced Andrew Gormly across a steel desk.

He delivered a complete account of the mission and resulting debate. He gave his best estimate of who would eventually line up where when the final report was submitted to the board.

"We have too much invested to make any decisions based on an experiment that might have been sabotaged by the travelers' bias," Gormly said after digesting Rose's analysis.

Rose felt a wave of relief. He'd been afraid Gormly would use the mission's failure as an excuse to recommend Hemisphere's immediate withdrawal. And that would initiate the fall of other key dominoes.

"Exactly," Rose said. "There's too much at stake here. If we stop now, we don't have any idea what we'd be walking away from."

"Oh, don't get me wrong. I've got no qualms about walking away," Gormly said. "The minute I'm convinced we can't get a very large return, I'll recommend that Hemisphere pull the plug. I don't think we can conclude that yet."

"Exactly. And as I said, Frank Altman's report suggested halfhearted efforts by the other three."

"Then next time we must get our people on that team and keep these three out of it."

"That's a lot easier said than done. They are the ones with the experience. It's doubtful that novice travelers could have completed the initial moments of the projection without succumbing to the disorientation and bailing out. Marta Hamilton is convinced if she had continued, her younger *Star Trek* counterpart would have suffered serious mental injury. And don't forget, we have to prove not only that we can profit from time travel, we also have to prove humans can survive the process."

"We'll use that to get Hamilton off the team," Gormly said. "She failed. She couldn't cut it. You can certainly make that argument."

Rose agreed that he could. He could hear himself telling Michael Huxtable with somber and studied judgment, *Marta Hamilton is simply not suited for time travel.*

Gormly continued. "I don't care who survives or who doesn't. We can deal with the human issues later. What you have to prove is that my company can make a buck here. You prove that, we'll deal with the other issues."

"So, we need a different group of travelers." Rose pondered the dilemma for a moment. "I can get Marta suspended from the team, at least for a while. But how do we deal with Marshall and Sheila?"

"Don't worry too much about Grissom. I'll handle that," Gormly said cryptically. "Our immediate problem is with Schuler. She's a political time bomb. If this project somehow goes public and these ethical issues become the province of open debate, we're dead in the water. If that happens, I will recommend Hemisphere distance itself immediately. We won't sit here and hemorrhage money while politicians and liberal crybabies argue."

"It's one thing for her to make a threat. It's quite another for her to carry it out," Rose said. "She really would be facing serious prison time."

"And she would become a hero to every anti-business pro-environment crusader on the planet. Never under-estimate a true believer. Martyrs are dangerous."

"We may not have to do anything," Rose said, "Sheila indicated at the meeting she would not be part of any more projections."

"As you said, there will be a powerful lobby to include her, and she could always change her mind. No, we must find a more permanent solution to Ms. Schuler, and we have to do it now."

"Um, wait a minute. I won't be a part of—"

"You're already a part of it," Gormly said, his gaze malevolent.

"Look, you don't have to harm her. She's already said enough to legitimize an arrest and confinement for violation of her contract. I haven't pushed for that yet, but if I go to the administrator and relay her threats, he'll have to—"

Gormly held up a hand, cutting Rose off. "Clearly, she has a support faction within the project. Once she's arrested and confined, that faction will coalesce into a campaign. And then it's only a matter of time before everything blows up. The resolution of this issue must be final. You say she's already told everyone she's leaving. That will cover her disappearance long enough for another mission to be conducted."

Despite the chill of the underground room, Rose felt dampness spreading from his armpits. He grasped the table's edge to keep his hands from trembling.

Breaking an uncomfortable silence, Gormly switched gears.

"What kind of a job do you think the three mission directors are doing?" he asked Rose. "Are they reigning in Detwyler at all, or is he running this program now?"

"The man is a menace." Rose's anger quashed his other emotions. "He takes credit for revelations he gets from other universes. The arrogant bastard lords it over everyone. And none of the mission directors will stand up to him. He's a lab tech, for God's sake!"

"Maybe what we need is a change at the top. Maybe Andropov and Allen and Naomi Hu simply aren't up to the challenge. Maybe that's why these missions aren't producing results."

Rose looked sharply at Gormly.

"That's right, Dr. Rose. I think you would fit Yuri Andropov's position nicely. To reach that point, though, we have this other problem we must resolve first."

Rose slumped into his seat. "I can't... I won't be involved with hurting anyone."

"Nobody will get hurt, Leonard. She'll just take a trip into the past."

As Rose made his way to his clandestine assignation with Andrew Gormly, Sheila was sneaking away as well. She wanted only to escape. She sought the nearest refuge she could think of—the women's locker room. She made her way to the last locker of the last row. She placed her hands high above her head and leaned heavily against the wall, its concrete slick with condensation.

When she heard the shuffle of footsteps across tile, she started to order the intruders away, then glanced to see Marta walking toward her, towing Marshall by the hand. Marshall's free hand shielded his eyes from a forward view.

"Relax, Marshall," Sheila said, smiling despite the anger still coursing through her. "There's nobody else here. You can look."

"How are you handling everything?" Marta asked her.

Sheila shook her head, eyes shining with a hint of tears.

"I think I'm done with this." She sat heavily on the bench facing the row of lockers. "I know you both disagree . . ."

"We don't disagree with your concerns," Marta said. "We . . . I . . . might disagree with you regarding how those concerns are represented . . ."

"If you can't continue," Marshall said, sitting next to her, "then I respect that, Sheila. If we knew when we started what we know now, who knows if any of us would have chosen to be involved. We are where we are, though. And given everything that's happened, I can't walk away. Not yet."

Sheila hugged Marshall. "I can't imagine what you must be going through. That's the most insidious thing. They've manipulated a tragedy for which you were in no way responsible and left you with guilt you'll bear all your days."

"I don't know about that. All I know is I can't just let it go. I have to stay involved here. Because sooner or later, if I work hard enough maybe I can convince them to let me try again. Maybe if we went back and stopped the sexual abuse . . ."

"What, you'll travel as a ten-year-old and keep Samantha's

father from assaulting his little girl? Marshall, that's ludicrous. And when that doesn't work, you'll recruit some ninety-year-old to return to *his* childhood and stop whatever abuse turned Samantha's father into a predator? You want to know what I think? I don't think we can change our past at all—not anything of significance. I think we're just screwing with the futures of everyone from these other universes when we try to change anything."

She hugged Marshall again and turned to Marta.

"I'm worried about this guy," she said, rubbing Marshall's back. "But right now, I have to get away from everyone and do some thinking. You take care of Marshall for me, okay?"

Marta linked her arm through Marshall's and smiled.

"I will. And Sheila, don't do something rash. Talk to me before you decide anything."

Sheila rose from the bench and walked toward the door. At the end of the long row of lockers, she turned and waved to her friends.

Walking through the corridor, Marshall glanced at Marta. "I'll be fine. I really will. You don't have to . . ."

"Look, I know I'm not the most sociable person. But even I understand there are times when it's better to be with someone than to be alone. And besides, I promised Sheila." Again, she linked her arm with his and steered him down the hallway, glancing up every few steps to check the somber face more than a foot above her. "We could stop at the Time Warp for a drink."

"I don't think so," Marshall said. "There'd be people

there. They'd want to ask me about the mission . . ."

"Okay, my place. We'll just hang out."

When they reached Marta's apartment, Marshall slumped on her couch. She stepped to the other side of a low bank of cabinets that separated the kitchenette from the living room.

"Beer, wine, tequila?" she asked.

"Do you mind if I pass? I just keep thinking of Samantha and the drugs and alcohol and . . ."

"Isn't it fading at all?"

"Not that I can tell. And what's more, details of other missions seem to be coming back. That's ironic, isn't it? When this is the one I'd want most to forget."

"Wow," Marta said, "see, the whole taser thing is already vague for me."

She poured herself a glass of wine and sat beside Marshall.

Not too close, though. Gillis's suggestion that she work her way into Marshall's life to discern his true purpose had left some emotional residue. Marta had a carefully tuned inner alarm about situations like this one.

Because she didn't *date*, she knew many people thought she was sexually indifferent. They were wrong. She was anything *but* sexually indifferent. And she wasn't above using sex as a means of gathering information. She was, however, disciplined.

That's what the alarm was for.

Marta certainly didn't operate under the assumption Marshall was sexually indifferent. His lack of indifference became more evident every time he took center stage on the projection platform. Marshall, she suspected, lived a life of limited sexuality, because he couldn't conceive that someone else might find him attractive. The attention Marshall had begun to receive from people like Wanda Mays, though, meant his self-concept was destined to change. And if Gillis was wrong and Marshall *was* the baffled, unassuming fellow he appeared to be, Marshall would probably change, too. Which, Marta thought, would be a shame. For all his physical and social awkwardness, Marta had to admit she'd been seeing Marshall differently for some time now. And it wasn't just the whole humongous dick thing. Most men posed and strutted and strove to out-gender any would-be rival to stake out territory. An unassuming, modest and simply good-hearted man was a refreshing exception.

If her instinctive impression was the truth about Marshall. *That's the real question, isn't it?* she thought. She considered her own sexuality. How the throes of genuine ecstasy stripped her of guile and deceit.

Hmmmmmm.

Marta drank from her wine glass and glanced at Marshall. Marshall fidgeted and offered a tentative smile. Marta smiled back. The alarm sounded louder.

Thank goodness for the alarm. Because, by God, she was horny! And who knew what might happen if not for that . . .

". . . fucking alarm," she said aloud.

"What?"

And Marta jumped him.

They were lips and tongues and hands and heat. A virtual blizzard of clothing littered Marta's living room. For the first time since that first projection, Marta noted thankfully, Marshall displayed not a shred of embarrassment about being hard as a nail.

She freed him from his pants, wrapped him with both her hands and said, "Finally!"

She pushed Marshall back and climbed aboard, easing herself down, slowly and carefully at first, then attacking with the rhythm of a jackhammer. Marshall exploded in a matter of minutes and reached up to still Marta while he caught his breath.

He wore an expression of awe.

In the aftermath of Marshall's release, Marta felt the impossible fullness within her begin to subside and thought with a smile that Nigel Smythe would have a lot to live up to.

Gradually she relaxed as well, lay on his chest and kissed him. The kiss was nice. Up to this point, kissing had fallen victim to more urgent priorities.

"Boy, did I ever have you read wrong," Marshall gasped.

"Disappointed?"

"I'd have to say I'm ... um ... thrilled ... right down to my toes."

"We'll get to your toes in a minute."

Marta began to rotate her hips with an almost imperceptible movement. Marshall's response was immediate. Marta's movements lost their subtlety. Marshall captured her rhythm and took over. Each thrust impaled her, and she responded with a groan that could have been pain, but whenever Marshall started to retreat, she answered with a short verbal burst.

"Go, go, go. For God's sake, don't stop now!"

In retrospect, Marta couldn't believe the performance.

They variously occupied the couch, the bed, the floor, two chairs—one of them on rollers—the kitchen countertop, a closet with a sturdy hangar bar, and the shower. Which was quite a trick because Marta was so short and Marshall so tall.

Still the waves of lust refused to subside.

Their passion was interrupted by momentary sweaty intervals during which they lay together in a state of astonishment. Then, one or the other would grow restless and initiate the whole process anew.

At last, with critical points of her anatomy raw and aching, Marta surrendered.

"You . . . um . . . you mind if I stay?" Marshall asked. "I don't know if I can make it home."

"Please," Marta said. "I'd be disappointed if you didn't."

Tucked into the nook between Marshall's arm and chest, she drifted to sleep.

34

LUST AND DECEIT

LOUD KNOCKING STARTLED Marshall from an incredibly erotic dream. His sleeping vision had been ... *Oh my God! It wasn't a dream. She's here. She's right here. And we ... we ... Wow!*

The knocking persisted.

"Mmmmmm," mumbled Marta without opening her eyes, "Marshall, go see who's at the door."

"Um ... okay ... but I'm naked ..."

"Me, too." She rolled over and sat up.

No question about it. Marta was incredibly naked.

"Um ... I would except ... it's your apartment ..." he apologized.

"Oh, yeah."

Marta slid out of bed and stretched luxuriantly. She pulled on her oversized t-shirt and padded out toward the persistent rapping. She opened the door to Gillis Kerg.

"Sorry to get you up so late," Gillis said quickly. "I knew you'd want to know I've identified our mystery man ... Oh, my."

He looked past Marta. She turned, following his eyes, and saw Marshall peek from the bedroom doorway.

"Um . . . Excuse me . . . I can come back at a later . . ."

"No, Gillis." Marta yawned and scratched at her side. "You're already here, and we're awake."

Marshall decided if Marta wasn't embarrassed, he shouldn't be either, though he did remain mostly hidden behind the door frame.

Gillis gave him a brief nod. "Mr. Grissom."

"Mr. Kerg," Marshall replied.

"I hate to be this way," Gillis nodded toward Marshall, "but I don't know if what we must talk about should be discussed with someone who isn't . . . uh . . . ?"

"Isn't what?" Marshall asked, feeling defensive.

Marta yawned again. "Marshall, I'm a spy. Gillis is a spy. There're lots of spies here. Are you okay with that?"

At this moment, Marshall was inclined to be okay with anything Marta wanted to be or do. "Um, sure, I suppose."

"Are you going to tell anyone what we talk about?"

"Not if you don't want me to."

"Good enough, Gillis?"

Gillis gave her an incredulous look, then nodded his assent.

Wrapped with a towel, Marshall scavenged the apartment for his clothes. He found his shirt easily enough, his pants a crumpled wad under an overturned chair. One sock hung from the ceiling light fixture, the other pulled over a wine bottle in lieu of a cork. His underwear was in the refrigerator. Marshall made a mental note to ask Marta about the refrigerator when Gillis wasn't around.

As Marshall searched, Gillis pulled Marta aside,

questioning her judgment with raised eyebrows and a nod in Marshall's direction.

"Don't look at me like that," she whispered. "You said I should get a little closer to him."

"A little?" he whispered back as he withdrew a photograph from his inside jacket pocket, showed it to Marta. "The gentleman is Andrew Gormly, Hemisphere Investment Group's liaison with the GRC project."

Glancing at the photo over Marta's shoulder, Marshall said, "I could have told you that."

Marta and Gillis offered puzzled looks.

"He introduced himself to me after he observed a mission a while back."

"What did he want?" Marta asked with narrowed eyes.

"He told me I was doing a good job."

"Did you see him in the company of Leonard Rose?" Gillis asked.

"No. He was waiting to catch an elevator to the surface. Why are you guys interested in him?"

"We think," Marta said, "Gormly and Rose are cooking up some kind of scheme and violating security guidelines while they're doing it. Having something to hold over Rose's head, particularly if he makes trouble for Sheila, would be a good option for us."

"I plugged both Gormly and Rose into my recognition software," Gillis said, "Gormly shows up several times over the past year . . ."

"You plugged them into what?" Marshall asked.

"Marshall," Marta said, "Gillis is an expert at surveillance. If you haven't noticed, security cameras record pretty much everything that happens here."

"Everything?" Marshall gulped.

"Not personal living spaces."

Marshall breathed a sigh of relief.

". . . and the security archive stores the video. Gillis is able to tap into that data with his recognition software and find almost anyone . . ."

"Wow," Marshall said. "They let you do that?"

"No," Gillis said. "They don't."

"Oh."

"As I was saying, they've avoided any contact. When they've been at the same place, neither has given any indication of knowing the other. When he talked to you, Gormly just said you were doing a good job. He didn't ask about anything else?"

"No. He started out really friendly, like he wanted to have a conversation. But I think I embarrassed him, and he left."

"You embarrassed him?" Gillis asked.

"Yeah. I brought up Raul."

Marta looked at Gillis then back to Marshall. "Okay, wait a minute. How does Raul fit this picture?"

"Gormly approached me by the elevators. I'd seen him somewhere, so I thought I was supposed to know him. You know how it is when you can't remember someone's name? Then he said Hemisphere Investment Group, and I remembered. Back at the travelers' reception during orientation stuff when we first got here. He was talking with Raul, and they seemed to know each other. I think he was a friend of Raul's. With Raul being a deserter and all, this Gormly guy got uncomfortable when I mentioned Raul to him."

"Gillis," Marta said urgently, "do you have your stuff? Can you run a cross check on Gormly and Raul?"

"Got it. I'll upload Raul's photo from personnel files."

Gillis withdrew his pocket computer and placed it atop Marta's desk. A three-dimensional display appeared above the device and a 3-D image of a keyboard materialized. A vague blur of humanity began to fly across the virtual screen floating above the device. They waited ten minutes before *No Matches Found* flashed across the screen.

"Damn . . ." Marta said.

"Oh, don't give up yet," Gillis said. He tapped a couple of virtual keys and a tiny X began flashing at the corner of the screen. "We've only seen the official video file. Now we'll find what my worm comes up as we see the hijacked footage I receive whenever a security camera is manually disabled."

A blur of faces streamed past for several minutes more before the screen resolved to a bit of video showing Raul walking from an office door, glancing quickly to his right, then facing the surveillance camera before walking into the hallway.

"So, where's Gormly . . . ?" Marta asked.

"Just wait. The software wouldn't have given us Raul if Gormly wasn't close."

Gillis pushed fast forward, and Andrew Gormly stepped from the same office door.

Marta noted the time and date stamp. "This is late evening. Right about the time Raul disappeared."

"Raul didn't just disappear," Gillis said.

"That's taking a huge risk." Marta nodded, meeting Gillis's gaze. "And the possibility that they could get past security to get off campus is miniscule. So, where's the body?"

"Body? What are you talking about?" Marshall asked with alarm. Before they could answer, though, he gave a gasp. "Oh, no!"

"What?" Marta said.

"Run that back."

"Run what back?" Gillis asked.

"The video. You guys missed it while you were talking."

Gillis did a quick rewind, and sure enough, a few minutes after Gormly disappeared from view, a third person appeared, walking the same direction Raul had taken. A man wearing a maintenance worker uniform and pushing a wheeled trash barrel.

"What?" Marta asked. "What did you see?"

"That janitor." Marshall's voice trembled. "If you're serious about there being a body, then I . . . I think maybe I helped that janitor get rid of Raul."

The call roused Sheila from a fitful sleep.

She fumbled with her phone.

"What?"

"Ms. Schuler?"

She recognized Leonard Rose's voice.

"What do you want? It's the middle of—"

"Ms. Schuler, we have what we fear is a critical situation, and we need you in the projection lab right away."

Sheila tried to push back the fog of sleep and make sense of what Rose was saying. *Critical situation? It's the middle of the night, for God's sake. Nobody would be in the projection lab at two a.m.*

"What are you talking about? What's happened?"

"Marshall," Rose said. "Apparently he's taken it upon himself to return to 2035 and keep his friend from dying. We've lost his lifeline. Someone must go back to find out what's happened."

Sheila immediately felt wide awake. None of this made any sense.

"Taken it upon himself? He couldn't operate the projector . . . Who helped him?"

"I'll give you details when you get here. But please hurry."

"What, did Elvin help send him back? That asshole—"

"Mr. Detwyler is very busy. Again, we don't know all the details . . ."

"How did you find out?" Sheila knew that Rose would be the last person whose help Marshall would enlist, and likewise, Rose would be the last person to give it.

"Please, we'll explain when you get here. You must come now. And don't tell anyone else. We want to keep this quiet to preserve the careers of the people involved."

Goddamn, Marshall, Sheila thought, *what have you gone and done?* "I'm on my way."

She threw on a sweatshirt and workout pants and grabbed her cell phone. She thought of who Marshall might have asked to help him and could only come up with people Rose despised. *Why would Rose want to protect their careers? He was right, though. The fewer people who know about this, the better. Except Marta. Had Rose called Marta, too? If not, Marta damn sure needed to know. She would want to help.*

Sheila spoke Marta's dialing code and heard only a loud intermittent buzz.

Shit! What a time for the cell relays to be down.

She dialed the facility's voicemail system, left a message that would go through when service was restored, and headed to the projection lab.

"You helped him kill Raul?" Marta asked with utter incredulity. "Marshall, unless I've misjudged you completely, I don't think there's any way—"

"I didn't do it on purpose."

Marshall told them about his late-night wandering through corridors, and the janitor with a trash barrel stuck at the projection lab entrance. "And something about it's been bothering me ever since. Something didn't seem right . . ."

"Why do you think Raul was in the trash barrel?" Gillis asked.

"That's what's finally occurred to me. Think about it. Why would a janitor be taking a full trash barrel *into* the lab?"

"And that's how you dispose of a body when you have a time machine," Marta said.

Gillis was back at his virtual keyboard.

"Security records identify the janitor as Jason Pratt."

"Check the work schedule."

"Mr. Pratt is pulling a graveyard shift right now at the computer labs."

"I think," Marta said, "we should have a talk with the janitor."

Gillis grinned. "My thoughts exactly."

Marta disappeared into her bedroom.

"Marshall," she called, "where are the phones?"

"Um ... I can't find mine. I think I saw yours in the sink."

"Can you get it for me, please?"

She returned wearing form-fitting stretch pants, running shoes, and a loose pullover shirt. She raised the shirt enough to tuck a pistol into a holster at the small of her back.

"That's a gun," Marshall said.

"Yes, it is."

"You can't have a gun. They don't allow guns ..."

"Yes, but I'm a spy, remember? We have guns they don't know about."

"Do you have a gun?" Marshall asked Gillis.

Gillis shrugged and nodded.

"I don't have a gun," Marshall said.

"If you ever need one," Marta said, "you can borrow mine. We'll be back—"

"No way. I'm not letting you go out there by yourself with a gun."

A smile tugged at her lips. "It's what I do, Marshall."

"Either you let me come, or I'll tell everyone about your gun."

She rolled her eyes. "All right. Just stay out of the way."

"What if she calls someone?" Rose asked.

Andrew Gormly gestured to a janitor who stood by the control panel for the time projection unit.

"Mr. Pratt has installed a device that will mask any signals in this quadrant of the complex," Gormly explained. "Everyone will simply think the cell relay boosting signals through all this concrete is down again."

"I've done my part," Rose said with a shudder. "I don't need to be here for the rest of it."

"Ah, to the contrary, Dr. Rose, I need you to stay right where you are."

Marta mentally ran the scenario as she, Gillis and Marshall navigated elevators and hallways. Initially, she'd seen the Gormly-Rose alliance as a simple security violation—and an opportunity to blackmail Rose into compliance when the need occurred. Now, though, the issue had become murder.

"Here?" she asked Gillis as he signaled his companions to stop outside a door marked *East Wing Computer Lab*.

"According to the maintenance schedule."

Marta took the pistol from her waistband and held it behind her back.

"If he runs, Gillis, you and I will stop him however we have to. Marshall, wait here."

Marta pulled Marshall away from the door, turned the knob, and pushed. Row upon row of computer stations filled the room. A vacuum hummed somewhere among the rows.

Marta and Gillis split up, each going to the opposite end of the room. Peering along the length of the third row Marta found a small man wearing headphones and fussing with an attachment to his vacuum. Gillis appeared at the opposite end. Still holding the pistol behind her back, Marta approached the man. When he noticed her, he jumped with fright.

"Holy sweet Jesus," he said, switching off his vacuum and pulling the headphones down around his neck. "You scared the crap out of me."

"I'm sorry. I'm looking for Jason Pratt."

"No, he got sick," the man said. "Couple hours ago. Sick as a dog. Threw up over by that last computer bank. They sent him home. I came to clean up the mess."

Surreptitiously, Marta tucked the pistol into her waistband. The janitor turned to see Gillis walking toward them.

"Anything wrong here?"

"No," Marta said, "we just have an issue regarding Mr. Pratt. Something about overtime. We were asked to speak to him."

"Well, you'll find him at his apartment, I'm sure. Looked like the living dead when I saw him last."

Only a few steps into the projection lab, Sheila knew something was wrong. The only people here were Leonard Rose, a janitor, and a portly man wearing a suit whom she'd never seen.

"Where's Elvin?" she demanded of Rose. "Why isn't anyone here?"

When Rose said nothing, she confronted the man in the suit. "Who the hell are you? You can't be here. This is a secure facility. We've got work to do."

Rose remained mute. He would not meet her eyes.

"You must forgive Dr. Rose," suit guy said to her. "He is not particularly enthusiastic about our mission."

"*Our* mission? I'll ask again: who the hell are you, and why do think you have any part in—"

"My name is Andrew Gormly. I'm employed by the Hemisphere Investment Group to see that its financial interests are best represented. And, with all modesty, I must say I—perhaps more than any other individual—can influence this program's future. The reports I make to select members of Hemisphere's board will determine whether they continue to fund time travel research."

"You can get out of here and tell your board members to keep their money. Time travel doesn't work the way they want it to. And if you expect me to be impressed by . . ."

She had stepped around Elvin's empty desk. The monitors were blank.

"Please, Ms. Schuler," suit guy said as he smiled. "Give me a moment to explain."

Sheila glanced toward the hallway. The janitor had positioned himself between her and the inner airlock door. He held a weapon of some kind.

"The monitors are not operating," suit guy said, "because Dr. Rose's call was a fabrication. Your Mr. Grissom is probably home in bed. We needed you here, because you have grown tiresome and we feel no matter what course you take, you will be an obstacle to the future of this program. So, you're being reassigned."

"Reassigned?"

"Yes. To another universe."

The janitor stepped toward Sheila. He pointed what Sheila recognized as an electronic weapon. "You can either cooperate, or not. I'll ask once nicely for you to disrobe. We don't want to hurt you."

At that moment, the plan became clear. Fright compromised Sheila's anger. As the janitor advanced, Sheila made a quick evaluation. He was older, probably late fifties, clearly in good shape. He moved with a comfortable athleticism. Sheila wasn't afraid of physical confrontation, but she knew she'd have to be lucky to get past him.

She searched for anything that could serve as a weapon. Pencils. A small jar full of yellow Ticonderoga #2 pencils sat at Elvin's computer station. Elvin obsessed over having sharpened pencils at his fingertips to fill legal pads with notes and unfathomable mathematical sentences.

Now she could read the logo on the side of the janitor's weapon. *Zap-Yo-Ass Taser Corp.*

"This doesn't have to be difficult," the janitor warned.

Sheila wondered how quickly Pratt could track her with the stunner.

She'd find out.

Screened by the monitors, she took a handful of pencils from the jar. She forced herself to relax, trying to communicate surrender through body language. She saw the janitor lower his weapon slightly. She made her move. She feinted to her left, as if to go around Elvin's desk. When the janitor raised his taser, she pushed off hard with her left foot and leapt to her right. She slammed into Rose as hard as she could. As she began her dive, she heard the crackle of the stunner's charge burn the air above her.

Rose collapsed with a scream. Sheila rolled him to a sitting position, her arm clamped hard around his neck, kneeling behind him for cover. She jabbed sharp pencil points onto his carotid artery. "Back off, or I'll shove these pencils through him! He'll bleed out before—"

The janitor laughed, moving around the desk toward a point where he'd have a clear shot. She maneuvered Rose as a shield. A red laser dot danced over his head and chest. His breath came with quick, panicked spurts just short of sobs.

"Ms. Schuler," said suit guy, "I could care less what happens to Dr. Rose. Run him through if you want. You'll accomplish nothing but a slight and messy delay of the inevitable."

The janitor kept coming.

Sheila felt Rose quivering in her grip. With disgust, she shoved him aside, dropped the pencils, and stood.

"Good choice," Gormly said. "Leonard, pull yourself together and go down the hallway to the equipment closet. There you will find a device installed by Mr. Pratt to disrupt cell service. We need to get the phones operating again. The last thing we want is for someone to complain and send a maintenance crew. And don't linger. I want you back here immediately."

Marta, Marshall, and Gillis walked toward the maintenance workers living units when Marta's cell phone vibrated. She glanced at the screen.

"Voice message," she said, putting the phone to her ear, "from Sheila."

"Hi, it's me. I'm afraid Marshall has done something stupid and talked Elvin into sending him to try and save Samantha again. Leonard Rose called me and said they've lost him. I'm heading to the lab now."

"Oh, no!"

"What?" asked Marshall.

Marta replayed the message.

"But I didn't . . . ," Marshall said.

"Of course, you didn't. Rose lied to get Sheila to the lab. And where do you think we'll find Jason Pratt?"

"We have to get over there!" Marshall said.

"Gillis," Marta called over her shoulder, "find Elvin and get him to the projection lab as quickly as you can."

"What are you gonna do?" Sheila asked Gormly with all the venom she could muster.

"We need you out of the way for a while. The corporation I represent must know exactly what is and isn't possible here. If we really can't manipulate the past, you'll get your way. Everything will stop because we'll pull our funding. We need accurate results, though, and I'm afraid your concerns will only complicate that process. You'll be sent to another universe, and I'm sure that, in time, your friends will come and get you. So please, don't fight us. I assure you, Mr. Pratt can be quite heavy-handed."

The janitor stood five feet from her. "Once again," he said, "this doesn't need to be difficult."

Sheila fixed the janitor with her most intense glare and felt a moment of satisfaction as the man hesitated, then backed off a step.

Behind Pratt, Rose returned.

"Please," the janitor said, gesturing again to Sheila with his weapon.

Sheila hesitated, then turned her back and pulled her sweatshirt over her head. She made the move with deliberation and felt the three men lean closer for a better view. She turned slowly, anticipating the moment when the janitor's eyes would fall to her bare breasts. At that instant she flung the sweatshirt and made a lunge for the door behind him. He jumped back, instinctively raising his hands to counter this assault. As she ran past, Sheila made a quick swipe at the taser.

Pratt fumbled the device but didn't drop it.

Only one step from the door and the safety of the hallway, she heard the crackle of the stunner's charge and felt a crippling sting bloom across her back.

Sheila crumpled to the floor.

She sensed someone standing over her. Her view was converted to the bright lights of the ceiling as the janitor rolled her to her back. Her peripheral vision absorbed a shaking Rose and the leering Gormly.

The janitor stepped from her view, only to reappear momentarily with a triumphant grin as he displayed the rest of her clothing like a trophy. Her vision spun recklessly as Pratt lifted her nude form over his shoulder in a fireman's carry. He hauled her to the projection platform where he laid her carefully on her back.

The first sign of recovery was an ability to move her eyes. She looked away from the bright lights to see the janitor walk to the projector control station. In the few minutes the projector required to cycle up, she was able to turn her head enough to see Rose step to Elvin's bank of tracking monitors.

"That won't be necessary, Dr. Rose," Gormly said.

"Without the monitors, there's no way to track her," Rose protested. "There will be no way to get her back."

"She won't be coming back."

"You . . . you told her . . ."

"Yes, well, I didn't want to frighten the young lady."

Sheila needed her legs. Now! She felt movement, but her arms refused to bear the weight of her upper body. Panic rose from her stomach into her throat as Rose tried to interfere with the janitor's hand playing over the dials.

"You can't go back that far! She won't survive."

The janitor shrugged Rose away. "Who knows. As I understand it, you haven't tried to send someone to a point prior to their birth. Let's test that theory. How about the 1960s? A prime era for a rebellious crusader if ever there was one."

Pratt made one more leering scan of Sheila's body as she managed to rise to a sitting position.

"What a waste," he said.

Rose, alarm written over his face, stared directly into her eyes, his own eyes begging forgiveness. Sheila felt herself evaporate into the blank white eternity of the limbo from which she knew she would not return.

35

OOPSIE

MARSHALL AND MARTA WERE thirty yards down the long corridor that led to the projection lab, running at a full sprint, when Marshall felt the thrum of the time projector vibrate through the concrete beneath his feet.

"Oh, no," he moaned, accelerating his ungainly stride.

"Marshall, wait . . ." Marta warned from behind.

He knew she was right. Marta had undoubtedly been trained in approaching dangerous situations. He should step aside and let her lead the way. She would have a plan, and who knew what sort of scene they might confront? He kept running. *Which makes no sense, because I'm not a brave person.*

Heedless of Marta's appeal, Marshall skidded into his turn to negotiate the projection lab doorway. He anticipated a grand entrance, distracting this evil janitor from his designs on Sheila long enough for Marta to follow with her gun.

That didn't work out.

As had happened several times before, one of Marshall's size sixteen feet failed to clear the airlock's lip at the bottom of the doorway.

He sprawled headlong, landing heavily and sliding face-first through a chair into the base of a computer stand. Undaunted by his entrance, though, and oblivious to the pain in one shoulder, he stood to do battle. He found Leonard Rose next to Andrew Gormly. Sheila was absent.

"What did you do, Leonard? What did you do?" Marshall demanded.

When Rose didn't answer, Marshall vaulted the over-turned computer stand and grabbed Rose by his shirt. Rose stumbled under Marshall's assault and fell to his knees.

"Where is she, you bastard?"

Marshall heard the crack of an electrical charge as Rose twisted to escape Marshall's grasp. The move spun Marshall as his hands remained locked on Rose's shirt until Rose slumped to the floor.

Marshall found himself staring at Pratt and his taser.

"Looks like we can solve that other problem right now, Mr. Gormly," Pratt grinned. "I'm sure Ms. Schuler would want some company."

Marshall stood with fists clenched and repeated his angry question. "What have you done to Sheila?" Any fear he might have felt was supplanted by hatred for the janitor, who loomed closer.

Pratt glanced to Gormly, who offered his approval with a shrug.

Marta recognized that charging into the lab without knowing exactly who waited and how they were armed would be the worst thing to do. The projector's hum told her Sheila was probably no longer a hostage. Marshall had stumbled through the doorway, though, so he would be at risk.

She stopped just outside the door, pistol at the ready, taking a moment to steady her breathing. She wanted to wait for Gillis, but the verbal exchange between Marshall and Pratt told her she couldn't delay.

She considered risking a quick glance to see who was where. But she needed the element of surprise. *Better to go all at once.*

She took a deep breath and stepped through the airlock. Her pistol pointed at Marshall. To Marshall's right was Gormly. Directly behind Marshall, Rose sat inert, his back against the wall. To Marshall's left stood the janitor, pointing a weapon and advancing toward Marshall.

The janitor's quickness surprised her.

If Marta's sights had gone first to Pratt, she would have the upper hand. But her brain had directed her to the knot of three people to her left, rather than the single person to her right. Now her mind calculated that the janitor would bring his weapon to bear before she could complete the short arc to swing her aim from Marshall to Pratt.

She dove as Pratt discharged his taser. Her right elbow struck the floor with a jarring pain, sending her pistol skittering away. The sound of air sizzling just next to her head told her Pratt was armed with electricity rather than bullets.

The taser will take a few seconds to recharge. She could rush the man, but Pratt was twice her size. A direct assault would be pointless.

Did he realize his shot had missed? She had felt the heat at her ear. Her best ploy was to play possum and hope Pratt would make a mistake.

Face down, unmoving, Marta sensed Pratt closing the distance between them. Heard the slight whine of the taser as its recharge neared completion.

"Marta!" she heard Marshall scream.

"Take one more step, and I'll kill her," said the voice above her.

Pratt nudged her with his foot. Not a kick. Just a rough shove. He reached to roll her over. She stared with blank eyes.

"We've got all of them now, Mr. Gormly," he said. "What should we—"

When Pratt glanced to Gormly, Marta rolled to her side for leverage and shoved herself up, driving her shoulder into Pratt's groin. She didn't get as much power into the move as she wanted. She knew he wasn't hurt badly, but he crumpled forward just enough for her to drive an elbow toward his temple and slap at the taser, which clattered across the floor toward Marta's pistol.

The janitor roared and backhanded Marta across her face. Her vision went sparkly and sounds around her became muddy as she fell.

This scene unfolding before Marshall jerked along like a video display on fast forward, then came to an abrupt halt. And there, in the space between Marshall and Pratt, Marshall saw both pistol and taser.

Pratt remained bent over, his face distorted with anger and pain until his eyes drifted ever so slowly to the weapons, each only a couple of yards beyond Marshal's grasp.

Everything clicked back into real time. Marshall lunged!

As he jumped, though, he took a quick glance to ascertain that Pratt still suffered the effects of Marta's assault. So, he fumbled the weapons like an infielder rushing to turn a double play before he has control of the ball.

Somehow, he managed to come up with both gun and tazer and, as a bonus, realized by feel they pointed the right direction.

Pratt froze.

"Um . . . okay," Marshall said. "Put up your hands and . . . and . . . put up your hands!"

Pratt took a step forward.

"I'll shoot you if you don't . . ."

"Bullshit," said Pratt. "You won't shoot anyone."

Pratt took another step.

Marshall suspected he was right. "In the knee. I'll shoot you in your knee . . ."

"No. Shoot him in the chest, Marshall." Marta's voice sounded firm and cold. "He'll kill us all if you don't."

Still Marshall would not look away from Pratt, who had now raised his hands.

"I . . . I think he gives . . . Do you give?"

"No, Marshall. He's waiting for you to relax. Then he'll jump at you. Just shoot him."

"I . . . Marta . . . I don't think I can kill someone."

"Then use the taser."

"Oh. Oh, yeah. I forgot. I can do that." Marshall raised his right arm.

Pratt recoiled. "No, you idiot, that's the wrong—"

A loud boom reverberated through the projection lab.

"Holy shit . . ." shouted Marshall as he dropped both weapons.

"Oopsie," said Marta.

Pratt staggered against the projection platform with the force of the bullet's impact and sat down hard. He stared at a hole leaking blood from his chest in little spurts.

"You shot me, you skinny asshole," he managed to say before sliding carefully onto his back.

Wild-eyed, Marshall swept his gaze from Marta, to Rose, to Gormly and back again to Marta, who stood next to him.

"Honest to God, I thought the gun was in my other hand. I didn't mean to—"

"Don't feel too bad, honeybunch," Marta said. "I was gonna shoot him if you didn't."

Horrified, Marshall stared at the bleeding janitor. His mind would not accept the concept of shooting someone. He felt an overwhelming need to apologize. Jason Pratt wasn't paying attention, and Marshall didn't want to talk to Rose or Gormly right now.

Still . . . he turned to Gormly where he saw the fat man standing, arms outstretched, hands shielding his ruddy face as if they could ward off the bullets from Marta's pistol.

"Um . . . Marta, what are you doing?"

He didn't see the woman with whom he'd just spent the most remarkable night of his life. Or even the woman who'd gradually become his friend over the past two years. He saw the distant, surly being he'd met all those months ago on a bus headed into a desert wilderness.

"Cleaning up," Marta answered.

"Please, that won't be necessary," said Gormly, his voice

no longer calm. "I'm sure we can work this out."

"What the fuck is going on?"

Marshall jerked his head toward the airlock to see Elvin—wearing a Motly Crue bathrobe and slippers shaped like bananas—followed by Gillis, who stepped to Marta's side where he, too, trained his pistol at Gormly.

Marshall ran to Elvin and began pulling him toward the bank of monitors.

"They've sent Sheila somewhere. We've got to find her."

"Who . . . who sent her? You can't just bop in here and use the projector—"

"Well, that's just what the dead guy over there did." Marta nodded at Pratt.

"Dead guy?"

"We're not sure he's dead," Marshall said. "Maybe he's just . . . anyone know CPR?"

"That's an awful lot of blood, Marshall," Elvin said. "He seems pretty dead to me."

Elvin stepped to his workstation and scanned the equipment.

"You know, you're right, Marta. So long as you don't care where . . . and he disabled the recording and monitoring equipment. You'd just have to know how to erase the history . . ."

"Leonard was here when they did it," Marshall frantically pointed to Rose, who remained incapacitated against the wall. "Leonard knows—"

"Leonard's not looking too helpful," Elvin said. "Is he dead, too?"

"I didn't do that," Marshall said.

"I can explain—" Gormly started.

"Shut the fuck up!" Marta barked. "If you say another word before one of us asks you a question, I'll shoot you in the balls."

Involuntarily, Gormly tucked his legs together and backed up a couple more steps.

"You have to find her," Marshall urged again as Elvin powered up his systems.

"They shut off the recorders," he said.

"So, she's lost?"

"I didn't say that. I have an independent system I've kept hidden."

He opened his secret program and hit playback. The scene unfolded—tracking data, lifeline activity and silent video of the projection platform playing on three separate monitors.

Marta told Gormly to sit on the floor with his hands beneath him. The big man struggled to get down as the seat of his pants ripped loudly.

The video display showed Pratt placing Sheila on the platform and running his hands over her body.

"No question," Marta said under her breath. "I would've shot him."

She pointed her gun again at Gormly who flinched, closed his eyes, and turned his head away.

"Marta, don't," Marshall said.

Elvin switched his gaze between the other two monitors and scribbling quick notations.

"Looks like," he said slowly, "looks like... yep. *The Lawrence Welk Show* universe. We've been there before. Once. With Frank and one of the secondary teams. It's a relatively close universe. Very similar to us—"

"So, bring her back!" Marshall commanded.

Elvin scribbled some more, studied the monitor, glanced back at his yellow legal pad, and raised his eyes to Marshall's. He shook his head. "They sent her to the 1960s. I can't pin it down any closer. The distance is just too great . . ."

He pointed to the middle monitor, conspicuous by its absence of a bright red line.

". . . three decades before her birth. She couldn't have survived."

"It's just a theory, Elvin," Marshall pleaded. "She might be hurt. She might not remember who she is. Send me there. I'll bring her back."

"All we'd be doing, Marshall, is killing you, too."

Marta turned away from Gormly and pulled Marshall to face her.

"It's over," she said. "I can't lose you, too."

Gormly sat, back against the wall and hands tucked under his ample bottom.

"Please, I—"

"The lady ordered you to be quiet," Gillis said through his menacing smile.

"Don't we need him to tell us what happened here and why?" Elvin asked.

The question jarred Marta. She found the emotion she felt for Marshall amidst this mayhem disorienting and unsettling. She needed cold outrage in order to find herself.

"No, we don't." She aimed her gun again. "Nothing he

tells us will be the truth. We'll wait for Rose to recover. I'll haul Rose into Yuni's office and see what he has to say. After that, we'll listen to fat ass over there."

Gormly peered anxiously at Rose, who began to stir.

"Please, that man, the janitor, he . . ."

Marta felt her finger tighten on the trigger. She also felt Marshall's eyes and was again compromised.

This won't work. I can't just abandon who I am . . . who I need to be at moments like this.

Elvin sidetracked Marta's internal debate.

"May I remind you folks, we also have the issue of a dead janitor to deal with."

"Has anybody checked to be sure?" Marshall asked. "Shouldn't we call an ambulance?"

"No, Marshall," Marta said. "He's too dead for that. Elvin, can we park him in some other universe?"

"Hmm, that's a fascinating prospect. A dead guy intersecting with his living counterpart. We don't even know if we can project non-living tissue."

"What are you two talking about?" Marshall protested. "If we really have a dead guy here, we have to notify someone . . . I have to turn myself in."

"That gets complicated, Marshall," Marta said. "We'll be in a lot of trouble."

"But after what he did to Sheila, everyone will understand."

"That's a risky assumption," said Gillis.

"We won't be subject to the regular legal system," Marta added. "Regardless of whether they decide the shooting was justified, I am still in violation of my contract by having a gun. They could confine me. And maybe you, too. Our lives could be in the hands of the same people who wanted to get rid of Sheila."

"Aren't you afraid of projecting a dead guy?" Marshall asked Elvin. "Dead guys might blow someone up. If . . . if we want to get rid of the body, why don't we just do it the old-fashioned way?"

"You say that as if you dispose of bodies all the time," Marta said. "The public relations business must be a lot more cutthroat than I thought."

"No, of course not, but, well, I watch television. We have a whole desert out there, and coyotes . . . and . . . and . . . pumas . . ."

"Pumas?"

"So how you gonna get him out there among the pumas?" Elvin asked. "This is a secure facility. They're just as picky about what goes out as what comes in."

"Clearly it's not as secure as everyone thinks," Marshall said, pointing to Gormly. "How did he get into the interior campus? And where's the security that's supposed to be protecting the lab?"

"Marshall, you can buy anything if you've got money," Marta said.

"And we have the best way ever to dispose of a body," Elvin argued.

Leonard Rose's groans interrupted the debate.

Marta felt her rage kick up a notch as she knelt beside Rose and slapped his cheeks.

"Leonard, look at me. Look at me. That's right. Let's sit up. Deep breaths, deep breaths. Can you talk to me?"

Rose blinked and gasped like a hooked trout.

"Are you gonna survive?" Marta asked.

"Yes. Yes, I think so . . ."

Gillis pulled Rose to his feet and shoved him into a rolling chair.

At Marta's direction, Marshall pushed the chair toward Yuni's office. Marta told Gillis to be sure Gormly stayed put.

Marta closed the door behind them. "One chance, Leonard. One chance to tell us what happened."

"Please, you must believe me! I didn't think they intended to kill anyone. I thought they'd just send her someplace for a little while."

"Who is 'they'?"

"That man out there is some kind of hired gun for the Hemisphere Investment Group. He says he's here to protect their investment."

"And you know this because . . . ?"

Rose stared at the floor.

"Leonard?" Marta demanded.

"I've been his informant."

"How much did he pay you?"

"I didn't take money. Well, not much. He used his resources to increase my influence here. But you must understand, I was protecting the program. Gormly has a lot of pull with Hemisphere's board. If he recommends it, they'll withdraw their funding. Our whole program will go down the tubes."

"And what did you have to do with this thing tonight?" Marta probed.

"I called Sheila and asked her to come to the lab. She thought Marshall had gone back—"

"You *told* her Marshall had gone back."

"Yes. Yes, I did. But I didn't have any idea—"

"When I question Gormly, do you know what he'll say?"

Rose regarded her blankly.

"He'll lay this on you. He'll say you misunderstood what he wanted. That you were trying to impress him. That he didn't have any idea anyone would be killed."

"That's not true!"

Marta shrugged.

She turned and opened the door. Over her shoulder she said to Marshall, "Bring him. I want to make sure he sees this."

Elvin sat at the control panel tinkering with settings. Gillis's pistol remained trained on Gormly.

Marta told Rose to sit next to the fat man.

"Elvin, are you about ready?"

"Uh huh, just a few more adjustments . . . and . . . okay. *The Honeymooners*. About ten years ago."

"What about his clothes?"

"They'll get burned up in the wormhole," Elvin said. "He won't know the difference. And . . . now."

Plasma oozed over the big globes and Pratt's body, along with every trace of blood, disintegrated into the familiar wisp.

"Okay," said Elvin. "I guess we can project a dead person, at least while the cellular structure is still sound. I'll bet if we waited until more decomposition had set in we'd have had problems."

Marshall felt as if he'd held his breath for the full ninety-seven seconds of the transport gap until Elvin announced, "I've got *The Honeymooners'* theme song. I don't think we blew anybody up."

Marta walked to Gormly. "Now you."

"Wait. None of this was my doing—"

"What did I say about speaking?"

"Am I to be given no opportunity to defend myself? This man—" he pointed to Rose.

"Liar, liar, pants on fire," said Marta.

"Dr. Rose told us what happened," Marshall added.

"And you believe him? Just like that?"

"Yep," Marta said.

She knew herself again. She summoned rage and aimed the pistol between Gormly's eyes.

"Stop it!" Marshall stepped between Marta and Gormly. "We can't just kill everyone."

"They just killed Sheila."

"We're not them." Marshall peered into her eyes. "At least, I hope we're not. Marta, I found something tonight, and I want to see where it takes us. If you do this, though, I think . . . I'll have a hard-enough time dealing with . . . haven't enough people died tonight?"

Marta felt her rage melt into an ugly lump. She could either reclaim it or cast it aside. She knew the cold professional within herself well. This other woman, though—this woman who could laugh with friends and care for them and dare to savor the possibility of a shared journey—this woman was a stranger. Vulnerable. Dependent.

But she was not lonely.

Marta lowered the gun, hoping she'd made the right choice.

Marshall stepped aside.

Gormly closed his eyes and took a deep breath.

Until Marta said, "We won't just let him walk out of here, though."

When Marshall opened his mouth to protest, she raised a hand to cut him off.

"If ever anyone had enough influence to manipulate a political or judicial system, it's the Hemisphere Investment Group. A guy like this, who has probably done their dirty work for years, is smart enough to protect himself. He'll have dirt on Hemisphere stashed somewhere, and they'll pull out all the stops to get him out of whatever charges he faces just to keep him from making a deal.

"The only justice he'll confront is what we'll dispense right now."

Elvin called from behind his monitors, "I'm thinking he'd fit right in with the lizards."

"Reptilian Americans," Marshall admonished automatically.

"What?" Gormly said with a quivering voice.

Ten minutes later, Andrew Gormly—a man who spent his days schmoozing with the world's wealthiest and most influential men and women, a man who had at his total discretion millions of dollars to protect himself and his constituents, a man who, as much as any other, held the future of time travel in his chubby hands—stood naked and quaking between two bright silver globes.

Each time he attempted to argue his case, Marta leveled the pistol at his balls.

"I don't care to hear your denials or your version of anything. We know now that dead bodies transport just as well as live ones. It doesn't matter to me one way or another."

Finally, though, as Elvin sorted through the ether to find the theme song from *My Mother the Car* and made the final adjustments that fine-tuned the projector's focus, Gormly spoke.

"All right, I'm not making an excuse or alibis."

Marta raised the gun.

"I can make you rich. How about five million apiece? Ten million?"

Marta snorted. Marshall scowled. Elvin stood a little straighter and seemed to consider Gormly with more interest.

"If I disappear, they'll send someone else to do my job. Or they'll cancel the program. I'll promise to keep it going. I'll tell them your efforts to change the past worked. I'll get you through the five years, so you get that payoff, too. If the program is canceled, there's no guarantee enough funds will be left to meet the contracts . . ."

Gormly couldn't keep the hint of a smug grin from touching the corner of his mouth. He had Elvin. He knew he had him.

Marta swung her gaze to Elvin.

"I have to be honest, Marta," Elvin said. "I really want this thing to continue."

"Not under these circumstances," Marta said. "If this program goes forward, it does so on its own merit, not this asshole's manipulations or his bribes."

Elvin glanced from Marta, to Gormly and back to Marta.

"Elvin, I won't threaten you. I'll only ask you to do this,

because you understand it's the right thing."

Gormly's fleeting moment of smugness reverted to raw fear as Elvin turned to him with a shrug, his hands spread— a "what can I do?" gesture. "Marshall," he said, "we've got an investors' representative here. I think we're supposed to have someone at the periscope."

Elvin pushed a lever, and Gormly felt himself being swallowed by the oblivion of time.

"Where'd you put him?" Marshall asked.

"*My Mother the Car*, six years back."

Marshall recalled his encounter there. "You should have let me brief him first."

"Oh, he's a bright guy," Marta said. "He'll figure it out."

Still holding her pistol Marta turned to Rose, who cringed.

Marshall tensed, then expelled a breath of relief as Marta holstered her weapon.

"You could send me to prison, Leonard," she said. "I don't want to go to prison. I want to continue to work here, and I want us to be a lot more careful in how we go about the research. I need an advocate for that point of view."

"Of course," Rose said.

"You're crazy," Elvin said to Marta. "How can you possibly consider trusting this guy? Your ass isn't the only one hanging out here, remember?"

"Security is already investigating too many mysterious disappearances. I'm afraid one more might be too much for the authorities to digest. What I figure we have here is a stalemate. Sure, he could cause difficulty. But he's an accessory to Sheila's murder. I have Sheila's voice message to prove it. If we go down, he does, too."

"That's right," Rose nodded. "I'd be crazy to say anything."

"And you do understand what I'll do if I even suspect you are passing any kind of information to anyone?"

Rose nodded. "Thank you, Ms. Hamilton."

"Get out of here before I change my mind."

"So now what?" Marshall asked. Suddenly, he felt exhausted. The adrenaline that had coursed through his body had dissipated, and he was left with dark realizations.

Sheila was gone.

A human being had died at his hand.

"Now we each act according to our own conscience and go ahead with the work of this program," Marta said.

"What about Sheila?" Marshall begged.

"We can look for her. Maybe there are other universes out there where she survived."

"I'll try, Marshall," Elvin said.

"It's all we can do," Marta added.

Marshall knew she was right.

"Elvin, good night," Marta said. "And thank you."

Elvin gave a bow. "You two do understand that I believe we have to continue."

"That's the way it should be," Marta said. "I'm not so egotistical to think I know the answers. All voices need to be heard. We just have to do our best to keep the greed out of it."

Hours later, after they'd carefully constructed alibis, and coordinated their stories so they might all survive the investigation into Sheila's death that must certainly occur, Marshall and Marta walked alone through the gloom of concrete corridors. Every few steps, Marta felt Marshall's need to say something, although the words never escaped his lips. Likewise, she knew she should address this strange new wrinkle in their relationship, but she couldn't, given the loss of their friend.

Finally, Marshall sighed deeply. "Marta, I'm sorry."

"Sorry? For what?"

"I messed everything up. I should have listened to you and not rushed in that way. I just . . . I just . . . I'm not a brave man, Marta. You'll figure that out sooner or later. I don't know what to do when—"

"Whoa. Not a brave man? Marshall, courage assumes many forms. The best kind is all about just trying to do what's right. I am amazed at your courage every day."

She slipped her arm into his. They continued along the hallway, heads bowed.

"Um . . . Marta?" Marshall again broke their silence.

"Yes?" She stopped and raised her eyes to meet his.

"If you were going to ever, like, kill me . . . you'd at least let me know why, wouldn't you?"

She laughed. "Well, probably."

She saw a shadow of alarm pass over his face until she took his arm again. They resumed their stroll.

As they walked, her mind kept stumbling over the same thought. *Is anyone really so inept they'd confuse a pistol with a taser?*

"And what about you, Marshall?" she asked. "Would you give me some warning if you were ever going to kill me?"

"What?" he said. "I wouldn't . . ."

She fixed her hardest stare into his eyes.

"... Yes," he said. "Of course."

She pulled his face to hers and kissed his cheek. "So, we're agreed we won't murder each other without fair warning. I supposed that's a better basis for a relationship than a lot of people have."

MEANWHILE, AT ANOTHER dimensional plane of time and space, a thoroughly disagreeable Amphibian American—bigots would have called him a toad—oozed his way along a crowded New York City sidewalk. His three-piece suit further elevated his discomfort in the heat and humidity, and he knew he would have to duck into an air-conditioned rest kiosk stationed along the street to lower body temperature of cold-blooded creatures.

Andrew Gormly was headed to an off-the-record gathering of key board members of Hemisphere Investment Group where he was to learn of his next assignment. He only knew he was going to Arizona—not a particularly pleasant prospect for an amphibian, but he'd endured worse.

He stopped at a cooling kiosk with a "Platinum" label set discreetly above a wireless data port. He passed the toadish appendage that was the equivalent of a hand over the port and a door slid open. Unlike public kiosks, this one was spotless and scented with *Midnight Swamp* air freshener. He waited while an injection of organic coolant flowed into his bloodstream, then tugged at his lapels to straighten his jacket. He stepped outside to cover the last block to the Hemisphere building.

He took only two shuffling steps onto the crowded walkway when a force he couldn't begin to describe rocketed into his head. Gormly collapsed, his toady body spreading like Silly Putty around him.

Momentarily, the crowd along the sidewalk paused to stare.

Inside the amphibian brain, the all-too human Andrew Gormly commanded his amphibious counterpart to glance wildly around and terrified himself.

He peered directly into the surprised stares of a half dozen reptiles with a strangely humanoid air about them. They resembled giant chameleons and geckos, dressed mostly in black. Some part of Gormly's being was particularly repulsed by the chameleons. "You can't trust an ethnic minority that can be *all* those colors," came the telepathic explanation.

When Gormly fell, five of these creatures reached automatically inside their jackets and formed a shield around the sixth who wore a black fedora, sported a white silk tie and held a cigar.

Gormly's sticky amphibian tongue rolled limply out of his open mouth and spilled across the concrete. The surface was hot, and he retracted his tongue with a painful splat.

"XSPSGGGLFRT!" he heard himself say with trepidation. "Fss grndrxxprats ne Liszpllfssftes!"

Which his human counterpart understood as, "Oh my God! They really are lizards!"

The five bodyguards produced handguns, all aimed at Gormly.

The one with the tie and cigar took a menacing step. "Hey, you frog motherfucker, who the fuck you callin' a lizard?"

Gormly made no response.

He couldn't.

His mind was a riot of images, each half of himself wholly and viscerally repulsed by the other. His future and past were two medieval armies closing with lighting speed, spears and swords drawn, intent on carnage. And when they met, his final coherent sensation was that of his amphibian brain collapsing into something his future counterpart would have compared to a small pile of grits.

Eventually, although confined to an assisted living facility specializing in treatment of mentally dysfunctional Amphibian Americans, Andrew Gormly would be able to recover enough motor control of his tongue to live out his days parked in a wheelchair by a pond on the bucolic grounds of his nursing home, happily catching flies.

ACKNOWLEDGMENTS

I love baseball and have devoted much of the past thirty years to playing at an amateur level. It is a pursuit in which you must embrace each success you find, because, at its core, baseball is a game of failure. That experience has been a great help as, almost a decade ago, I decided to try my hand at writing. Writing is also a game of failure.

Unlike baseball, though, writing cannot be measured objectively. Statistical confirmation in the form of batting averages, earned run averages or on-base percentages don't exist to calculate the quality of one's work. One reviewer will embrace your book, and for a day, you sit on a shelf with Mark Twain or Christopher Moore or Tom Robbins. The next critic will crucify you, saying he couldn't survive the first hundred pages, and you wonder why you even tried.

Eventually, if a writer is lucky, he or she finds a group of people to offer validation that can be trusted. These people guide you through the obstacles of failure and rejection.

My guides are Holly Youmans and Jessica Therrien at Acorn Publishing, my fellow Acorn authors, and my editors: Laura Taylor of the Southern California Writers Conference, and Shanna McNair and Scott Wolven of The Writers Hotel in New York. Six years ago, Scott and Shanna took on the first sad version of *Taking Time* and, with characteristic honesty, pointed out its shortcomings. At the end of that conversation, more than a little discouraged, I asked them where I should go from here. Scott gave me the best advice I will ever receive.

He said, "Write another one."

Mike Murphey Books

Tales of Physics, Lust and Greed

Taking Time
Wasting Time
Killing Time

www.mikemurpheybooks.com

AUTHOR'S NOTE

Thanks so much for reading *Taking Time*, the first book in my Physics, Lust and Greed Series. Writers write for a lot of reasons, but one of the most important is to be read. With a couple million new titles to choose from, believe me, it's a tough market out there. If you enjoyed this book, or even if you didn't, you can do one more thing to help. Write a review and post it on Amazon here:

http://www.amazon.com/review/create-review?&asin=B087PP8DPL

Thanks again for reading Taking Time, and I hope you will be on the lookout for Wasting Time, the second install-ment in the Physics, Lust and Greed series, appearing soon.

Made in the USA
Las Vegas, NV
03 October 2021